Dedication

For Grandpa, who made writing way to earn a living.

Acknowledgements

I'd like to thank everyone, family and friends alike, who helped me get this book written. Whether that was by creating and holding the space I needed while the story took shape, or by reading and commenting on the manuscript, or simply by grabbing a review copy as soon as it was available, you all made it happen.

I'd also like to thank my copy editor, Rebecca Coffindaffer, not just for the awesome job she did eradicating my many mistakes, but also for her encouragement throughout the process.

Author's note

When I was small, I had books about fairies (as you do). There was *The Violet Fairy Book* with its beautiful baroque illustrations, a style I still admire. The stories themselves, in hindsight, always seemed a little too worthy. You know what I mean? Just a bit too neat, with everything wrapped up and evil banished to everyone's satisfaction. The fairies themselves were all polish and no edges, god-like, in the same vein as Tolkien's elves.

On the same shelf there was Lamb's *Tales From Shakespeare*. His fairies seemed both more like actual people and, at the same time, more like genuine gods. If we're using Pratchett's definition, that is.

... a brief resume of the lives of most gods suggests that their origins certainly couldn't be divine. They tend to do exactly the things people would do if only they could, especially when it comes to nymphs, golden showers, and the smiting of your enemies.
Reaper Man, Sir Terry Pratchett

Then, one year at Christmas, a kind relative gave me *Faeries* by Brian Froud and Alan Lee, and that changed everything. It felt *right*. Here were fairies as people, with wants and needs and preferences, with humour and habits and pernickety quirks. The illustrations, from marginalia pencil scribbles through to full-page colour paintings, showed a level of not just skill, but real affection, a regard for the subject and an interest in how they would like to be portrayed.

Even as a small child, I knew they weren't real, but with the book in my hands, that didn't matter. They *felt* real. More than that, their stories taught me something very important, which is this: to create a story, you must eventually learn something about how your characters would like to be treated. In this I also learned so much from the writings of Sir Terry, and the main lesson there was that it's possible to describe people in all their glorious imperfections, all their foibles and vulnerability, while at the same time portraying them with huge affection. To hold up a mirror and say, *People, eh? Aren't we odd? Aren't we lovely?* That's skill.

So why is this the story I chose to write?

The first and most compelling reason is that it wouldn't leave me alone until I did. Even now it continues to leak out, desperately trying to spawn new edits.

Beyond that though, tales like *The Green Children of Woolpit* suggested to me that there was something of a theme around lost children being taken in by lords — and lost girls, in particular, being married off practically at random once their magical sheen had worn off a bit. I began to wonder, if these were based in any way on true stories, just how those girls might have felt about that, and whether their opinions were in any way prioritised or even invited by the men in control of events. One thing led to another. I wrote a fairytale of my own and then filled in the gaps from the perspective of the other side. As you'll discover, they had a great deal to say for themselves.

This isn't a love story; although if you look closely, you may detect hints of emotional attachment here and there. It's also not a fairytale, even if otherworldly creatures will wander through it from time to time. If you absolutely must have a theme, let's say it's about being where you need to be. Whatever that looks like.

I hope you'll enjoy reading this book as much as I enjoyed writing it.

LAURIE MATHER, 2023

Introduction

History is written by the winners, so the saying goes.

So are fairytales.

Whether you believe in fairytales or not, it doesn't change the fact that there's probably a grain or two of truth in them somewhere. After all, somebody took the trouble to write them down. Some of these heroes and villains must have existed in some form, the events must have happened, even if it was once upon a time and far, far away, and there's nobody still around who might be able to confirm or dispute the telling.

Nobody on the "winning" side, that is.

BOOK 1

The Past

The Legend of the Moon Princess

LONG AGO, a prince was out riding when he crossed the path of a fairy hunt. He quickly hid in the trees to watch them, and to his amazement, as the moon rose, a magical door opened in the rocks and one by one the riders disappeared from sight until only one was left. A princess, as it seemed to him, pale and proud with pearls bound in her hair and the sound of tiny silver bells when she moved.

So beautiful a maiden he had never seen, and his heart was filled with longing to see her again. Try as he would, he could not forget her, and as he was approaching the age to be married, he began passing that same spot night after night in hopes of wooing her. When the full moon approached, he heard the sound of silver bells once more and hurried to the rocks just in time to see the hunt passing through the door. He could not reach it before she vanished, and although he called out to her, she did not look back.

In desperation, he consulted a wise man who lived in the woods. The wise man was reluctant to help, warning the prince that no good would come of it. But eventually, seeing how deeply in love the prince was, he relented and shared the secret.

"To stay the princess on this side so you may speak with her, you must wait beside the rocks. Just as the rider before her vanishes from sight, step forwards and cast your shadow across her path. If you do this, she will be unable to pass until you move aside."

The prince thanked the wise man, promising him many rewards in return for his advice, and hurried to carry out his plan before the moon began to wane. That night, he did as the wise man had said and cast his shadow across the princess's path.

Her horse stopped dead and she cried out in alarm, "Why are you standing in my path? Let me go home."

But he led her to his castle and declared his love for her, begging her to marry him. She would not agree, crying for her home and beseeching him to let her go.

Soon, he returned to the wise man and demanded he help him once again.

"There will be a price," the wise man warned him. "But if you truly love her, then do exactly as I tell you now. First, take your bride to the church and be sure she is not left alone. Second, she must be baptised before the next full moon. And finally, you must destroy the door to the land of Faerie. If you fail even one of these three things, she will escape through the door, and you will never see her again."

The very next night, the moon would be full again, so the prince hurried to follow his instructions. The princess was taken to the church and baptised before the sun was down, and the prince went to the place where the fairy door would appear and recited the charm the wise man had given him. Just as the moon rose, the stones creaked and groaned as if the very earth was in torment, and a sound of such thunder came from within that the prince was afraid for his life. But he held fast, recited the charm three times, and each time took one of the three iron spikes the wise man had given him and drove them into the stone with all his might. To his astonishment they passed into the solid rock as if it had been soft clay, not even needing a hammer. As the third spike went in, there was a mighty crash and all went still. The door was closed forever.

When he returned to the chapel, his bride was waiting for him, calm and content just as the wise man had promised. He took her to wife that very same night, and they lived happily together. After a year, she gave birth to twins, a boy and a girl. The prince was delighted, saying, "Look at my son! He will be as strong and as brave as his father. And see my daughter! She will be as fair and as generous as her mother."

But the princess only smiled sadly, turning her face away and saying, "Treasure them, for they are all I can give you."

She fell gravely ill soon after. The prince was distraught, for he loved her dearly, but no matter how many doctors he called to her, there was nothing to be done and she died.

The twins thrived, delighting all who knew them with their

charming smiles and quick wits. The boy grew strong and brave, just as his father had said, and the girl became more beautiful with every passing day. Soon, however, the nursemaids came to the prince in great distress, saying the nursery must be haunted. On the night of every full moon, they would hear the babes wake and start talking, and when the maids would rush in, they would see the children smiling and laughing at thin air as if there were some invisible visitor that only they could see.

The prince lay in wait one night, and as soon as he heard the children wake, he rushed in to confront whatever sprite was troubling them. But to his astonishment he saw only a woman, tall and slender and dressed all in shining silver, bending over the crib. Alarmed, he begged her not to hurt the children, but she replied, "Shame on you, for I would never raise a hand to a child, much less so to one of my own blood."

He was terrified, for he realised this must be his bride's family, come to see what had become of her. The woman kissed both children tenderly, saying, "Grow strong, and be well."

But to the prince she said, "Good fortune shall not favour you, for you have taken something very dear from us. All your ambitions will be dust, your name forgotten. This is the price."

With that she vanished, and he never saw her again.

Chapter 1

A MAN LAY sprawled in the suffocating dark, half-buried in broken stone and scattered soil.

"Shit shit shit, don't be dead . . ."

Against the black, a darker black shifted, glossy wings swooping down and fluttering frantically against his cheek. "Don't you dare die on me down here, you feckless arse. Wake up!"

The faceful of feathers roused him, or possibly it was the insults. Either way, he flinched away, jerking upright with a fending arm across his face. "Get off, will you? I'm not dead."

The wings withdrew, and the voice with them. "Fucking move then, eh? Reckon we can still get through—"

Too late. It came again, the clash of iron on iron and iron on stone, a hateful splintering sending a spray of dry mud and stone chips stinging into his face. He staggered back over the debris, flinging out one hand to find the wall for guidance and reaching for the Path with the other.

Take me home, he willed.

The tunnel flooded with light, all colours and none, a silent shockwave shoving him backwards still fumbling for the tunnel wall. The stone under his grasping fingers faded obediently away, and he tumbled over the threshold into the blessedly calm shadows beyond.

***

High above the sleeping village, the air in the stone circle curled in on itself and spat him back out.

The stench of disaster came with him, the stink of blood and rot clinging to his clothes and coiling up around his face. His stomach heaved, and again, and he dropped to his knees alternately retching and sucking in lungfuls of cool clean air, clutching at the ground for support. It seemed to go on forever, but eventually there was nothing left to purge. He sat back on his haunches, wiping his mouth with the back of his hand.

"Don't worry, I'm alright. Where the hell are we?"

Not that he needed to ask. By pale moonlight, he could make out the familiar shapes of the stone circle at the top of what the locals called "Fairy Hill." Nowhere near where he'd intended to bring them, but it was better than where they were.

The portal hanging in the air above his head rippled and sealed itself again with a smug curl, like the tide turning. Time to go.

"You alright? We'd better get moving. They said she'd be at the church."

But there was no reply. He strained his senses, listening for any sign that Sweyn might be nearby. A rustle, a twig breaking in the undergrowth, a string of swearwords and some scurrilous assumptions about his ancestry. . . But there was nothing. Not a sound other than the cheerful gurgle of the spring feeding the water leat and beginning its journey down the hillside to the village.

After all that, Sweyn didn't make it.

By rights, he ought to throw back his head in dramatic despair, shaking his fist and howling his fury and loss to the shrouded stars. He would too, if only for dramatic effect, but what was the point without an audience? Instead he stared blankly into the dark, muttered, "Shit," and struggled to his feet, brushing at the mud caking his knees.

As he passed out of the ring of tumbled stones, he kicked one in passing, hissing something under his breath that made the dry weeds at the edge flare into brief bright flame.

Chapter 2

THE NIGHT'S GAME was nearing its end.

It was seldom enough that these five could come together, and rarer still that it should be a social occasion rather than a crisis. The empty bottles along the dresser neatly demonstrated how ably they'd responded to the call—that along with the neat stacks of coins and the jewel-bright cards heaped in the centre of the table.

At the edge of the pooled candlelight, their host sat almost invisible, only the amber gleam of the liquor in his glass idly swirling as he watched the play. At last, he leaned forward and picked up his own cards, running a fingertip thoughtfully along them before selecting a single card to lay down.

"You sneaky bastard," the sculptor muttered. "Have you been holding on to that queen the whole time?"

"Oh, you know me. I always aim to have a queen in hand." The observation was accompanied by a tight smile, an allusion that the others understood all too well. "Would anyone care to counter?"

To his right, the smith fanned out his hand again and reviewed each card in deep concentration, sweeping his fair hair back off his brow impatiently. "I believe I am out," he conceded at last. "I do not recall you having such skill the last time we played."

The scribe returned at that moment from the dresser with their glass freshly filled and the bottle in hand. "He's been getting some practice lately," they commented, tilting the bottle to indicate the finder.

They should know, too, since they're the one called in to tally up the aftermath and see things drawn up all right and tight. Not saying the baron couldn't be trusted to keep track of his losses, but it never hurt to have some neutral third party keep score. If young Lord Vernon could have seen the grin that flashed between his recent opponent and his bookkeeper now, however, he might well reconsider where he'd placed his trust.

The finder leaned across the table to start gathering up his winnings. "Almost enough to buy myself a manor," he said cheerfully. "Something tells me there'll be one on the market soon."

That raised a shout of laughter even from the disappointed losers.

"Job's nearly done then?" the sculptor asked eagerly. "'Bout time you left this benighted mud puddle to its own devices. I never understood why you didn't just raze the hall to the ground and be done with it."

"There were the children to consider," the finder reminded him. "Besides, I tend to prefer a longer game myself."

"Is that some kind of cipher for doing nothing? 'Cause that's what it looks like from here."

"He always looks like he's doing nothing. Right up until he pulls a queen from his arse." The smith smiled to show no hard feelings and raised his glass in a toast. "To our finder, who I have every confidence will make things right."

"To our finder," the sculptor repeated, raising his glass but not drinking. "How much longer, though, is all I'm asking?"

"I have my instructions," the finder said mildly. "When the last of them goes into the ground knowing nobody cares who they ever were, that's when I'll be done. You know how she is."

It was as if the shadows around him grew momentarily colder. His companions exchanged meaningful glances at the mention of the *she* he carefully didn't name.

The sculptor alone seemed blind to the mood change. "What instructions, though?" he prodded. "She said to ruin 'em, right? Don't look like they're ruined to me."

The scribe opened their mouth to correct him, but subsided at a warning glance from the finder. "She told me to bring them to nothing. What that looks like, how long it takes—that's my business. You want I should come down to your workshop and instruct you on slip-casting?"

The sculptor shrugged and set his untouched glass back down. "Ah, there's no arguing with you. I just miss how things used to be, don't you? Time was this place was a proper playground. You recall that time Carney's dog got loose on the moor? I still hear them telling their children not to play up there or the beast will get them."

"Excellent stock, that one. Could have sired a whole pack," the huntsman agreed. "But no more hunt means no more hounds. I, too, have my instructions."

He tipped his glass a fraction in the finder's direction before taking a sip.

"What, so you just gave up? Seems a waste," the sculptor sneered.

"More of a waste to create the beast and then give it no outlet for its talents. Would be cruel to constrain it so."

There was a note of patient reproof in his tone; this conversation had evidently been had before.

"Some things can never be made the same," the finder said pointedly, though whether he was talking about the hounds and the hunt or something different wasn't clear. "We mend what we can and tolerate what we cannot. Isn't that the way?"

A subtle glance around the table invited them all to pick up his cue and divert the topic to something more neutral; they swiftly obliged, turning with relief to news from Home and other gossip carried by those few of their kind that still travelled this way.

By the time dawn crept over the rooftops, the finder was alone again, his companions disappearing one by one into the night, and the end of his day overlapping the sound of the bakers behind his tiny lodging beginning theirs. He took a deep breath in and held it, looking about the room and considering. Maybe his friends were right. Maybe he'd done enough. On the other hand, the deeds for the bakery and the several properties on either side laid even now in a secure lockbox behind the dresser, surrendered by the young baron in lieu of his gambling debts. The finder already spent more time here than at home, and he'd long since established to his satisfaction that the border could be watched equally well from either side. He wasn't entirely joking about the imminent sale of the manor house up on the hill, either. That grand property might be beyond his touch right now, but the departure of the last Vernon from this region would cut the unseen link and leave this little town entirely without a guiding hand.

More to the point, though, the world was changing, what with wars and civil strife and a distant government looking to wring every last penny from a population ill-equipped to provide it. It made it so that mysterious strangers—and travellers and tinkers—got asked far more awkward questions than used to be. If he was going to be here at all, he needed a base to call his own.

Chapter 3

CHARLES HAD ALWAYS coveted this room, particularly the massive walnut desk his grandfather used to sit behind. On taking possession, he wasted no time having it cleaned up and making himself at home. Most of the contents would have to go once he'd learned the final extent of the death duties, but the desk, he resolved, would stay even if that meant he had to personally buy it back from his own damned inheritance. He felt every bit the stern patriarch his predecessor was, leaning back against the worn leather upholstery of the chair and reading his paperwork by lamplight under the approving stares of his ancestors.

The banker's lamp should stay too, he rather thought, with its ornate base and bottle-green glass shade. Anything more modern would only look foolish in this setting. He leaned forward and peeled away the auctioneer's red sticker, rubbing at the circular smear of gum it left behind on the polished brass. He abandoned the attempt after a couple of futile passes; one of his people could deal with it later.

Picking at the sticker, leafing through papers he'd already read a dozen times, these were symptoms of a deeper unease. He was more than a little nervous about what was coming next, and he'd spent enough time this evening worrying about how to set the scene to place himself firmly in control of the upcoming conversation.

To his annoyance, he hadn't really been able to come up with anything that would improve on the original arrangement. The lighting, for example — a pool of warm light serving only the desk and its occupant and leaving the rest of the room in gloomy shadow. And the desk itself — placed at the farthest end of the room from the door, flanked by a display of past wealth and acquisition, forcing visitors to cross the expanse of carpet like supplicants to a throne, with centuries of Vernon lineage silently judging them every step of the way.

It bothered him, in a way he couldn't quite define, that he could only seem to tread in the old man's footsteps rather than make his own mark here. It would have to do though. If it wasn't all some huge joke, if it really was going to play out as his grandfather seemed to think it would, he'd need all the stage-dressing he could muster. Just twenty-three years old, newly qualified in his chosen profession, he was all too conscious of his receding hairline and dreading the day it reached the already quite pronounced thinning spot on his crown. His grandfather, blessed in his youth with the signature thick auburn waves from the Vernon side, maintained an impressive snow-white mane well into his nineties. Charles, on the other hand, was the disgruntled inheritor of flyaway chestnut wisps and male pattern baldness via his Warrington genes, still working his way through supplements advertised in the *Times* in the hope that one of them might prove to be the cure-all it confidently promised.

If only there were a cure for penury. The desk's polished drawer-fronts had been hiding unpaid invoices, sorrowful letters detailing the collapse of various business interests, court summonses ignored and judgements in absentia ditto, as the last of the Vernons counted down his final days. With nothing of consequence to leave and no son of his name to leave it to, it would appear he had simply stopped caring, the family curse opening its maw and swallowing one more victim whole. Everything with any intrinsic value was already lined up downstairs to be appraised and taken off to the auctioneers, even the kitsch Wade figurines Charles was personally convinced no sane adult could ever love. "Very collectable," the auctioneer's man assured him; he'd have happily paid someone to take the blasted things away, but if they were worth something to someone, all the better. The bare shelves reproached him, but what choice did he have? The fellow had hinted delicately that the family portraits might also fetch a decent sum if Mr Warrington were so inclined, but he'd shut that suggestion down immediately. Things might be desperate, but never that desperate.

Finally, there was the one remaining item in the cabinet behind him: the massive silver serving platter depicting the family's founding legend. At least the old man had enough sense left at the end to include that as a personal bequest, "To my only grandson, the honourable Charles." The way things were going, his final net inheritance could well be nothing more than the plate and some pocket change.

And the curse, of course; an even more bitter legacy. *He'll show up when he sees the obituary*, the old man had assured him during their final, incredibly awkward conversation. With that prediction ringing in his ears Charles seriously considered not even having one published. Let the miserable old bastard slide into obscurity, why not? He'd gone beyond caring after all, and what he'd left behind was more than enough to worry about without adding dark fairytales into the mix.

Charles was still clinging to a faint hope that it would all turn out to be nonsense, one last joke at the family's expense, but that hope died to nothing when the door swung open and a man strolled in unannounced, idling his way along the portrait wall as if greeting old friends.

The Nothing-Man, his grandfather always called him, as if it would be bad luck somehow to speak his name. Not that they seemed to know his name; at least, there was nothing in the family records that hinted at it, and no doubt that's how he preferred it. So the Nothing-Man he remained, a bogeyman conjured to impress generations of Vernons with the appropriate sense of duty and foreboding in equal measure.

It was an apt name. He looked like nothing, middling-tall and middling-build with nondescript features and plain, workmanlike clothes all in the same dusty black. You'd pass him in the street without a second glance. Only his eyes were remarkable; deep-set, endlessly dark, they seemed to reflect nothing back that he passed—not the lamps, not the mean little fire glowing in the grate, not the bright gilt of the picture frames on the wall nor the silver oval of the platter behind Charles' head. He ended his unhurried approach at the very edge of the lamplight, tilting his head to look up at the fairy hunt scene.

"A nice piece, eh? It was my favourite when I was a little boy. My grandfather used to tell me the story."

Charles couldn't help but congratulate himself on the perfect opening. A greeting as equals, a cordial tone, no sign of the jangling tension he was feeling—the old man would have been proud.

The man huffed faintly, half a laugh and half not, and with the sound he came into focus somehow, the lines of his face and clothes sharpening imperceptibly as if he'd stepped out of the shadow without ever moving.

"So you're the new one."

Charles didn't care for the inference, as though the Vernons were some kind of tiresome vermin that wouldn't stop breeding under the floorboards. He clamped down on a sharp retort and determinedly steered back to his script.

"As of my grandfather's passing, yes. I was hoping we could dispense with the formality of your visit, since the Vernon name will end with him. The curse is done, yes?"

"That will be up to you." The Nothing-Man's tone was unexpectedly gentle. "Are you prepared to make amends?"

Exactly what the old man said he'd say. *Don't back down, boy. Never back down.*

"Where would I start? There's no money, if that's what you're hinting at."

"No, it is not." Any suggestion of gentleness vanished, the words slamming into place like nails into a coffin. "Every time, you disappoint. You're all so like your ancestor."

Charles screwed up his face in confusion at the non sequitur. Was that supposed to be some kind of twisted compliment? "I'm very gratified to hear it," he said stiffly.

The stranger's brows quirked up in bitter amusement. "You shouldn't be. He was a coward, a man who reached for more than he had the talent to earn. A man who kidnapped a child for ransom and then let her die."

"It was for love," Charles interjected. "My grandfather said—"

"For ransom," the man cut him off forcefully. "Don't try to argue the facts with me, lordling. I was *there*. He took her hostage, and to escape the consequences, he destroyed our door. Until one of you works out what it takes to make amends, there will be no end to the curse."

"It was centuries ago! Why should I suffer for his actions? Why should my grandfather?" Charles objected, cursing the outraged whine in his voice. "It's not like it was murder!"

"It wasn't murder, no." The shadows at the stranger's feet rose up, spreading behind him like dark wings, and he faced Charles down with a glitter of fury in his eyes. "Murder requires intent, and I doubt he ever so much as registered the little lives he destroyed. But since you want to argue technicalities—it was abduction. It was rape. And at the very last, when she could have been saved, it was neglect."

He spat out the words one by one, a bitter litany of reproach. If not for the leather seat of the chair nudging the backs of his knees, Charles might well have taken a step back, but that would have been unacceptable. The family motto, after all: *Habemus Tenemus. What we have, we hold.*

"Very well," he said, grandly waving aside the tedious details. "Let's say, then, if I were ready to make amends, what must I do?"

The Nothing-Man paused, scanning Charles's face as if searching for the truth of his statement or the intent behind it. "You only have to do what's right," he said at last, as if explaining playground rules to a particularly dense participant. "If you don't know what that looks like, then honestly I don't know how to help you."

He cast one final glance up at the fairy hunt scene winking in the lamplight.

"One piece of advice, for what it's worth. Turn your life to something useful. Perhaps you'll figure it out along the way."

BOOK 2

The Here and Now

Chapter 4

EVERY HUNDRED YEARS, the legend goes, the Devil goes down to Alfriscombe. Why? The legend is a little hazy on the details. Perhaps he has a fondness for the place. Perhaps, as some wit suggested, Beelzebub likes his day at the seaside as much as the next man. Other, darker rumours suggest he comes by to collect what's owed by the Vernon family after a disastrous wager made long ago.

Either way, stories and sightings abound. A tall man dressed all in black with coal for eyes, he roams the town greeting people by name that he's never met, asking questions about things that nobody should know. If he's satisfied with the answers, he goes away again after spending his gold freely. If things aren't going so well, somehow they start going better. Rents fall and wages rise, families fallen on hard times receive an unexpected windfall or run of good luck.

Not the Vernons, of course, since the last one with any ties to the place drank himself to death in a debtor's prison hundreds of years ago. No, the Devil's regard (if that's what it is) flows entirely to the common folk of the town.

***

And there are plenty of those.

Imagine every stereotype from any seaside town that you can remember, all rolled into one, and you'll have a fair mental image of Alfriscombe. Buckets and spades, beach cricket sets in net bags, and racks upon racks of cheap plastic flip-flops in every colour. Twenty-three flavours of ice cream between seven ice cream parlours, four fish and chip shops with identical stern warning signs about not feeding the seagulls, sweetshops and tat shops and ugly souvenir shops with yellow cellophane shielding the windows from the sun's bleaching rays.

The place has barely changed in the last sixty years, and why should it? Sun, sea, and sand — a winning formula that needs no updating, as the thousands of visitors who flood the area every summer can testify.

The town sits on the south coast, a middling-small settlement nestled in a fold of the hills sloping down to the sea. A sheltered natural harbour attracted humans to make their home there since before history began, a tiny fishing hamlet of the same name even getting a passing mention in the Domesday Book.

The present-day town is considerably larger, of course, spreading its skirts over the years to absorb a handful of villages inland and down the coast to the west. Back in the day, this was a hotspot for quackery, fraud, and pseudoscience, new money flocking here to take the waters or breathe the air as a cure for whatever ailed you. All of their grand houses are now hotels, dental surgeries, nursing homes painted in tasteful variations on off-white and cream.

All except one. You'll see it if you come in by train, one single subversive soul who rejected the tyranny of beige and opted instead for a vibrant Mediterranean sky-blue. It looks joyously awful against its more refined neighbours, a football shirt at a wedding, but it stands out.

Alfriscombe isn't overly fond of things that stand out, nor things that change, still clinging to the image of the perfect family resort from sometime in the 1950s. The town's steady decline into obscurity is a direct result. It's neither old-fashioned enough to be quaint, nor modern enough to be vibrant. Not big enough to be lively and not small enough to be peaceful, designated "urban" only by contrast to the rural hinterland it's surrounded by. Unless something more exciting than the biannual waste management conference happens here one of these days, it'll remain forever stuck in a bland no-man's land.

Chapter 5

SOMEWHERE NEAR VICTORIA, tucked down a narrow side-street, there's a tiny hole-in-the-wall café bar that appears in no tourist guide to the city.

The owner is unconcerned. Her prices wouldn't suit the idly curious, nor tourists on a budget, but they're perfectly pitched for her actual target demographic. For example, the man currently sitting alone at the pavement table outside, chair angled to collect the afternoon sun. Passersby might take him for a senior civil servant stopped for a moment's respite between meetings. This neighbourhood is stuffed with them, after all. They'd be almost completely wrong aside from one single point; he is, in fact, patiently waiting to meet someone. The superb espresso in front of him, black as a churchman's conscience with a perfect galaxy-swirl of crema, is merely an indulgence, an excuse to sit while he waits.

He reaches over and claims the newspaper abandoned at the next table, shaking it out and turning to the back page. Crossword half-filled in — in pencil, he notes with a baffled lift of his brows. Either commit or don't, what's with the half-measures? Typical mudside, though. People claim to care about things, but they'll abandon the quest if it proves too complex. They want, but their heads are soon turned by the next want, and the next; shallow desires pursued with misplaced determination.

The day's headlines are a depressing but grimly satisfying case in point. People sick and dying because of sub-standard housing. Yet another politician caught in the wrong bed. Possible insider trading at an investment bank, management issuing strenuous denials. Negligence, greed, and lust. Speaking of which . . . He reaches for his pen and flips back to the crossword. 16 down — *Fur in disarray, Danny starts a scam. (5).* Ah, yes: 'FRAUD'.

Scanning the next few clues provides no further inspiration, and he turns his attention back to the crowds crossing the main concourse, heads down and wrapped up in their own thoughts. A rolling tide of humanity, lifeless and disconnected.

Exceptions prove the rule, though. A girl comes past, pretty in the sunshine, with hair dyed bright red, multiple silver piercings in her ear, knitted rainbow sleeves warming her arms. Other than his coffee, she's the most interesting thing he's seen all morning, a bright counterpoint to the dreary background she moves against, and he watches her until she disappears out of sight behind the buildings before turning back to his headlines. City councillor suspended for misconduct, criminal investigation ongoing — good. It took long enough for justice to catch up with that one.

His satisfied smirk turns thoughtful, and he examines the crossword again. 3 across — *Attack on Lot's wife removes support, we hear (7)*. The pen is deployed again: 'ASSAULT'.

He sips his cooling coffee, letting the flavour roll over his tongue and debating internally whether he has time for another. The sun has moved round behind the office blocks now, putting him further and further into the shadows, and he's almost out of time. There's a sudden edge in the air, though — a brightening of the dreary street and the impression of a melody just beyond the edge of hearing, which tells him his wait is over. He doesn't even need to look up to see who's joining him.

"Good to see you back," he says, leaning back to catch the barista's eye. "Can I get you something?"

"No, I can't stop. I'm surprised to find you still here, to be honest. Did you not hear?"

"I heard." Mainder smiles bitterly. "They finally made the connection. It made the papers and everything."

"That's it then, isn't it? He'll be moving on the Fold before we know it. People are wondering when you're going to step in."

"Are they?"

The quirk of his mouth politely hints at disbelief, drawing a reluctant smile from the scribe. "Alright then, *I'm* wondering.

Couldn't you do something?"

"I am doing something. The long game, remember? Half of progress is made by standing still." Mainder grins over the rim of his cup. "You'll just have to trust me. How was it, anyway?"

The scribe sighs. "It was a mess, honestly. I'm amazed nothing went wrong, the way they were picking it over—like children digging for worms! What if there'd been something active down there?"

"Was there?" The bland query is delivered with a knowing smirk.

"I know, I know. You'd have said if there were. No, it didn't feel like any of it had ever even been used, at least not that I could sense."

"There you go then. A trade drop maybe? Anyway, it doesn't matter what they found. Never has. They'll put it all under lights and behind glass and write about it until they get bored." Mainder sounds indulgent rather than irritated, like a parent discussing the latest crayon-on-the-walls incident. "Were his people there?"

"All over it, yes. He's the last, isn't he? Surely it would be easy enough to finish it here."

"Easy, yes. But where's the elegance in that? He'll have his chance, just as all the others did before him. If he chooses to over-reach, that's on him."

"You'll let him ruin himself." The scribe smiles as understanding dawns. "Elegant indeed."

Chapter 6

MANOR HILL HOTEL and Day Spa sits up past
Alfriscombe's headland, a decorative shell formed gradually
over the centuries around the core of the original medieval
manor house. For centuries, this was the family home of the
Vernons, able to trace their noble line back to the Norman
conquest and beyond, but a combination of expensive tastes, a
series of disastrous investments, and a few unlucky runs at
cards forced them to sell up and retreat long ago.

It still has the air of a grand house, if you can overlook the
Michelin star plaques screwed to the stonework beside the main
entrance and the "[NO] Vacancies" sign creaking on its gibbet
down by the main road. The sweeping carriage drive still
follows the curve of the manor's boundary wall, taking new
arrivals past well-kept gardens and grand views over the bay
before dropping them at the front door. The frontage is all late
Regency, clean and white in the spring sunshine with row upon
row of identically sized sash windows, while newer extensions
at the rear house guest bedrooms overlooking the back lawn,
neatly clipped evergreens, and — beyond that — ancient
woodland with the crown of Fairy Hill rising up out of the trees
in the distance. In short, picturesque as all hell from every
possible angle. Little wonder the first Baron Vernon chose this
spot to cement his triumphant land grab post-Conquest.

The grand ballroom jutting off the southeast side is a
Victorian addition from the family who owned it briefly until
their only son was lost in the Great War. One of the bedrooms is
still preserved as a shrine to his memory, the life's work of his
grieving parents, even his uniform laid out as if ready for him to
return and don it before he heads off to victory.

Mainder struggles to remember that family's name, to his
occasional shame. Not Vernon, certainly, and he had nothing to
do with their misfortunes, but still. Maybe he'll drop by the

display later and remind himself. It feels like the right thing to do.

The only visible remnant of the medieval hall in these modern times is a wide Gothic arch just inside the front door. The old lord's motto just manages to assert its presence, if not its meaning, shallow scratches in the fragile sandstone barely legible now. *HABEMVS TENEMVS*, it used to say. A brief smirk ghosts across his face as he passes under the inscription and wipes his muddy feet thoroughly on the logo woven into the doormat. The hotel had initially decided to adopt the Vernon coat of arms as part of their branding, but between the spectre of possible lawsuits and the enthusiasm of the fancy graphic designer they hired it ended up almost unrecognisable, with details like the lion *passant* the Vernons were once so peacock-proud of replaced by nothing more than a stylised scribble beneath the shield. The absolute cherry on the cake is knowing that it appears not just on doormats, not just printed on restaurant menus and crockery and the tiny guest soaps in the rooms, it's even embossed on the luxury quilted toilet paper. Odds are that someone at that very moment is wiping their arse on the Vernon crest, and Mainder couldn't have devised a more fitting use for it if he'd tried.

This early in the year, it's sparse business, with the Valentine's Day offers over and done with and the Spring Bank Holiday trade yet to materialise, but those guests who do make the trip tend to be heavily susceptible to impulse buys from the trinkets displayed at the treatment centre desk. He stops to admire, as he always does, the sheer artistry at work in arranging the showcase, each shelf in the display containing precisely the correct number of tempting items, not too crowded and not too sparse, all angled to sparkle just *so* under the cabinet lights.

Looking more closely, though, there are a few gaps.

"You managed to shift that geode," he remarks, reaching into his coat pocket and flipping open his notebook. "Want me to send up another? Anything else you're out of?"

The young woman at the desk holds up a finger and darts

into the tiny office behind the desk. "All of the rose quartz," her voice echoes back to him. "Most of the pendants . . ."

She reappears with a handwritten list which she pushes across the desk for him to review.

"Pretty much all of the fossils. Here you go. We had a big rush on over Valentine's Day."

He raises his eyebrows, scribbling swift notes as he works his way down the extensive list. "No kidding. Who says romance is dead?"

"Certainly not me!"

The cheeky smile she shoots at him doesn't go unnoticed, but he lets her flirting pass without comment. Gratifying as it was when he overheard that the young ladies at the spa reception desk "totally would" even if he is "like, *really* old," the days are long gone that he'd consider taking them up on it.

Back before the Closing, his two chief duties had been monitoring the Fold for strays and wanderers and keeping track of the *yasim*, the half-bloods seeded year on year by the constant traffic between the two sides. He'd barely had to stir himself on that front in the last two centuries. Maybe there are more green eyes in Alfriscombe than you'd expect in such a small population, a bit more luck on the scratch cards or the horses — Realm blood leaves its mark. But these days, there isn't one that he could pick out of a crowd with the aura about them that says they're someone he needs to watch over. Certainly there are none of his get. He hasn't even had a relationship on this side for who knows how long for precisely that reason, and he's not about to start now.

Business concluded, he ducks down the corridor in the direction of the events suite. Hotel management chose to decorate this section with a selection of tasteful prints in unfussy dark wood frames showing scenes from the history of Alfriscombe. He stops to admire what's, in his opinion, the best of the lot: delicate ink lines and cross-hatching showing a view of the town from, if he remembers correctly, 1857. Yes, that'd be right; the pier hadn't been built yet, and the old Abbey schoolhouse, one of the only victims of the fire of 1860, is still standing. Memory supplies the scene: the blaze and its aftermath; nobody hurt, but the building itself reduced to smoking rubble, handwringing from the diocese and mutterings from the vicar about God's mysterious ways. In truth God had very little to do with it, but he's confident She would have approved of the outcome, if not the methods. No more kids being singled out at the teachers' whim. No more mysterious discipline delivered behind closed doors, strictly one on one, leaving boys pale and tearful and resolutely silent. Not in his town. He still counts that as one of his better days' work.

A couple of steps onwards he halts again, head cocked as if listening to an unseen navigator, and apparently on impulse takes a sharp right into *Hotel Staff Only* territory, a service corridor providing hidden access to the function rooms and the restaurant. As such, it's an unloved, undecorated space designed for actual work to get done, safely out of sight of paying guests. Plush carpet underfoot gives way to easy-to-mop vinyl in dull blue. Utilitarian plastic skirting protects the bare plaster walls from the heavy catering trolleys, inclined to rumble on unchecked if you let go even for a moment.

One such appears as he reaches the bend, and he stops close into the wall to let it go rattling past. The tiny young woman struggling to steer the beast nods breathless thanks and carries on her way. Further down, there's the murmur of voices from an event in progress. More of the staff are in full action mode here, smartly kicking open the kitchen doors to bustle past and around him with water jugs and trays of coffee cups, but they pay him no attention beyond the occasional nod of greeting. They all know him — local kids grown up playing hopscotch or bulldog in the alley behind his shop — and for all his many faults, he never could bring himself to be a dick to children. It works out nicely; they have nothing but positive associations with him, and this wouldn't be the first time he's taken advantage of that fact to use their domain as a shortcut.

He emerges precisely where he needs to be: the atrium at the centre of the function rooms. They're busy laying it up for the first break, and he drifts aside to keep out of the way, helpfully picking up a discarded lanyard from the floor. A sign propped on the easel by the other door proclaims that today's series of seminars are on the subject of "Alfriscombe: Past, Present, and Future," and are kindly sponsored by the Warrington Institute.

He barely glances at it. There's news to be had here today, but that isn't it.

Chapter 7

"THE TOWN OF Alfriscombe has long been of historical interest. First recorded in the Domesday Book as a manorial hall in the possession of one William Vernon and featuring heavily in many of the fairytales and folklore of this region, this location has seen many events over the years . . ."

True of any place that's a place, Mainder grouches silently, easing into the back of the room. Why mudsiders place so much faith in sticks and stones was always beyond him. Like somewhere isn't a real place until they've been there and smothered the living earth in stone and steel.

The current speaker is an almost pitch-perfect stereotype of the absent-minded professor, even down to his choice of clothes — unfashionable jeans paired with a fussily patterned shirt and a sage-green tweed jacket. He hardly seems like a formidable adversary. Mainder can only hope there's more to him that meets the eye — or indeed the ear. Half his audience sits with arms folded, frowning down at the ground, a pose that says they're listening only because they can't think of a compelling reason to get up and walk out. The other half appear to be surreptitiously composing emails on their laptops.

"After a promising start, William took possession of the parish in 1103 as a reward for his family's assistance in the Norman invasion. He promptly built a simple hall, the remains of which you will of course have noticed in the hotel's reception area. His grandson Robert was one of the architects of the Treaty of Wallingford and, as a result of his endeavours, was able to considerably enlarge the original structure and add two new wings, with building work spanning twenty years from 1157 onwards. Sadly, by the late 1500s records suggest the Vernons had fallen from royal favour, and the manor saw no further expansion from that point."

Of all the people in this room, Mainder is the least in need of a potted history of Alfriscombe, and if he ever felt the need then this rambling word-salad wouldn't be it. Nonetheless, he keeps his thoughts firmly to himself and schools his face into an expression of polite attention.

"Of course, it's not the Vernon family who have brought us to Alfriscombe — although their descendants are certainly interested in what we may find!" The speaker chuckles weakly, and when there's no answering ripple from his listeners, he pretends not to notice and continues. "This period in Alfriscombe's history also coincides, as far as we are able to establish, with the charming story of the Moon Princess. Of course it's no more than a children's tale, but there may well be some historical basis in fact. Rather more mundane than the story would have us believe, but it was hardly uncommon for a young woman to be carried across borders, quite possibly against her will, to be married into a neighbouring tribe!"

He twinkles happily, as if abduction and forced marriage were some quaint regional custom on the same level as cheese-rolling or Morris dancing.

"What little evidence we have of such a person as our mythical princess existing is limited to the Moon Brooch, part of the Vernon Collection. As you know, my own specialism is not in metalworking or jewellery, so you may be asking yourself, why on earth am I so interested in a few trinkets?"

He breaks off to take a sip of water and possibly to allow his listeners a moment to ponder a hypothetical scenario where they might be persuaded to care about what he's thinking. Mainder's view from the back of the room suggests the majority remain focused on correcting typos in their email drafts.

"The Moon Brooch, while sadly damaged, still bears the trace of a stamp on the underside, a maker's mark in the very distinctive form of a triskelion. By itself this is interesting, but with the recent discovery by my colleagues of the Alfriscombe Hoard bearing the exact same mark — ah, I'm sure you can see the implications! It strongly suggests the items were made somewhere nearby, rather than a single item being an import from elsewhere. Now, this is where it gets really interesting.

Using some very new techniques - some of you may already know this next part, of course; we're not quite ready to publish but, aha, no surprise that the odd snippet will have slipped out! - a very new technique, as I say, we believe we may have discovered a very significant connection."

The slideshow advances to an artist's impression of Fairy Hill from pre-history. Lively, imperfect pencil strokes describe a wooden palisade and rough huts clustered at the bottom, a grand circle of standing stones at the summit, and ragged stick-figure inhabitants — who don't appear to own a razor or a comb between them — leading a reluctant ox to ritual sacrifice.

"The significance of the barrow and its stone circle, of course, cannot be denied. No question, no question at all, there must have been some ritual function connected to Alfriscombe during that time. The Hoard's component parts — what must have been a magnificent harness, or perhaps a collar, we are still, ah, discussing that question, of course — but as I say, a magnificent high status object broken into scraps and placed — with immense ceremony, I have no doubt! — in an attempt to gain favour with the deity attached to the region ... uh, where was I? Oh yes. What brings us here today is something many have missed, which is the very clear connection between the objects in the Hoard, the Moon Brooch, and the town itself."

The slide advances again to display a 3D model of the landscape, monochrome blocks just recognisable as Alfriscombe's bay with the town in the foreground and the hill rising up behind it.

"The Lidar scanning technique we have been utilising on a larger scale to capture the landscape topology, you see here the clear evidence of a structure at the foot of the hill, which I am certain has some connection to ritual worship. This technology can also be deployed at a much finer resolution. So, for example, we might scan a surface to see what is underneath a layer of paint, dust, or what-have-you. On an impulse, I directed my team to test this on some samples around the Hoard site, and . . ." He holds the projector control high, as if he's about to perform a magic trick, and triumphantly presses a button.

The result is underwhelming. Due to some technical hitch or other, the layout has been horribly mangled, so what should have been a neat gallery has become a jumble of images stacked on top of each other. The top of the pile shows two young men standing on either side of a very ordinary-looking section of dry-stone wall, grinning at the camera with thumbs up and a heap of equipment at their feet.

"Ah. That's . . . uh, I don't quite know what happened there. What we should be seeing is — ah, perhaps I could have a moment to fix this?" He appeals to the timekeeper in the front row, who returns a firm head shake. "Of course, yes, we must keep to time. Perhaps it's best if I simply describe the results. The scan revealed a carving on the stone here, at the centre of this frame — a very distinctive design that almost exactly matches the triskelion we saw on the objects in the Hoard!"

Evidently from his breathless delivery, that was intended to be the climax of his presentation. Without the scan image as proof, though, the only reaction he gets is a handful of people glancing up briefly from their screens and immediately looking down again.

"So, ah, in conclusion: while many continue to advocate for more traditional methods used solely in isolation, I can safely say we have demonstrated how effective the newer technologies can be at assisting the early phases of a project. I am sure your home institutions will be as keen as mine to explore the efficiency angle there!"

That, at least, prompts a murmur of ironic laughter from the audience, and he preens for a moment before advancing to his final slide.

"We look forward to testing our approach over the summer with a little, ah, proof of concept here in Alfriscombe. A few minor details to wrap up, ah, very promising talks with the landowner and, um, yes. We expect to have an agreement any day now. Thank you, ladies and gentlemen. I think we possibly have time for a few questions?"

There it is. Mainder stretches his fingers out to loosen the tension in his hands and pushes away from the wall. It's almost unsporting. The universe may eventually see fit to send him a challenge, but today is not that day.

Chapter 8

PROFESSOR PATTERSON ISN'T a terrible person, on balance. Maybe he does switch focus according to which way the money is flowing, and perhaps he occasionally adds his name to work he didn't contribute all that much value to, but he's very far from the worst of the breed.

For example, while he naturally delivered the keynote in a way that suggested he was personally responsible for all of the key insights, he did at least make sure his team of students could attend the event with him. The cynical might say it was so he doesn't have to man the stand constantly, freeing him to network and sniff out new funding, but that's hardly a crime. Somebody has to keep an eye on the landscape.

He has valid reasons to be focused on the money, too. The 3D modelling alone ate up a quarter of his budget, and if his current spread of grant applications aren't successful, the institute might well go over his head and put someone else in charge.

Luckily, the model is proving to be quite the draw, curious visitors crossing the room to watch Alfriscombe's contours spin in slow motion against a dark background. A point scored against his nemesis on the audit committee, he congratulates himself and beams benevolently at the crowd as he answers another question.

"Ah, the Lidar, yes. Government data, the environment scans they use for flood modelling. Fascinating what they can uncover! The classic barrow shape, of course. We'd expect to see at least one high-status internment. And —" indicating a semi-circular line of bumps in the ground at the foot of the hill " — this could be something very exciting, perhaps a ritual site for preparing the deceased for their journey to the underworld."

One of the crowd of visitors leans closer and examines the screen with a scholar's frown. "I can see why that's an appealing theory," he says judiciously. 'Given the history of building in that area, though, I don't know. What have you done to rule out the other options?"

Patterson's smile stays pinned to his cheeks, but the rest of his face fades to blank incomprehension. "Other options?" He peers at the man's chest, searching for the cardboard rectangle that will help him decide whether his inconvenient questioner is someone he needs to be polite to. He's out of luck; the badge appears to have been lost somewhere, though the empty lanyard dangling around his neck says he must have had one at some point.

"The old shrine, for a start. First contemporary mentions from about 1620, if I recall correctly. The chapel site around the same time. Then there was talk of a folly with a circular tower in the early 1800s . . . I could go on. You weren't aware?"

"Sorry, who are you?" The words emerge from Patterson's mouth before he has a chance to soften them. "Ah, I mean to say, who do you represent? What organisation?"

The stranger seems amused by the slip rather than offended. "Mainder. Alfriscombe Historical Trust. Forgive me, I was sure I heard you say just now that you'd been talking to us."

"Talking to the Trust? I'm sorry, I—I mean, we may have been?" Patterson is utterly adrift, floating in a sea of uncertainty.

"You said you'd been talking to the landowner. That's the Trust."

Back on surer ground, Patterson smiles patronisingly. "Ah, no, I think you'll find it's part of the Vernon estate. One of our board members is a direct descendant of the family. I assume he should know!"

"There is no Vernon estate," Mainder says coolly. "And if we're thinking of the same man, he's getting on a bit now, isn't he? He might be a bit confused. The manor and anything else that hadn't already been lost at cards was sold off around 1820. Apart from anything else, that whole area has protected monument status, so I don't see you getting permission to dig it up."

"There must be some misunderstanding." Patterson looks up and down the line of faces; far from the crowning triumph he'd anticipated, it's fast becoming a sideshow, this amateur nobody showing him up in front of all the people he'd been hoping to impress. The room is practically creaking with second-hand embarrassment. "Mr. Vernon was very confident there wouldn't be a problem."

"Well, his ancestor was pretty confident, too. Right up until he tried to play his fifth ace." Mainder rolls his eyes dramatically, eliciting a ripple of unpleasant sniggers from his audience.

Patterson wants nothing more than for this to be over. "Indeed," he says tightly, scanning the room for one of his students to hand off to. "I'll check in with our people and see if there's an official position on your query. I'm sure there's a perfectly good explanation."

"I'm sure there is," Mainder agrees, granting him a cordial nod, and strolls away without waiting to hear what it might be.

***

The official position — when Patterson finally manages to get through to a person rather than a voicemail — is both much briefer than he expected and far less helpful. Rather than answers, it's more questions. *Who's asking?* they want to know? And what exactly did this mysterious local history buff look like? Mystified, he does his best to provide a description and then asks plaintively, "Is this going to impact the project?"

"We're looking into it," comes the short reply. "The board is confident everything is in place." The line goes dead.

"Well, that's all right then," he murmurs sarcastically and heads back to the stand to work out where he's supposed to be next.

Chapter 9

SQUIRREL'S DREY, ANNOUNCE faded silver-grey letters in gothic script painted on the dusty fascia. Under that, in far more prosaic and legible lettering: *Est. 1863. Prop. E. Mainder Esq.*

The shop itself is something of a local landmark, a navigation point for those unfamiliar with the area. *Head up until you see Mainder's, then turn right,* the locals tell tourists looking for the church. *The loos? Oh, they're down past Mainder's and towards the sea front. You can't miss it.*

Not that it's in any way remarkable; it's just one more cluttered window smack in the middle of the row of shops, a higgledy-piggledy mashup of what used to be fishermen's cottages back before Victorian engineers decided they could push back the sea. Like all the buildings on that street, it's an architectural mongrel, uneven lumps of red sandstone at the back and spartan neoclassical from assorted eras rising up above the modern shopfronts, additions and extensions sprouting in all directions. No, what makes it a waypoint is that it sits right on the junction with the broad avenue of Bishop's Walk, once the imposing approach to some long-dead churchman's long-fallen palace. From that direction, the shop is front and centre, clearly discernible from a hundred yards away.

If you had an hour to kill and nowhere to be, the shop is perfectly placed to take advantage of your curiosity. Bullseye panes in the bowed bay window show distorted glimpses of the treasures inside, narrow shelves cluttered with coins, arrowheads, and fossils. To the left and to the right, round baskets of trinkets placed haphazardly on every flat surface. Mainder doesn't make it easy for you to find the good stuff. *Let 'em search,* he always says. Let the customer feel good about discovering the perfect gift or outright bargain in amongst the dusty tat.

Stepping inside, the first thing that hits you is the smell. It's not awful — quite the opposite. It's something like slipping between the pages of a book, warm and dry with a faint papery rustle on the edge of hearing. Underneath that are notes of dust, bergamot, and charcoal, though what causes this peculiar blend is impossible to say. Certainly, there are books — row upon row on crowded shelves from floor to ceiling, disappearing into the gloom at the back. Cardboard labels in hand-written capitals sellotaped to the edge of each shelf suggest the topics you might expect to find there, including local history, reference, folklore and "Fiction – Local Author." Lower shelves dispense with labelling and instead entice smaller customers with the colourful covers of the books themselves, a sample turned face out to display distant worlds, talking animals, twin suns and magical doorways. Mainder knows his audience.

Well, he ought to. As he likes to say, he's been in this business long enough. Distant contacts are constantly surprised to find the shop is even still going. *Must be the son,* they say, *or the grandson. Or the old man finally retired and handed off to someone else who kept the name going, like Dread Pirate Whatsisname from that movie.*

Every once in a while, some tourist will laughingly enquire if "Mister Mainder *Ess*-squire" is available, and he'll grin along with the tired joke and come out from behind the counter, indicating himself with a showman's flourish and asking what he can do for them. How good a mood he's in depends on how long he lets them stew before explaining that the shop was founded by his great-grandfather back in the day. It never gets old, the frozen horror on their faces dissolving to foolish relief, and the haste with which they fumble to buy something just so they can get out of here.

The woman who picked up the book her hand happened to be resting on and blurted, "Just this, thank you!" — she's still his favourite memory. He's just sorry he never got to see her face when she opened the bag later and realised she'd bought *An Illustrated History of Faerie Congress,* the collector's edition with full colour plates in glorious anatomically graphic detail. Even Jen, running the sweetshop next door and as strait-laced a matron as he ever met, got a chuckle out of that one when he told her.

He likes Jen. She's that rare combination of genuinely sweet-natured and incurably curious and keeps him well supplied with accurate gossip on the lives of everyone in the town. He can't break her habit of calling him *Mister* Mainder, though, no matter how many times he gently corrects her. To everyone else, he's just Mainder. In theory, there must be a first name floating around somewhere in his history, but nobody ever gets close enough to know it. It just doesn't seem necessary somehow. Taken with the longevity of the shop itself, it cements the impression of an eternally benign presence, forever and always a Mainder with a hand on the helm, and it's been that way for so long that nobody questions it.

Sometimes, if he's honest, he does wonder if it's time to pack it all in. He doesn't need to be here all the time. In fact, he could probably get away with not being here at all, barely ever required to man the actual shop, perfectly able to leave day-to-day operations to the cheerful Krzysztof. Perhaps it genuinely is time he went home, even just for a visit.

He could, of course. There was never anything stopping him; it's just that every time the idea crosses his mind, he finds he somehow just doesn't really want to. He's far too comfortable with things the way they are.

Chapter 10

KRZYSZTOF ISN'T TOO surprised when Winter Street starts filling up before the season really gets underway. There's still a couple of weeks to go before the Easter tours start dropping coach-loads of cantankerous pensioners at the north end car park and dispatching them in search of cream teas and postcards, but he's already seen the usual uptick in traffic thanks to conference season. Business has been brisk all weekend, and he's barely had time to straighten up a bit before the bell over the door is jangling yet again.

It's immediately evident they've come via Jen's shop, since half of them are clutching the retro candy-striped paper bags she uses to dispense pear drops and humbugs from the glass jars on the shelf behind her. Before the bell has even finished jangling, he pointedly clears his throat and pushes the "Patrons Are Kindly Requested Not to Eat or Drink in the Shop" sign an inch farther forward on the counter, and a couple of guilty hands shrink back and put the sweets away into pockets and bags. Satisfied, he nods a vague welcome and returns to his book, occasionally letting his eyes flick up to see what they're doing. Kids like these rarely buy anything; they just waste his time raking through everything and making a mess for him to straighten up after they leave.

He's unwillingly intrigued, though. If they're anything to do with the conferences, they're far from the usual demographic. Far too young, for a start. Barely out of their teens some of them, all skinny jeans and floppy hair and scuffed rucksacks slung carelessly over one shoulder.

First one in, he mentally names Ponytail, for the thick brown hair pulled back off his broad forehead and hanging down his back. Behind him is another youngster with a distinctly indoor look about him, pale to the point of being pasty and dark eyes filled with resignation, like a teenager dragged unwillingly away from his Xbox to take a nice walk in the fresh air. Krzysztof quietly chuckles at how he touches the door handle as he comes in, fingertips delicately extended as if trying not to catch anything. He knows for a fact it's spotless, since he personally polished the bloody thing to a shine only this morning.

Third in line is something of a switch-up, slightly older or a superior of some kind. Or perhaps that's the effect of how he's dressed — a pale pink dress shirt with the sleeves rolled up a little way, blue jeans pressed to sharp creases, polished brown brogues. Dark hair dips in a perfect glossy wave over his forehead, impeccably styled, and meets thick sideburns shading to a neatly trimmed beard. He looks nothing like an academic, student or otherwise. He looks more like the junior doctors up at the county hospital, well-educated and whip-smart Indian boys putting in their residency on this backwater rotation until they can get a placement somewhere more lively.

Last through the door is a shorter figure of indeterminate gender. A black knitted hat, a ragged fringe of ashy-pale hair, and a thick scarf wound double around their neck hide the majority of their face, and an oversized sweater in broad stripes of black and grey covers their shape entirely down to the knees. Skinny legs encased in dull grey jeans end in scuffed black leather boots loosely laced up halfway. This one can't be anything other than a student, not dressed like that.

Gradually, the book occupies less and less of his attention, not that they'd know it. The deceptively random placement of framed maps and posters around the shop is actually carefully designed to give the cash a view of almost the whole shop floor without turning. The smart young man disappears between the bookshelves, where he can be heard exclaiming occasionally over some of the titles, while the other two wander around, peering curiously into the glass-fronted displays and turning over the boxes of cheaper curios.

Finally, the sour-faced one comes up to the counter with a small handful of flint arrowheads. "Are these all found locally?"

"Indeed they are, up on the edge of the moor. Kids pick

them up when they're up there playing."

That clearly wasn't the answer the boy was hoping for; his face rearranges into a displeased frown. "You shouldn't let people just take artefacts away from a site, you know. Ruins the archaeology. Very irresponsible."

Krzysztof leans back a little and widens his eyes in fake dismay. "Oh, is that right? I'm very sorry. I'll be sure and tell the kids whose families have been here since Doomsday that they aren't allowed to turn over rocks anymore. I can't promise it'll go down too well, seeing as I'm not from around here myself." He plays up his accent to full effect, ending the sentence with a friendly smile.

Ponytail calls over from his corner. "We've talked about this, Aaron. No lecturing the locals. Leave that to Viktor."

The sour one grins ruefully at the correction. "Good point. Sorry, and I'll take them, please. Oh, and a gemstone lucky dip as well."

Throughout the whole process, the last of the group hasn't said a word, just loitering by the counter idly looking through the rack of carved soapstone pendants.

Krzysztof likes to think he's good with youngsters, even at that difficult age, so he goes for the upsell. "What about you, young man—nothing take your fancy today? Must be something on there that suits your style. Souvenir for your mum perhaps? Good value, only £2.99."

The face crinkles into what's probably a smile under the swathes of fabric. For a split second, he's reminded of the boss, the warming of the lad's expression making him feel momentarily like a better version of himself. The questing hand turns over several of the designs on offer before there's a quiet "huh" of triumph and he extracts one with a pale stripe and geometric design.

"Oh, good choice," twinkles Krzysztof as he wraps it in tissue paper and secures it with a tab of sticky tape. "This one is my favourite." It's not, but it's a useful sales spiel he's employed on many occasions. Make them feel good about it, just like the boss says.

The transaction is completed in silence, the child handing over a handful of still-warm coins extracted from a pocket hidden somewhere under the jumper, but he nods thanks as the neat package is placed in his hand.

"Nice kid," Krzysztof mutters to himself as the shop empties and the bell finally stops swinging.

Chapter 11

BERYL HAD JUST decided she could get away with nipping out back for a smoke when the cafe door rattles in its frame, signalling that someone has just fallen foul of the sticky latch. She's told Andy a dozen times that he needs to get that fixed, and he's waved his hands in his typical excitable way and assured her that it'll be done by the time the season starts. Well, he's the boss — but she's the person who has to soothe the customers who've bashed their heads against the door when it failed to open the first time. She almost turns tail again seeing the four young people filing in. Bet they take forever to go through the menu, and then they'll order four diet Cokes and a piece of cake to share. But they've seen her, one of them giving her a friendly smile while he grabs four laminated menus from the stand by the till, and she busies herself tidying the cutlery tray until they make a decision.

It does take a while, but she's pleasantly surprised. Two plates of chips, three sandwiches, tea for four, and on top of that, they one by one wander up to the display to review the selection of cakes. Healthy appetites and decent manners — who'd have thought? More than you can say for a lot of so-called adults, especially the old folk who waste her time bitching about extra jam portions.

As soon as she heads back to the kitchen, they crowd together again and strike up a lively conversation. It's incomprehensible for the most part, full of side-eye and sniggering, whatever it is that's amusing them so much. In between snatches of conversation, they're glued to their phones as well, apparently carrying on several interleaved conversations at once with absent friends.

In their group chat, however, the topic is far more focused.

weatherwax92: you guys done yet?

scrublord: @weatherwax92 just

weatherwax92: and?

AJ: he want there
*wasnt
interesting tho

weatherwax92: duh
client wants him on the project, i need more than ¯_(ツ)_/¯ yeah we think
he's interesting
did we gt his family history

AJ: yep, bit sparse
great-great-something grandfather settled here back in the 1840s. possibly
gypsy settling down with local girl

weatherwax92: roma, not gypsy
incredibly unusual if so

AJ: roma yep sorry
anyway we went back to 1828
always a mainder on the deeds
and several others too
deeds I mean. he owns quite a chunk of that street

xXpaganXx: @syco you're very quiet
what's your take? specialist subject and all :P

syco: loving the all-black vibe
alfriscombe's final boss, Edgelord the Unflappable

scrublord: lmao

xXpaganXx: lol, trust you
missing your gaming rig yet?

syco: wdym 'missing'
brought my steam deck

xXpaganXx: of course you did
think you can handle him?

syco: possibly

scrublord: any of us could.
old man runs a shop ffs
when's the last time you think he had to deal with anything bigtime?

syco: you're hardly big time pumpkin :)
miniboss at best

xXpaganXx: burn

scrublord: thats it, i'm calling childline

syco: you know we love you really bby

scrublord: sure you do
anyways, isn't it weird tho? several hundred years of a man with the same name
always being there?
sounds like a movie pitch

xXpaganXx: Highlander, yeah
except connor mcleod was smart enough to use stolen identities every time he
faked his own death, and will his stuff to his new persona

weatherwax92: oh we think he's immortal now? you watch too much tv

xXpaganXx: nah, but he's definitely interesting

syco: make sure we get that in the report, aight? 'interesting, possibly immortal.
not as smart as Connor McLeod'

The burst of laughter that greets this startles Beryl, and she
whips around to stare at them suspiciously. She wonders if
they're laughing at her somehow, even though they haven't

spared her a second glance. But when they get up to leave, they're politeness itself, even going so far as to stack their dirty plates and sweep up crumbs while the tall lad with the ponytail comes over to pay the bill. Clearing the dishes, she even finds a neat stack of coins in one of the untouched saucers — the unanticipated tip.

Chapter 12

THE LETTER IS waiting in the hall, crisp and clean and utterly blank. No stamp or frank in the top-right corner, so it must have been hand-delivered early this morning before he got moving. He carries it through with him to the tiny kitchen, tossing it on the table while he coaxes the stove to light and sets some coffee on to brew.

Only after he's taken his first appreciative sip does he sit down and pull the thick envelope towards him, extracting a pearl-handled penknife to slit the paper and extract the contents. A single sheet of heavyweight cream paper slides into his hand, crackling genteelly as he lays it flat. He frowns at the embossed heading and coat of arms, then at the two lines of elegantly handwritten script.

Your presence is kindly requested at your earliest convenience on a matter of significant interest to both our principals. Failure to act could result in an opportunity lost.

There's no name, no salutation, and that, along with the absence of an address on the envelope, delivers a message of its own. They know who he is and where he can be found. And as for what he's being invited to discuss, they know he knows that, too.

The letter ends with some unreadable scrawl of a signature, but that's irrelevant. The embossed letterhead announces in crisp, square-cut capitals that this comes via the private office of the Honourable Charles Ernest Warrington Vernon.

"Well. Here we go," he muses out loud to the empty kitchen. Then he leans comfortably back in his chair, one hand still resting delicately on the paper, and finishes his coffee.

Chapter 13

FASHIONABLY LATE, LINDEN lingers in the doorway for a moment of people-watching.

You can always tell the ones who were born into status and wealth. Every overt signal of the power imbalance between them and the people around them, every benefit and opportunity, is accepted as just fundamentally how the universe is supposed to function. If sometimes they're aware of their massive privilege, as the man they're currently watching would like to think he is, it's still mostly a performative affair. Like making a point to smile and thank the server gliding past as he deftly claims a refill from her silver tray.

Moreover, that smooth charm — from overling to underling — is a fragile veneer over a deep well of entitlement. Break the compact, fail to be suitably grateful for the condescension, and the charm can vanish. They've seen it. *Caused it, too,* they recall with a lopsided smile swiftly suppressed, and they push off the doorframe to go and greet their host.

He turns as he registers their approach, arranging his features into a warm overling smile masking his mingled apprehension and relief. On paper, Linden currently works for him, but the Archchancellor is entirely aware where the power balance would lie if it came down to a challenge. He's far from the only client with the correct combination of money and requirements.

"It never gets old, you know," Linden says. "Mission briefings in the back room of the fundraisers' ball. Are they really so boring that you need to spice them up with covert operations?"

"You've attended enough by now, you tell me." He takes a sip of his own champagne to mask the smile twitching at the corners of his mouth. "Have you reviewed the brief?"

"Only the outline. I thought it was very similar to the Ely project, apart from — well, you know. Is he serious?"

"Well, we shall see." He nods at the figure in sombre grey livery lurking pointedly in the entrance to a side corridor, a signal that their host is ready to see them now.

***

A very select handful of guests is enjoying a more intimate view of their benefactor's residence, dotted about the room in twos and threes, admiring the artwork and talking academic politics in hushed tones.

It's a grand setting, certainly. The room must be fifty feet long, with elegant panelling at the far end open to reveal yet more space beyond. Deep blue velvet, fringed and tasselled and draped, adorns the floor-to-ceiling windows running down the right of the room, while a cheerful fire crackles in the massive marble fireplace on the left, presumably for the comfort of the frail figure huddled in one of the armchairs there.

Time has not been kind to the honourable Charles. The receding hairline he once tried so vainly to ignore is ancient history, just a bare iron-grey fringe clinging on somewhere around the level of his ears. Dark pink lesions dot his scalp and forehead, and an unusual pallor gives him a drawn, weary look despite his many comforts. He stares into the fire, face settled into heavy jowls, with a petulant quirk to his mouth that recalls the spoilt child he used to be.

"Finally," he snaps at the new arrivals. "The paperwork is on the desk."

One crabbed hand swirls imperiously in the direction of the double doors and the study beyond. Linden receives the hint with unruffled good humour and retrieves the documents, offering them to the old man, but he waves again impatiently.

"No, no, that's your copy. I have no desire to read the blasted things ever again."

Linden settles in the wing chair opposite the old man, leafing through the folder to check the contents while the archchancellor fidgets irritably. Etiquette is a consideration here, in the private home of the Institute's founder and most significant donor, and he hasn't actually been offered a seat. But then neither has Linden, and Vernon didn't comment.

"This historian," Linden says thoughtfully, breaking the silence. "You expect him to be a problem?"

The old man wheezes, a painful parody of a laugh. "I expect him to try, certainly. He'll hate not having the upper hand. Had it all his own way for far too long. Cooper tells me you'll keep him under control. I should damn well hope so, considering your outrageous fee."

"Forgive me, sir," Archchancellor Cooper interrupts. "Are you serious about bringing in this man? He may claim to be the local expert, but he's hardly the sort of name that will enhance the project's reputation."

"He is considerably more than that. Didn't you read the briefing material my people put together?" Charles gives him a sour look. "I'm deadly serious, believe me. Fifty years ago, he stood in my study and told me I was wasting my time, damn him, and if there's a way to cause trouble, he'll find it. Better we have him on the inside pissing out than on the outside pissing in. He's essential."

"Essential," in Cooper's considered opinion, is exactly what the man is not. Vernon has some very odd ideas that he's prepared to spend very generously to pursue, and that sort of obsession attracts exactly the type of lowlife charlatan willing to indulge — or even encourage — the old man's delusions. It's another matter entirely that that the university happily continues to cash Mr Vernon's cheques, of course. Not the same thing at all.

"Of course, sir. If you're satisfied that you have the right man — " a significant glance at Linden clearly signals his own opinion on that score " — might I recommend that you leave the negotiations to my people? I see no reason for you to be troubled with the details."

"You'll allow me the pleasure of bringing him to heel first," Charles shoots back, with a flash of bitter humour. "If I'm right, he'll be appearing before you have a chance to summon him. If there's one thing you can count on with these creatures, it's their curiosity. Remember that!" he adds, jabbing a finger in Linden's direction.

Linden scans the blurred photo on top of the pile: a dark-haired man striding down a crowded street with his long coat billowing out behind him, gaze fixed straight ahead and apparently unaware of his surveillance. Their client seems utterly convinced, but it's not possible. Fifty years ago, the man in this picture probably wouldn't even have been born.

"Your other guest has arrived, sir," a deferential voice murmurs, and Charles begins the painful process of extracting himself from his chair.

"As I thought. Show him up once I reach the study."

***

No shadows to lurk in this time; Charles can clearly see the Nothing-Man strolling across the room towards him. Still tall, still dark, still dressed head to toe in dusty black. Still approximately forty-something years old even though more than fifty years have passed since their last meeting. It may be the nature of his kind not to age, to wear any face they take a liking to, but still, it stings to see it.

On the other hand, his very presence here, unchanged after so many years, is a strange sort of comfort, a testament to the truth of his obsession and validation for the task ahead of him. In a moment of rare introspection, Charles wonders what the creature sees, lightly fixed in time as he is. Does he see him as he was? Or as he is now, the fractious old man his own mirror shows him, weaker and paler with every passing day?

Those fifty years haven't been wasted at his end, however. Clearing the debt attached to the estate swallowed up the first decade and most of the comfortable profits from his first practice, but that was only the beginning. Reviving the Vernon name and influence demanded enough expensive favours to keep him at a standstill for a decade more, but now? Now he stands as financially secure as any of his noble ancestors.

"Well, here I am." Mainder smoothly claims the chair on the other side of the desk and makes himself comfortable, adding conversationally, "It's a little strange to be meeting the same Vernon twice. You know how it is, you come and you go. Anyway, what can I do for you?"

Bored already, his eyes flick to the private party going on through the huge double doors. A couple of young men uncomfortable in rented black-tie; one older chap in considerably better fitting and better-quality ditto; and an expensive-looking blonde in an expensive-looking dress, blood-red lips and nails echoing the wine she accepts with a dazzling smile from one of the youngsters. He winks at her just for the hell of it and grins ruefully when she blanks him with well-bred disdain.

"You didn't come all this way to sit there and ignore me," Charles says sharply. "Does it surprise you to learn that I'm ready to make amends? As soon as they find the door, I will have it repaired, no matter the cost. I've told my people to expect you, to save you the bother of trying to sneak in."

"How very thoughtful of you," Mainder murmurs, eyes crinkling in amusement.

"Kindness has nothing to do with it. I assume you intend to meddle."

"I intend to observe," Mainder corrects him casually. "Thank you for making it easier. I don't suppose for one second you've given any thought to the implications if your little project goes wrong?"

Charles chooses to skirt the question. "My people have everything in hand. Just show up and make yourself useful—or is that too much to ask?"

"Not at all."

Charles almost sags with relief. Braced for a fight, expecting denial and anger and outright mischief, and yet it was so easy! He hates to think less of his grandfather, the disciplinarian terror of his childhood, but he feels just a little smug in that moment. Generations of cajoling, negotiating, even outright begging, when all that was needed was a little firmness.

Mainder's attention has wandered again, this time to the illustrious ancestors staring down from the walls. One in particular, he keeps returning to with a lurking smile. An unattributed oil-on-board of a young woman in a dark red gown, pearls in her hair and lace at her throat, her merry dark eyes sparkling out at the viewer as if inviting them to share her triumph. '*Margaret, Lady Vernon, c.1540*, says the nameplate set into the heavy gilt frame. The painting is beautifully done, even if the subject herself were less engaging; the delicate patterns and knots of the lace glow creamy-pale against the darker folds of the dress, picked out in individual strokes and dots as crisp as if the artist's hand had only just placed them there. Mainder looks from the portrait to Charles, eyes suddenly tawny in the light.

"A question in turn," he says curiously. "If you manage to get the door open, what will you do next?"

"That needn't trouble you.," Charles says dismissively. "Do your part and we will be even."

"I suppose we will."

Chapter 14

IN MAINDER'S LATEST absence, the shop neither caught fire, fell down, nor disappeared into an eldritch dimension — none of which was a surprise since he left it in very capable hands. If those capable hands didn't exist, he simply wouldn't be travelling, certainly not on his customary month-long jaunts to London and farther afield for collectors' fairs and auctions and catching up with old friends from "back home," as he calls it.

He lets himself in at the back of the stockroom as usual, poking his head around the adjoining door to give Krzysztof the nod that he's back and continues up to the flat. On the top landing, a little oak table with barley twist legs has the usual scattering of post waiting for his attention. Not much to show for his time away, maybe four or five items that Krzysztof decided he couldn't deal with or that didn't need dealing with at all. He suspects his assistant leaves a few random items for him to look at just so he doesn't start to feel redundant. Today's crop certainly bears out that theory. A couple of glossy cards offering broadband upgrades — he's never even owned a computer. Discard. One limp brown envelope addressed to "The Occupier" — same. Safe to ignore. One official-looking letter addressed to him personally by name and franked by machine — that could be something. He opens the flat's front door and, with the letter clamped between his teeth, wrestles his luggage inside and dumps it in the hall. Unpacking can wait.

***

No heavyweight Basildon Bond this time, no embossed coat of arms or handwritten script. It's come straight off some office printer, spelling mistakes and all, transplanted from screen to dreary, grey-tinted recycled A4 and shoved into a fragile white window envelope with the address so misaligned it's a miracle it reached him at all.

"An opening has arisen for a consultant position which we feel would be well suited to your particular skillset," it advises him, and his eyebrows rise a notch. "Please advice at your earliest convenience if such a contract would be mutually agreeable. If you could call our office to indicate whether you can be available for the upcoming schedule of project briefings [see below]. Kindly allow twenty minutes ahead of briefing start time to be processed by security."

His face creases further into a you-cannot-be-serious grimace. Gods help him if the individual responsible turns out to speak the way they write. He'll be hard pressed not to laugh in their face. It's signed with an unreadable squiggle, cheap blue biro skipping over the terrible paper and tearing a notch at the final downstroke, and typed underneath is *Dr. Bryan Patterson, FRSA EdD MArc, Project Director, Warrington Institute.* The "upcoming schedule" is a solitary appointment slot for the next morning.

Well, now. At this short notice, he could easily get away with being unavoidably busy. He could send his apologies in the same atrocious style as this invitation, a stilted mockery of polite corporate communication. The notion makes him laugh out loud, alone in his tiny kitchen; he drops the letter on the table and spends a few pleasant minutes brewing coffee while composing increasingly more ridiculous and convoluted responses in his head. *We regret that our availability at this time is unconfirmed, and request that a further schedule be considered,* perhaps. No, an *alternatively convenient schedule.* Oh, that's good. Or how about, *We appreciate your consideration of our potential suitability for the role mentioned and will be in touch at the earliest opportunity.*

Nice. That has to be good for raising somebody's blood pressure, and he has no doubt that whoever is responsible for this travesty will not only deserve it, but they won't even register how ruthlessly they're being lampooned.

The coffee pot squeaks and rattles just then, the heavy lid

snapping up and down in a staccato plea for aid. He responds, deftly handing the pot off to the cork mat on the counter and pouring himself one perfect cup. These things matter to Mainder; if you're going to choose a vice — a visible and socially acceptable one, that is — you should at least put the effort into doing it properly.

At last, he sits down again with his steaming cup to peruse the letter one last time and shakes his head in resigned amusement. He'll go along; of course he will. It's exactly where he needs to be.

***

"You okay there, boss?"

Krzysztof peers around the door. The thumping and swearing from the stockroom started shortly after lunch, and he was more than half-expecting to find his erratic employer trapped under a toppled shelf.

"Fine. I'm fine." Mainder waves an irritable hand. "Just trying to recall where I put something, that's all."

That something must be both important and urgent, judging by the state of him — hair sticking up at all angles, shirt smeared with dust and cobwebs, and the usual lurking twinkle in his eye banished by a grim focus.

"Maybe I can help." Krzysztof comes fully into the room to find the tall shelves pulled away from the far wall, books and boxes on the floor in a haphazard pile to expedite the move. The newly cleared wall is a patchwork of brick and stone from different phases in this room's history, and a neat hole in the brickwork at roughly chest-height is almost exactly the dimensions of the rusted lockbox now resting on the shelf beside Mainder, showing all the signs of having been wrenched open by a man in too much of a hurry to remember where he put the key.

"No, it's done. Do you have a minute?"

"Sure." He darts back out to the shop to flip the sign on the door to "Gone to Lunch."

Mainder half-turns as he reappears, eyes flitting between the door and the lockbox and pursing his lips as if deciding how to begin. "So . . ." He trails off, staring at the box with a faraway frown. "I thought it would all be okay, and I don't know, maybe it still will. But I don't want to leave anything to chance. You understand?"

The cautious look of bafflement on Krzysztof's face clearly signals that he absolutely does not, and Mainder backs up a little.

"Okay. Right. You and Aggie, you're happy here?"

"Sure. It beats picking fruit." That old flippancy, the one he and Aggie use at home between themselves, slips out before he can stop it and he hastens to clarify. "Seriously though, yes. Very happy. Aggie just got the flat nice, just the way she likes it, and we put the children's names down for the school just last month. We were hoping to settle down here. Is something wrong?"

Alarm crosses his face, and it's Mainder's turn to reassure.

"No, nothing. Nothing that affects you. It's just — how can I put this — there's a possibility of my past life catching up with me, and I might need to disappear for a while. Possibly a long while. If that happens, I need to be able to leave someone I trust in charge."

"How long exactly are we talking about?"

"I can't say. But if one morning I can't be found, if I'm gone for more than one full moon without getting word to you somehow, I need you to know what's up."

One full moon . . . A strange way to specify a month, but Krzysztof doesn't question his employer's funny little ways anymore.

"And what is 'up'?" he asks, though he isn't sure he's ready for an answer. If it turns out he's been working for a criminal all this time, some tawdry front for something dreadful, he — actually, he doesn't care. If Mainder needs his help, after everything he's done for him and Aggie, he shall have it, even if it means Krzysztof has to perjure his soul to do so.

Mainder looks at him keenly, as if effortlessly reading the

thoughts ticker-taping across Krzysztof's honest forehead, and his usual spark of mischief reappears. "I wouldn't dream of troubling you with the details, my friend. If it happens, there'll be a letter in this box for you, alright? It'll explain everything."

No less mystified, Krzysztof nonetheless nods firmly. This he can do. "You leave it to me, boss. If it comes to it, I'll take care of the place for you."

"I know you will."

This is accompanied by Mainder's smile — the real thing, a warming of approval and confidence that's honestly the main reason Krzysztof agreed to work for him in the first place, and furthermore, the reason he'd never consider leaving. It's like — as he once tried to describe the man to Aggie, before she'd met him herself for the first time — when he smiles at you like that, it's like sitting beside a comfortable fire in a safe place. Like that.

To his surprise, she hadn't mocked his foolish words, just nodded in that way she has and murmured, "Ah, *dusza*." He let it slide, not having been raised in the same ways as her, but it wasn't long before he'd come to realise she was probably on to something. There's something not quite here-and-now about the man he calls "boss."

If anything, Krzysztof was too diffident. He flat-out *loves* working at Mainder's, especially compared to the other jobs he's had since they came to this country. Picking fruit is all very well, and it kept them fed and housed (barely) to begin with. He didn't precisely hate waiting on tables, either, though he could have done without the finger-snapping and the casual xenophobia from a small minority of customers. But this now, this suits him down to the ground. He gets to use the degree he studied so hard for back home — mineralogy and geology, writing neat little cards explaining the properties of the carved trinkets on the racks and the baskets of loose gemstones. The customers are easy to deal with.

Most importantly of all, though, his treasured Aggie has finally lost the haunted look that she used to wear, anxiously counting up their combined pay packets and parceling notes and coins out into the row of jam-jars on the mantelpiece against future bills. Now, what he brings home alone covers the essentials, and they can look ahead further than the next rent payment.

Braced for signs of trouble, it's an odd sort of relief mingled with disappointment when the rest of the day continues in the usual prosaic pattern. The predictable afternoon rush of disinterested holidaymakers looking for something to do before they wander back to the B&Bs for dinner. The pre-closing checklist, flitting around the shop, tidying the quick and easy areas like the bookshelves and the baskets of trinkets. Flipping the sign to "Closed," counting the takings, stashing the next day's float in the tiny safe behind the counter, and finally sweeping the floor, with a quick once-over to make sure everything is in order for the morning.

The shelves are firmly back in their place in the back room when he goes through to empty the dustpan, all the mess swept up and no sign of ever having been disturbed. If he'd not seen the hole, he'd never have known it was there, and that ancient lockbox looked like a genuine antique. Strange.

He flicks off the lights, locks the door behind him, and heads home for his own day's end ritual: dinner, a precious hour or so playing with the children before bedtime, and then curling up on the sofa with Aggie to watch TV.

Chapter 15

REVEREND MERRETT WAS always delighted to receive a visit from his friend Elias. Goodness only knows where the man came from, but every so often he would appear with a cheery, "Just passing!" and stay for several hours drinking endless cups of tea and sharing tall tales of his travels. Who knows? Some of it may even be true.

Certainly, the housekeeper didn't believe a word of it, depositing a fresh pot of tea and a plate of macaroons on the table with a disapproving sniff. The curate resolved to have a private word with her later; it wouldn't do for his guests to feel unwelcome. And this guest, in particular — the only decently educated man for miles around, someone with whom he could discuss the Germanic folklore translation he'd been working on and the antiquities he acquired last month.

This new piece — a Celtic standing stone — he had shipped up from Cornwall and placed in the corner of his sheltered garden in hopes it might attract some visitors from what he delicately called "the other realm."

That's the other reason he liked Elias. The man didn't sneer or dismiss his wish as childish, as so many of his peers might. He nodded sagely, steepling his fingers and touching them to his lips, and agreed that such a splendid object was sure to catch the eye of the Shining Ones. He went further, saying that if it were to be placed near still water and perhaps some other treasures added to the lure, he might find himself playing proud host to a water spirit or two. *Like the magpie*, he said, *they adore to line their nests with treasures that shine.* Certain metals that keep their lustre were held to be the greatest draw.

An intriguing idea, but the curate secretly wondered if that might be taking the notion too far. A curate's income didn't stretch to treasures in silver and gold, not to the extent that he could afford to leave them lying around in the garden. He turned the conversation back to his progress with the translation and accepted with delight several suggestions on the precise meaning of a passage he'd been finding troublesome.

In the weeks following the visit, however, he found himself distracted from his research by a new project: directing the small brook at the foot of his garden into a pond. Framed by two trees on the border with the lane, an elder and a rowan that predated the vicarage itself, the tiny brook filled in the hollow dug out by the gardener in less than a day.

With his treasured face stone sunk into a deep hole at the far corner, only the very top visible through the irises and rushes planted around the edge to give the shy spirit some privacy, before too long he had as handsome a dryad's abode as he could wish for. As a final flourish, he gently lowered a small bronze torc to the dark water, guiltily mumbling a few words of welcome to whomever might find them and be pleased enough to stay.

Chapter 16

ALFRISCOMBE'S TOWN MUSEUM is easily the nicest site any of the team has ever worked on, especially compared to the bland university campus most of them have recently been transplanted from. In a former life it was the vicarage, built in the same pale-streaked granite as the magistrates' court and the imposing town hall at the top of the main street, and gifted to the council under covenant "for the good of the townspeople" in 1921. It retains much of its original grand character, including the famous sweeping curve of the double staircase rising up from the entrance hall. It's a *happy* place to work, something above and beyond just the aesthetic. There are both grander and prettier buildings in Alfriscombe, but this one somehow generates a glow of contentment in its inhabitants, as if over the centuries the house has absorbed happy memories into the very brickwork and releases them back into the air bit by bit.

The cleaners may roll their eyes sometimes, hearing the praise heaped on the house, but it's more indulgent than exasperated. That eternal gloss on the banisters, the glowing patterns on the floor tiles in the hall — it's not invisible midnight pixies making that happen. A building this old demands sustained and expert effort to make sure it shines. But they're every bit as happy as the office personnel, seeing their efforts rewarded every day by the smiles and appreciative comments of the occupants and by the responsive glow of the building itself as they bring it to life.

Today in particular the house seems determined to put on the best possible show. Just yesterday the glass panes of the side porch and inner door received a thorough cleaning using an old-fashioned concoction of vinegar, newspaper, and elbow grease, encouraging this morning's broad sunshine to flood though into the hall and highlight the tiles to perfection. Off to the right, on either side of a little fireplace, two upholstered armchairs in a deep red velvet invite guests to wait in elegant comfort. There's no fire laid there today, not with the weather turned so warm recently; a tasteful arrangement of dried flowers in shades of pink occupies the tiny iron grate instead. To the left of the door, a rotating team of volunteers man the front desk in a pokey cubbyhole where the cloakroom once would have been, dispensing old-fashioned paper tickets and taking payment under the flirtatious gaze of a marble bust depicting *Miss Amelia Waldron, aged 18yrs, on the occasion of her coming out.*

Despite its small size, the museum contains some impressive collections. A former son of Alfriscombe donated a significant proportion of the artefacts during his career as an Egyptologist, a collection stretching across the whole ground floor of the east wing. On the other side of the house, there are smaller displays of Alfriscombe's own history, from eighteenth century watercolours of the fishing boats on the harbour through to Second World War gas masks and ration cards.

Upstairs, the prehistoric collection is richly populated by finds from the caverns under the top end of town, a tourist attraction in its own right. It's been less popular in recent years, there only being so many flint scraps and mammoth molars you can look at before you head for the gift shop, but the word is, it's about to receive some very significant new exhibits.

Today's visitor has yet to appear to appreciate the museum's delights, despite having been informed that the briefing is scheduled to begin promptly at a quarter past ten. The tall clock beside the door is showing a few minutes after the hour already, and the welcoming committee has been ready and waiting since a quarter to.

Raj fidgets by the door, peering out periodically to see whether there's any sign of someone coming up the drive. "I know we didn't think he'd be bang on time, but this is ridiculous. What's the plan if he doesn't show?"

The second member of the committee is feeling less welcoming by the second. Jonas has one anxious eye on the clock, conscious that he's already going to be late for the daily site security meeting. Not that he likes attending the blasted things and there are never any surprises, but by God does management ever make a fuss if you're not there on time.

"Give it 'til ten past and then I'll have to pack up and take the kit back to the office," he announces. "You'll just have to start without him."

The kit under discussion is a hastily assembled photo setup: backdrop screen, lighting rig, camera and tripod in one corner, along with the triply secure laptop and the special printer, a small but disproportionately heavy box in yellowing plastic that transfers images to plastic cards. Dragging it down here and getting it all set up just right was, to be frank, a massive pain in the arse, but their instructions were clear. Every possible effort must be made to smooth this particular consultant's way into the building and on to the project, and if this means bringing the entire setup down to the hall to save the man the bother of climbing a couple of flights of stairs, then so be it.

With precisely one minute to go before Jonas makes good on his threat, Mr. Mainder at last strolls through the door. Reports varied as to what to expect, ranging from local gossip about a harmless middle-aged shopkeeper, through to a shady and possibly criminal dealer in artefacts—this from overheard fragments of the Archchancellor's embittered rant on his most recent visit.

The man now approaching quite frankly defies both of those neat pigeonholes. Tall, dark—well, two out of three isn't bad. Rather than handsome, his face is better described as "interesting." High cheekbones and a wide mouth hint at Slavic ancestry somewhere down the line, and the bridge of his nose kinks in a way that suggests it's been broken more than once in his lifetime. A neat four-day beard is a strange contrast to his hair, clipped short apparently at random and showing all the signs of wanting to curl if just given enough leeway. Deep-set eyes are clouded blue-grey, the colour of flint. A shade over six feet tall and lean with it, with shadowed hints of tattoos and a hint of muscle under his long-sleeved shirt suggesting he's in halfway decent shape for a man his age. What that age actually might be is harder to pin down; he could be anything from a weathered thirty-something to an incredibly well-preserved fifty.

He halts on the threshold and takes in the scene in the hall: Jonas, glowering with one guilty hand already on the release catch of the tripod, and Raj, hovering with an uncertain smile. After a moment's hesitation, he accepts the offered handshake, and those clouded eyes brighten momentarily. Raj catches himself checking out the man's other hand, inexplicably cheered to see no wedding ring. He can't help but feel a spontaneous surge of attraction, however difficult the man is being. For all that he's dressed for a day's work down in his shop, he moves and stands like someone who'd be entirely at home with a blade in his hand and a horse under him. That kind of confidence is a powerful draw.

Jonas, less impressed, gestures for Mainder to hurry up and be photographed for his security pass. He does so, flipping the tails of his coat out from behind him and settling on the plastic chair with the leisurely air of royalty deigning to sit for a formal portrait. At least he's cooperating for this part, and a suitable image is quickly captured and transferred to the laptop for it to do its thing. Meanwhile, Mainder rises and submits without complaint to being scanned and patted down, obligingly raising both arms to shoulder-level to facilitate the latter, all with a faint smile on his face.

He isn't carrying anything remotely like a weapon. In fact, he isn't carrying anything at all. Not a wallet or a mobile phone or even a set of house keys. Polite attempts at small talk falter under that flint stare and the half-smile. He answers readily enough, but it's all one-word answers establishing that, yes, he's been to the museum before; no, he didn't drive here; and yes, it's certainly a lovely day. It's very much a relief when the printer rattles to life and disgorges his pass, the laminated image faithfully like him, but at the same time strangely unlike and forever fixed in that same unsettling smile. At last, with the clock now showing twenty-three minutes past ten, he's finally ready. He thanks Jonas with solemn courtesy, even as he drops

the rectangle of plastic into the pocket of his coat like he's
forgotten its purpose already.

Chapter 17

THE BOARDROOM HAS been laid out exactly as instructed, even down to the refreshments tray waiting on the polished sideboard — the distinguished guest edition that only comes out when they want to make sure somebody feels special. Given that today's only external visitor is a local shopkeeper, that raised some eyebrows.

Tall silver urns reflect their passing as they enter, hand-written labels on crisp white card proclaiming their contents. Actual porcelain cups and saucers are laid out enticingly in a neat line, a small box in polished dark wood propped open to display a tempting array of herbal and fruit teas, and as a finishing touch, a plate of fresh shortbread waits at the very end.

Mainder wastes no time heading for the urn marked *Coffee*, even before Raj thinks to tell him to help himself, pouring himself a small sample and passing it under his nose as if assessing the quality of the blend. It seems to pass inspection. The corners of his eyes crinkle in a sudden smile, and he fills his cup all the way and retreats to the bay window overlooking the back lawn.

It used to be a lawn, anyway. What it is now — well it's a tragedy, is the only possible word. The once impeccable green, centuries-old turf expertly kept, is now a crisscrossed mess of shallow pits and muddy paths worn between them, red clay tracked all about and over the brick terrace off the kitchen. The curate's charming little pond was filled in long ago by a resident with an eye to the safety of his young family, but even with the deep water gone it remains an unappealing prospect, a waterlogged dip in the ground overshadowed by the twin pillars of the marker trees. The pooled dark between the trees reassures him, at least; somehow it appears they've managed not to disturb anything. Not yet anyway.

Once this was the curate's dining room, its former function echoed now by the long oval table in polished wood, its glossy finish a dark mirror reflecting the contents of the room. That includes the nervous fidgets of the smart young man from reception, loitering near the door and casting anxious glances between the clock and Mainder himself as if expecting trouble.

He can't bring himself to care, to be honest. So much for a ten-fifteen prompt start, but he knows a power play when he sees one. His own lateness was half-laziness, half-mischief, but if he'd stirred himself to arrive precisely at the designated time he doesn't doubt the director would have been unavoidably busy until fifteen minutes after that. For coffee this excellent he's prepared to sit still and be patient, anyway.

In the end, there's time to despatch that first cup and begin another before the door finally opens and Patterson enters.

"So sorry to keep you waiting," he lies briskly, taking up position at the head of the table. Behind him follows a bland young woman wearing a scarlet blouse that clashes horribly with the shapeless floral cardigan hanging from her shoulders. *Secretary*, Mainder assumes, judging by the bundle of folders clutched to her thin chest. After her, a steady stream of people of all genders, all in jeans and T-shirts and hooded sweatshirts, all early twenties at the absolute most. All self-consciously checking their shoes and trouser legs for mud as if it's only just occurred to them that they might accidentally track their working dirt across the plush carpet.

The last man in closes the door and takes his seat, and Patterson places both hands palm-flat on the table before he claims their attention with a practiced lecturer's *ahem*.

"Welcome, Mr. Mainder. Ah, I believe we spoke briefly at the conference? The board were very intrigued by your insight—a little local expertise, so to speak. I wonder if perhaps we could deal with the formalities before we discuss the details."

A folder appears at Mainder's elbow while he's still mulling over the implied sneer in that "so to speak." He decides he won't rise to it; he's feeling generous today. He pats his pockets absently, reaching inside the front of his coat on one side and then the other until he finds a pair of delicate metal-rimmed glasses which he settles fussily on his face to examine the documents.

There's not much to examine: two copies of the same thing, a non-disclosure agreement printed double-spaced on every other line and still only covering three sides of A4. Purely for the hell of it, not that he intends for a moment to abide by anything it contains, he takes his sweet time reading both copies, occasionally laying them down again to drink more coffee or flicking back to refer to a previous page, eventually laying them both side by side and comparing them line by line to make sure they're identical.

They are. What's more, this is no generic template; his name is typed in the same font as the rest, several standard clauses are missing, and some new and very specific sections have been added to cover "artefacts, spoil, etc." that he is under no circumstances to examine without a team member present. And even more stringently, he is not to take away or remove any such items from the site. Presumably, Vernon has hinted at treasure under the lawn—academic, if not monetary—but how exactly do they imagine they'd stop him if that's so?

His attention is momentarily caught by the secretary. She's not actually doing anything, which is the strange thing; just staring down at her hands resting in her lap. A pensive Madonna, her pose suggests, humbly waiting to be glorified. It's strangely calming, the way she sits at perfect rest. He can almost see it spreading out in gentle waves and subduing uneasy fidgets around the room. He warms to her even as he forgets her existence again. That ought to be enough time to—yes, there it is; the unmistakable rhythm of someone tapping their foot under the table. He neatly shuffles both documents into their separate piles and looks up.

"I don't suppose you have a pen?"

Patterson almost launches his own across the table in his haste, and Mainder reviews the cheap disposable biro for a frozen moment. It could be worse—at least the end hasn't been chewed — but it could also most certainly be better. He puts it aside and searches his pockets again.

The fountain pen he at last produces puts Patterson's offering to shame, as he very much intended. Capped in old gold, its bullet-shaped body in midnight blue lacquer, once upon a time it would have been the only conceivable choice for the serious man of business. He developed a strong preference for the style as soon as he was in a position to try it out and hasn't found a good reason to change it since. He uncaps it and rests the hooded nib on the edge of the folder, teasing out the ink flow and testing it with three short strokes. The ink gleams on the thin cardboard, deep forest green, and he pulls the paperwork back over and signs both documents with an unreadable flourish. Too much to hope these people would have blotting paper to hand — if they even know what that is any more — so he holds the papers in his hand and waves them gently until he's satisfied the ink has dried.

There's a marked change in the atmosphere when he lays the papers back down, as though the room collectively had held its breath and is just now letting it out.

"All done. What's next?"

The secretary rises and passes him another thin stack of paper, shrinking away when his fingers accidentally make contact with hers, and then retakes her seat.

She's forced to stand up again instantly when someone on the wrong side of the room realises he's supposed to be setting up the display screen, and an awkward few seconds follow of people getting up, pushing in their chairs and pressing up against the table to allow him to pass before sitting back down, like a painfully polite slow-motion Mexican wave.

"Thank you, Viktor. Ah, does anyone have the controls? Ah, yes, here we are. Now. . ."

The screen lights up with what looks very much like the same slide deck as Patterson presented at the conference. Mainder feels entirely justified in ignoring him after the first few seconds; if the man is going to narrate every single bullet point, he might as well just read it himself. Especially since the first thing in the folder is a full-size print out of the exact same slides. "The Fairy Hill: a centre of late Bronze Age worship and commerce," the title of the presentation proclaims, and Patterson's monotone retelling adds nothing of value. Mainder lets it wash over him while he reviews diagrams, photographs, and blueprints, reading every detailed note. Everything he needs to know is right here.

". . . unexpected results as you can see, but I believe we've exhausted that area now. In phase two, we'll be investigating what appear to be significant structures under the lawn here, spreading east and extending under one corner of the current building. Possibly an earlier dwelling, cellars, or foundations belonging to the current building, or earthworks relating to civil war defences."

All solid theories. All very feasible. All of them completely and utterly wrong, which is his favourite thing about them. If you know what you're looking for, the scans clearly shadow the structures beneath, but since they don't appear to know what they were looking for . . . Well, this must have caused significant confusion. He almost smiles — unexpected results, indeed — and turns over the sheet to check the back.

The urge to smile drains away, and he tenses, fingers pinching a crease in the edge of the thin paper. This page shows an image so clear that, for a moment, he's almost convinced they're simply playing dumb. There's no way they can't see what they're looking at: the Fold's ancient chambers, right down to the slight narrowing where one spiral arm was damaged in the Closing. He can still recall as clearly as if it were yesterday how it felt — the pain in the moment, the loss, and the dreadful aftermath as they pieced events together and discovered exactly what had been done to them all.

Chill fury rises in him like bile. Sweyn is still trapped down there somewhere. Not that there'll be anything left of the poor little sod by now, but still. If by some miracle they do get anywhere near that section, it's on him to see if he can retrieve anything.

"Ah, does our guest have an opinion?"

Patterson has to repeat himself before Mainder raises shadowed eyes to sweep the room. A muscle jumps in his cheek, but all he says in a quiet, flat tone is, "What's your favoured option at this point?" A neat deflection to disguise the fact that he really wasn't paying attention.

Patterson seems delighted with the question though, gesturing eagerly at the presenter to rewind the slides back to the image of the lawn scan marked up with arrows and boxes.

"We thought—could I have the pointer again please? Thank you. We thought here—" And he indicates a dark blob on the far top left of the marked areas. "It looks very promising, wouldn't you say?"

"As good a place as any, yes."

His lukewarm approval sparks a burst of activity, half the table pushing back their chairs and leaving the room, the other half talking past each other in a rising babble.

For his part he keeps his eyes down, the table's polished surface a convenient mirror for him to observe the room. There's more to this dynamic than meets the eye. There has to be. His dark eyes flick from person to person, evaluating. Patterson, already dictating a detailed to-do list to Raj. The unlucky volunteer on tech support duty, powering down the display and extracting a storage drive with a pained grunt from the awkward socket hidden somewhere on the back. Youngsters gathering in the hallway outside, waiting for the last stragglers, self-consciously sweeping the chairs clean of the traces of mud they've brought in with them. The secretary, still seated and leaning forward on her elbows . . .

. . . watching him. Using the table exactly as he is, the angle of reflection letting her observe him indirectly, with her colourless brows pinched together in faint concern. She holds his gaze for just a split second, then rises without a word and is instantly lost in the crowded corridor.

Dammit. He didn't actually get a decent look at her, not for all his staring. There was nothing of her to hold on to, easily the least interesting person—visually speaking—in the room. All he can recall is mousy hair, nondescript features—and the terrible fashion sense, of course. If she discarded that awful cardigan somewhere, he'd likely walk past her without a second glance. Intrigued, he rises to follow and nearly collides with Patterson stepping into his path.

"So pleased to have you on board, Mr. Mainder. Ah, can I interest you in a little guided tour?"

Chapter 18

"AND THIS IS where the magic happens! Not my personal area of expertise, but I'm pleased to say that my little team of technicians here has everything well in hand."

Patterson's air of smug ownership is very much beginning to grate by the time they reach the little office at the back of the museum. Their arrival doesn't even turn any heads until Patterson pointedly clears his throat and a young man rises to greet them.

Lanky and pale, thick dark brown hair pulled back off his face and into a ponytail hanging down his back, his faded red T-shirt proudly proclaims "HAIL SAGAN." Patterson introduces him with studied vagueness as, "Ah, Chris looks after the technicians here," and Mainder doesn't miss the faux-casual skipping over surnames and specifics. The security pass on the bright orange lanyard around his neck clearly identifies the boy as *Dr. Christian Taylor, Technical Director, Non-Invasive Archaeology Unit*, which sounds considerably more senior and more qualified than Patterson made it out to be.

"Mr. Mainder, isn't it? Sorry we weren't at the briefing. Aaron had a batch script just about to complete."

Aaron is presumably the young man hunched over the next desk who mumbles something vaguely like welcome without looking away from his array of screens. A dozen coloured traces blip across one of them in sync with rapidly scrolling numbers on another, and periodically he types something into an open tab on the third.

The next two desks in the row are currently unoccupied, but sheets of paper and bright sticky notes cover every inch of available flat surface and extend up the walls on either side.

"Janice sits here, she's our project manager. I wouldn't ask for details unless you really, *really* like Gantt charts. Viktor spends all his time knee-deep in mud, so Janice uses his desk as overflow. Um, kitchen through there, help yourself to tea and coffee . . . Oh, will you need a desk? We can probably shuffle up and make room somewhere. Did they issue you a laptop yet?"

Mainder searches his memory and comes up blank. There wasn't anything in the document he signed, that's for sure. It could have been mentioned while he wasn't paying attention, but either way it doesn't matter. There's no way another desk is going to fit anywhere in here unless they sacrifice the little couch and coffee table in the bay window, and if they did decide to give him any kind of computer, he wouldn't even know how to turn it on.

Patterson, still talking, has carried on down to the far end of the room, arranged like a lab with worktop running the length of one wall and an array of tall metal cupboards on the other. Shallow trays laid out along the worktop display finds from the work so far: beads, bones, and pottery shards, nothing momentous. Much more interesting, to Mainder at least, is the brief glimpse of scarlet beyond the open door of one of the cupboards; if he's not mistaken, this could be the invisible secretary from the meeting. He covertly stares as they pass, trying to commit her to memory this time. Oval face, high forehead, mousy hair cut in a chin-length bob that falls over her face no matter how often she tries to tuck it behind her ear. Lightish grey eyes - oddly familiar somehow, that's going to bug him. No wedding ring, no engagement ring, not that that means anything these days. No other jewellery that he can see, and either no makeup at all or an incredibly understated and undetectable no-makeup look.

On balance, he's inclined to think it's the former. If she had any interest at all in making herself more attractive, she'd do something with her hair, dress in colours that suited her better — literally anything would be an improvement on her current outfit, especially that eye-draggingly awful cardigan, leeching attention away from her until her own features are reduced to mere background noise.

"Of course I'd expect you to recognise most of this," Patterson says, gesturing at the trays. "Lovely little mix, fantastic extraction and cataloguing experience for the interns. All the evidence points to some kind of rubbish pit beside a relatively high-status settlement."

Mainder pretends to inspect the lacklustre collection of archaeological scraps; trash, just as the professor suspects. No surprises there.

"You'll recall, of course, that we could be looking at a late Bronze Age tomb complex extending to under the barrow to the east, your so-called 'fairy hill.'" The quote marks clip into place as clearly as if he'd raised his index fingers to sign them. "In fact, we all got very excited when this was uncovered." On the wall, a grainy black-and-white photo of a severely plain bronze torc has been stuck up, along with a terse red-pen annotation of "OUT OF CONTEXT!! :(". He taps the photo with a stubby finger and continues, "But as you can see, it was quickly discovered to be a hoax. One of the previous residents of the vicarage apparently fancied himself as an amateur archaeologist. Had, ah, a naughty habit of burying artefacts wherever the fancy took him to be discovered later."

"How very frustrating," Mainder soothes, bending his head quickly over the trays to hide the rogue grin quirking the corners of his mouth. "I'm sure he meant no harm."

"Possibly, possibly," Patterson acknowledges judiciously, "but still, it was quite the red herring."

"And is this all you've brought up so far?"

"Ah, you should see our star find." Patterson taps his nose in a faintly creepy display of confidentiality and gestures for Mainder to back up. "Some of the more unusual artefacts require slightly more specialised treatment, as I'm sure you'll understand. Evie, would you mind pulling the chieftain's brooch for Mr. Mainder to see?"

Evie. Mainder tastes the name silently. It doesn't suit her. A childish diminutive, surely short for something more imposing. Evangeline? Evelyn? He boggles momentarily at the unbidden vision of her responding to either of those names — something similar to his reaction if somebody tried to call him "Elias," notwithstanding that it's the name on his official documentation. Evie it is, then.

"I must have missed you in the introductions, Evie. What's your role here?"

She barely manages to open her mouth before Patterson answers for her. "Evie is our asset management specialist."

An awkward silence spins out while Patterson waits expectantly for the girl to pick up her cue and fill in the gaps. Somehow though, without moving a muscle or making a sound, she couldn't have signaled more clearly if she'd written it on one of those sickly-coloured sticky notes and slapped it on his forehead that, since Patterson had started answering for her, he could feel free to carry on and supply the missing details. Mainder hadn't expected to feel sorry for Patterson, today or any other day, but honestly, it's like watching someone dispatch a wasp with a rocket launcher. He can't help but smile, safely behind Patterson's back, and comes to the rescue.

"Asset management, right. What does that involve?"

"Spreadsheets, mostly," she answers, so blandly that he feels almost like he's ceased to exist too, vapourised in Patterson's blast radius. No, this won't do. She's too interesting to be allowed to fade into the background again.

"What happens if someone tries to make off with an asset? I hope for your sake you're stronger than you look!"

It turns out he was mistaken. Her expression before wasn't bland; it was simply polite-shading-to-neutral. At his ill-chosen attempt at humour, it transforms to total, absolute stillness, a null, as if invisible shutters had slammed up between her and everyone else. He could swear the tacky lino under his feet trembles faintly, so physical is the *frisson* of uncertainty that runs through him. He retreats to safer ground, turning with relief to the item under the magnifier.

"Beautiful," he murmurs after a frozen pause.

He's absolutely sincere. It's one of Smidur's, one of his best at that, and has to have been for someone high up in one of the old Fire houses. Maybe even at the very top. Shaped like a stylised sword, the blunt tapering blade and the pommel both heavily inlaid with precious stones, polished cabochons of garnet and deep-hued amber reflecting the bright ring of the magnifier light back up at him. Around them, red-gold and silver wire inlays chase each other around the borders and up over the arch in a leaping flame pattern.

Homesickness washes over him, a sickening wave that curls his fingers around the edge of the bench for support. He has one of these—not nearly so fine, of course—tucked away safely somewhere until it might be safe to use it again. He can feel the potential still stored in this one, a journey unfinished, hidden under mud and stone for so long, waiting to shine again. The scribe was right; this beautiful piece has never crossed the Divide.

Glancing up, he finds the girl watching him again, and again with that faint hint of concern she showed in the meeting. It unsettles him, far more so than if she'd been openly hostile. He won't deny he's off-balance, but what's it to her?

"Well, thank you for the viewing," he says lightly. "What else should I see while I'm here, Professor?"

***

The dig supervisor is waiting for them at the far corner of the house, a gaggle of young interns clustered around him like imprinted ducklings.

It's not hard to see why. Viktor is an impressive specimen whatever your personal preference. Tall and tanned, he's blessed with the face of a young Valentino and the physique of a gym rat.

People always fail to guess correctly what he does for a living, to hear him tell it; they go for fitness instructor, rugby player, even Navy SEAL, long before they get anywhere close to his real specialism. It's netted him many free drinks on a Saturday night from giggling young women who've failed to guess correctly, not to mention getting him laid more times than he can count. He has no interest whatsoever in seducing Mainder, obviously. In fact, he has strong opinions about old farts posing about the place dressed all in black like they think they're cool or something, but he prides himself on remaining professional. If there's one thing he cares about more than his image, it's his career prospects.

"I was just taking everyone through the dig schedule," he hails them as they catch up to the group. "As I was saying, our scans show some very strong signals towards the back of the house, but we'll be warming up with a look at the anomaly over by the hedge first. Depending on what we find there, we'll decide where to dig next, and of course, we have to have an eye on the structural integrity of the building. Any questions so far?"

This is pointedly aimed only at the students, so Mainder fades to the back of the group to let them raise their points. The young woman next to him doesn't appear to have anything to ask, not related to the dig anyway. She watches the magnificent Viktor with shining eyes and murmurs confidentially, "This is so exciting! Have you done projects like this before? Oh, you must have done hundreds. This is the first one I've done. I can't wait to get started! I wonder what we'll find?"

Mainder accurately gauges that she's not looking for a meaningful dialogue, rather chattering from a combination of exhilaration and nerves, and confines himself to encouraging nods and murmurs of assent at appropriate intervals. He can't remember the last time he was that excited about something; it would have been so long ago that now he can't even remember how it would have felt, that's how long.

"What happens if we don't find anything?" one of the students near the front asks. "Maybe the same person who buried the torc buried the stuff from the Hoard as well, and it's all just a big joke."

"It's possible, but of course we hope not," Viktor says stiffly. "There's more than enough evidence of the site being worth investigating, even without the Hoard so close by, and whatever we find will tell us more about how it was used. Does anyone else have a question?"

Since nobody does, they move on to the next part of their briefing, leaving Mainder and Patterson staring expectantly at each other. A moment of awkward silence descends, as if Patterson was hoping Mainder would simply disappear of his own accord at this point, and when that fails to happen he glances at his watch.

"My goodness," he murmurs vaguely. "Well, ah, I do have other appointments this afternoon. Just let the team know if you need anything."

Chapter 19

MAINDER DOESN'T GO looking for trouble, not if he can help it. It's less effort all round to sit still and wait for it to come to him, as it invariably does once he's found the right place to be.

His instincts are currently insisting that the right place to be is the office. *Something in here, it's something in here,* the subtle itch sings to him. Something in this place is *wrong.*

He quickly finds several possibilities, perusing the whiteboard propped against the wall. It looks like a conspiracy theorist's work-in-progress, red threads connecting random scraps of paper and photographs in no discernible pattern.

He's more entertained by the nonsense on display than he'd care to admit, though. *HOARD Qry link between Bronze Age chieftain ?? & shrine votives found nr. Home Farm 1800s,* reads one offering in tiny, looping handwriting on a garish pink sticky note. A thread joins it to a faded sepia postcard showing not the farm, but a watermill which—unless he somehow managed to sleep through a century or two—has nothing whatsoever to do with Alfriscombe. He turns the card over, looking for a caption or attribution to confirm his suspicions. Yes, there it is. *The Old Mill, Keston, ca. 1850.* Not even the right county. He turns it back and nudges it into its former position.

Up above that there's a snippet of dense text photocopied from a book.

. . . evidence of significant Roman activity but later found to be the result of widespread looting over the following century and a half. This lawless region was finally tamed by the emergence of a local chieftain of possibly Celtic roots, the famed Severin (see also Svenn*, Sweyne**, Sarin***), whose exploits live on in local legends. So many deeds are attributed to Severin that most scholars believe he must be an amalgamation of more than one individual, with the details sadly lost to time. One of Severin's legends describe him being transformed into

a bird on the orders of a witch, presumably as punishment for some slight or injury, though the legend goes on to describe his many acts of mischief while in this form.

Tacked to that, grainy depictions of Norse ravens carved in stone from the British Museum. *Close,* he heckles silently. *Not quite, but close.* The silence at his shoulder is a constant reminder of what should be there; Sweyn would have adored this scenario. So much pomposity to puncture and so much potential for mischief, he almost wouldn't have known where to start.

Choosing a thread at random from there, he lands next on a garish school textbook illustration of a Roman legionary, a fearsome snarl on his face and a shortsword raised above his head at a wildly impractical angle. It seems to have no function that he can fathom beyond aesthetics, apparently only there to fill a gap in the display.

Next is something that's actually relevant—or at least related to the right place.

In the winter of 1442, a dairymaid was discovered sheltering in the church porch, blue with cold and her clothes all in in rags. She swore on the Bible to have been chased by a terrifying imp or demon that mocked her the whole way, pulling her hair and tearing at her clothes. She eventually banished the evil apparition by entering the churchyard and laying her hand on the door handle while reciting the Lord's Prayer.

From there, another thread leads to a faded salmon-pink leaflet from the Tourist Information shack. *Make a wish on the Alfriscombe Imp!* proclaims the chirpy headline, with a cartoon of an aggressively cute demon twirling his arrowhead-tipped tail and sticking out his tongue. The souvenir shops sell Impey keyrings, pot-metal charms, and plastic pencil toppers by the dozen during high season, but it's a line of merchandise he's always flatly refused to carry. The original carving, leering out from his overgrown niche in the garden of the old Lodge, can only be accessed these days by prior appointment and by kind permission of the current owners — which they almost never give. That doesn't stop locals and visitors alike from tossing a coin into the fountain on the green, as if there's some way Impey can detect their mundane desires from a mile and a half away and make them so. The bottom of the basin glitters with many years and many wishes worth of pennies, trapped under the thin steel grid installed by the council, a deterrent to the occasional enterprising soul who decided to wish simply for a pocket full of soaking wet pennies and was willing to act directly to make it a reality.

Mainder completes his baffled circuit by claiming the couch and flipping through the pile of books on the low table next to it. The offerings here continue the theme of the whiteboard, an eclectic collection designed to entertain rather than to instruct. An ancient issue of *Crystals Monthly*, the free gemstone sample long gone. *Hill Forts of Britain*, a hefty coffee table book that's mostly hills and precious few forts. *Lords of Mischief Through the Ages*, a hardback treatise with a fetching medieval woodcut of Loki looking suitably villainous on the front cover. Incongruous even in this pile, a paperback novel: *American Gods*. He flips it open and reads a few pages at random before dropping it back with a smile. Window dressing, without a doubt. But who's behind it?

***

Tawny eyes flick up when the office door bangs open once more and admits Evie, carrying yet another stack of folders. Is her entire job simply moving paperwork from one place to another? If he were a cynical man, he might wonder if it's simply a prop, a way to look busy.

He'd be wrong on this occasion. She manages to divest half of her burden working her way down the line of desks, delivering whatever's required to whoever needs it with a bright smile and a comment for each person. It's considerably more animation than he's seen in her so far, and he wonders idly if he might expect a similar greeting. On the face of it they're colleagues of a sort, aren't they? At the very least, she has to be polite.

Deep down, he knows he wants more than just "polite," though. Now he's seen it happen, he discovers he'd quite like to be the recipient of one of those unexpected sunshine smiles. The effect is contagious, the mood in the room brightening with each stop she makes. Part of it, now he comes to consider it, is how much Patterson's presence damped everyone's spirits — his own included. That's not it though, or not wholly. Patterson is certainly tedious, but he's hardly a monster. And yet between his absence and Evie's presence, the whole office seems lighter somehow, the air clearer, even the lighting taking on a warmer tone. Whatever it is that's jabbing at his subconscious, she has something to do with it.

By the time she passes him, she has just one folder remaining. As much as he despises pointless paperwork, he almost hopes it has his name on it if it means an interaction. She keeps her hold on it, however, heading past him without an acknowledgement and seating herself at the kitchen table. In profile her face is solemn and classical, a funerary angel in pale marble, and he finds himself staring in honest fascination. It's not that she's pretty, not in the traditional sense, although a hundred years ago they'd have had her sitting for saints' portraits with that solemn gaze and enigmatic half-smile. How on earth does she manage to transform that bland mask to bright welcome so effectively? Not that she's wasting the effort on him right now, but she clearly possesses the ability to charm at will. As one charmer to another, he salutes her skill.

Time to try out the smart coffee machine beside the sink; he can oh-so casually offer to make her a cup while he just so happens to be getting his own, the perfect opening. Intense study of the machine's many buttons and the nearby rack of colourful pods turns up no option for espresso, but the lightest roast and the smallest cup size might just produce something he can live with.

The device kicks off with a dreadful graunching and

grinding, and he mouths a contrite "sorry" when they all look up, startled by the sudden burst of noise. It subsides at last to a bathwater-down-the-drain gurgle, with an unappealing spit-bubble of brown foam expanding out from the nozzle. That doesn't look right. Is the thing broken?

Chris comes through from the office, retrieving his lunch box from the fridge while continuing a conversation with Aaron.

"I'm just saying, though. *Crystals Monthly*? Why?"

Since Mainder had much the same question, he shifts subtly closer to hear the answer.

"Laying a paper trail, duh," Aaron says triumphantly. "'During a desk review of popular literature, the team established several possible avenues of investigation for the next phase . . .' And then we get to spend a month in the lab recording how carnelian or whatever it was responds to a range of voltages and frequencies. You never know, one day you might be using technology like this to detect different materials while they're still buried. Like, this trench only has jasper, that one over there has rubies."

"That actually might work," Evie adds, looking up from her folder. "I mean, maybe not the tech, but as an academic angle of attack. 'Expanding on the piezo-electric effect and its significance in lapidarial settings,' or something like that. You know Patterson wouldn't question it."

"He wouldn't understand it, you mean," Aaron stage-whispers, and Mainder is startled to hear a raucous and frankly quite filthy laugh from Evie that he wouldn't have believed could have come from that colourless girl if he hadn't seen it happen with his own eyes.

The coffee machine buzzes just then, heralding a burst of dark liquid splashing into his waiting cup. Once . . . twice . . . and with a metallic death rattle, three times. There. It appears to be done, but he eyes it cautiously for a few seconds before retrieving his prize.

The tragic quarter-cupful of froth staring back at him is enough to confirm that he'll need to look further afield for his caffeine fix. Blending in is one thing, but there is no way he's making do with whatever this swill is for the foreseeable future. He pulls a face at his own comically distorted reflection in the scarlet enamel — no classical beauty detected there — and idles his way up the room to place himself in Evie's line of sight.

If you asked him, he couldn't tell you what he's angling for with that manoeuvre. Some subtle tell maybe, confirmation that she's his unlikely nemesis. Catching her eye and exchanging a meaningful glance, making certain she knows that he knows that she knows. Honestly, he'd settle for one of her smiles. Anything, any sign that she's aware of him and open to negotiations.

But he might as well not be there, not the slightest change in her expression or posture suggesting that she's even interested in his existence. He never used to have to work this hard to gain a lady's attention. Is he so out of practice? He glances at the imp on the leaflet, its cheery grin mocking his desperation. *Make a wish!* Well, if he thought for a moment that it would work . . . But when you've lived as long as Mainder, you've either worked out how to make something happen or learned to stop wanting it.

Chapter 20

ROOM 103 AT Manor Hill is listed on the website as a "junior suite" — more than a bedroom, but at the same time not quite a full suite, equipped with a gracious sitting area of two cream-brocade sofas and a highly polished coffee table currently covered with grab-bowls of cookies and sweets. When Linden calls a team meeting, it's worth your while to show up.

"You don't seriously believe it's real," Raj scoffs, selecting a handful of sweets.

"Do you seriously believe it's not?" Evie counters. "Security searched him when he arrived, yes?"

"Yes.", he says firmly. "Nothing in his pockets whatsoever.".

"Fair enough. But in the meeting we all saw him pull glasses out of those empty pockets, and a vintage Parker 51 I'd cheerfully sell you all to the Devil to own. Any way you could have missed them?"

"I don't see how. Could he have grabbed them from somewhere when we weren't looking?"

"Antique spectacles that fit his face perfectly?" she lifts a hand to forestall the anticipated objection. "Yes, I'm certain. He was never out of our sight, unless anyone would like to confess now to something different. Anyone?"

Blank stares and slight head shakes greet her searchlight glare.

"Well, then. And even if he did pick them up in the museum or the grounds somewhere, how would they have got here?"

There are no satisfactory answers for that question either, and she settles back on the couch with an exasperated wave of her hand.

"He's something. I don't know what, and I don't think he's the Devil himself, but Vernon isn't entirely crazy. As much as I'd like that to be the truth of it."

It's past midnight before the movie night breaks up. They

ended up watching *Highlander* at Chris's insistence, although Evie spends most of the film staring into space and occasionally leafing through the pile of paper scraps she had the team write down their thoughts and ideas on. Periodically, she shuffles the little deck of insights, pulling out two in particular and frowning at them.

I felt transparent, one says. That's unmistakably Chris's writing, tiny and round and sloping backwards due to his left-handedness. She still remembers the day she innocently asked why they were making him hold the pen in his right hand. Seven years old he was, falling further and further behind at school and scheduled for testing for a whole raft of learning disabilities. People are so blind sometimes.

Good coffee makes him smile, says another in sharp energetic spikes. A doctor's handwriting, as they always used to tease Raj back in their uni days, and the reason nobody ever wanted to borrow his notes. Nobody apart from Evie herself, who rose to the challenge and learned to decipher it as a matter of principle.

She snorts quietly as she puts the comment back on the pile. Raj is openly and joyously bisexual, equally openly against settling down before he's good and ready, and always on the lookout for new experiences. However he's also an uncannily good judge of character, a sad but necessary byproduct of the troubled environment he eventually escaped. If he feels a man should smile more, generally that man deserves to have something to smile about.

She has the same feeling, she has to admit. The more they learn about Mainder, the more she's drawn to him. It wouldn't be the first time the mark turned out to be more appealing than the client, and it never ends well.

She takes herself to bed with that question rattling around in her mind.

Chapter 21

SURFACING FROM DEEP sleep, Evie idly wonders what woke her. Not her alarm—it's nowhere near morning yet—and she gradually becomes aware that this is very much not the bed she laid down in. One hand twitches and curls, fingertips exploring the heavy weave of the sheet and the plump softness of the mattress beneath. This is nothing like the smooth, aggressively over-sprung slab on her hotel bed. In fact, it's a blissful contrast, and a silent huff of laughter escapes her. Is she seriously so stressed that she's dreaming about feather beds?

It's a delicious sensation, luxurious even, and she nestles back into the softness with a contented hum and a resolution to do nothing that will make this dream end before she's ready. If feather beds are even still a thing these days, perhaps she should see about getting one as soon as this job is over.

A faint rustle behind her alerts her to the presence of company, and her eyes spring open again. She turns in meltingly slow increments, fighting the lure of the mattress the whole way, to see exactly who her dreaming mind decided to conjure as her bedfellow.

Indistinct shadows resolve into a shock of black hair sticking up at all angles, dark eyes with a momentary flash of gold in their depths, and heavy brows drawn together in a sleepy frown. Unmistakably Mainder, even if he looks markedly less sinister than usual. Significantly less clothed, too. The dream even supplies his unseen tattoos, intricate geometric tangles in a many-rayed sunburst on one shoulder spreading along his collarbone and down the arm flung out over the covers. Under the dark ink his skin looks almost golden, lit from within, and she blinks rapidly to clear the sudden impression of flames swirling just under the surface.

Strange tattoos aside, he looks—and she can't quite believe that's the word queuing up first—inviting. There are better words, surely. Safe. Comfortable. Approachable.

No. None of those words go far enough. He looks rumpled and warm and, quite frankly, snuggleable. The sheer ridiculousness of it all sparks another quiet laugh, of disbelief this time.

"What the hell are you doing here?" he rumbles indistinctly, raising a hand to rub his face. He sounds surprised rather than annoyed; the frown deepens, but there's a hint of a smile glittering in his eyes.

"I have literally no idea. Where is 'here'?"

He glances around the room. "Home. My home, in the old country."

A spectacularly unhelpful non-answer, but exactly what she'd expect from the real Mainder. Looking at him lying there so relaxed, all sorts of possibilities present themselves — but honestly she'll have to look the real version in the eye at some point tomorrow. There's only one appropriate option here, and she regretfully starts extracting herself from the warm hollow of the bed. The dream has supplied her with her clothes at least — well, the sweats and vest she went to bed in — so that's something. No shoes though.

"Where are you going?"

She flaps an impatient hand at him. "Exploring."

She doesn't even get her feet to the floor before that tattooed arm snakes around her waist. It's not an aggressive move, despite the speed of it; it feels entirely protective. Definitely capable of holding her if she chooses to resist, though. All of Raj's wistful speculation about exactly how he's built under that coat didn't come close to describing this version. There's muscle, yes, but it's whipcord and steel rather than strongman bulk.

"Not so fast, child. It's dead of night, and there's worse things out there than me."

Child, he calls her, an oddly archaic form of address. She'd shiver, but he's so warm, scorching almost, pressed close up against her back to murmur that caution in her ear. She swears she can feel a tremor of uncertainty run through him at the contact, as if now he's caught her, he's not sure what to do with her. She half-turns her head to reply, freezing when his lips make accidental split-second contact with her ear, and this time the tremor is no delusion. He backs off instantly, but that warding arm stays in place.

"You need to just wake up nice and safe in your own bed now, before anything happens."

Again, it's clearly a caution rather than a threat. Why does she feel so safe, in a strange bed in a strange place with this undeniably strange individual? It's such a surreal under-reaction; it has to be a sleep thing. No adrenaline in dreamland.

"How? Do I click my heels together or something?"

"Make the sign for home. Like this."

The bed creaks as he brings his other arm around in front of her, raising it to show her his hand. A moment's hesitation, as if he's only just registered this means he now effectively has his arms around her, then he makes a motion like turning an invisible key in a lock. Where his fingers move, they leave a faint trail, a spiral of dull red-gold light that hangs in the air for a second before slowly fading.

"You're still here," is all she can think of to say.

"Well, I'm already home." She wishes she could see his face right now; he sounds like he's trying not to laugh. "Your turn."

"How do you know it's going to work for me?"

"My dream, my rules. Try it."

He sounds so certain that automatically she obeys. She lifts her hand and does her best to mimic his action—thumb and forefinger extended wide, turning and drawing them together in a smooth curve. Blue-white light follows the path they make, and she lets out her breath in an awed "whoa."

***

Mainder wakes with a jolt in the comforting dark. His hand clutches at nothing, searching, and meets only cold fabric and the rough plaster of the wall. Dawn light is already creeping around the shutters, and with a muffled curse he pulls the covers over his head and tries vainly to go back to sleep.

Chapter 22

THE SHRINE HAD been there for as long as anyone could remember, marking the spot where the spring bubbled up through the rocks: a single standing stone as tall as a man with grey-green lichen filling its carved spirals, and a second stone laid flat at its foot like an altar. There used to be a third stone, but that was smashed to pieces years ago, its scattered fragments buried somewhere in the weeds.

Some villagers kept to the old ways still, a fact evidenced by desiccated posies scattered on the stone, dark splashes of wine in clay cups, and antlers hanging off nearby branches like a particularly gruesome crop. All to be cleared away now at the baron's command, all of it—the stones, the rotting timber hut behind, and those disgusting relics as well. No superstitious peasant nonsense must remain to sully this holy site.

As the ground was cleared, the remaining stones pushed over and broken down, a wanderer emerged from the forest path. Tall and swarthy with a heavy pack on his back, he looked like any other gypsy the stonemason ever saw, but since he was a decent man at heart he wished him a good day, enquiring after his health and his travels, even offering a cup of water and a bite of his own meal if the man would care to share.

It bore an unexpected dividend, and not just the warming gleam in the tinker's eyes as he stepped out of the shadows. He accepted the water gratefully but wouldn't take more than a sip. "Your men will be needing this more," he said with a glance up at the sun. "As for your meal, let me contribute." From the depths of his pack he produced a well-wrapped haunch of venison and cheerfully shared it around. "It'll spoil before I can finish it," he insisted against their protests. "It's you who's doing me the favour, or would you have this go to waste?"

Over the meal they were happy to discuss the chapel's plans, since the fellow was so polite and so curious. He particularly admired the design for the roof bosses, a rosette with deep-cut petals that the mason was particularly pleased with. Just as well, as four dozen in all would be needed for the ambitious vaulted ceiling before they were done, and a few gargoyles besides.

"It'll be a fine chapel indeed," the tinker said with a lopsided grin, "if it ever gets finished."

Long afterwards, the mason reflected on that day. It seemed from the moment the tinker said those words, nothing went right. Sinking foundations, cracking lintels, and collapsing walls — before too long the men flatly refused to return to work, even for triple pay. Some curse lingered over the site, they agreed, and as soon as other jobs arose, they moved on with relief.

The chapel fell to ruin so quickly you'd barely know there'd ever been a structure there at all. Fine-dressed stone gradually got robbed away for doorsteps and windowsills and mounting blocks until there was nothing left but a tumbled mossy outline of the tower base. A generation later, you'd barely know it was there unless your horse stumbled on one of the hidden stones. The only sign a chapel was ever planned was the jeering stone demon carved by the stonemason after a heavy night drinking the tinker's ale. Its twisted grin seemed to be mocking the whole endeavour, perched up on the wall where he left it until the brambles eventually claimed it.

Chapter 23

DAY ONE OF the dig dawns on a fine, sunny morning. Rain clouds are massing out to sea, but with barely any breeze, it'll be hours before they reach the museum.

The site manager consults her clipboard — mainly for show, since she knows everything is in place, from the permits acquired and carefully entered into the system, to the license for the skip out in the drive, right through to decades of blueprints consulted in case of underground cables. The interns are busy stacking find trays and hand tools ready beside the paved path bordering the lawn. On the other side of the garden wall, a catering truck is dispensing a breakfast fit for people with serious work to do: bacon rolls, crumbling dark fruitcake by the slice, scalding builder's tea in chipped china mugs. *Vegan Option's Available On Request*, according to a handwritten addition to the menu, but a second bulk pack of bacon is already out to defrost in anticipation of the morning's bestseller.

Approaching eight-thirty, the lawn fills with people shouting incomprehensible instructions at each other, collecting cones and pulling up stakes, winding up orange tape as they go to clear the way for the backhoe rumbling along from the main driveway.

Archchancellor Cooper himself has graced the occasion, a forty-something man with the shaved head and solid build of a prop forward and with much the same immovable air. Despite his bulk, he's wearing a beautifully cut suit in heavy charcoal wool. Spotless white cuffs emerge precisely half an inch from his jacket sleeves, no more and no less, and the silk tie around his thick neck displays the colour blocks and badge of the local Rotary Club. He's not here to dig, obviously; the presence of the local newspaper signals he's here to be photographed shaking hands and possibly holding a polished silver trowel that's never touched dirt.

Mainder maintains a lowkey brooding presence somewhere on the edge of the action, leaning against the high stone wall that borders the lane on the far side. He wasn't expecting roll-away-the-stone levels of discovery, but despite the scattered cheers from the assembled crowd, it's distinctly anticlimactic. The driver takes up position and, with a theatrical hand raised high for all to see, brings it down on the lever to lower the bucket. It's some skill, delicately breaking the surface and cutting a neat strip of turf, that he grudgingly agrees is worthy of applause. But after that it's just doing the same thing another three times before turning the backhoe in a neat manoeuvre and trundling back across to the driveway. The trench is begun, six feet long and roughly the same wide, and all of three inches deep.

Mainder takes a hint from the sudden unobtrusive bustle of multiple people realising there'll be nothing more to see for several hours, all simultaneously and spontaneously deciding they have something they just need to go and check on and good Lord, is that the time?

He himself has nowhere in particular to be, but there's no point loitering in this spot until something is uncovered. The office looks to be open for the day already, a suitable haven, and no sign of the girl yet.

Good. He's more than a little uncomfortable with what it might say about his psyche that he'd be dreaming a half-naked woman-child into his midnight bed. That requires some self-reflection, ideally before he next has to look her in the eye. He claims the couch and stretches out for a power nap, still fuzzy from his pre-dawn waking.

***

'Ssshhhh.', Chris mimes as Evie comes through the door. "You'll wake the baby."

Confused, she follows his glance to see Mainder stretched out on the couch.

"Wow," she mouths, and tiptoes up the room. "He really

made himself at home, didn't he?"

"I know, right? I keep wanting to fetch him a blanket."

Sleeping Mainder is a treat to behold, she has to admit. The brooding tension that he usually radiates is entirely absent, with his lean face perfectly relaxed and his long body twisted awkwardly half-on and half-off that much-too-short couch. He looks — there's that word again — safe, when all the information so far suggests he's anything but.

Chapter 24

"IMPOSSIBLE TO SAY, really, until it gets cleaned up."

Mainder shifts, floating back to consciousness. *Impossible to say.* What's impossible?

"They must have theories though, right?"

"They always have theories," he hears Evie comment tartly. "Right now, all they'll say is it looks like bronze, maybe a cache of some kind."

Mainder levers himself upright, blinking, and scans the room. All desks are bare save one, a huddle around Aaron's bank of monitors carrying on a hushed debate.

"Really? From the way they carried it in here, I thought it was gold at the very least."

"It's a very big deal apparently. Viktor's going to be insufferable."

"He already was — oh! Mainder's back with us." The huddle parts, an opening inviting his presence. "You slept through all the excitement I'm afraid."

On screen is a hasty photo of the object just uncovered in the new trench. It doesn't look like much, mainly a clod of mud with some odd nubs of something sticking out at one end and a vague cross shape.

Mainder frowns at the mess of soil and corrosion, slowly leaning over and bracing himself with a hand on the edge of the desk, and any trace of sleepiness vanishes. He sharpens somehow; Chris has the strangest impression that if they brought a blanket near him now, it would likely burst into flames.

"They found this about two feet down," Evie offers. "They think they have postholes, too, so a timber structure of some kind, and this buried under a clay floor."

"Just this? Where is it now?" Mainder demands.

"There was more, but it's all gone for cleaning. You won't

get in there."

"Right. Okay. And postholes." He glares at the screen again. "Right."

***

The trench is markedly deeper in the corner where the cache was found, but the diggers have abandoned that part for now to spread out and see how far the signs of the wooden structure go. The trays lined up along the path display a collection of broken clay pipe stems and bowls, two-tone shards of a stoneware bottle, a few unpleasantly organic-looking shreds of some dark material, and a half-carved stone rosette about the size of a man's fist.

Mainder crouches down by the trays, picking up the rosette and turning it over in his hands with a black scowl. *Four dozen of these, my lord says, and then he wants a few gargoyles.* And before that was the shrine and—

The hermit's hut. That *bastard.*

Buried in that lump of soil is a bronze fibula, he'd put money on it. Unmistakably a Realm token for crossing the Divide. Stashed——*hidden*—under the floor of the hut the so-called "wise man" occupied right up until his disappearance in the aftermath of the Closing. One of their own the whole time! He must have known he wouldn't be able to use the doors again, otherwise he'd never have left it behind—or he'd have come back for it long since. Mainder replaces the rosette in the tray and slowly straightens, dusting traces of mud off the hem of his coat and sneering silently at Viktor, hovering anxiously over the finds tray with his keys swinging at his belt. *Go ahead and count them if you like,* he grumbles to himself. The only interesting thing here now is what else is in that cache.

"One current theory is more mischief from the Reverend," Evie prompts. "Is that feasible?"

It's not an idle query, nor conversation for the sake of it. The way she says it is as though there's no question he wouldn't be in a position to confirm it. One eyebrow just quirks at him, a face that says, *Well?* Having her full attention is remarkably disconcerting. Not like when she was observing him covertly in the meeting room or meeting his challenge in the office. This is—well, like he's suddenly interesting. A searchlight strafing past him in the dark, far too close for comfort.

On the other hand, he could certainly use her security access and her connections if he hopes to do anything about this latest development. Besides, she's actually talking to him. No smiles yet, but maybe he can work on that.

He considers all the angles before giving in to impulse, answering briskly. "No, entirely the wrong place and context. He would have used the pond like he did for the torc. This has to be something else." A hint of the tinker's swagger reasserts itself, and he lowers his voice conspiratorially. "I think I might have an idea, but I can't be sure. Any chance I can persuade you to let me have a look at the brooch when they're done cleaning it?"

He pours every ounce of appeal he possesses into the earnest, hopeful look he gives her.

"A brooch," she echoes. "You think that's what it is?"

"What else could it be?" he dissembles, as if it's obvious to a man of his vast knowledge and experience.

She doesn't answer that question, but after a thoughtful pause says, "I can arrange that. Where will you be later?"

Chapter 25

TRUE TO HER word, she has the brooch ready for his inspection just before dusk, laid out under the same magnifier as last time.

It's unrecognisable as the muddy blob from earlier. Bright metal gleams back at him as he angles the light over the intricate angular patterns that cover the whole surface. It's far more sparse than the so-called chieftain's brooch, the only gems a trio of pale ovals at one terminal. He brings the magnifier closer, stooping to get a better look: common banded agate and one off-white quartz with a deep crack across it.

If he'd hoped to identify his betrayer from this single clue, he's out of luck. It's much too common a style. Earth affinity, certainly, but it's been too long. What was the name of that stoneworker, the one who used to harass the girls in town before Mainder packed him off Home? Could have been him. He can see the face as clear as anything, but the name eludes him. And what's-his-name — Alaric? Roderic? The huntsman would remember, the lad rode with the Hunt for a while before the Closing. If he can get a hold of him or the sculptor somehow . . .

"Any idea why there are so many artefacts in this style buried around these parts?"

He stares blankly, dragged back to the present. Does she expect him to know? Of course he does know, but how could she know that he knows?

"You must have a theory," she presses. "It's very unusual, most digs this size will only find one high-status piece like this if they're lucky, and we have two without even a single grave site. And there's the dolphin brooch, isn't there, the one in the museum. Is Patterson right? Was this place actually like a Bronze Age brooch factory or something?"

Damn. Of course they'd have to make that connection

eventually; he'd be a fool to have thought otherwise. He toys with the idea of supporting her line of questioning, staring at the blank wall ahead. It could work, if he can find a way to come back later and seed something else that supports it.

"Mainder," she says softly, and there's a note of compulsion in her voice. What is it about the girl? He finds himself wanting to give her answers, to make her happy, to maybe even see the glimmer of her smile, and compresses his lips to prevent words from tumbling out before he's had a chance to review them.

"No," he says with finality. "Not a production centre, just a lot of people used to have one of these, and —" he catches himself just in time " — maybe something happened."

Chapter 26

"AND WHAT ARE you doing in here so late, young lady?".

It's probably a good thing the security guard can't see Evie's expression when he comes up behind her. She's not startled, having heard his heavy footsteps coming long before he arrived, but his overbearing paternal tone could almost be calculated to irritate. She finishes returning the brooch to its numbered shelf and locks the cupboard door.

"I'll be done soon."

"It's not a question of how long you'll be." The floorboards creak in protest as he brings his bulk farther into the room, taking up a position just behind her left shoulder. It's altogether too near for her comfort. If she turned now to look at him, judging by his cloying-sweet breath ruffling her hair, they'd be nose to nose. "You understand me, love? It's a question of whether it's on my schedule. I'll need your name and your manager's name." The clipboard is flourished, pen poised, ready to take names and make trouble.

Chris's return couldn't have been better timed as he steps through the open doorway and says coolly, "That would be me. Who left this door open, please? This is supposed to be a secure site."

The man steps smartly back, and Evie can finally turn to review him. He doesn't look like a predator, but then the worst of them never do. He radiates an instantly forgettable bloke-next-door vibe, with a mop of iron-grey hair combed in a swirl around his very obvious bald spot and a fussy toothbrush moustache recently committed to. His uniform jacket and high-vis vest fit remarkably well considering he's about twenty years older and several stones heavier than the rest of the security crew. There's no menace in him now, on the surface at least; now there's another male in the room, he's as affable and as harmless as a tipsy uncle at a wedding. His official security pass announces him to be *T. Clegg (Night Shift)*. Fixed in the glare of the camera's flash, he looks like an unrepentant Mr Toad caught joyfully speeding, florid cheeks merging into his non-existent neck and what he probably imagined was a friendly smile. Evie can still feel his breath on her neck, goading her to turn around and open herself up to assault.

He shrugs off the question of the door left open — security is on the case, no need to be alarmed — and delicately hints that, even with his mighty protection, foolish little girls shouldn't be sitting with their backs to doors after dark. He flourishes the clipboard like a token of power and ends with, "If it's not on my schedule, it's not happening. I don't make the rules."

"There's a schedule?" Chris says blankly, glancing at Evie to see if she knows what Clegg is talking about. "Is this a new thing? It's the first we've heard of it."

"The professor and I discussed it this afternoon. You're supposed to let security know if your people are going to be on site after six. Don't want anyone getting into trouble now, do we?"

Exactly how overtime they didn't know they needed could be submitted to a schedule they didn't know existed isn't specified; Chris is about to point this out when Evie intercepts.

"Of course not," she says smoothly. "We'll check in with the Professor's office first thing."

Clegg gives her a patronising nod. "You do that, sweetheart. Can't be having your boss always running around to get you out of trouble, eh? I'm sure he has more important things to do."

He makes a show of peering into each corner of the office, doubles back to rattle the cupboard door handles and, apparently satisfied all is secure, ticks off something on his clipboard with heavy emphasis and departs.

Chapter 27

IT'S STANDING ROOM only at today's guest lecture, hinting at either a popular topic or compulsory attendance. Possibly both. The Archchancellor himself is at the lectern, and beside him is a blonde giant of a man Mainder hasn't seen in a very long time. According to the schedule, this is one Dr. Tor Sónnarson, expert in prehistoric metalworking and jewellery making techniques, flown down from Reykjavik after the discovery of the second brooch. Sónnarson isn't the name Mainder knows him by, but this isn't the time — nor the venue, and most definitely not the company — to remind him of that.

He quickly spots Mainder taking up a relaxed slouch against the wall at the back, nursing a cup of scalding hotel coffee, and a grin lights up his face. Fortunately, this coincides perfectly with the tail end of the Archchancellor's introduction.

". . . and I'm delighted to introduce our guest, Doctor Sónnarson. I'm sure you'll all join me in giving him a warm welcome."

He pointedly raises his hands and leads the applause while Sónnarson lumbers to his feet.

"That is indeed a warm welcome." His English is impeccable, precise if faintly accented. "I am not a man given to long speeches, so I will simply say that I am very excited to join you all on this project, and I look forward to talking to you all individually in due course."

He beams at the room in general and takes the lectern to more applause, possibly for the sentiment of his speech but equally likely for its commendable brevity.

"I understand you have been wondering why you are finding so many of this style of brooch. If we include the splendid specimen from the Vernon collection, which is claimed to be the brooch of the famous 'moon princess' of local folklore, that would make three. A treasure trove!"

There's a ripple of uncertain laughter; after all, you're not supposed to laugh at the speaker unless you can be absolutely certain they're intentionally cracking a joke. Maybe he only meant to be enthusiastic?

"Ah, you are allowed to laugh," he advises with a knowing nod. "I mean to be sarcastic, and now I will tell you why."

Relieved smiles at this. Damn him, for all his diffidence, the smith always did know how to have the punters eating out of his hand. It doesn't hurt that he's put together like the gods saved all the best bits for last: tall and broad-shouldered, with pale blond hair sweeping back off his forehead like some Icelandic hero from the sagas. Girls used to practically fall at his feet.

Maybe they still do—a horrible thought in the present context. Evie is down there at the end of the second row, leaning against the wall and occasionally turning back to scan the crowd. Looking for someone? Himself, possibly? A brief warming of her expression lets him know she sees him, but then she's all solemn attention as the lecture begins in earnest.

The first slide is a simple drawing—a diagram, really—of a typical fibula-style brooch. "Of course this style is very common," Sónnarson says. "Very common for the period. Think of it as being the equivalent of coat buttons for our era. This is how we hold our clothes together, nothing more, and if one day archaeologists dig up Saville Row, I am sure they will be very excited by the ritual significance of the tailor's shop and the many buttons sacrificed there to the minor deities of Finance!"

He twinkles with delight at his foolish joke—twinkles directly at Evie, as it happens—and expands his chest pridefully when she grins back. Mainder will have to give him a warning. She's off-limits, he'll have to tell him, because . . .

Because why? She doesn't belong to him. She's an adult—by mudside standards, anyway. She can do as she pleases. He'll warn him off anyway. If it would be inappropriate for Mainder to pursue her, the same goes for him. There are rules, aren't there, about relationships in the workplace? That ought to cover it.

"You are very lucky indeed to have discovered so many such beautiful examples."

His slides advance to show the two recent finds. The contrast between the magnificent red, amber, and gold piece against the mud-coloured and pitted bronze is shocking now that they're side by side. Garnets versus pebbles, silver flames versus empty channels.

"I hope to examine them more closely later, but from what I see here, I can tell you that you are looking at — how should I put it, a Versace next to a Walmart?" Blank looks greet him. "You do not have Versace here?"

"We don't have Walmart. Primark, maybe?" Evie volunteers, and he bows slightly in gratitude for the clarification.

"I see. What you would have, then, is your cheapest clothing store of reasonable quality. Where you may buy something that is similar to whatever Versace was showing on the catwalk five years ago, but of course in much cheaper materials and a much poorer fit."

Confused faces clear, smiles of understanding dawn, and he smiles happily at Evie again.

"There, we have an analogy — thank you, miss. This is the same thing. A fine lord may command a beautiful bespoke piece in the colours of his choosing, using the most expensive materials he can afford. He wears it, the lower levels of the feudal nobility observe, and a fashion is born. They ask their craftsmen to make them something similar."

The slide advances again, just the bronze and agate version now. "And so this is the next step. Lords and ladies bring the fashion home and any skilled metalworker may observe the design, how cleverly it fits its purpose — for holding the cloak together, you see? Perfectly designed."

To make his point, he advances to the next slide where a sallow young man stares awkwardly just off-camera as if trying not to laugh. He's wearing a swathe of bright red fabric over his T-shirt and jeans, with a replica of a simple one-piece brooch in thick bronze wire gathering the material at one shoulder and holding it in place. Behind him, the outlines of ugly concrete buildings and a patch of tragically uncared-for lawn suggest the photo was captured in haste at Sónnarson's home institution, with an unlucky student co-opted as the model. His next words confirm it.

"My thanks to my lovely assistant Klaus for modelling for this picture," Sónnarson intones with another twinkle. "And also my apologies to him for having him wear red, which is most definitely not his colour."

This raises a roar of laughter at poor Klaus's expense, but presumably it's okay since he's not here to endure it. Sónnarson flicks back to the previous slide.

"And so, these clever metalworkers make many more now in the most basic materials. For bronze, there will be scraps remaining from making larger pieces — weapons, torcs, drinking vessels. Agate and quartz may easily be found in the riverbed if you are prepared to sift the gravel for them. What we would call, an easy profit."

He beams at his clever analogy, regarding his audience's obvious approval with pride. "I will be happy to say more about the specific techniques after I have seen them more closely, perhaps a little talk at the end of the week?"

Chapter 28

THE HOTEL'S RESTAURANT is a safely anonymous venue, with the busy clatter of cutlery against plates and other diners' conversations to mask what these two have to say to each other. In any case, who would question the two experts, the local historian and the distinguished specialist, sitting down over lunch to compare theories?

Mainder isn't astonished to see the smith occupying this new role. His wily friend has apparently been hiding in plain sight for the last few decades, literally writing the book on early Romano-British metalworking techniques. Which makes perfect sense once you know that he personally invented most of them.

"So you haven't seen the brooches in person yet? I was pretty sure the jewelled one is one of yours."

"It may be.," Smidur rumbles. "I think it was a young miskin with a commission for his master. Such a long time ago! If this is the same, then I recall he said, 'As fine as you please, and you may be sure he will pay well if he's satisfied.' So I did, and so he did, and I heard no more."

The waitress bustles up at that moment to deliver the list of today's specials, followed by the other, slightly longer list of things they've run out of. Smidur listens attentively, leaning forward and giving her a look of deep approval until she starts to blush and fidget, before solemnly announcing that he believes he'll try the salmon. Mainder settles for the same, and she disappears off to the kitchen to place their order.

"And when were you going to tell me you'd come into town?"

"Right after this, I promise you." Smidur barks a laugh, throwing his head back and making nearby patrons turn to stare briefly. "I knew you would not be far away. This is still your place, yes?"

Mainder meets the jibe with a gleam of challenge in his eye.

"Yes. This is still my place."

He endured some teasing from them all back in the day for being here so often, for taking an interest in the folk that lived here, but he never regretted the time spent. It needed done, he would argue. If you break a system (and that's what destroying the Vernons effectively was, bringing all their feudal plans, however benign, to dust), then you have to be ready to make good any damage down the line. The Queen would have her way, but she wouldn't see innocent folk suffer either — and as long as she approved, he was in the clear. He could never seem to make them appreciate that crucial point. Or perhaps they did, and they simply didn't place the same weight on it that he did.

In any case, Smidur has already shifted to his next thought. "The girl at the side, the clever one, what are your thoughts? I think I saw her looking for you in the lecture."

Trust him to notice. "That depends on what you mean by 'thoughts,'" Mainder deflects.

"Perhaps I should say, intentions. Is she yours?"

"Not exactly."

Mainder isn't ready to be having this conversation, not until he's resolved the same question in his own mind. But that cautious non-answer isn't what Smidur is digging for, and they both know it.

"Not exactly — what is that? It is a yes-or-no question, my friend. Do you lay claim?"

The formal language, the old language, gives Mainder pause. Technically he could, since he saw her first; and if he did, then Smidur would have to back off gracefully and without question.

It's not that simple, though. Living among the people here for so long has changed him, changed how he sees them. They're not animals to be branded. Anyway, even if he laid claim with all formality, would it make a difference to her? What if his handsome friend suits her taste better?

He can't explain, and chooses to ignore, the twist in his gut at that idea.

"She's just a child. Between you and me, I'm not sure she

even likes me."

Smidur leans back and ostentatiously makes a show of looking right and left at the people around them.

"My friend, from where we stand, they are all children. It seems to me that you have been here too long."

Mainder shifts uncomfortably under the truth of that statement. Both of those statements.

"If you say so," he responds at last. "Take my advice and watch your step around her."

And I'll be watching your step for you, just in case, he mentally adds.

Chapter 29

"FIVE PLACEMENTS IN two years? That's quite the history."

"You agreed to take her, pal. You can't back out now."

Naz is only teasing. Roger didn't just agree to take the girl on; he's keen to do so. If he does say so himself, he and his partner have something of a knack for working with the so-called "difficult" teens, even if they only discovered it because that's all they ever got offered. The difficult ones, the damaged ones, the constantly-in-trouble-with-the-law ones, the ones that all the nice, "normal" families would pass on. Him and David, they might not be normal, but they are—as the social care function up in Aberdeen has come to realise—an excellent foster family. For this girl, galloping towards adulthood without ever having known real stability, they could well be the last chance she has.

"Tell me what I need to know then. Is she really that much trouble?"

"Not at all! To be fair, none of this is really her fault. We've had a string of problems lately—oh, you didn't hear this from me obviously. We've got several carers under investigation. At least one of them will never be allowed to work with children in any capacity ever again, if you catch my drift. The others—well, you don't need all the details there either, but let's just say there are questions about their treatment of the children. This last one complained to me constantly that Evie was eating her out of house and home, so we upped the food allowance. You know how teenagers eat, right? I assumed she meant the kid was grazing, midnight snacks and the like."

"I do indeed," Roger agrees, glancing meaningfully at the massive fridge he and David went shopping for shortly after their second foster son arrived.

"Well." Naz sighs, shaking his head, and it's clear he's still furious about what happened. "I popped in on my way home to drop off one of Evie's homework sheets that got mixed up with my paperwork, and obviously they weren't expecting me. Arrived bang on dinner time and she was sat there with a Pot Noodle. For her bloody dinner! Turned out that's all they ever got, and if they complained, they went to bed without."

"Holy crap — and nobody ever suspected?"

"Never. She was always lovely when there were scheduled visits. Went on about her famous home cooking. Should have known when she kept making digs about teenagers and their eating habits, but — yeah. I completely missed it. If I hadn't had found that bloody homework, I might still never know. Anyway, she's doing fine at school, no worries there. Doesn't have many friends, but those she does have seem solid. She's a good judge of character, I'll say that. If she likes you, you're golden."

"And if she doesn't?"

"Then you're screwed, I'm afraid. Sorry. Even the placements that didn't end in disaster, they all say the same thing. She'll run rings around you until you're exhausted."

Roger makes as if to hand the paperwork back, but Naz smirks and steps smartly back out of range.

"Too late! Anyway, you'll be fine. You two must be the most authentic people I know, and I've seen you go through some shit. The worst I can say about you is your bloody awful taste in music."

That's all the conversation — and warnings — they have time for, as a tidy red hatchback pulls up and the assigned social worker gets out of the driver's seat.

As she fusses her way around the car and opens the passenger door to let her companion out, Roger realises she must have had the child locks on. Every precaution, eh? The youngster stares straight ahead at the quiet cul-de-sac, not acknowledging the woman until she finally takes a step back; then she unfolds herself and ducks past without a glance or a word.

The paperwork claims she's now fifteen years old, date of

birth unknown, but assuming she was around eighteen months the day she was placed in care. Honestly, he'd have assumed no older than eleven or twelve if he'd passed her at random in the street, pale eyes over-large in her face and a short snub nose making her look very much still a child. He can instantly see why Naz was so concerned about her — she'll age out of the care system in less than a year, cast out on her own the day after her sixteenth birthday, and looking like that she'll be a prime target for the worst kinds of predators.

Even if he hadn't had the history from Naz, he'd have had questions about whether she was eating enough. She's all angles, with the coltish long-legged look of a child in the middle of a growth spurt, elbows and knees and distressingly sharp shoulders very evident even through her shapeless clothes. Her face would be oval if it weren't for her hollow cheeks and sharp cheekbones, and there are faint violet shadows under her eyes. He mentally doubles the quantities for bread, cheese, and cereal on his weekly shopping list for a start. If she has any favourite snacks, he'll be stocking up on those as well. And maybe a stash for her room . . .

His musing is interrupted by the social worker, apparently satisfied Evie isn't about to immediately bolt, heading to the back of the car and saying, "You go ahead, I'll bring her stuff."

Roger turns to lead the way, then freezes in disbelief when he sees what's in the boot. A bin bag, a black rubbish sack, flimsy plastic tied up in double knots at the top and already tearing from where it had been carried to the car. It's barely half full, and that apparently is all the child has in the world to bring with her to a new home. That and a canvas satchel slung across her thin body and held protectively close in front of her.

"I thought you were supposed to get suitcases for placement moves," he addresses Evie directly.

"Hardly worth it!" the social worker says cheerfully, hefting the bag to demonstrate and squeezing past. The look in the child's eye dares him to make a scene, dares him to pretend he cares, and he swallows whatever ugly retort he imagined would put the woman straight. No need to cause a scene out here in the street, and she'll be on her way soon enough.

Perhaps not as soon as everyone would like, however. First there's the necessary busyness of inspecting the bedroom Evie will be occupying, touring the rest of the house like an estate agent conducting a viewing—all formality since all the paperwork was signed and sealed, but she likes to be seen to be taking an interest in case anything later comes back to trouble her.

Job done, she drinks a cup of tea at the kitchen table, chattering on mainly about herself, while the child stands in the doorway ignoring the mostly rhetorical questions aimed vaguely in her direction. Isn't this a nice house? Isn't she a lucky girl to get a placement in this lovely area, so close to a good school? Isn't she grateful to Mr. Deen for arranging all of this, and Mr. Linden for offering the placement? And so on, and on, until her mug is empty and none of her wistful glances at the pot seem to elicit the offer of a refill.

"Well, I must be going!" she announces at last, leaning down to her overstuffed handbag on the floor at her feet and extracting her keys from its drooping maw. "Do let us know how she gets on, won't you?"

At last it's just the two of them, and Evie finally claims a seat at the table. Roger makes more tea and joins her, pushing a cup across the table to her with the usual ritual—milk? sugar? say when—and waiting for her to wrap her hands around the cup and take a sip.

"I hear you've not been having the best time.," he offers carefully, opening up his body language and mirroring her grip on the cup. "Did Naz tell you why you've been placed with us?"

"You mean the reason I was given, or the real reason?" she counters. "It's a test, isn't it. You're a policeman, Naz said, a 'fine upstanding member of society.' Seems to think the sun shines out of your arse."

He's momentarily shocked by her bluntness, but it's a good sign. He hopes so, at least; she feels safe enough to speak her mind. "Well, it's very kind of you to say so," he quips and is rewarded by the briefest gleam of amusement.

"It is what it is. He said, 'Evie, if you manage to fall out with Roger, I'm going to hand in my badge and retire.'" She mimics Naz's tone and cadence perfectly, making Roger chuckle. Without a doubt she'll be doing the same to him before too long, but that's parenthood for you.

She lifts her cup at last, taking a deep swig and staring at him over the rim. If he's not mistaken, there's finally something like a smile lifting her solemn expression.

"I see. Alright, one thing you should know: I'm not in the police anymore. But when I was a detective, I was very good at my job."

The cup goes back down on the table, and she leans forward, cupping her chin on her hand. "Oh. You want to know about the homework sheet."

He laughs faintly, shaking his head. "God, Naz was right — but don't ever tell him I said that! Yes. I want to know about the homework sheet. Not an accident, right?"

"I like Naz," she remarks, apparently at random. "He pays attention to stuff, you know? All his paperwork in order, that sort of thing."

"Which is a good thing."

"Which is a good thing," she agrees. "And he always sees the best in people, which is nice. But some people just don't have a 'best.' All they have is . . . is camouflage. He needed to see."

A good judge of character, Naz said; that has to be the understatement of the year.

"Why hasn't he put you on the payroll? Seems like you're doing his job for him."

She doesn't answer that but raises her cup for another sip and stares a challenge at him over the rim.

"Got it," he says ruefully. 'I'll have to be on my best behaviour, eh? My daughter's at college right now, but when she comes home, she'll be able to fill you in on exactly what kinds of dads we are. The good and the bad," he adds with a wry twist of his mouth. "And my partner will be home soon. I challenge you to fall out with him. He's the most easy-going man in the universe."

"Oh, right," she says thoughtfully. "Why do you call him your partner? Why not boyfriend?"

"Boyfriend . . ." He considers the shape of the word. "No. Makes him sound like a temporary thing. We've been together nearly eleven years now."

"Husband then?"

"Not until the law changes," he answers shortly. "May be a long time before we get married."

"Laws are stupid," she pronounces with all the certainty of youth. "But you must love him, right? You want to grow old together?"

"Yes. Very much." Even as he says it, he realises this might be the first time he's said so out loud — to anyone other than David, of course.

"Yes," she echoes faintly, and the smile is unmistakable now. It feels like the sun coming out from behind a cloud, like he's aced a test, though for the life of him he cannot figure out what or why. "Let's not fall out, then. I want to dance at your wedding."

Chapter 30

"IT'S NEARLY MIDNIGHT, kiddo. Shouldn't you be in bed?"

Evie rolls her eyes at the chiding tone. As if that ever worked, honestly! From the very beginning, even in the early stages of settling in and being on her best behaviour, she'd treated direct orders as suggestions and suggestions as no more than background noise.

"Don't change the subject! Pops said you'd been to the specialist today?"

"Ach, same old nonsense." David, usually Mister Sunshine himself, sounds uncharacteristically grumpy. "I have to cut out sugar and fat and alcohol and all the things that make life worth bloody living . . . He said I should join a gym, for crying out loud!"

"It'll do you good!" Roger's voice echoes from the kitchen.

"The hell it will!" David's voice briefly goes distant as he holds the phone away from his face to yell back at his husband. "I bet you'd love to see me jumping around on a treadmill, eh? At my age! One broken hip and it's all over."

"Dad, you had a heart attack," she says sternly. "Most people aren't lucky enough to come back from those. Do I need to come home and make sure you're behaving?"

"No, of course not," he says hastily. He's every bit as invested in her career as she is. The idea she might abandon her biggest project to date just to fly back to Aberdeen on his account horrifies him. "What is it now — couple more weeks before you're due for a visit?"

"Four and a bit," she corrects him. "Angie's coming up too, with the baby. But I can fly back tomorrow if I hear you're running Pops ragged."

"You know I wouldn't really," David sighs. "Silly old fool's all I've got."

"Oh? And what about your favourite daughter?" The mock-outrage in her voice sends him off into a gurgle of laughter, echoed by the impish grin at her end. "That's better. You be good now, and I'll see you soon."

Chapter 31

THE THING ABOUT taking an interest in a mudsider —
claimed or otherwise — is that while you're free to neglect or
ignore them as suits you, you do tend to find yourself watching
out for them in a wider sense. Like — oh, purely for example —
shielding them from the influences and actions of others of your
kind. The uncomfortable implications of Smidur's interest in
Evie have been parading through Mainder's mind for hours
now despite his best efforts to ignore them. It's not that that's
making it impossible for him to sleep, but it is making his
wakefulness far less pleasant. Sometime after midnight, he
abandons the attempt and goes to track down whatever it is
that's making him so on edge. Perhaps the walk will resolve his
complex emotions on the other matter, who knows.

With his old friend back in the vicinity, he knows that at
least part of it is the distinct energy, long absent, that signals the
presence of more of his kind. But even that's not it — or not
wholly. There's something more. It may be benign, others like
him and the smith drawn to the spot when the mudsiders
disturbed the earth over the Fold, but it's not a feeling he can
dismiss unexamined. This is his place, his charge. He needs to
know.

A walk down and along the seafront gives him a fine view of
the moon riding high over the water, something he'd normally
stop to appreciate, but the sense of urgency only grows.
Something is out of phase, but not here. Two other possibilities
remain: the girl and the Fold.

Approaching the museum, he can see nothing out of order.
Nothing obvious, anyway. The coaxing dark between the
ancient trees is devoid of any sign of the Path, meaning energy
levels are still just where they should be. A bulky figure in the
distance paces a slow circuit around the perimeter of the lawn,
using a torch to light their way and to shine in dark corners, and

when they reach the back of the building they stop and check their watch. Darkness fades their bright green vest to a vague grey, but that, along with the clipboard in their hand, clearly identifies them as official site security making their scheduled rounds.

He doesn't expect them to be able to pick up on whatever it is that's keeping him from his bed, but their very presence is a reassurance. He can leave it to them to raise the alarm if need be. Besides, if he tries to get any closer, the alarm they raise will be on his account, some stranger dressed all in black sneaking into the museum in the small hours of the morning. He'd rather not get embroiled in that, even with his official pass to smooth out any little misunderstandings.

That only leaves Evie. He skirts the house and turns into the lane behind, letting himself through the rusted gate at the end to pick up the footpath through the woods.

The skin on the back of his neck instantly prickles, telling him that it's somehow at once both the right and the wrong direction, like there's more than one thing going on here. He dithers momentarily and resolves to check the museum again first thing in the morning. For now, he continues the steady climb up the gently sloping track, keeping to the shadows.

The footpath takes him in a vague zigzag between back gardens and meadows, an ancient trail that nobody has ever tried to annexe for the meagre few feet of lawn it would give them. Being untouched for so long has made it a haven for the wildlife, too—from the owls calling to each other in the woods beyond to the irritable rustle of a badger asserting his right of way through a hedge.

He himself doesn't disturb them, his quiet footsteps barely rustling in the overgrown grass of the path. It's a soothing route, perfect for thinking through whatever's on his mind at the time and no need to watch his steps after so many years coming this way.

The transition from narrow track to woodland to well-kept arboretum is so gradual that he finds himself standing at the edge of the hotel's immaculate back lawn almost before he realises it. Nothing is wrong here either, as far as he can sense. Not a thing. The hotel is mostly sleeping, only a scattered handful of bedroom windows glowing with the overspill from bedside lamps or late-night TV and otherwise absent of any sign of activity. He makes a conscientious circuit of the shadow-filled back lawn nonetheless, stopping and turning full circle at every corner as if calibrating a compass.

He comes at last to the southeast corner behind the ballroom restaurant, long since closed for the night, dark and deserted inside with the chairs stacked up on the tables for easier sweeping. Someone is still up though, a lone figure huddled in a wicker chair out on the terrace. Fairy lights strung from the parasol above them cast a soft glow over the tableau. A wine bottle and a single glass sit beside them on the table, both half full, and they themselves are almost hidden by the high back of the chair and the soft blanket in the hotel's signature blue pulled around their shoulders.

"Shouldn't you be in bed?" he calls, stepping out from the shadows.

Evie turns, startled, but the surprise fades to welcome instantly. "Shouldn't you?" she counters.

He laughs, holding up a hand to acknowledge the hit. "I couldn't sleep. Thought I'd go for a walk."

"Same, except for the walking part." She picks up her glass, indicating the bottle in the process. "I decided I might as well come down and finish this."

He helps himself to the neighbouring chair, settling himself comfortably and staring out across the silvered lawn. The moon, fully risen now, casts pools of black shadow under every shrub and lamppost alongside the drive.

"So, why can't you sleep? Something going on?" Perhaps it's only his imagination that she seems faintly troubled.

"Oh, there's always something going on, but no, no particular reason. Sometimes I think I'm just actually nocturnal. Everywhere's different by night, like . . . like you own the space. Like anything's possible." She takes a thoughtful sip of her wine. "That sounds stupid, doesn't it."

"Not at all. It's—what do they call it—liminal."

She nods, approving the word choice, and twists to reach the bottle for a refill. "If I'd known you were coming, I'd have brought down another glass."

He waves off the offer. "Don't worry about it. What are you drinking there, anyway?"

She peers at the label. "Shiraz, I think—no, that was earlier. This is the Malbec."

"Two bottles in one night?" His eyebrows go up in not entirely fake concern. "Are you going to need walking to your room?"

She laughs, a filthy chuckle that sparks an answering smile despite his current preoccupation. "That's the second offer of an escort I've had tonight. I'll be fine, thank you anyway."

Truth be told, it wasn't a serious offer, not entirely. He's more than happy to sit here indefinitely, even if they run out of things to say and have to sit in total silence. This is easily the longest interaction they've had that isn't overshadowed by what's going on at the museum, and she seems entirely happy—not just neutral for a change, but actually positive—to be talking to him.

Besides, he discovers her face is enchanting by moonlight, the soft folds of the chenille throw framing her like a medieval drapery. Left to itself, her expressive face shines out, and he feels again the tantalising suspicion that he's seen her before, somewhere so far away and so long ago that he can't even recall the specific circumstance. Possibly she reminds him of somebody he already knows, maybe even someone back Home. There are only so many unique faces in the universe, after all.

Backtracking over her last remark, it seems he might not be the only person to have noticed how appealing she looks by the light of the moon. Her second offer, she said. Smidur is staying up here as well, the wily bastard. Has he made a move already? If so, it sounds like he overshot, or so Mainder can hope.

Before he can probe any more, she passes his own question back to him.

"So what about you? Something on your mind?"

"No, just a feeling. Like when you're on your way somewhere, maybe running late, and you bump into someone you want to talk to, you really do, but you can't because you don't have time? You say, 'Look, I'd love to stop, but I have somewhere to be.' Yes? It feels like that."

"Somewhere to be—yes, I get that. And is the feeling always right?"

"Pretty much."

They lapse back into a comfortable silence. There's nothing wrong here. Everything is fine. He stretches his senses one last time, just to be sure—no, nothing. This must be one of the rare occasions when the feeling was actually wrong somehow.

And yet he feels somehow reassured, as if whatever it was got settled while he was searching for it. He should go. Especially since he's now feeling a foolish urge to invent something, to introduce another topic of discussion—a clear sign that he needs to get moving right now before he manages to make it really awkward. He rises from his chair with a not entirely put-on pained grunt and places a gentle hand on her shoulder as he passes.

"I'd better be going. Sleep well, child." The touch feels like a blessing or a prediction. He's lost in the shadows before she can respond.

Chapter 32

THE BACK DOOR slams open as Viktor stalks in from the lawn.

"Your bloody scans are useless!" he snarls at Aaron. "I thought you said we'd find something in trench six?"

"Trench six . . ." Aaron repeats calmly, tabbing through several windows on his screen. "Trench six. Yep, loads of signals. You not finding anything?"

Viktor blows out his breath in frustration. "Nothing. Not so much as a broken bottle. I've got them sifting everything that comes out and you know what they've found? Fucking nothing. Not even stones or roots or anything, just soil."

"Maybe whatever it is, is just buried a bit deeper," Chris suggests. "I mean it's possible there's an error with the scans, but they've been spot on everywhere else, right?"

Viktor opens his mouth to say something—nothing good judging by the condescending sneer on his face—but before he has a chance, he's interrupted by Mainder.

"How far down have you got? Trench six is up against the back wall here, yes? They'd have dug all that out when they were putting in the foundations, back when the house was built. Won't be a lot to find yet."

Viktor subsides, unable to fault the logic, and huffs his way back outside again.

As the door closes behind him, all eyes turn to Mainder, and Chris voices what everyone's thinking.

"Thank you," he says firmly. "Viktor can be a pain in the arse sometimes, and we're not in a position to argue since, you know, he's the *proper* historian here." The emphasis makes it clear that Viktor hasn't made many friends with that distinction.

"What I was hired for, right?" Mainder replies casually. "Speaking of which, is Evie in? I found something about the chapel."

Evie emerges from her corner and takes the book, running careful fingers over the faded gold lettering on the cover. *A History of Alfriscombe.*

"Oh, this is perfect. I've been looking for this one." There are several other reference books already stacked next to the printer, fat with scrap paper bookmarks, and she places his offering on the top of the pile. "Is this your personal property? I need to scan the page, but I'll try not to damage the spine."

"I'd appreciate that," he says solemnly. "Not many copies of that one left, I don't think."

He quietly congratulates himself on a successful overture and hovers while she lifts the lid of the machine and arranges the book on the glass scanner plate. It takes some contortions, but eventually she finds a way to arrange the page she needs on the plate without stressing the book's fragile spine, hanging the redundant half over the edge of the machine and supporting it with her hand until the scan is complete. She twists to the side to peer at the copy the machine spews out, checking she's captured the right section of text, then lifts the book back off the plate and closes it with care.

"I'd love another look at that later, if that's okay," she remarks, flicking an invisible speck of dust off the cover and handing it back.

"Sure," he says casually, a move which would astonish Krzysztof if he'd been there to hear it. *We're not a lending library,* is the more common response to anyone who's asking, and this book and several other volumes of similar vintage and rarity are usually kept in a locked glass-fronted bookcase up in his flat.

***

The afternoon wears on with little progress out on the lawn. Viktor reappears several times to make himself coffee, and with each fresh cup, his mood gets worse. The culprit isn't caffeine overload, but rather that every time he comes in to complain about his still-empty trench, he for some reason finds Mainder in his direct line of sight blandly watching him. Something about that smug nothingness gives the impression that he's just waiting for Viktor to sound off specifically so he can correct him again. *I could take him,* Viktor assures himself. He may know Alfriscombe, but he's no archaeologist. But Mainder's polite, expectant half-smile diverts him each time, and each time he swallows whatever he had lined up to say and re-routes to the coffee machine instead.

Just as dusk approaches, a trowel *tinks* against buried stone.

And that's when the real excitement begins.

Chapter 33

A WEEKEND'S DEDICATED overtime uncovers enough to make it clear this is no cellar; at least, not one belonging to the museum. Entirely the wrong materials, for a start, pale blue-grey stone banded and streaked with quartz that's wholly unlike the granite and sandstone more commonly used in Alfriscombe. The trench now reveals a deep-cut channel lined with stone, wide enough for three people to walk abreast and easily deep enough for a man to stand upright. The floor is currently packed clay, but the seams in the walls suggest they haven't hit the original floor yet. What the purpose of the tunnel is and what it leads to is still a mystery as it comes to an abrupt end after two metres, blocked by a heap of broken stone. There's just enough room above the blockage to shine a torch in and get a tantalising glimpse of the chamber beyond, a long rectangle roofed over with massive slabs and supported by simple pillars.

Given the position of the blockage and the curve of some of the shattered pieces, the engineers think one of the roof slabs fell in after its supporting column shifted. The cause of that, they're deeply apologetic to have to suggest, is probably the sheer number of people who've been standing and moving around on the earth above. If something isn't done, they delicately suggest, the whole thing could fall in and then there'll be nothing left to excavate. Patterson, unusually, wastes no time making the decision to protect the site with every possible precaution. A tent is hastily erected over the tunnel opening, fibre matting laid down to protect the fragile surface all around, and barriers for good measure to keep everybody off it until they can find a way to support the structure.

***

A tableau of serious men talking serious matters, all hard

hats and clipboards, greets Mainder when he makes his appearance on Monday morning. A lively debate is in progress, to his mingled irritation and delight, Patterson and some visiting colleagues each stoutly defending their pet theories.

"... seriously out of context. Just look at the quality of the stonework! Are we sure of the dates on the main structure?" he overhears as he flanks the engineering team, attempting to find a better viewing angle. Fantastic. Let them argue. Let them talk over each other and go around in circles all damn day.

"... ceremonial avenue, are you serious?" sneers another. "It's always 'ritual' with you people ..."

Oh, yes, *please* let the debate devolve into fisticuffs. That'd be perfect. The longer it takes them to agree on what they're digging for, the closer it gets to the end of the workday and his chance to slip in under cover of darkness.

"Of course, we actually have an expert on the scene. Mainder! Could you pop over here for a second and settle an argument?"

That's Patterson, claiming his time and attention as if he has some kind of right to. On the one hand, to hell with that pompous little prick. On the other ... Well, he's bored.

"Of course." He smiles serenely at the little assembly, the adult adjudicating a playground disagreement. "How can I help?"

Five minutes of attentive listening, thoughtful *hm's* and *uh-huh's* sprinkled in at appropriate intervals, and he's managed to convince two academics with completely opposing views that they're both absolutely correct without actually saying so in so many words. He's delicately seeded the idea that a ceremonial tomb complex is remarkably feasible, with half a dozen local figures of note who might have qualified for such an impressive burial, and also raised the completely so far unconsidered possibilities of an ice house for the old manor, a Vernon family crypt abandoned due to cave in, and the foundations of some part of the medieval abbey. That should keep them busy.

Now all he has to do is wait for sundown.

Chapter 34

MAINDER RETURNS AFTER dark and watches the security guard pace the perimeter, making silent note of the timing. If that's the standard circuit, then he should have at least fifteen minutes once the man passes out of sight around the corner. In any case, it'll take seconds at most to cross the few feet to the tent.

Anyone looking in the right direction at precisely the right moment might have noticed a patch of shadow detach itself and flit across the lawn, but no more than that before he ducks under the flap covering the doorway and moves swiftly to the tunnel entrance. Someone has left a warning lamp at the near end, a faint amber glow outlining the sharp drop where the trench begins, but it stops short of illuminating the far end.

Well, that's where he needs to be. He drops into the hole and strides to the end with his hand already raised, a faint blue-violet flicker of flame between his finger and thumb lighting the way.

The mess of jumbled stone has halted the mudsiders for now, waiting on daylight to assess how best to document and clear the blockage before they go any farther, but beyond that he can make out the distinctive outlines of the old chamber. With casual disregard for the damage to his clothes he hoists himself up on the rubble and slithers over the top, taking a few of the smaller stones with him. They clatter down as he lands, skidding across the floor a short way, and come to a halt against the build-up of silt against the far wall. Accumulated damp seeping in, dripping down the roots and the walls, has formed layers of mud against every edge, but that seems to be the worst of it. He's able to stand upright, holding up his tiny flame and examining the walls carefully.

Faint sparks follow the movement of his hands, a single smooth line tracing the outline of an archway that isn't really there. Just for a moment though it is — or appears to be — and then again it's not somehow, fading behind a faint net of pale-gold threads.

Now for the other task. He crouches near one of the battery lanterns, unfolding a drawing and comparing it with the layout of the chamber. He's pleased to see he has the dimensions more or less correct, and the construction of the pillars and roof supports is almost exactly as he remembered it. The tiniest bit of pressure in the right place would bring the rest of the ceiling down quite nicely.

But will that stop them?

It seems a long time that he stands there, wavering between action and inaction. This is probably his one chance to reduce the whole thing to rubble, to cover it up and make it safe once and for all. It won't, though. He sees that now. He can almost see the likely future unfolding inside his head. It won't matter to Vernon, whose only focus in this world is being proved right. It won't matter to Patterson, who'd likely continue the dig out of sheer spite. It won't matter to those energetic youngsters; they'll treat it as a challenge to be beaten by the application of yet more shiny new technology that he hasn't a hope of understanding. They'll keep digging until the whole thing is laid bare. Like — heh, exactly like children digging for worms. He offers a silent apology up to the scribe. The only possible course of action, then, is simply to leave it standing and keep an eye on it, managing events as they go. *I'll be here*, he argues with himself. *Here to guide, to guard. To make sure they don't do anything stupid.* Intuition, call it the pricking of his thumbs or whatever, says that the right thing to do right this second is . . . nothing.

With the decision made, he feels a calming certainty, like he averted a disaster simply by standing still. He's lived too long to make a habit of second guessing himself; whatever the moment was is past now, and the fallout is in the future. He heads back over the tumbled stone to climb out. All quiet up there, all dark still, apart from that single lantern, and he's been down here ten minutes, if that. Security will still be on the other side of the building.

"You're not nearly as sneaky as you think you are," says a voice from behind him as he hoists himself out of the trench. "Must be losing your touch, old man."

He spins to face the voice, calling a flame up in something like panic. The brief flare illuminates a stocky figure in security uniform, a round face, tousled grey hair, a self-satisfied smile, and, at last, his memory supplies a name.

"Clegg? When did you get here?"

The sculptor snickers and waves his clipboard. "You're definitely losing it. I've been here for a week—no, more—working the night shift. I heard, you know, they were opening up the old place."

"And you didn't think to stop by and say hello?"

"Well, I was going to," Clegg says almost sulkily. "You beat me to it."

"Have you been down there for a look?"

"Not yet. This lot love their bloody schedules, don't they, and I have to be in the right place at the right time or they start asking questions." He chuckles to himself. "Should have picked a different cover story, but hey ho. Reckon they'll get it open?"

There's something about the eager way he asks that makes Mainder suddenly cautious. He may be of the Realm, and they have known each other a long time, but they were never exactly friends, not as such. Acquaintances, rather.

"I very much doubt it," he dissembles. "They don't know what they're looking for, do they?"

"Honestly, I figured you'd be helping them. Nice little boost for business, yes?"

The sharp moment of doubt fades, but he's beginning to remember precisely why they were never particularly close. Mainder's no paragon of virtue himself, as he's well aware, but he's never managed to pinpoint what it is about Clegg that puts him on edge. He's just, for some reason, exhausting; an energy leech, putting people around him on permanent alert without knowing quite why.

He dodges the question, gesturing at the clipboard. "Look, I should get going. You need to stick to your schedule, right?"

"Yes, unfortunately," Clegg grouches. "Catch you later."

He stomps away to pick up his circuit, and Mainder watches him until he turns out of sight. Too late he remembers he could have asked him about possible candidates for the betrayal, the original owner of the bronze brooch, but—well, it'll have to wait.

He's all the way home before he realises he doesn't have his diagram any more.

Chapter 35

ABOVE GROUND, THE sun is high overhead, evaporating all traces of yesterday's heavy rain off the grass. Heatwave on the way, according to the forecasts, so it's almost a relief to be able to head down into the dark.

Some kind soul has replaced the flimsy ladder with proper steps now, wide wooden treads creating a safer route down. Not for the team's benefit, but rather for the very important visitors anticipated to arrive towards the end of the week. Bundles of electrical cables and daisy-chained extension leads run down into the darkness for the same reason, to power the floodlamps augmenting the flickering battery lanterns lining the tunnel and scattered around the chamber beyond.

Progress has been remarkably rapid over the last few days. Timber props now brace the sagging tunnel, and the debris is being ferried topside one precious bucketful at a time to be probed and sieved for hidden treasures. Nobody can really say what they expect to find, but not even the smallest clod of soil will be left unexamined just in case.

Beyond that, there's no need for further reinforcement since the tunnel opens out into a natural cavern, its walls scoured smooth by long-vanished water. It feels oddly like a cathedral down here, hushed and holy, reinforced by the illusion of pillars. Smooth Gaudi-esque outcrops rise to the domed roof and sub-divide the cave into three irregular lobes like a lopsided cloverleaf. Where the three sections meet, there's a rounded dip in the ground, a shallow bowl choked with silt that's being held as evidence of the underground spring said to have fed the ancient shrine.

Patterson is making his presence felt nearby, expounding at length on his tomb complex theory. Listening to him with the face of a man goaded to almost the limit of his endurance is Mainder.

Evie moves to the northernmost edge of the cavern, trying to stay out of everyone's way. Nobody is working over on this side; a handful of lanterns are scattered at random, all casting their fragile glow in the opposite direction, but there are no tools or trays in evidence. All efforts are being directed at the far wall where they think they're uncovering another tunnel half-buried in the accumulated debris, a wide arch water-carved from the rock long ago. Beside the tunnel mouth, the rock is streaked with an odd pattern of rust-coloured stains eerily like a watching face, two lopsided eyes with a mouth below forever frozen open in a soundless "O" From the hushed chatter of the diggers, she gathers that the watcher in the rock has been dubbed "Bob" and is henceforth to be regarded as part of the team. You don't work underground in near darkness for hours at a time without developing a certain armour against weird phenomena.

Where she's standing must be under the hedge, thick roots twining over and around each other across the ceiling and tracing down the wall. Two sets of roots meet and cross over with almost perfect symmetry to one side, framing a bland section of rock in a precise Gothic arch. They must have been growing there a very long time; the pressure of the growth has forced a deep crack all the way round where they've embedded themselves into the stone. It looks just like a door, a magical portal to Fairyland. There's even a thick vein of quartz at just the right height for a door handle. She could reach out and lay her hand on that crystal seam and the rock would shift in its frame, swing inwards at her touch. On the other side, there'd be something magical, mystical, yet at the same time safe and comforting. So the storybooks would have you believe, anyway. A different place, where none of your mundane worries exist. Not dinnertime nor tidying your room nor foster-siblings pulling your hair and hiding your stuff. A place where you're powerful, special, useful. Above all, a place where you're welcome. All you have to do is lay a hand on the stone and hope.

"Don't."

Mainder is somehow beside her in the time it took to raise her hand, gripping her wrist and glancing between her and the door.

"You can see it?"

She manages to move her head in a faint nod, shocked rigid by how fast he appeared. She didn't even see him move.

Nobody else is reacting to his unexpected departure, all clustered around the new tunnel opening and debating how best to clear it. Patterson doesn't even seem to have noticed he's lost his audience, carrying on an animated discussion as if Mainder were still next to him.

He releases her arm and leans against the wall beside her.

"Interesting. Been a while since I was taken by surprise like that," he says in a casual tone, just as if he'd cornered her at a party and is making small talk over the canapés like a normal person. It's hardly a stretch to imagine him holding a glass of room-temperature white wine and working his way through a plateful of mushroom vol-au-vents, all with that wicked gleam in his eye. The only element that doesn't fit is how intently he's watching her still, searching her face like he's mapping it against a memory.

"Are you alright? I didn't mean to scare you, but there's a very good reason nobody's paying it any attention. I'll explain later, but for now, leave it alone. No one else will go near it. Alright?"

He walks away again, looking weirdly pleased. Unconsciously, she rubs her wrist where he grabbed it, surprised to find it unmarked. There's nothing there, nothing but lingering heat from the contact with his hand.

Chapter 36

THE STEEP INCREASE in progress fetches several VIPs to the site, including the great Mr. Vernon himself via video call. Too frail to make the journey himself, and certainly not in any state to climb down into muddy holes in the ground, his pinched face fills the screen of the tablet being carried around by the Archchancellor's assistant, leaning forward eagerly to take in every detail of every angle as they proceed around the chamber. He doesn't look at all well, and the shadowy figure occasionally visible hovering around him is dressed in medical scrubs.

Patterson contrives to be in every frame somehow, claiming a guiding hand in every discovery. Mr. Vernon can afford to fund many such projects, after all, and it doesn't hurt to be certain he remembers a distinguished lecturer's name when he comes to write his next set of cheques.

Cooper allows it, if only because he knows just how futile the brown-nosing is. Patterson has very publicly scoffed at several of Vernon's favoured theories in the past, and if he imagines this would be overlooked come the next funding round, he's very much mistaken. Let him make a fool of himself, while the real work continues in the background.

Speaking of which, Mainder is keeping carefully out of video capture range despite having been invited to offer his insights directly to Vernon. He catches Cooper's eye, effortlessly reading the hint of reprimand, and faintly nods in Patterson's direction. *I would, if that idiot weren't*, the gesture clearly signals, and Cooper almost smiles despite his abiding distrust of the man. He may be a charlatan, but he at least knows how to behave. Surprisingly, he has no interest in milking Vernon for money either, which is more than can be said for the project director right now.

"Cooper! Where's Cooper?" the tablet squawks, cutting

Patterson off in full flow. "Yes, thank you, Professor, we're done here. Cooper!"

The archchancellor smoothly steps forward and positions himself in front of the screen, indicating he's present and listening.

"Go ahead with whatever needs doing. Whatever it costs," Vernon wheezes. "I shouldn't need to spell it out for you. I want it open, cleaned out, and ready for me to visit as soon as may be."

"Of course, Mr. Vernon," Cooper agrees, but he's already talking to a blank rectangle. Vernon has ended the call.

***

"Mr. Vernon is very pleased. Very pleased indeed," Cooper announces gravely, the focus of rapt attention from the entire project team now crammed into the conference room. "What we have uncovered recently is incredibly important, both in terms of our understanding of the site and in the implications for some specialised areas of research. Mr. Vernon is very keen to support further work on these topics, so many of you can look forward to having your contracts extended until at least the end of the year."

But not all of you, is the unspoken rider to that statement, and there's a faint murmur of disquiet from some corners of the room. Cooper raises his voice slightly and ploughs on. "As you know, our benefactor is a distant cousin of the original Vernon family, who founded the manor here. Furthermore, he is a very strong proponent of some of the possibly supernatural explanations for the strange activity recorded over the last few centuries. Whether he's right or wrong in this, I couldn't possibly say, of course."

A ripple of laughter, swiftly suppressed, greets his all-too-clear non-verbal indication of which option he favours.

"But as long as Mr. Vernon is happy to fund the research, we, of course, are happy to continue it. I'll talk you all through the outline schedule for the coming months . . ."

The screen behind him flicks on, and he reaches for the projector controls.

Gods help me, he has slides. Mainder glances wistfully at the door. Beside him, Aaron whispers "For ten quid, I can go and set off the smoke alarm in the hall, no questions asked."

"Son, if I carried cash, you'd have a deal," he murmurs out of the corner of his mouth and settles down to endure the slideshow.

***

It turns out to be worth sitting still for. Mr. Vernon is so very pleased, apparently, that he's prepared to pay for the entire project team to get shitfaced at his expense. Obviously, that's not how he phrased it, and it's nowhere in the wording of the instructions filtered down to Manor Hill's events team. But "open bar" only has so many interpretations, and none of them end in uniform sobriety.

As for the details, it's nominally black tie with a five-course sit-down dinner, followed by a disco, resulting in a scrambling exodus to the nearest town of a size likely to have a gentleman's outfitter and a department store with a ladies' formal wear range. Ballgowns and cummerbunds aren't high on the list of things to pack when you're heading south to work on a dig site for six months. The steadily rising tally of half-days and flexitime hours taken to expedite shopping trips has the HR team chuckling, even as they struggle to get everything correctly logged with payroll in time for the reporting deadline.

Chapter 37

MAINDER STIRS, OPENING bleary eyes on his cabin.
Beside his chair, a fire he doesn't remember lighting collapses to
glowing ash, the last remnants falling softly through the grate
with a whisper of finality. He could swear he just sat down a
second ago to ponder the day's problems. Must have been more
tired than he thought.

And the girl is back. Not in his bed this time, but sitting over
in the window seat, examining the cards scattered on the broad
sill. She's wrapped herself in the massive fur throw from the
bed, almost totally hidden apart from one bare leg dangling idly
over the edge of the seat and her pale face bent over the cards.
As he watches, she shivers and pulls the fur tighter around her
against the creeping cold, looking over at the fireplace.

"I tried to keep the fire going, but there was no more wood."
She gestures to the window with a face of comical dismay.
"And it's snowing out there."

He snorts a laugh and hoists himself from the chair, rubbing
his numb face to chase away sleep and peering out of the
window. It's late in the year for snow, but fat flakes are drifting
slowly down and settling on the ledge. Beyond the thick clouds,
the sky is lit by the aurora, red and gold wings beating against
the atmosphere. A rare sight even here — and telling of
something or other.

"Can't keep away, huh. Come to tell my fortune?"

"If you like."

She gathers up the cards and holds them out as he comes
alongside, looking up at him with her sunshine smile. The only
people who get that treatment in real life seem to be the ones
she's genuinely happy to see, which hasn't seemed to include
him so far. Proof, if he needed it, that it's only a dream. The
cards, too; he hasn't owned a set like this for — well, for a very
long time, unless he left a forgotten deck in storage somewhere

over on this side.

He takes the deck and shuffles, laying down a single card and offering the rest back to her with a magician's flourish out of sheer habit. Always used to make the girls smile, and tonight is no exception. She chuckles at his whimsy and gets to work laying out a simple pattern on the sill.

"Okay, let's see." She turns over the first card: the Moon. "You're feeling your way right now. Governed by intuition."

"Yeah, that sounds like me." Intuition chooses that moment to elbow him sharply in the ribs. *She's naked.* Not a stitch on under that fur. He tries desperately to focus on the card, the face in the pale circle leering knowingly at him. He swallows heavily and moves back a fraction. "What else?"

She reveals the World, reversed. "You're challenged by . . . a task, incomplete. Unfinished." The next card is the Star, reversed again. "In your past, a betrayal." The Hermit, reversed. "More recently, isolation. You're far from the people you want to be with."

A faint edge of cold fear nudges him, the beginnings of caution, like the dark lakes under stone lapping at his feet.

"Maybe I gave you the deck upside down," he offers in a weak attempt to lighten the mood. "Can we start again?"

The ghost of her impish grin flashes across her face, but she turns over the next card. Death, upright. "In your future, change. The end of a cycle perhaps." She glances up and smiles. "Things are going to get better, okay? Trust me."

"I like the sound of that," he agrees. "Keep going." *And keep smiling. I like that smile aimed at me for a change.*

She turns back to the pattern and the next card. The Lovers, upright. "Whatever it is you're searching for, you need help to find. You can't do this alone."

She seems so sincere, so reassuring. He has to remind himself that it's not real, however much he wants it to be, however much he'd love to be able to talk to her about all of this and have her understand. The cold, hard reality is that she's nothing but an insertion into his dream state so that he has someone to listen to while he talks to himself. She's only telling him what he already knows.

Better make the most of it, then. She might just tell him something he hasn't been paying attention to up until now.

She turns to the final row. The Devil, reversed.

"You have freedom to act. The next steps are up to you. I wonder . . ."

She looks directly at him again, and now there's no levity, just concern.

"I wonder if that's the same as your isolation. You've been dealing with something alone for a very long time. In control, but unsupported. Does that sound right?"

It sounds so very right that he nearly wells up. Should he pinch himself? He has no idea if that old tale really does wake you from an unwelcome dream, but he'd be willing to give it a try right now.

On the other hand . . . maybe his idiot subconscious has the answer, just waiting to be revealed. He leans on the sill and gestures at the remaining cards.

"You're gonna make me cry if you keep this up. What's next?"

That sparks an answering grin at least, and she turns over the next few cards. The Magician, reversed. "Some things aren't what they seem. Be careful of assumptions, or you may be caught out." The Tower, reversed. "Things could go very wrong. I — you know this already." Her brows twitch together in concentration. "A disaster, averted," she adds softly.

Now, the final card. Strength, upright. She stares at it for much longer than she did the others before admitting, "I'm not sure — focus or control? In the end, it will be down to you, I think. God, that's vague." She sits back and swipes her hair back off her face, laughing at herself. "No need to cross my palm with silver for that one, that was rubbish. Call it a free sample."

Crossing palms with silver — now there's an ancient idea. Even the old people only say it occasionally, maybe when they meet proud parents pushing a brand-new baby on their first outing. *For luck,* they say, touching the coin to the infant's chubby hand before passing it to the adult. *For luck.*

And despite her denial, her reading is scarily accurate. But then it would be, wouldn't it? If it's not real, if it's not really her, if it's only the thoughts in his head given shape so they can be spoken back to him. If it's just a dream.

He settles down on the seat next to her and takes possession of her hand.

"No silver," he says gravely. "But in this place, my thanks are worth something."

On impulse, he raises her hand to his lips in ancient courtesy. She looks faintly surprised but doesn't object. Idly he wonders what else he could get away with right now. It's his dream, after all.

"This isn't real, is it," he says.

He's not sure who he's trying to convince. It feels very real, so much so that it's unnerving. Way beyond faint misgivings now, far past discomfort, he begins to feel the cold waters rising, chill to his knees, to mid-thigh, and he's stepping forward blindly into the dark and reaching out for certainty. He's still holding her hand like a lifeline, and she's letting him. He could let go. He *should* let go. But somehow he doesn't, sitting there staring into her calm eyes.

"This isn't real," he repeats. "Right?"

She'll vanish any moment. He'll wake again in his dark nest above the shop.

"Who knows?" she says softly, gently disengaging her hand at last, reaching back for a card at random and tucking it into the breast pocket of his shirt. She's too close and somehow not quite close enough, and he couldn't be more grateful to his dream for giving him something to wear right now. The idea of her cool fingers touching his bare skin — well, it's very much *yes* and also at the same time absolutely *hell no.*

The movement dislodges the fur a fraction, carrying her scent up to him. How is it that she smells like moonlight? Moonlight and sweet moss crushed underfoot, still water under stone, long cold nights back home in the dark. Somewhere under it all, more ordinary scents: soap, perfume, a hint of fresh sweat. He wants to breathe it all in, get closer and find out how she tastes. He wants what he doesn't know he wants — or didn't before he wanted it — and by all that's holy why is the dream wandering off down this blind alley? He needs to know what to do about the Fold, about Vernon, not fantasise what he might do with this absurdly engaging woman-child if he thought he had a chance.

Yet he can't look away, transfixed by the line of her bare shoulder, her neck, skin shining pale and perfect against the dark fur and begging to be marked.

Her strange move with the card is a fleeting distraction at best. He squints down at the edge of it poking out of his pocket.

"What's that for?"

"Ask me in the morning."

There's that smile again, the one you have to know is there in order to know it's there, and that's a feed line if he ever heard one. Unmistakably an invitation. He can barely breathe, frozen by sudden certainty, struggling to form a coherent thought beyond I want. It's not lust that's making him weak at the knees, surely. She's just a girl, an ordinary mudside girl, no matter how intriguing. It's not love. It's not magic; he would know the taste instantly if it were. It can only be homesickness of a kind, a longing for simpler times and easy access to girls like her, lithe and pale and strong beyond imagining. It's not love, it's . . . it's just time he went home.

Even so, he closes the gap, tracing the line of her jaw with a careful hand and drawing her closer. Where his fingers touch her skin, faint trails of gold follow, a dull glow like the moon edging behind cloud, just like once upon a time when the magic in his partner would leap up and blend with his own. Something he hasn't been in a position to experience for far too long. He stares, fascinated, running his thumb across her cheekbone, and still, she allows it. Still. If he just . . . if he can . . . maybe he could . . .

Shit. This is wrong, even in a dream. But somehow, she smells like the memory of moonlit nights, like home and safety and better times, and there's no more fight in him. He lets the waters close over his head.

Chapter 38

HE SHIVERS AWAKE in broad daylight, shifting his head sharply to escape the sun in his eyes. Must have fallen asleep right here on the couch. Slept several hours past his normal rising time, too, judging by the sun's angle, but he's not in the least relaxed. In fact, he's almost painfully aroused, hands balled into fists across his chest, clutching something that's not there anymore. He swears he can still feel the texture of the sable fur bunched up under his palm, still feel the edge of the window frame digging into his hip. Still breathe the scent rising off her skin. He arches back on the couch and gropes for his waistband, vainly trying to ease the pressure on his groin. Couldn't the dream at least have let him get to the good part? No, the better part. Even if he didn't get to the finish, it was still a sweet taste of something he wasn't even aware he'd been missing. But this now, the aftermath, the *wanting* — this is going to be a problem.

He hauls himself to the bathroom and turns the shower on. Already shivering in anticipation of the cold shock to his system, he fumbles for the hem of his shirt and struggles out of it, balling it up with both hands to toss aside. His hand meets unexpected resistance, something with corners, and he halts in confusion. Could have sworn he left that stupid security pass in his coat . . .

He extracts the offending object, and a chill washes over his skin. It's a tarot card. *The* tarot card, the Tower — the one she gave him in the dream. He gropes for the controls and turns off the water, scowling at the card the whole time. A cold shower is redundant now.

Chapter 39

WITH THE ERRATIC hours everyone's keeping at the moment, Evie isn't surprised to find the office empty today. Anything before nine o'clock in the morning counts as cruel and unusual punishment in her mind, but today she has a hand on the door handle at 8:12 a.m. precisely. With some flexitime hours saved up and a light workload, she's perfectly on track for a lunchtime finish and an afternoon's shopping up in Exeter.

At least, she assumed the office was empty, lights off and screens blank, but as she passes down the room, flicking on lights as she goes, she's pulled up short by the sight of Mainder sitting in the corner on the couch, idly turning something over and over in his hands. Never exactly elegant, today he looks like he got dressed in the dark, shirt rumpled with buttons and holes mismatched, and the hollow-eyed stare of a man who's just received terrible news.

"You're in early," she says cautiously. "Is everything okay?"

He smiles sadly. "Honestly, I have no idea."

He flips the colourful rectangle in his hand again and hands it to her. She looks at the tarot card with dawning horror.

"What—"

"You tell me. I found it in my pocket this morning." He holds out his empty hand like he's asking her to dance. "Walk with me?"

It doesn't occur to her to wonder why he'd need her hand until it's too late. The Path sings open behind him, and he pulls her through.

Chapter 40

THEY LAND TOGETHER on the other side, staggering inelegantly; he finds his arm already tight around her to hold her steady, an unthinking impulse to avoid causing further harm. It brings her too close, much too close. Worse, she really *does* smell like moonlight, even here in the weak sunshine of a mudside morning, and without thinking he takes a deep breath in to savour it again. Except now this is real, really real, and it carries consequences he's not sure he's ready to deal with. He sets her firmly at arm's length and paces in a tight circle, mustering his defences to deal with whatever she turns out to be.

She backs away, a warding hand held out, to review her new location — the standing stones at the top of Fairy Hill, empty of anything except her and the scorching fury of the man who just magically transported her here. The protective cloak of mundanity he usually wears is dissolving, shadows pooling at his feet and wreathing up around him, plucking his long coat into tatters as they go. A sullen red-gold shimmer glows on his shoulder and creeps across his chest, up his neck, down his arm, and when he flicks his fingers to place a ward around the circle, it sends tiny short-lived sparks spiralling down into the weeds.

"What are you?" he demands curtly.

"Nothing!" she insists, backing up towards the nearest gap in the stones. "I mean — Jesus, I don't know, *normal*. What the hell are you?"

Another step back brings her up against his invisible barrier, a high-pitched hum palpable against the skin of her neck and arms. Where she makes contact, it becomes momentarily visible, a fine lattice of pale gold lines like a net dropped over the stones, and she tests the strands curiously, watching the glittering threads distort under her fingertips. There's no escape until this is resolved, one way or the other.

At least he's still holding human shape, whatever he really is. What's more, his body language in general is screaming defence not offence, panic rather than rage. Frightened people can be dangerous, of course, but given that display of power just now, it's not fists she needs to fear, not hands circling her throat. At least, not yet. Nevertheless, her heart jolts when he closes the gap, looming over her with his companion shadows curling around her as if to hold her still. She feels the strangest desire to step forward to meet them, to let them surround her and welcome her into the dark and be done with it.

"No. *Normal* people don't just wander in and out of my dreams."

The subtle flame beneath his skin intensifies, curling along his jawline. By contrast, his eyes are cold, clouded flint replaced with coal. *Get it over with*, she urges, squeezing her eyes shut and trying to turn her head away from his empty stare. Jesus he's strong, just like the dream. And warm — not scorching, not burning, but she can sense the furious fire, barely contained. What if she can't convince him? What if he lets it loose? She got burned once when she was small, playing with matches she wasn't supposed to be able to reach, and she still has the scars. Not just physical either. The pain of it, the searing and the stink of burned hair, and the dreadful siren of her own screaming, the roar of panic as the adults came running . . . She flinches, dragged back into the memory, and abruptly the pressure of his hand is gone.

"Damn," he says softly, more to himself than to her. He looks almost ashamed. The shadows retreat back wherever they came from, and abruptly he's just a man again, standing tall in his dusty black overcoat.

"Relax, child. I'm not going to hurt you."

It's a little late for that reassurance. She lowers herself to the ground and hugs her knees, willing her aching chest to expand and allow her to breathe. *Five things I can see*, she tells herself. One: Mainder, hovering like he wants to say something, apologise maybe, but she refuses to make eye contact, to give him an opening. *Just shut the fuck up*, she advises fiercely in her head. *Not a fucking word. Just don't.* Stupid supernatural bloody shopkeeper, that's one.

Green grass under her feet, springing back up from where she trampled it trying to escape — from where she trod, she firmly corrects herself. Grass. That's two.

Tiny flowers in the green, clover and forget-me-nots and dainty lilac-white stars upturned to look at her. She doesn't know what those star-shaped ones are. Do they have a name or are they just a weed? Flowers, anyway. That's three.

What else? The lace on one of her boots, frayed at one end. Time to buy some new ones. Four. One more.

The tarot card, dropped face-up between them when he grabbed her. The cracking Tower, lightning flashes and flames and tiny figures spilling off the parapet to the ground. This way up it means disaster, a tragedy to come.

Focus, Evie, that's five, what's next, what's next . . . Four things you can feel.

The fizz of the magical barrier behind her, blocking her escape. Not helping. The sting of her fingernails digging onto her palms. *Relax, breathe, stretch out your fingers and lay your hands flat. Better.* The stone behind her head, cool and gritty and solidly certain. Good. One more. A sudden breeze humming between the stones, ruffling her hair and making the tiny star-blossoms tremble among the grass blades. Was that there before?

Mainder reacts to it too, turning in place and peering out over the hill at the distant seafront. "Something's about," he murmurs. "You feel that?"

She ignores him. Three things you can hear . . .

A buzzard keening overhead, quartering the hilltop for prey. That's one. Air moving across the circle, murmuring between the stones, that's two. Mainder wittering about the fucking weather after he just scared her half to death for fuck's sake. *Three, goddammit,* and a bright flare of irritation renders the rest of it redundant. It's very difficult to be afraid when you're furious.

He seems to sense that she's recovered a little and crouches down to peer at her. "Evie, I'm sorry. I thought . . . never mind. Doesn't matter what I thought. Listen, though, if I'd known last night was real . . ." He abandons whatever awkward denial he was about to attempt, meeting the disbelieving eyebrow arched at him with the glimmer of a grin. "Well, I'd at least have offered you a drink first. You knew, right? That's why you gave me the card. Why didn't you say something?"

An excellent question. *Because I didn't want you to stop* seems like the least helpful thing she could possibly say right now, for all that it's the honest truth. He must be deeply embarrassed by what should have been a consequence-free moment in the privacy of his own head.

More than anything, now that her short-lived panic is subsiding, she hates that he should feel that way. In the moment, maybe he acted on impulse — but she allowed it, didn't she? She's as certain as she can be that if she'd objected, it would have ended there. The memory is oddly calming. It didn't feel wrong last night, not in the slightest, and here in the cold light of day, it still doesn't. If that was really him last night, if the desire was genuine, then so was his solemn courtesy and his exquisite gentleness.

Evie's gift, if you want to call it that, is simply this: her first impressions of people are always accurate. It's been that way since she was old enough to speak and possibly even before that. She put it down to growing up in care, an environment stuffed with both the best and the very worst of humanity. Seeing how people behave when the only witnesses are small, powerless, voiceless — it gives you a certain perspective. Mainder doesn't feel like an enemy. Last night, how he behaved — that's who he is when he thinks nobody's watching.

"I wasn't sure, not totally. I haven't had a lucid dream like that since I was little. Besides, it wasn't terrible. It was pretty good actually." Petty revenge perhaps, but the medley of expressions crossing his face — from earnest to gratified to mortified all in a split second — warms her all over. Serves him right for going off like that, scaring her half to death over a stupid misunderstanding.

"You've dreamed like that before? I mean, not exactly like last night, not . . . you know . . . " His boots must be very interesting, the way he's examining them. "But it's happened before." He abandons the intense study of his toecaps and peers at her face again. "Right. I should have known when you saw the door. If I'm right, you'd just get pulled in exactly as you were, wherever you happened to be, if the conditions were right. Even down to your clothes or . . . you know, whatever." His mouth quirks up again despite himself, thinking about the sable fur.

"That would make sense. I'd just had a bath," she agrees, refusing to be embarrassed. "What makes it happen?"

"For a start, there has to be a connection. I'd have to be thinking about you, you'd have to be thinking about me. I mean, *really* thinking about . . . you know. Is that . . .?" He stares desperately up at the sky, entirely failing to suppress a grin. "I cannot believe I'm even asking you that question."

"We're both adults here, Mainder. It's allowed. And that's all?"

"You're only just barely an adult. What are you, twenty-something?" he shoots back. "And I'm . . . I've been around longer than you can even imagine. Anyway. The other thing is, you must have an ancestor from where I come from."

"Seriously?"

"Seriously. Well met by moonlight, yes? Shakespeare knew what was up. We used to meet up for celebrations and trade and, you know, the inevitable." The twinkle in his eye invites her to fill in the gaps. "Nine months later, there'd be a moonchild on one side or the other, and no telling what gifts they'd get from our side. It all fits."

Moonchild. Huh. She finds she likes the word, likes the shape of it in his mouth. He makes it sound mystical, magical, a circumstance to be celebrated and cherished. Which, now she comes to think of it, is exactly how he's made her feel with every interaction they've had so far. Even the way he transported her up here, a courteous invitation with his hand out waiting for her to consent, then supporting her on landing and waiting until she was steady on her feet. If there's an etiquette guide somewhere for kidnappers, surely this would be a textbook case.

"Are you okay?" He seems to have taken her silence for dismay. "It doesn't have to be a big deal."

"No, it's fine. It's just a lot to take in."

"Of course," he agrees solemnly. "I expect you'll have all sorts of questions once you've had a chance to think about it. Come and find me when you're ready. And, um, could you do me a favour and keep this to yourself? I'm not supposed to go around abducting mortals. It's kind of frowned upon these days."

She snorts a laugh. "Right, who am I going to tell? Do I talk to your manager?"

"I'm sure she'd be happy to hear your complaint in person." The notion makes him laugh, too. She absolutely would, and he'd never live it down. "Perhaps you'll get the chance one of these days, but one thing at a time. We should get you back before you're missed."

Before he gets tempted to try his luck again, is the real reason. If he doesn't get a grip, he might just end up seducing her all over again right here in the circle—and all the signs indicate she might just let him. It's a compelling vision. And would it be so dreadful? For a second, he feels an odd spark of hope. If she's *yasim*, maybe this can be something after all.

Back up there, Romeo, his inner voice jeers, so clearly that he almost checks behind him for Sweyn. There'll be nothing there to see, and how could there be? He collects his scattered wits and holds out his hand again in invitation.

"Let's get you back. I'll explain everything when you're ready, alright? My people have a tradition of looking out for yours, especially the ones who cross our path without shrinking. Think of me as your—I don't know—fairy god-uncle or something."

Summoned by that ridiculous comparison, her impish smile breaks out.

"'Uncle' Mainder? If you say so," she murmurs, grasping his

hand, and hearing it said aloud, he knows instantly it was the wrong offer to make. There's absolutely nothing avuncular about the ideas in his head when she smiles at him like that.

Too late now, dickhead, crows Sweyn's echo. Deal with it.

Chapter 41

HUMAN BEINGS ARE strange and complex and, above all, *resilient* creatures. They see sorcery in shadows and malice in happenstance, but when the truly magical crosses their path, they have an enviable ability to enlarge their world view to include it and carry on with their day.

To be fair, Evie's in-tray this morning could almost have been designed to drag her back into the minutiae of project priorities, especially this spiteful little memo from the security office. It asserts on precisely zero evidence that the lock on the asset cupboard isn't up to the required standard. An approved replacement is on order and will arrive within the week. Approved by whom? And she's to empty the existing cupboard, it says here, and have everything laid out ready to be audited and transferred as soon as it arrives.

"I very much think I will not, thank you so much," she mutters under her breath, holding the paper slip up to the light to examine the unfamiliar handwriting more closely. The purchase order for her current setup had to go all the way up the chain of command to the board since there was a significant cost difference, and she went right along with it to defend her choice in-person. No one in the senior team could possibly be unaware; even Patterson is crystal clear where he stands when it comes to her area of responsibility.

She doesn't quite crack her knuckles before she starts typing, but she might as well have. Security team lead, CC the board's secretariat, and furthermore, whomever it may concern are kindly reminded that artefact storage for this project is not included in the remit of on-site security. Asset management is surprised to receive this morning's memo (scan attached for their information). It would be appreciated if any further concerns were raised with the on-site asset management specialist directly in person. Regards, etc.

She leans back and considers the text on her screen. Too forthright? Hardly. If anything, it's far more polite than this little power play deserves. Just one tiny edit required, on consideration. *Kind* regards — there we go. Now they'll know they've really pissed her off. She hits send with just a little more force than is strictly necessary and pulls a face at the cheery *whoooosh* that sends the email on its way.

She sits still for some time after that, staring unseeing at the wall opposite. That stupid memo has shaken her. Hurt feelings? Wounded professional pride? Somewhere in between perhaps. It feels very much like an attack on her authority, and she feels confident she can see it off without breaking a sweat, but still. One of her favourite and most closely held lessons from her dads is this: *Never ascribe to malice that which can be adequately explained by incompetence.* She had the motto beautifully cross-stitched and framed for them for Christmas a couple of years back, and it now hangs in pride of place above the kettle back home. It's faintly possible this is just a stupid misunderstanding, a new manager getting their wires crossed and thinking they need to do something to make their mark.

The rest of her paperwork is less challenging, thankfully; a few new candidates for the whiteboard, and several of them guaranteed to raise Patterson's blood pressure a notch. It's a childish game they've been playing, she'll allow, but since he couldn't take the time to be courteous about their domains of expertise, they've been actively hunting for wildly unrelated and yet almost convincing scraps to fill in any gaps in the display. Watching him trying to make sense of the nonsense is entertainment enough. Listening to him attempting to take credit for it and explain it to the occasional distinguished visitor is a whole new level of unholy joy.

Given that context, this snippet from Mainder's book is almost too mundane.

Alfriscombe's village church stands just half a mile from the site of a pagan shrine, and contemporary writings as late as 1632 confirm it as the focus of local ritual. Which gods were thought to visit is

unknown, but there was almost certainly a connection with the nearby
spring. The fourth Lord Vernon earmarked the site of the shrine itself
for a private chapel. However, the removal of the standing stone to
make way for its foundations appears to have intensified the so-called
Vernon curse. After a string of disasters, including alleged hauntings
and a direct lightning strike, the attempt was abandoned and he
poured his funds instead into refurbishing the main church. The
'Alfric's Coombe Impe' found embedded in the manor's boundary wall
during the late 1700s was almost certainly intended as a chapel
gargoyle or roof finial.

The imp's stone face leers out of the photo beside the text,
and Evie smiles at how much it looks like Mainder. He was
probably there though, wasn't he, no doubt hiding tools and
starting fires to frighten the hapless builders off his
metaphorical lawn. It's entirely possible he annoyed them so
much they were inspired to caricature him for posterity.

Next in the heap is something she doesn't recognise: a torn
and stained copy of the lawn scans marked up with scribbled
lines in forest green ink. It looks like it's been dropped in the
mud and then kicked around the floor a few times for good
measure, so most likely the cleaners found it in a corner and put
it on the nearest desk to be dealt with. Odd symbols here and
there could be annotations, but either they're in code or a
language she's not familiar with. On one corner, almost
obliterated by a smear of mud, there are the remnants of a
drawing vaguely similar to the stonework down in the
chamber, and if she squints, she can make out a couple of
arrows pointing in at one of the lines. It reminds her irresistibly
of the diagrams David used to draw when she was younger,
helping her with her homework. *Here,* he'd say. *Pass me that pen.*
Right. Imagine you have two forces acting on each other . . . And he'd
draw a row of fat little arrows advancing in parallel, pushing on
this or pulling on that to make things move.

Or to make things shatter. It's force calculations. Has to be.
But why? And the strange door — it *is* a door, Mainder actually
said so back on the hill. *Should've known when you saw the door,*

he said. That phrase is beginning to bother her. He didn't expect it to be seen, perhaps didn't want it to be seen. How far would he go to ensure it stays hidden? How carefully would he calculate the level of stress required to make people abandon a site? *Hauntings and a direct lightning strike* . . . People would have been hurt, even if the book doesn't mention it. It must have been terrifying.

It doesn't feel right, though. She's never felt anything but safe around him, even when he's been as angry as she's ever seen another human—person—whatever he is. It just doesn't fit.

At the same time, she can't afford to be wrong.

***

The passage down to the cavern seems subtly smaller than she remembers; darker, more cramped, and more threatening. Halfway in, she slows and stares around, wondering why it feels so different to yesterday when everything looks exactly the same. Same thick bundle of cables running down to feed the flood lamps, same scattered lanterns flickering against the line of the wall. Same cleated bootprints underfoot, same pale roots hanging like threads from the roof above and stirring faintly as she passes. It's all the same.

The interns are all crouched at the new tunnel opening, debating in hushed whispers, and the reason is resting on top of the rubble on the ground in front of them. It looks like iron, a remnant of some object nearly two feet long now rusting away in flakes.

"Right, so it's not a blade," Viktor is saying as she comes closer. "Evie, come look at this! We thought maybe it was an early Iron Age piece, a dagger or part of a sword, but it's the wrong shape. And it was embedded in the rock, here." He picks up his trowel and carefully nudges at the tumbled stone underneath. "It all came out when we cleared the weeds away. Nearly buried Claire."

The little heap of spoil is barely three feet high. "Hey!" the diminutive intern objects, laughing along with everyone else.

"I'm short, but I'm not that short!"

Evie joins the huddle and crouches to get a closer look. The object has none of the attributes a blade would have—no tang or hilt and no flattening along its length. What remains of its shape under all the rust looks more like a massive nail, the kind blacksmiths used to make by hand, with a triangular cross-section and a diamond-shaped head slightly flattened from the blows of the hammer.

It can't be that, though, surely; there's no horse so large that it would need nails that size for shoeing, and even if it was intended for a door, it would be far too long. More than anything else, it makes her think of something from one of her university textbooks, the famous case of Phineas Gage and the tamping spike that was driven clean through his skull and changed his personality forever.

"That is odd," she murmurs thoughtfully, strange engineering diagrams forgotten for the moment. "Let me just grab the camera, okay? I'll get as many pictures as I can before you move it."

***

At the transition from cavern to cellar, again her skin prickles; it suddenly feels *wrong*, much colder than usual, gritty and dry like a memory of ancient stone long since gone trying to reassert itself, pushing her back and denying her passage. Even the air tastes wrong. Foul like danger, like decay, dark and bitter in her throat. *Somewhere to be*, a long-dormant instinct whispers. *Not here*. It's too strong to ignore.

Above her head, one of the roof slabs subtly shifts, dusting a handful of loose soil on to her shoulder. She makes a hasty sidestep, staring up at the slab, and jumps when the next one along does the same thing, only this time it droops so low it nearly touches her head and the soil starts to pour out from above it. She lunges back to get out before any more comes down, but the next slab drops free and slams to the floor, earth cascading down on top of it and blocking her escape entirely.

Chapter 42

THE STRANGE THING about Mainder's flat—well, one of the strange things—is that it's considerably larger than it ought to be. Considering the size of the shop beneath, it shouldn't have quite so many rooms or run quite as far across the row of buildings as it does.

The fact is that, over time, with all the extensions and additions and changes to the street, nobody is quite sure where the lines are drawn. All the properties are tenanted rather than owned, managed by a property firm somewhere upcountry and let on long leases, and if anything needs doing, some cheerful workmen appear and take care of it without fuss or delay. It's an arrangement that suits everybody concerned. It suits Mainder, certainly, gradually claiming forgotten rooms and attics and expanding his protective borders to subsume them into his dwelling.

What does he need the space for? Nothing you wouldn't expect to find. A sitting room of sorts mostly given over to clutter, boxes stacked against three of the walls stuffed with books and artefacts that aren't ever going to see the light of day in the shop downstairs. Off the hallway, a tiny alcove under the attic stairs serves as an office, angled shelves wedged into the awkward space any way they'll fit and holding ledgers, receipts, a battered tin cash box, a pot of pens. No computer, not even so much as an electronic calculator.

His bedroom hardly merits the name, being not a room containing a bed as such but rather a space where, once he's done for the day, he drops on the untidy nest of feather-stuffed cushions and blankets until he's rested. The blinds in here stay down, the curtains drawn, shutters closed at all times, so that no light gets in even on the brightest of moon-bright nights.

The tiny bathroom contains an unexpectedly modern fitted suite in severe, spotless white. A shower cabinet, toilet, and sink all in the same square style, the walls tiled from floor to ceiling on all sides. Lazy Mainder may be, but like all exceptionally efficient lazy individuals, he doesn't see any point in making it hard to clean up after himself.

The kitchen is the next best kept room up here, equally spotless and minimal, with the only items on display a metal coffee pot on the tiny stove and a bottle rack stocked with tannin-rich dark red wines. The contents of the shelves suggest that he apparently lives on bread and fresh air, and the little fridge in the corner isn't even plugged in. Unlike the bathroom this room is curiously old-fashioned, with an oak dresser pushed against one wall where you might expect to see fitted cupboards, and a small square table in the centre of the tiled floor with a single straight-backed chair pushed up under it.

At the top of the attic stairs is where the limits of the original end and the annexation begins. To the left, he's taken over what would be part of the extension over the back room of the sweetshop — if they knew there was a door hidden behind the brickwork, that is. To the right, the attics above the pasty shop and Magick Krystals, respectively. Those tenants have never had use of the roof space, although they do know it exists. All they know is that their absent landlord specified the doors to both should be kept firmly locked, storage or some such, and since everything else is so convenient and the rent so reasonable, they see no reason to make a fuss.

The dividing walls between the sections have long since been removed, just a trace of brick arch marking where they used to be. Tiny windows high on the street side admit limited light — though, to be fair, they could do more if someone could reach them with a rag. Years of accumulated grime and cobwebs suggest that optimal natural daylight probably isn't the chief resident's main concern.

At the far end, furniture rejected from every other room over probably several centuries is stacked in haphazard piles, stored until needed.

Under the windows, a cluttered workbench stretches along almost the entire wall, a rough timber construction heavily braced at intervals and holding a careless scatter of hand tools giving the impression that someone will be right back after a quick smoke break. Candle stubs sit pooled in mismatched saucers around one workspace, a massive slab of stone polished smooth by constant use. Beside the door there's a faded armchair with the stuffing leaking from the cushions, a half-full bottle of whisky on the floor beside it. A thick layer of dust covers workbench, floor, chair, and bottle. Nobody has been in that attic in a very, very long time.

***

So when Mainder hears a slithering crash from somewhere up above his sitting room ceiling, he's up those narrow stairs much faster than you'd think wise. He could swear he's left nothing up there that should go bad or blow up, at least he thinks not, but it's been a while. He slides across the threshold and corners with a hand clutching the door frame, braced for disaster—and deflates instantly when he sees Evie, wild-eyed and dishevelled, at the back of the furniture stack with her hands raised to fend off a toppling chair. She lets out a held breath on an angry sob and lowers her hands; the movement dislodges a dusting of soil from her hair, fine grains like desert soil trickling into the folds of her collar and dropping to the floor.

He swears softly, half-alarmed and half-relieved, and places gentle hands on her shoulders.

"Alright, you're okay. How'd you end up here?"

"I did the—" one shaky hand sketches a facsimile of the glyph "—the thing. From the dream."

He goes ice-cold all over just thinking about all the ways her unconventional arrival could have gone wrong.

"What—? You shouldn't even be able to— You could have ended up anywhere."

He stops short of delivering a lecture; now is not the time. Under his hands, he can feel her shaking, adrenaline surging through her still from whatever chased her up here.

"Better than staying where I was. I thought you said it was the sign for home?"

"Or the nearest safe space," he clarifies. "Depends what you were thinking of when you did it. What happened?"

"Cave-in at the dig. I went down to look at something and it — the roof just — "

The trembling intensifies. *Idiot*, he chastises himself. *Let her recover first.* Since these are special circumstances, he allows his cautious hold to become something more, gathering her in with exquisite care.

"Okay," he murmurs, muffled in her hair. "Tell me in a minute. It's okay."

He wouldn't have been offended if she'd pushed him away, but instead she accepts the offered support and leans into him with her arms wrapped around herself. It's all too easy, too natural, for her head to rest on his shoulder, for him to raise a hand to stroke her hair, gently carding the fine strands to soothe her panic away.

Outside of the dream, and discounting that moment that he carried her to the top of the hill, this is the closest they've physically been. It's an oddly sweet feeling to be here at the right moment to help and knowing that she allows it, she trusts it, and he lets his swell of contentment expand to reinforce the reassurance he's still pushing outwards for her benefit. *It's okay,* he projects as hard as he knows how. *Everything is okay now. I've got you.* Everything is very far from okay, he's certain, but here and now she's not in danger. Not while he's here to make sure of it.

"That's some trick," she says at last, shifting against his chest. "Is that some kind of mind control? I couldn't panic right now if I actively tried."

He dodges the question, releasing his gentle hold and fetching his coat with a smug flick of his fingers. "Let's go and see what's going on up there."

"Wait. I needed to ask you something first."

She's calm now, but beyond that, there's something more: a hint of the guarded nothingness he saw the first time they met.

Whatever lingering contentment he was feeling dissolves instantly.

"Go ahead," he says cautiously.

"I found this. I mean, I think the cleaners found it and put it in my in-tray. Must have thought it fell out of one of our folders or something." She unfolds the mud-stained paper and holds it out to him. "What is this?"

"Ah," he says distantly. "So that's where that went."

He reaches out, but she keeps her hold.

"I know a stress diagram when I see one, Mainder. Does this have anything to do with what happened?"

"Absolutely not," he says hastily. "I mean, I had an idea for getting the dig closed down, but I would have made damn sure there was nobody around to get hurt! Look, I talked myself out of it pretty much straightaway. I know the people behind this dig, Evie. I know what they're like." He leans across in his eagerness to make his point. "You don't know how far they'll go to get what they're after. They'd send you all back down there tomorrow to dig it out with your bare hands if they had to."

He feels uncomfortably exposed, all his concerns out in the open, and she watches his face in silence while the echoes of his words die away. He could almost believe time had slowed if it weren't for his steady heartbeat marking the seconds. Does she even believe him? He wouldn't believe him if he were her. If he could only come up with a more convincing denial, but what is there, though? He's told her the truth. There's no more to it than he's already said.

"Alright," she says quietly, releasing her hold on the paper. "Let's go then."

As much as he was desperate for her to believe him, that feels too easy.

'Not that I'm not grateful, but . . . really? Knowing what I am and what I can do? What if I really were some big bad villain? How would that have gone down? And then you just believe me, just like that—" he waves a hand airily " —when I tell you it's not me. Why?"

"I *don't* know what you are," she objects. "We still haven't had that conversation, remember? I know you're . . . something, and I know you can do things that make no sense to me, but . . . *shit*. I don't know." Frustration gets the better of her. "I know you could, if you needed to, and I assume you wouldn't do it without a very good reason. But if I thought for one second you'd put innocent people in danger—well, that would be the end of this friendship."

Friendship. The word stings out of nowhere, a pale parody of what he'd like there to be between them. But then, even her friendship is a reward he never expected to earn and probably doesn't deserve. "That is fair," is all he says, swallowing the bitter taste of disappointment and turning towards the door "Let's talk about it later. You ready?"

***

Two ambulances stand blinking in the road out front, with a blanket-swaddled casualty being gently loaded into one of them on a stretcher. Evie's face crumples in sudden realisation.

"Shit," she whispers. "I just left them behind, didn't I. I didn't even think."

He lays a gentle hand on her arm, a reassuring squeeze that quickly turns to warning when he sees Smidur striding over with grim purpose. Jacket discarded, sleeves rolled up to display his impressive arms, he looks ready and primed to lead the heroic rescue and dig any imperilled maidens out singlehanded if necessary.

"Are you all right?" he demands, grasping Evie's shoulders in dramatic concern. "They said you were down there!"

On the surface, it's much the same impulse as Mainder's own, a simple expression of worry and an invitation to take comfort if needed. She chooses not to, to his very great delight, rejecting the implied offer and stepping back out of Smidur's grip immediately. He seems quite put out when she lies smoothly, "I'd just stepped out to fetch my camera, luckily. I must have missed it by seconds." Admirable, how she summons that calm dishonesty as if bare minutes ago she wasn't on the edge of hysteria in his dusty attic. "Sorry, I need to check in with the team." She ducks her head and hurries away.

Mainder lets her go for now and navigates his way around the crowd of gawking onlookers. A hasty cordon is going up all the way around the trench and for an extra six feet in every direction, barring spectators from compromising the unstable ground any further. It actually doesn't look too bad from here. One of the visible roof slabs is drooping down at a slight angle, and the slump of the fibre matting further along suggests the earth beneath is maybe a foot lower than it should be, if that. But Evie described a full cave-in, slabs falling to the floor and soil pouring down, and what's more, the fine, dry mud in her hair and on her clothes confirms what she saw. This simply isn't possible. *Shouldn't* be possible. Alfriscombe's thick, red clay soil does not trickle, not ever; one of the reasons it makes both for solid trenches and for backbreaking gardening. It makes no sense.

Chapter 43

MAINDER HAD HOPED that keeping his hands busy would allow his brain to work on the problem at hand—and it has, sort of. Just very much not in a helpful direction.

Since Evie appeared behind his forgotten furniture, he's curious. Why there? Why his attic in the first place, obviously, but then why that particular spot? There are Paths all over Alfriscombe, most of them dormant and safely hidden, but this was never one of them. Somehow, she signed for home and safety, and it brought her straight there.

Hang on a minute. Right where she appeared, he'd have been sitting precisely under her feet at the moment she stepped through.

He paces from the end wall to the first joist, the support for the wall between the sitting room and the hall. One pace back from that would be right above his shabby sofa. The Path wouldn't have been able to place her safely anywhere in the sitting room because of the clutter; she'd have ended up trapped in the stack of boxes or out on the window ledge, so it must have routed her instead to the level directly above him.

Which means—she must have thought of him.

The realisation makes him giddy. At a moment of life-threatening and inexplicable danger, he was somehow the safety she sought, even after this morning, even after he grabbed her and dragged her through the Path and threatened her and exposed his true nature, flames and all.

He slowly restacks the chairs, his mind working furiously. One stack safely against the wall, that way, if it happens again, they won't fall. He has to make sure there's no chance of it happening again. If it does happen again, he has to be here to catch her, hold her, reassure her again. *No.* Stop that. It can't happen. It *won't* happen. She won't be going anywhere near that tunnel, and so he'll tell her when he sees her next. And as for other dangers . . . Well, he'll deal with those. Just as soon as he figures out what they are.

Tables next. Maybe if he pushes them up against the opposite wall and puts this other chair on top, and this little chest of drawers? Fits underneath, that's good, and why the hell does he even have an umbrella stand? Not like he owns an umbrella, nor ever did. Anyway, under the table it goes. What if the trench falls in completely, undermines the house, takes the whole back lawn with it? If she's there when it happens — well, he may be getting on in years but he can still move when he needs to. A dash across the lawn to reach her just in time before the earth closes over her head, clutching her outflung hand and hauling her to safety —

He slams the stool he's carrying down to the floor and leans heavily on it, exasperated with himself. Inventing scenarios now? Wishing her in danger so he can imagine himself playing hero? What is wrong with him? It's ridiculous. The only way he can be sure she's safe is if he's with her one hundred percent of the time. *You'd like that though, wouldn't you*, snarks his hindbrain. Yes, he would, very much, but would she? Impractical, anyway. She has a job to do, he has a task at hand, quite apart from the more mundane concerns of running the shop and managing his own life — such as it is — and eventually this whole fiasco will be over and done and she'll move on, and what will he do then? Follow her?

A vision of himself doing exactly that unfolds in his head before he can stop it. *No.* He will leave her the hell alone to get on with her life, and he'll . . . ah, who cares what he'll do. Mope, certainly, but he'll get over it.

He shoves the stool away in frustration, ploughing a trail in the thick dust, and stomps back downstairs just in time to hear the knock.

Chapter 44

IF KRZYSZTOF IS surprised to learn the boss is receiving young ladies at home, he's far too polite to show it and waves Evie through on her sunny assurance that Mainder is expecting her. The full implications don't dawn on him for a minute or two, and he stops dead in the doorway, shaking his head and chuckling to himself. Girl's a little on the young side, sure, but old enough to know what she wants. Anyway, plenty of locals take advantage of the summer influx every year to indulge in no-strings holiday romance, so why shouldn't he? Good on him.

Since she doesn't reappear after a couple of minutes, he assumes Mainder let her in and other than resolving to find no reason whatsoever to disturb them, he thinks no more of it.

***

Technically, Mainder did let her in. That is to say, he opened the door wide expecting it to be Krzysztof with some query, and on seeing Evie instead just . . . froze. Visions of mortal peril, heroic rescues, and happy-ever-afters are still chasing each other round in his head, and now that the real deal is standing in front of him, they seem more ridiculous than ever. If he'd imagined she'd be back so soon, he could have cleaned up a little, maybe shoved some of the sitting room clutter out of sight.

Ah well, at least the kitchen is tidy. He leads her through, batting at the dust stuck to his shirt and taking hasty stock of what he might have in for visitors. Bit early in the day for wine; it's probably five o'clock somewhere, but not quite here. If she wants coffee, he'll need another cup, and if she opts for water, it'll have to be in a wine glass.

That's it. That's the limit of his provisions right now. Either way, everything except the single cup he himself uses every day is covered with a thin film of dust, so whatever happens, he has to wash something up. He sighs and collects one of each to rinse out in the sink.

"How did you get over here?"

Perhaps he imagined having his back turned would be enough to fool her into thinking that was a casual, social question.

"I walked, before you start with the lectures. After the way you freaked out before, I guessed it would be a bad idea to start zipping around town the same way you do."

"Damn right." He smiles at the implied rebuke in her voice. *Mainder, you're a hypocrite.* Well, he may be, but he's a hypocrite who's been using the Path for centuries without mishap. "How's your colleague? The one in the ambulance?"

"Oh, she'll be alright. She had a panic attack and that set off her asthma, but she's fine now. She's determined not to miss the party."

It's fine. Rather, he can pretend it's fine. If he doesn't have to look her in the eye, if he doesn't see her smile, perhaps he can dampen his enthusiasm long enough to have a serious conversation. Maybe he's over-reaching anyway; it's not like he's going to forget himself and proposition her over the kitchen table.

He definitely shouldn't have allowed that idea to surface, not even inside his own head. Antique or no, that sturdy little table has seen some action in its time, along with just about every other suitable flat surface in his lodging, but that was back when he was more social, more impatient, and less . . . *Boring*, his impulsive inner critic supplies, which he resolutely ignores and substitutes with: *responsible.* He's responsible for her well-being whether he likes it or not. More importantly, if she's mastered using glyphs already, then she has to get some basic instruction before she gets herself into real danger.

"Mainder, what's going on? What's under there that you're so keen to protect?"

"Something very old." He sets the clean glass on the drainer and turns back to her, drying his hands. "Between our side and yours, there's a significant energy gap, the Divide, and when we cross it there has to be an exchange." He tips his hand one way then the other like a seesaw. "The Divide has a sort of a cycle so that sometimes it's easy to cross, sometimes it's impossible, and so we built something under there to store the energy and discharge it in a more even pattern."

"A regulator," she suggests.

"Exactly. A regulator." He nods, approving her insight. "When the cycle was at its high point, anyone could walk through without even knowing it. And with the power differential, a few hours on our side could be years or decades on this side."

"Did that happen a lot?"

"Sometimes. By accident, mostly. It got to be a problem, especially kids wandering around and getting lost. If they cross without a token, they can end up literally anywhere."

"Are you telling me that every fairy story I ever read is based on some idiot child wandering through your invisible magic doorway?"

"Not all of them," he protests. "Only the true ones. Used to be my job to chase them down and get them safely home, since I lived so close to the door."

"Why didn't you just mark the door? Wouldn't that have kept people safe?"

"Not really. People see doors and they want to walk through them, you know? Especially magical doors to Fairyland. You people are incurably convinced there are pots of gold under our bed or something. In the end, I arranged it so nobody could pass through by accident anymore. That was a little while after the Closing."

"How?"

"Persuaded the curate at the time to build a pond over it. You wouldn't believe how pleased with myself I was when I came up with that notion." He chuckles reminiscently. "It's perfect, right? Nobody's going to go wading in there for the hell of it, they're going to keep their kids well away from it, all would be well. It's been dormant for centuries now."

"But if it's dormant, how come I used it earlier?" she asks, examining her hand as if traces of magic might still be seen clinging to her fingertips.

"That's something different. Hold on. I need props for this. May I?" He reaches for the floral cardigan hanging from the back of her chair. "This—I'm sorry to say—absolute monstrosity now represents all of space and time. Okay? The patterns are people. This hideous tea-rose thing here can be me, and this . . . What is this supposed to be? Anyway, that's you. Yes?"

"Hydrangea," she supplies helpfully, choking down laughter.

"Hydrangea, sure. And if we do this—" He folds the knit so the two flower patterns touch. "That's us meeting, interacting, whatever. With me so far?"

"Barely. Explanations are usually supposed to make things clearer," she hints.

"I'm getting to that! See, if we interact, then there's a trace, an energy between us that persists. Call it memory or emotion or attachment, whatever you want, but the important thing is that if we keep meeting, then the trace keeps getting stronger. Like if I stitched this together, then ripped the stitches out again, the fabric would still be marked somehow, distorted, where the thread went through. If I put those two parts close to each other, the holes would line up again. It's like the fabric remembers."

"Alright, that sort of makes sense. Does it only work for people? Between people, I mean."

"Not always. Sometimes it's places as well. It depends which glyph you use. There's *siket*—you already know that one. That's for home or safety."

"But it didn't take me home," she objects. "It brought me to you instead."

"The Path is funny like that," he agrees, avoiding meeting her eyes. "The nearest safe space or the nearest person who can help, I suppose is the longer version. If you keep that in mind when you use it, it will put you where you're most likely to be safe."

"Okay. That sounds like it covers most things."

"Mostly. The only other one you're likely to ever need is *tren*, but I can't imagine you'll ever have to use it."

"I'll take your word for it, but just in case, what does it do?"

"It takes you where you need to be. I know, it sounds like the same thing as *siket*, but it's different. If you've lost something, or you know who has it but you don't know exactly where they are, *tren* will get you to them."

"So if I use it now, will I disappear and reappear somewhere else?"

"No, you'd still have to step into the Path to make it happen. It looks like this." He traces the shape slowly in the air for her, two short strokes down and a curve like a stylised P. "Like that."

"I'll remember that one," she says solemnly. "I expect I'll be needing it more than you think. Are you done insulting my poor cardigan?"

He twitches it out of her reach. "Not even close. What on earth possessed you to buy this travesty? I mean, it's hideous. Every time you wear it you disappear."

"Well, yes. That's the idea."

He gapes at her. Of course it is. Of *course* it bloody is. Roll up, ladies and gentlemen, roll up and take your seats for Protective Camouflage: The Masterclass! How to be the most ordinary person in the room, bonus points for making sure everyone can feel just a little bit superior to you. If you're in the room, nobody notices. If you leave the room, nobody cares. Between that and the overpowering brightly coloured blouses and the instantly forgettable hairstyle . . . *Damn* it. One of these days he'll stop underestimating her, or so he very much hopes. Glamour was always a guaranteed moonchild gift to greater or lesser degrees, but this might be the first time he's ever seen it applied in reverse. Hiding in plain sight the whole time.

She grins triumphantly and whisks the cardigan out of his grasp. "Thank you. So what are we going to do about this? I mean, it could happen again, and this time we might not be so lucky."

"Tell me exactly what happened," he counters. "Was there

any warning?"

"No. No noise, no vibration or anything. It just came out of nowhere. Except the air tasted strange, like—I don't know, like there was a gas pocket or something. Maybe that's why it fell in?"

His eyes flick up to her face, suddenly intent. "Did it smell like gas to you?"

"I don't even know what that would smell like. It was sort of bitter, like . . . like rotting metal, if that even makes sense."

"Old blood and rust," he says faintly, and it's not a question. "No, that wasn't gas. That's *tros*. Old magic."

"So someone *is* doing this on purpose?"

He could kick himself. All the ease in the air disappears; just when he'd got his wayward mind back on track, just when she'd started to relax, all that inconsequential distraction and making her laugh just for the satisfaction of seeing the guilt and strain in her eyes melt away—all undone just like that. It's neither right nor fair, none of it. It's not her fault.

"I can't know for sure. It might be something left behind from a long time ago, some sort of safeguard."

It works as a theory, but somehow he isn't convincing himself. He needs to get in there and see for himself.

"Why would they? What exactly are we getting into?"

"Oh . . ." He lets out a long breath. "It's ancient history, mostly. Up on the hill, the church and the old town, it's pretty much built on a Fold. A persistent link in the Path," he clarifies, seeing her confused look. "Used to be a lot of coming and going up there back when things were better. The people are long gone now, but the Fold remembers."

"When things were better," she repeats slowly. "When we were talking about the brooch, you said to me, 'Maybe something happened,' and you looked so sad." She looks sad too, remembering. "I felt like something had gone horribly wrong and you'd been personally involved, then I told myself that was a stupid notion."

"Not so stupid, seeing as you were absolutely right. Something did go horribly wrong, and I was stuck in the middle of it. There was one nasty little lord in particular who'd heard about the pots of gold and decided that wasn't enough. He wanted it all — you know, the Realm and everything in it — and he abducted one of ours as leverage. 'Merging the dynasties,' he called it. I was on my way to fetch her back when he nailed the door."

"But that's the moon princess story," she objects. "It really happened? I thought that was supposed to be a love story."

"Love story, my arse," he says bitterly. "See those kids out there? That one, the one with the pink bag."

Evie obediently looks out of the window at the schoolchildren idling home up Bishop's Walk. The girl he's pointing at can't be more than eleven years old and dainty with it, swamped in a school blazer bought two sizes too big to grow into. A candyfloss-pink rucksack dangles carelessly from her hand to scuff on the pavement.

"The girl he took? She was no older than that one. Still playing with dolls, for fuck's sake. Can you honestly look at that infant and tell me a grown man would be overcome with romantic love at the sight of her? Bullshit. She was an easy target is all. He dragged her off her horse and had her locked in his hall before her friends could even raise the alarm."

"Jesus," she murmurs, wide-eyed. "And then he sabotaged the door so you couldn't get her back? Like in the story?"

"Exactly. And what he did threw everything out of phase, mangled parts of the mechanism. I nearly didn't survive it."

Pain is replaced by anger, his hand spasming into a fist, and she reaches over in a brief touch of apology mingled with reassurance.

"God, I'm sorry. You don't have to talk about it. Shall I make the coffee?"

He nods curtly, still struggling to contain the flare of ancient fury and hurt. It wasn't her fault, she wasn't even born, and he'll be thrice-damned if he takes it out on her just because she happens to be here asking the wrong question. He stretches and flexes his fingers to dismiss the fist, watching her bustle about his kitchen.

She maintains a blessed silence while she rinses out the coffee pot and starts a fresh brew, lighting the stove and lingering on the far side of the room while it boils. Deliberate distance, it feels like. Either she's considerately giving him some space, or else she's keeping out of range of that ill-timed fist.

The idea that it might be the second, that stings him. Anger sparks again. *What the fuck is wrong with you, child? Don't you know that I'd never hurt you?* But just as swiftly, it subsides, quenched by a memory. Years ago, a man whose name he never bothered to learn, standing over a sobbing woman in the alley behind the shop and screaming at her, flecks of spittle on his chin, raging that she was a stupid bitch for thinking he'd ever raise his hand to his woman. Worthless whore, he'd called her, hysterical, delusional and more besides, until she was begging his pardon, clinging to his arm and sobbing for permission to be allowed back over the threshold into her own home where her child was crying for her in the tiny back bedroom. Observing this display, Mainder had known with a cold certainty that the woman knew all too well when it was time to flinch, and the man had learned that her flinches made him look bad in the eyes of the neighbours. This was her lesson: that flinch or no, he would find a way to punish her if she showed him up again.

That man didn't come home one night shortly after. Lost his footing while drunk and went into the harbour, they said, and to this day, Mainder feels not a shred of remorse. Some cancers are best excised.

But he hears the man's echo in his own head in the lashing out, the shame of the ugly reflection in the mirror being held up to him. This whole thing is getting beyond him. He needs to bring an end to it, and he needs help before it crushes him. And most of all, he just wants to go home.

And there she is, carrying the scent of home, leaning over to place a steaming cup on the table.

"I couldn't find milk, so I'm guessing you take it black," she says and seats herself opposite him again.

He wraps his hand around the cup and stares at his reflection in the dark liquid. Wounded eyes stare back, asking what the fuck he's thinking. He can't answer, so he forces a smile to his face.

"I keep forgetting to turn the fridge on. I got tired of lumps of cheese in my morning coffee, so I gave it up."

Her watchful air dissolves instantly into laughter, that filthy chuckle filling the little kitchen like a cleansing.

"Poor Mainder," she says, reaching for his hand again. It seems to be okay.

"Look," he says heavily. "I'm sorry if I scared you just now. It's just that—when it happened, a friend of mine, he didn't make it out. What's under the house is no danger to anyone, but Vernon's obsession with it might be. The only reason I'm helping is to make sure he doesn't get anyone else killed trying."

Her hand tightens over his, and he gratefully clasps it back. What's said is said and what's done is done, and she's still here.

Chapter 45

FAIRY HILL LANE, 1815

A MAN CAME down off the hill one dusty hot day. It'd been a while since he came this way, but the weeds looked to have been cut back recently, and the hedges trimmed too. That was promising; people were still around, people with time and grace enough to spare to look after the place.

Out front of the first cottage he passed, just where the dirt path widened out, a small child in a grubby dress scowled at him from the front gate. He gave her the briefest nod and a smile, mentally assessing the danger of approaching, whether she'd run inside to fetch her mother. He had no desire to be chased off with a besom, not for the sake of begging a sip of water and some news.

To his surprise though, the child called out as he passed.

"Hey, mister!"

He turned and looked a question at her. "You mean me, child?"

"Don't see any other mister around here," she snapped back, and he laughed.

"Very true. What can I do for you?"

"My nan says she remembers you."

He came right up to the gate and stared down at the child's face thoughtfully.

"Does she now."

"She does. Saw you coming down the track back a way, said I should come tell you she remembers the last time you came by. She was just small like I am now. But you're not old like her. How can that be?"

"Some things bear no explanation," he answered, which was no explanation at all, and stepped up to the door. "Mind if I come in?"

She made a rude noise at the unexpected courtesy, as if to mock him for offering such grown-up manners to a child, but stepped aside with a toss of her head.

"I s'pose. She's in back."

Inside, a tiny front parlour gave on to a narrow passageway, then a cubbyhole of a kitchen. A woman stepped out and barred his path, wiping her hands on a rag and looking him up and down with distrust.

"My husband will be home any time now, so don't you get any ideas."

He did his best to look unthreatening, though privately he doubted the husband would be back today or any day. The whole place, sparse though it was, had the spotless order and air of comfort that marked it as a women's space. If there ever was a husband he was long gone, and quite possibly good riddance to him.

"I don't mean to trouble you, ma'am," he soothed. "The child said I was wanted, but if that's wrong, then I can keep walking."

"My mother," she huffed in explanation. "Won't be satisfied until she's talked to every stranger that comes over the hill. I don't know what you are, but she's just a foolish old biddy with an idea in her head. Don't upset her, you hear me?"

He ducked his head in amiable agreement, and she finally stood aside, gesturing sharply at the door at the end of the passage.

"She's in there. Mind your head as you go in."

It would be easy to miss the old woman, cocooned in blankets and tucked into a faded armchair next to the window. It had a fine view looking up at the hill and the winding path down from the crown; she must sit here all day long, noting comings and goings.

Not much else to do, not in her state. The child hadn't overstated the case; she was ancient, hunched over and propped up with cushions so she wouldn't fall forward. Fragile hands clutched and worried at a corner of the covers, every knuckle and vein visible through her crumpled paper-white skin.

Her eyes, though—as she registered his presence, she tracked his steps across the room, gaze sharpening and pinning him with a stare that saw across the years.

"It is you." Her voice came in a rasping whisper, almost a sigh. "I remember you."

"Oh?" He smiled encouragingly, pulling up the low stool beside her so he could sit. "What do you remember?"

The door behind them swung open before she could answer, and to his surprise the daughter came in with a tin cup of water. "It's a hot day. You could use a drink, I expect."

He took it and thanked her, but didn't miss her swift glance between him and the old woman. Come to check on him, of course. Fair enough.

"You came when I was no bigger'n Milly is now," the old woman interjected sharply. "Came with the gypsies, sold my mum a kettle. Still got that kettle." She tailed off into a pained wheeze, the daughter hovering in concern, but she recovered herself, swallowing in odd small gulps as if taking in air for her next sentence. "You gave me a ribbon for free. Said I needed cheering up. I was crying 'cause I'd skinned my knee. Kettles are all well and good, you said, but a girl needs something to brighten her day."

He chuckled at the detailed recital. "Such a long time ago. Sure you got the right man? Eyes can play tricks."

For all the implied denial, his voice was gentle, coaxing. Behind him, the younger woman blew out a breath in affectionate despair and disappeared back to the kitchen.

The grandmother shifted in her cocoon and glared at him. "I'm sure. Maybe I can't get out of this damn chair anymore, but I know what I know. Nothing wrong with my eyes or my mind, *tinker*. Gave me a ribbon, sky-blue it was, and said you'd been saving it for a moonchild. Said you'd see me again before the end."

He didn't bother denying it, now it was just the two of them. "Well, and here we are. Seems I was right."

She held very still, watery blue eyes meeting his tawny stare.

"Here we are," she echoed. "I *knew* it was you. You'll see things right, won't you? That's what you come for."

"That's what I come for," he agreed, placing a gentle hand

on her shoulder like a benediction. "The little one—Milly is it? I
see a spark in her. She'll do great things."

He left her sitting there, staring out at the hillside with a
faint satisfied smile warming her lined face. On his way back
down the path, he ran into the child again, now clutching a
ragged posy of wildflowers from the verge beside the lane.

"Those for your nan? Better run in and give them to her.
She'll need to rest soon."

Chapter 46

THE RUN UP to the dinner dance is a haze of bright anticipation and gossip about who's likely to show up with whom. And of course, who's likely to go home with whom, which may or not be the same pairing in every case. Luckily for Mainder, it takes the focus and the resources away from the dig. Mr. Vernon is already happy, which means the Archchancellor is happy, which means nobody will mind if the work slows down a little and people fit in extra shopping trips on quiet days to track down the perfect accessory to complete their outfits.

It seems to be all anyone can talk about. Good thing nobody was hurt in the tunnel slippage — we'd have missed the party, eh? Thank goodness we weren't digging under the hotel; we'd have had to move the party somewhere else!

It's a strange level of focus. Hasn't anyone ever been to a formal dinner and dance before? Do they think this is their only chance ever to go to one? It starts to feel like there's something else people are looking forward to, like back when the Path's cycle would build up to its high point and the village (as it was then) would gradually brighten, smiles would widen in anticipation of goods and friends and lovers to cross the Fold. Well met by moonlight indeed.

But that's not what's happening. For one thing, the Path is absolutely stable, fixed indefinitely at its lowest point. They made sure of it. Nobody comes over from the Realm side; no delegations or trade negotiations, not for a very long time. Not since the child was taken. If anything had changed on that front, he'd have heard.

The buzz continues to build nonetheless.

Maybe it's just that it's the end of the project for roughly half the people on site, their last chance to shoot their shot with whoever they've had their eye on or to blow off some steam. In that respect, he has to admit it's exactly like the moonlit crossings of old.

Chapter 47

THE DAY ITSELF dawns with rain, miserable and persistent, causing not a few last-minute changes to footwear and a rush on taxis booked to bring those staying elsewhere safely to the hotel. Mainder isn't among this number, walking up the drive in the steady summer drizzle with only his long coat for protection. He's not dressed in black tie, for the simple reason that he wasn't invited. That's not going to stop him from showing his face later, but for now he has a prior engagement.

In passing, he takes a moment to peer into the restaurant to see how the party's going. Dinner is done with, stacked dessert dishes coming in by the tray load to be deposited by the dishwasher, and handfuls of silver coffeepots going out the other door. He gets a brief glimpse of the action each time the door is kicked open and swings shut again. Some sparse groups are still seated, finishing their wine and their conversations, while the younger members of the project are already up on the floor doing something he supposes he could charitably describe as dancing, technically. His knees hurt just watching it. Been a long time since he last had the opportunity to dance, and that would have been back when a simple waltz was considered dangerously intimate and avant garde.

Smidur emerges from the restroom, fearsomely impressive in black tie that surely has to have been tailored specially to accommodate his broad shoulders and huge arms. He looks magnificent; as he strolls through the crowd, there's a ripple of interest, heads of all genders turning to appraise him. He's on the hunt though, scanning the mass of bodies on the dance floor and passing up all other possibilities in search of someone in particular.

He zeroes in on a lively crowd standing at the bar, sampling the obscure top-shelf liqueurs, and the crowd parts to let him get near. Looks like he has his hand raised in greeting, gesturing over the noise. Then his arm crooks invitingly to offer a lady an escort. The lady accepts, because of course she does. Why wouldn't she? He smiles to himself; same old Smidur. In the unlikely event she'd turned him down, no doubt he had a backup. Several backups, judging by the envious faces turned to watch the scene. And the lucky lady is . . .

Shit. Of course would have to be her.

If Mainder thought Smidur looked the part, then there has to be a new way to describe Evie's transformation. He's seen her in smart skirts and blouses, he's seen her in t-shirts and jeans — he's seen her buck-naked other than his sable fur sliding down her pale shoulders, his treacherous memory supplies — but he's never seen her like this. She should wear plain colours always; the simplicity of the backdrop lets her features shine out, and some stylist has worked sheer magic with her hair, lifting it high up off her face into a braided circle like a coronet. No fading into the scenery tonight. Elegant in shining, silver-grey satin, deceptively simple drapery sweeping down to the floor and leaving her shoulders bare, she looks expensive and polished and feminine and several million miles above his touch. Mucking about the office, laughing at him across his kitchen table — there he might believe she's someone he could aspire to engage. Looking the way she does tonight, that flicker of hope dies away to nothing. It's never going to happen.

Smidur places a proprietary hand on the small of her back to guide her along, smiling down at her with that earnest, open face the conniving arsehole does so well; easing a path through the crush with her held protectively in the crook of his arm, he looks like the prince claiming his Cinderella. *You scumbag,* Mainder silently rages. There are more than enough pretty girls here tonight; even with his own partiality, he's not blind. Why couldn't Smidur pick one of them? Anyone, any single one of all the other options, he could effortlessly walk in and captivate with minimum effort right now. Why her?

Because he let it happen. Pretending he wasn't interested; outright telling Smidur he wasn't interested, effectively giving him the go-ahead; telling *her* he wasn't interested, of course. He all but said she was no more than a child to him.

A sour taste rises in his throat, the bile of bitter envy. Pissing Vernon off by showing up late doesn't seem so important anymore.

Chapter 48

HE FINDS THE old man huddled in an armchair by the window, staring out at the shadowed lawn.

He looks considerably frailer than the last time Mainder saw him mere weeks ago, and no doubt the wistful air about him has something to do with wanting to be elsewhere. Not down in the ballroom, Mainder is willing to bet. More likely the muddy trench behind the museum. He's shrouded in blankets, one of them the same soft blue chenille Mainder last saw draped over Evie's shoulders down on the terrace. She definitely wore it better.

But that's not the only connection trying to spark in his brain. The old woman in the back room of that tiny cottage, she had that same look on that long-ago dusty hot day, waiting by the window for a dark stranger to come down off the hill and give her permission to rest. It's that same look, even the same pose, with his desiccated hands plucking at the folds of the blanket in his lap and his eyes fixed on what he can never reach. Shallow, uneven breaths barely lift his chest, and when Mainder is announced, it's an effort for him to turn his head to look.

Mainder settles himself comfortably in the other armchair. "Well, and here I am," he says, in the same gentle tone he used all those years ago. "It's nearly time."

Time for what, he doesn't clarify, but Vernon obviously has his own interpretation. "My people tell me you've been extremely cooperative," he says. So many words at once seem to exhaust him, the last syllables ending on a pained wheeze.

Mainder quirks an eyebrow but otherwise doesn't comment, and Vernon summons more energy from somewhere.

"Of course I don't believe a word of it. I assume you used your powers to charm them into believing it. But I haven't had reports of any serious trouble, so I suppose it will have to do. Tell me you're close to opening the pathway."

It's a command that Mainder has no desire to obey. He easily could, though it would require him to lie. Uncharacteristically though, he chooses the truth. It's not like Vernon will accept it in any case.

"Nowhere near. We've only uncovered the very first chamber so far. I don't even know how much of it is still active yet, let alone safe to use."

"You'll forgive me if I'm disinclined to take your word for it," Vernon counters with a flash of bitter humour. "I intend to see it for myself, as soon as they've finished making the tunnel accessible."

"You can please yourself."

Mainder feels the familiar creeping boredom he always experiences around each successive generation of the Vernon family. Pointless petulance, talking in circles, always trying to find a way to be right and have their will be done and to hell with the laws of space and time. Tiresome and a waste of everyone's energy.

Vernon shifts forward with the first real animation he's shown and extracts a shaking hand from the blanket's folds to point at his guest. The movement dislodges the folds of chenille, and uncovers Vernon's other hand clutching something, bright red-gold and silver flames and a sullen gleam of amber catching the light.

"Don't sneer at me like that, damn you! I've never understood your atrocious attitude. According to the legend we're related, aren't we? If the girl was so precious to your folk shouldn't that extend to her children and her children's children?"

Mainder freezes in place, eyes fixed on the brooch.

"Seriously? There's no gentle way to break this to you, but you're no relative of mine. I know for a fact there's not a drop of Realm blood anywhere in your line."

"Of course there is!" Vernon snaps. "You're walking proof of the curse, and the records say she bore my ancestor twins."

Mainder raises his hand, and Vernon finds the words die in his throat. "Your records lie. She died in childbirth, and the boy with her."

"No," Vernon wheezes. "No, it was a boy and a girl. Stephen and Agnes. Their names are in the family tree, I can trace myself right back . . ."

"The boy died, Vernon. Died before he even drew breath. The birthing was a bloody mess, let me tell you, because she was no more than a child herself and that bastard wouldn't let a midwife near her for fear of 'witchcraft.' By the time he realised his mistake, he'd lost them both."

"No," Vernon repeats in a ghost of a whisper. "A boy and a girl. The legend says."

Mainder can almost see the lights going out behind the man's eyes, the cherished belief crashing down like cliffs surrendering to the sea.

"Then who are we tracing our line from?"

Possibly Vernon intended that to be a triumphant rebuttal. *Explain that, hah!* As if human babies are some rare commodity impossible to procure or create. Well, if he wants the truth, he can have the entire ancient sordid truth, for all the joy it'll bring him.

"Are you sure you want to know? He installed his mistress in the east wing before his beloved 'wife' was even cold. Already pregnant, luckily enough. Margaret, her name was. I think she was his bailiff's daughter. Pretty little thing, red hair — you have her portrait up on your wall."

Vernon shakes his head ever so slightly, but he's not seeing the man in front of him anymore. In his mind's eye, he's seeing the exact portrait, Mainder knows. Margaret, Lady Vernon; from sidepiece to mistress of all she surveyed virtually overnight. A remarkable young woman in every respect, her sudden elevation was, in his opinion, the only good work her brat of a husband ever achieved.

"Anyway, if I recall correctly, there was a hasty wedding, and she delivered a healthy boy not two months later. Vernon had him installed in the nursery, claimed him as legitimate. Convenient as all hell."

"You're a damned liar."

Still, unbelievably, denial, creaking out as a faint fraught whisper. Vernon shrinks so far back into his nest of blankets now that he's barely visible, and against his pallor, his lips are disturbingly close to the blue of the chenille lying in folds across his sunken chest. Mainder idly wonders if he should stir himself to call the attendant to see to him, bracing himself to rise from the chair just in case.

"What does it matter? It doesn't change anything, does it, if all you want to do is lift the curse. Nothing's stopping you."

Vernon doesn't answer. He may be recovering from the physical shock, but he remains fixated on something out there in the dark.

"Let's be honest now, lordling."

Vernon's eyes dart to Mainder when he speaks, an uncertain flicker as though he can't quite remember who this is and why he's here.

"I believe you may have thought I didn't know your true goal. Did you seriously think I would allow you to set foot in the Realm?"

"It's my right . . ." Vernon chokes, forced to a halt by Mainder's warding finger.

"Your money doesn't buy you passage. And neither does your stolen token."

"This is *mine*," Vernon creaks. "Made for my ancestor to cross, to meet his bride's people."

"Is that so."

Mainder sits back and stares at the old man's face. Searching for what, he doesn't know, but all he sees is utter conviction, complete and concrete. Whether it's the truth or not, Vernon believes it absolutely.

"Well, be that as it may, it changes nothing. If you were planning to stomp into fairyland and demand your birthright—well. I've just saved you from a short lifetime of embarrassment, if not worse. You should thank me."

" . . . damn you . . ." Vernon manages.

Despite himself, Mainder is impressed. Such tenacity the man has, even now, in the face of cold facts. Such strength of will, such *spark*—all sadly applied in negative polarity to chase an impossible aim. He shakes his head, gently sorrowful.

"I warned you, lordling. If you'd have just turned aside and spent your life doing something useful, I'd have happily left you to your moneymaking and never lifted a hand against you. You chose to revive the name. You chose to stake a claim to something you neither earned nor deserve. You invited the curse inside and gave it a seat."

"The curse is dead," Vernon spits. "My success, my reputation—you call that nothing?"

"Not yet," Mainder says calmly. He rises from his chair and leans across, falsely cordial, to touch the old man's fragile hand in farewell. Just a fingertip, just the faintest touch, but Vernon flinches at the sudden flicker of heat when Mainder murmurs, "*Your works to nothing, your name forgot.* Your house of cards is about to collapse."

The attendant smiles uncertainly when Mainder strolls back though the door and glances expectantly at the bedroom, as if expecting a report of some kind.

"I'll be going now," Mainder says with a solemn nod back at the still figure in the armchair. "I think the old man's a little too tired for any more company tonight."

Chapter 49

MAINDER STROLLS AROUND the edge of the ballroom, flint eyes raking the crowd. An idea is forming in his head, one he's not at all happy about, and before he takes himself away, he needs to settle something. If he's right, his evening is about to get a lot worse.

While he was busy upstairs, the dance floor completed the transformation to full late-night party disco, multicoloured lights strobing and spinning across the mass of bodies so that it's hard to make out the real colours of what they're wearing. Flashes of pale grey or silver shift to white, to pink, to gold, to green in a dizzying kaleidoscope of thrashing limbs. Perhaps his best bet is to sit still somewhere visible and think happy thoughts until she seeks him out by herself.

He selects a suitable vantage point, an unoccupied table set a little back from the dance floor, and heads to claim it. Nobody challenges him as he skirts the disco, either on his lack of invitation or his lack of correct attire. In fact, he gathers a few genuine smiles of welcome and more than one coy glance of invitation, a tribute to the time he'd put in charming a few select individuals.

My people tell me you've been extremely cooperative, he hears again in Vernon's rasping whisper. The arrogance! The ignorance! As if the man thought he would show up and start — what, openly pushing vases off tables like some kind of attention-seeking house cat? Has the man never encountered a scenario where he had to actually make friends to achieve his goal?

Likely not. Money buys a great deal of cooperation.

Mainder doesn't really want to stop and talk to anyone right now, but not to be rude, he acknowledges them all with the same polite tilt of his head and remains focused on his goal. *Child, where are you? Show yourself.*

Either he's more powerful than he thought, or he's the luckiest man in Alfriscombe tonight. A flash of silver at the terrace door is his quarry, nipping out with her chiffon wrap trailing in one hand and what is definitely an unopened bottle of wine in the other. He detours to collect a tartan rug from the neatly folded stack behind the cutlery station, kept to hand for the comfort of guests sitting outside in the evenings, and by the time he appears she has the bottle open and a full glass beside her.

"Thought you might be cold," he offers, hefting the rug in both hands like a supplicant approaching an altar. "That's a damn fine frock, but I don't see it keeping you warm for long."

She accepts his tribute with mock solemnity, arranging it around her shoulders and settling back with a contented sigh. There's a second glass standing ready on the table, and he swallows a sudden pang of anxiety.

"Expecting company?" he enquires in his best attempt at a casual, none-of-my-business tone.

"Yes, actually." She offers him the glass, to his confusion. Her brow furrows in sudden doubt. "I saw you come in. You do like the Rioja, don't you? I thought I saw some in your kitchen."

"And there I was thinking I'd managed to sneak in unnoticed."

His first mouthful confirms that it's exactly to his tastes, not that he should be surprised by now. She's remarkably observant when it comes to him.

And now he finally understands why.

"Sorry I wasn't about earlier. Had a meeting, you know how it is."

She nods, drinking from her glass and staring out over the view. It pains him to realise that, even if it doesn't come to a fight, this might be the last time he gets to sit with her like this, at perfect ease and in perfect trust. More than anything, he wants to freeze this moment, to just let this be one of the good memories, with her snuggled into that hideous tartan and the pale oval of her face shining out in the moonlight. It could be an acceptable ending to the whole affair to just drop it, to leave it here and let this be how he remembers her.

But he knows deep down that this conversation has to happen, no matter how much he's dreading the outcome.

"I'd ask you to dance, but I really didn't come dressed for it," he begins, feeling his way across the silence.

"Shame." She looks him up and down in his habitual head-to-toe dusty black, a frank and appreciative assessment, and adds, "I'd love to see you in full formal. You'd rock it."

Despite everything, the compliment warms him. He's too old, he tells himself, too old and too bitter to be affected by a simple snippet of flattery like that. But he can't deny that it's good to hear.

"Well, I don't know about that. You certainly do. Fairly took my breath away when I saw you just now."

One thing he hadn't mistaken—she's not the type of girl to simper at empty compliments. He'd have got up right then and walked away if she had, to be honest, but true to form she wrinkles her nose at him.

"Don't bullshit me, Mainder. You have to know by now it's my job to look the part."

"Yes." He sighs heavily, looking anywhere but directly at her. "Do you want to know how pissed off I am that it took me this long to figure it out?"

"I can guess. How did it go with Vernon?"

"Well, he's still alive, if that's what you mean. Still an arrogant dick, too."

"Yes to all," she solemnly intones, raising a finger to tick off imaginary boxes on an imaginary checklist and making him laugh reluctantly. "He would have it that someone needed to be on site to keep you in line, and once I read the files, I knew I couldn't risk anyone else."

"He actually put it in writing? He told you what I am, I mean? I'd have thought he'd have been laughed out of the room, even with his fat chequebook open."

"You'd be astonished if you knew how much academic funding involves keeping a straight face until the ink is dry on the contracts." She drains her glass and reaches for the bottle to refill it. "He had a whole dossier, if you can call it that. A collection of contemporary sightings of 'the Devil of Alfriscombe,' and some ranting about how this seaside town shopkeeper is the real reason his family never amounted to anything."

She shivers and pulls the rug tighter around her, and he quells the urge to offer her his coat as well.

"At the risk of damping your ego, you weren't even in the top five strangest contracts I'd been given. As long as you were human-shaped, I knew I'd take the job and see what I could do."

"I might just go home and cry." He sighs and raises his glass in a silent toast. "How would I make it into your top five, out of interest?"

"You screamed to the top of the leaderboard when you started shooting fire from your fingers," she deadpans. "I wasn't going to tell you that, though. You're big-headed enough."

Oh, she's a joy to talk to. A pure visceral joy. It's a cliche, but where has she been all his life?

Nevertheless, it's a strange conversation. Very strange indeed. He ought to be furious, indignant, betrayed, and vengeful. And the only reason he's not is — well, this: as far as he can tell, she never stood in his way. Not once did he find himself unable to make his next move because of her, and with the benefit of perfect hindsight, it's clear that she must have been smoothing his path from that very first meeting.

"So you were supposed to — what, observe? Monitor? Keep me in line? What on earth did they think you were going to be able to do?"

She raises a hand and waggles it in a seesaw motion. "'Security' is how we describe it. We monitor vulnerable personalities, keep an eye on the dynamics, advise of problems before they arise. Close any gaps that might be used for social engineering. Reading between the lines, I think Vernon was hoping we could manipulate you into doing as you were told, but that was never going to fly."

"Quite. Not to be obtuse, but what *have* you been doing?"

"I'll tell you a secret," she announces, leaning forward and lowering her voice to a stage whisper. "I actually stopped caring about the details of the brief pretty quickly. Right after I saw how you reacted to the lawn scans. I knew then that there was more to you than the stupid cartoon villain Vernon described, and you must have some motivation beyond mischief."

"Too kind," he murmurs. "Mischief is pretty much what I am."

"More bullshit," she announces. "You hurt, back in that meeting. It was as clear as day. You loved, and you lost, and you *hurt*. Vernon only wants to win, so he can settle some centuries-old score. You—I don't know. After reading all the briefings and then seeing you, all I could think was that if you were what he said you were, then you settled here and looked after little people—ordinary, unimportant, nobody people that Vernon wouldn't even step on in passing—and you kept on doing it for centuries. And on top of it all, you suffered, and you're still suffering, and I decided right there to . . . I suppose to manage things. To see what you were actually up to, and if it made more sense to me, then I would help."

Her glass is empty again, and she eyes it with an irritated sniff.

"I'm drinking this too fast. Stop making me so comfortable."

"No," he objects with a grin. "I like you comfortable. Comfortable and talkative." He drains his own glass, gesturing suggestively at the bottle. "We should see if there's any more of that inside."

"I'm happy out here—" she starts to demur, but he rises firmly from his chair.

"You're shivering, even with the rug. And if I give you my coat, then I'll be cold, and you don't want to see me suffer more now do you?"

He fixes her with a quizzical stare, eyebrows raised and eyes twinkling, and she snorts a laugh.

"Don't push it. Alright, let's take this inside." She rises from her chair, gathering her shining train with a practiced sweep of her arm. "Better yet, how about we take it upstairs? We can get room service."

He doesn't dare hope that this is the invitation it sounds like. Doesn't *dare*. He'd been so certain she'd choose Smidur, for one thing. As much as he hates to admit it, his old friend makes a far more fitting foil for her elegance tonight.

And if not Smidur, then surely there's someone in that ballroom more to her tastes. Somebody younger, better looking, better dressed. Better able to offer her something that has a chance of going somewhere. She shouldn't be standing here on the terrace, regal in silver and bathed in moonlight, casually inviting him to bed. It feels somehow wrong, out of phase.

She takes his hesitation for something else.

"Never mind. I thought . . . " She compresses her lips briefly, as if to contain whatever she was about to say, and turns instead to pick up the tartan rug where it dropped to the floor. As she collects it back up into a rough bundle, she comes over to him and presses it into his hands, looking up at him with a shadow of doubt in her eyes. "I wasn't asking for your hand in marriage, Mainder. I'm well aware that this—you and me—couldn't be anything serious, but there's no reason we shouldn't enjoy each other's company while we have the chance. But if that's not what you want, that's fine."

For some reason, her even acceptance hurts more than if she'd protested. *It's not right*, he howls miserably in his head. *I do want this. I want this to be something serious, for fuck's sake.*

But the moment has passed. She turns away and slips back into the ballroom, leaving him clutching the rug in suddenly numb hands. Without thinking, he raises it to his face and takes a deep breath in, savouring her scent left behind, and when he steps back into the Path shining behind him, he's still holding it.

Chapter 50

MR. VERNON IS very ill.

Word spreads uncharacteristically slowly through the site, what with the rain and the hangovers, and in a handful of cases, the morning-after regrets keeping everyone indoors for the day following the ball.

The general opinion is that the journey down from London was unwise at his age, almost certainly against the express advice of his doctors, and he's being hastened back up there for the best specialist care money can buy after a brief spell in county A&E to get him stable enough to travel.

Shame about the old man, people murmur in passing as they make eye contact in the breakfast queue. *Did you hear about poor Mr. Vernon? Such a shame.*

Shame about the money, is what they really mean. Vernon had plans to endow a foundation to carry his name—his legacy, as he would insist on calling it—and the Dean's office is engaged in tactfully investigating whether or not he'd actually signed the documents before he collapsed. A real shame about poor Mr. Vernon, of course, but where does that leave the project?

The answer to that question is, *It depends*. It depends who's asking, as there are complex layers to the project that only a tiny number of people have full knowledge of. It depends also on what you mean by "project," as parts of the programme continue unaffected, funded by a completely separate budget line.

And finally, it depends on whether your goal was to open the Fold or to bury it again forever.

***

The project goes into a state of limbo. Until the question of Vernon's endowment is settled, there's no point extending contracts or filling new vacancies. If Vernon pulls through, then of course the work will continue, and Cooper is already reviewing a very promising batch of CVs collated by his office in readiness, but if the old man doesn't make it, then the long-desired foundation remains a distant dream.

Word is that Vernon is lingering on, alive enough to merit the money being poured into keeping his heart pumping and his lungs filling, even exchanging a few breathless words with his nurses, but in no way fit to make major financial decisions or sign contracts. The university would be a pariah if they ever held up a document signed under such circumstances and expected it to hold water.

Besides, it would be wrong. Legalities aside and Cooper's own steamroller personality notwithstanding, there's an ethical boundary here that he's not prepared to cross. They will wait, and if Vernon recovers, they will talk. If not . . . Well, he already has a eulogy sketched out in his head on the off-chance that he'll be asked to deliver one. And then they move on. There will be other benefactors and other funding streams, and if he has his way, there will be no fairytale conditions whatsoever attached.

Chapter 51

FOR MAINDER, THE morning after the ball passes in a haze of miserable self-reproach. He barely slept at all, sulking in the shuttered gloom of his nest of pillows and playing imaginary scenarios in his mind. Bittersweet what-ifs where he swept her off her feet and told her how he really felt, where he gathered her in his arms and kissed away her doubts like some square-jawed cinematic hero. He's torturing himself. It didn't happen and probably never will.

He abandons any hope of rest when the sun rises above the rooftops opposite, a subdued pale glow working its way around the edges of the shutters, and emerges from his cocoon to face whatever the day brings. He indulges himself with a lengthy shower, lingering under the water with his face upturned to the scalding jets as if he hopes to dissolve his black mood along with yesterday's dirt. Rooting through the pile in the cupboard turns up halfway clean clothes, good enough for today's endeavours.

Stalking to the kitchen, still shrugging on his shirt, he takes his time brewing coffee and drinking two cups one after the other, seated at the table and staring into nothing. Maybe she's drinking coffee right now. Moving around her bland hotel room, boiling up water in the tiny kettle and wrinkling her nose at the sachets of instant Nescafe while she decides which is the lesser of the evils on offer. The mental image makes him smile a little, at least. Quite possibly she paid a premium — or more likely her wealthy client did — to get a room with a proper coffee maker. Hell, maybe Vernon is paying for her to indulge in freshly ground coffee from the restaurant right now, ferried up from the kitchen on her whim.

A most unwelcome image forms in his head: room service knocking on her door right now with a tray carrying not just fresh coffee, but two cups, one for her and one for Smidur. Of course he wouldn't be stupid enough to pass up the opportunity. He was likely just waiting for Mainder to mess up so he could make his move. He might be propped up in her bed right this second, tousled and smug and suggesting a morning rematch with a knowing smile plastered across his handsome face.

Mainder's hand tightens on the cup. With an effort, he forces it to relax again, stretching his fingers out and examining them sternly. It's none of his business, no matter how much the notion makes his stomach cramp. He's had plenty of chances.

There isn't a third cup to be squeezed from the pot, so at long last he rises from his chair and heads out the door to begin the walk up to the museum. It's a terrible day to go anywhere on foot, yesterday's rain continuing without respite and sullen clouds in all directions indicating it'll last for the best part of the day, but he hopes the walk will give him time to work out what he's going to say when he sees her.

If he sees her. The office at the back of the house is disturbingly empty when he lets himself in. More than unoccupied, more than lights off and screens blank—things are actively missing. He's no expert, but he distinctly recalls seeing laptops hooked up to these screens, along with all the usual peripherals. And the traditional office clutter, too—that's gone. Personal notebooks, pencil pots, mugs with cheerful slogans brought from home, bags and coats bundled into corners and cubbyholes. All gone. The reading corner tidied away, books dropped into a cardboard box on the kitchen table along with half the contents of the shelves. Even the flashy coffee machine has been disconnected, pulled away from the wall with its hoses and cables coiled up in a heap beside it. This place is in the middle of being cleaned out.

He strides to the nearest desk, pulling out the drawers one by one. Empty. Nothing but dust, a couple of errant paperclips, the broken stub of a locker key. It looks very much as if everyone who was working in here is finished with the project and won't be coming back. Have they been pulled off the job? Has she told Vernon that she's been made, that there's no point to her being here, that the whole deal is off? It can't be. She said she'd help. After everything, was that just another lie?

He steps back until his heels hit the wall and leans against the cool brick, closing his eyes in despair. It can't be. He hasn't lost his touch to that degree.

He raises a hand to glyph to her, then lowers it again slowly. He can track her down later for an explanation. Pushing away from the wall, he squares his shoulders and heads back out to the lawn and to the trench.

***

The hidden door is still untouched, his protections still in place. With a sweep of his hand, he clears them and the door swims back into focus, settling back into its niche as if it had never left. He closes his eyes and lays his hand flat on the crystal seam, and gradually a faint pattern appears, sinuous lines curling around each other and repeating the pointed arch until it looks like a tunnel disappearing impossibly into the distance. Where the lines meet the top of the arch, a pale green-gold glow seeps down, suffusing the rock inside the frame until the whole thing is glowing. It brightens suddenly, the entire archway filled with a single uniform sheet of bright gold light, and when it dies away, he grins triumphantly at the Path glittering in the tunnel a few feet beyond the threshold. It still holds.

The stonework shows slight damage here and there, but as far as he can see, it's cosmetic only, surface decoration chipped away by debris from the disaster. The walls themselves and the vaulting of the vestibule are intact, held in place by their own weight and the tons of soil pressing down from above.

A tiny ripple disturbs the shining portal, giving off a sharp buzz as it hits the side of the frame and bounces back on itself. Not the signature of somebody coming through—his first thought—but minor feedback from the disaster that blocked it off so long ago. It ought to stabilise if he leaves it to stand for a while. Besides, if he closes it now, he won't be able to show it to

Evie. Won't be able to have the conversation he's been rehearsing in his head for the last few hours.

Anyway, he has another errand here, one that takes priority over happily-ever-afters for the moment. He places one foot into the tunnel and crouches down to examine the mess built up on the threshold. This is all debris from the Closing. Flakes of damaged stone from the roof, twisted fragments of bronze sheared off from the torch brackets that used to be set in the wall either side. One or two lumps poking out of the soot and filth look to be discarded tokens, dropped here by some of those travellers unlucky enough to be mid-transit when it happened. He reaches over and digs them out of the mess, placing them in his coat pocket with the vague idea that he might track down their owners later. If he goes Home, that is. If he doesn't—well, he'll add them to the collection in his store, artefacts to put on the open market once he's made them safe for the hands of mudside collectors. Either way, it's a better fate than lying here forgotten here in the mud.

Where the Path's boundary begins, the walls are blackened and scorched, incongruous against the shining doorway. Paler gaps in the grimy overlay seem to describe the outline of a man falling backwards, one arm raised to protect his face, a frieze of long-ago disaster.

At the edge of the floor below that, there's a bundle of feathers and soot embedded in a deep crack in the floor. This must be where some of the debris came from, the force of the blast propelling some unwary creature into the stone flags and spraying shards in all directions.

Mainder swallows heavily, sick fury washing over him as he realises he's finally tracked down what remains of Sweyn. Even though he was expecting to find some trace, the sight of the tiny corpse shakes him to the core. He recalls their last ever conversation, the desperate calls to each other as they tried one futile attempt after another to find a safe way out. He wouldn't even be out if Sweyn hadn't roused him from his stupor after the initial shockwave. He hadn't deserved to be left behind in the darkness all this time, buried and forgotten, after that tiny act of heroism.

He inches forward, still crouched, and holds a flame up to light his way while he eases the stubborn lump out of its resting place. He breathes out shakily, cradling the fragile bundle carefully in his palm and blinking back something suspiciously like tears while he flicks his fingers to quench his light.

And then he freezes. In the hole he's just created, there's something else, something wholly unexpected. He leans back over for a closer look, strengthening the light between his finger and thumb to bright gold and holding it high over the hole.

"Well now," he says distantly to the empty cavern. "There's a thing."

What he's uncovered is a rough lozenge of part-fired potter's clay the size of a man's closed fist, still attached to the fragment of stone panel it was placed on. Paired symbols flow in a repeated pattern around the edge of the shape like handwritten script, scored into the surface using some thin sharp tool, and smeared dots of dark brownish-red decorate the centre in a clumsy spiral. Possibly accidental, the long-ago maker catching their finger on the tool they used to score the runes, but the spiral placement looks deliberate even if it was done in obvious haste. The soot shadow around it says it was formed and placed here before the Closing, misshapen thumbprints at the edges showing where its maker pressed it into position.

There's no innocent explanation for this, not with the bind runes running around the edge. Somebody made this to disrupt the Path — or, more specifically, to disrupt anybody coming through. He straightens up and searches the wall and door frame with methodical thoroughness until he finds a fracture that matches the fragment's outline, almost exactly level with his shoulder. A few inches above that, he finds another clay lozenge pressed against the stonework, unactivated as far as he can tell. It has the same spiral pattern, dabs of old blood radiating out from the centre, the same binding runes.

If the placement wasn't enough to give him a clue, the ragged scrap of dark fabric partially buried in the clay seals it. He cautiously touches the threads, twisting them between his fingers and comparing the texture to the fraying edge of his coat collar. This dark cantrip here came within an inch of putting an end to him just as the smaller version did to Sweyn. Someone — from his side, from the Realm, maybe someone he actually knows and who is still walking around to this day — someone wanted them both stopped, trapped down here in the dark forever.

The knowledge drains him of all certainty, and he sits down abruptly on the filthy tunnel floor, still carefully cradling Sweyn. He can't take Evie back Home, can't even raise the possibility, not with this hanging over him. Added to all his other worries, now he has to find out who did this and make sure they're never in a position to do it again. He sits for some time with his head resting against the stone behind him, staring up at nothing in despair. Yesterday his biggest problem was being too stupid to see what was under his nose.

Despite himself, he lets out a bitter crack of laughter. Today's no different then; it just turns out there's more going on under his nose than the tantalising prospect of true love.

He reaches over and levers the first clay shape free of its resting place, placing it in his coat pocket. If he's right, he still might be able to do something with this. As for the second . . . After a moment's thought, he removes that, too, pulling it off the stone in one piece and holding it in his hands. If it hasn't been fully triggered, it's too much of a risk to just leave it lying around. He glyphs out without a backwards glance, his mind working furiously.

***

The Path swirls in its frame as he departs, surging to the edge of the frame and bouncing back on itself furiously. The ripples cross once, twice, three times, each crossing amplifying their force and making them deeper and wider until the Path starts to bow outwards, a fierce crackle of white light collecting around the top and vibrating the stone of the containing arch. With a sad creak, the frame abandons its integrity and the top of

the arch collapses, the stones falling into the bright light and
disappearing altogether.

Chapter 52

HOME MAY BE on Mainder's mind, but it's a different Path he calls this time. *Take me where I need to be,* he wills as hard as he knows how, and *tren* deposits him neatly at the foot of his attic stairs.

That seals it then. He made the correct choice. This day has been black enough already; he couldn't have borne it if it had turned out that he was mistaken and, after everything, he'd ended up leaving Sweyn behind in the dark once more.

He takes the stairs two at a time, not even stopping to remove his coat. The magic he has in mind to try is simple enough, to the point that it barely merits that label. There's no chanting, no pentagrams nor candles, no release of sinister dark powers. If anything, it's more like cooking, with a pinch of this and a handful of that from the containers lining the dusty shelves. He really ought to thank his past self for being too lazy to clear up the mess of liquors and powders after he went through his apothecary phase. Not that he'd ever felt much of an urge to indulge in spring cleaning, but if he'd succumbed to it at any point he'd have been screwed now. Some of the ingredients casually lying around up here would be very difficult to source in a hurry.

He moves to the polished stone and wipes it clean with a corner of his sleeve before setting down his finds. A small paring knife laid beside the stone receives a similar cursory dusting, and then he begins the recipe by drawing the blade across the pad of his thumb and allowing a few beads of blood to form. Blood magic was always the strongest, and countering it requires something to be given.

He sucks absently at the tiny cut while he crumbles dry blue petals to a powder in his other hand and sprinkles it over the stone with a flourish. A pinch of silvery-grey dust follows, and the final touch is a fragment of elder bark—not added to the stone, but wiped across both sides of the knife blade before he uses it to mix the mess on the stone to an even paste.

He stares down at the stone, lips moving slightly as he ticks off the ingredients. Blood for blood, flowers for renewal, wood ash for the end of a cycle, elder for purging — that should be everything. If he's right, it'll counter the original cantrip and open up a pathway if anything remains to take advantage of it. The clay lump at last goes on top, firmly pressed down into the paste so it can start doing its work.

It won't go any faster if he stares at it, but at the same time, it feels wrong to turn his back and walk away, even if nobody would ever know. It'll be a strange vigil, but he'll sit it out. Sweyn would have done the same for him. He retreats to the armchair, grabbing the dusty bottle on the floor in passing and holding it up to the light to check the label. If this works, he'll celebrate with a small measure. If it doesn't — well, he'll see if he can't get blackout drunk.

Far below his feet, the faint sounds of a normal day continue their usual routine. Krzysztof greeting customers, the hollow jangle of the shop's bell, and the brighter treble trill of the cash register. Clatter and fuss from the little ones dawdling along the alley out back on their way home from school.

The sun creeps round, noise from the shop dying away gradually. The thump of the back door will be Krzysztof taking the bins out to the end of the alley for pick up tomorrow. Car doors and front doors banging, neighbours arriving home at the end of their work days.

The sun's rays reach the middle of the end wall and then disappear, the sun ducking behind the rooftops. One final jangle of the bell as Krzysztof heads home for his dinner. Mainder smiles vaguely to himself, the whisky taking effect. Krzysztof and his family will be okay. He's written the letter, tucked it safe into its hidey hole in the back room. That's all fine. Whatever happens to him, he's taken care of what matters.

His head bobs; he must have dozed, missing moonrise. Down in the empty shop, the phone is ringing, which is probably what woke him. He lets it ring out and lifts the bottle to squint at its level. Still some left. Good.

The phone rings again, and he ignores it again. Anybody who needs him knows how to find him. Anybody he cares about, anyway. He glares at the moonbeams slicing across the room, creeping along the floor towards him. Why didn't he ever put curtains up here? He can't remember. He must have thought it didn't matter. Maybe it doesn't. He shifts his foot out of the moon's path anyway and dozes again, cradling the now-empty bottle against his chest.

***

A faint fizzle from the bench jolts him awake, and he starts forward, squinting across the attic. Over on the stone the clay lozenge is rocking like an egg straining to hatch, a tiny puff of dust rising into the air with each movement. He half-rises from the armchair as it rocks again, harder this time, and then abruptly it drops into two neat halves with a whipcrack sound, obscenely loud in the dust-choked stillness.

It worked. It's done. The dust billows around the stone, rising into the air like a tiny stormcloud, and he holds his breath until the particles drop away again to reveal—

"You left me behind, you rancid fucking son of a b—"

Loud sneezing cuts off whatever was coming next, and Mainder hurries over in concern. The dark shape curled on the stone seems to be having some kind of fit, writhing and flickering through a rapid array of unpleasant shapes all punctuated by more violent sneezes and incoherent cursing. Mainder hastily upends the bottle in his hand over the stone, shaking out the last few drops. Whisky doesn't go off, does it? It should be fine.

And indeed, it seems to be just the thing. After a second or two, the shape slumps down and spreads across the stone, an oily puddle oozing over the edges of the stone. The sneezing at last dies away to nothing.

The cursing though, that keeps coming.

"—pox-ridden bastard son of an itinerant whore—"

"Steady now." Mainder raises an unsteady finger, stifling a grin. "Mothers are off-limits, remember?"

"Oh yeah." The shape raises what's probably its head and slowly pours itself into an upright position. "Shit. Sorry, I forgot. Not like you ever had one, anyway. Bet you I'm right about the pox, though."

As it settles down, it seems to be something like a cat in shape and size, with a tail flicking irritably behind it and pointed ears set back on its domed head. It sits more like a primate, though, and when it raises a hand to examine itself, there are short but distinct fingers and a human-like opposable thumb. Bright gold eyes shine like coins in its otherwise indistinct face, flitting around the room to take in its surroundings.

"Nice. I missed you, too." Mainder laughs out loud. "How are you feeling?"

"Like absolute fucking shit on a stick, thanks for asking. But at least I'm out of that. Did we do it?"

"No." The laughter fades. "They collapsed the Fold altogether. I barely made it out. Thought you were with me until the very last moment. They had this waiting for you."

He indicates the scattered halves of the clay seal on the bench. Sweyn picks up the nearest half, bringing it close to his face and testing it with a swipe of his pointed blue-black tongue.

"Well, fuck me. That's miskin handiwork, that is. I can taste them. Eugh." He tosses the clay fragment aside with a sneer. "What are we going to do about it? And where the hell are we, anyway? How long has it been?"

"We're right where I left you, more or less. And it's been about five hundred years on this side."

"So we missed the exchange?"

Mainder sighs heavily. "There was never going to be an exchange. They fucked us over, had it all planned out. There was one of those waiting for me, too. It's only thanks to you it didn't get me. They even nailed the door."

"No shit," Sweyn says faintly. He sounds small and lost, and

Mainder feels a pang of sympathy. It's a lot to take in all at once.

"Listen, let's go down and I'll find you something to eat."

"I can feed myself," Sweyn quibbles. "People still keep hens round here, right? Or ducks or something? That'll do me."

"Hens? No, not anymore. You might find a seagull, but you'll soon wish you hadn't. Come on. There's proper food downstairs."

Of course he doesn't mean in his own actual kitchen. He never really got round to keeping meals in the house. But down in the fridge in the shop's break room, he knows there's a stash of spiced sausage that Krzysztof brings from home for his lunch, and he's forever pressing Mainder to help himself to as much as he wants. He never has, but it looks like today's the day. The little sprite will happily eat anything, up to and not excluding actual garbage, but for the quickest boost to his powers, pure protein is the first choice. He waits until Sweyn is fully engaged in tearing chunks off and wolfing them down before he breaks the next piece of intel.

"So, listen—there's a girl here we need to keep an eye on."

"What for?"

Sweyn stares at him sullenly, chewing with his mouth open. He remains faintly transparent, but at least the sausage isn't visible as it disappears down his gullet. A tiny mercy in the grand scheme of things.

"Because I say we do," he says firmly. "*Yasim,* and I'm not sure what else. Anyway, you'll see what I mean when you meet her."

Sweyn bites off another chunk and mumbles through the mouthful, "Five hundred years, and you're still thinking with your dick." He swallows, examines the stubby end of the sausage clutched in his paw, and opens his mouth wide to toss it in whole. "If you ask me, it's time we went Home. See if we can't get you laid while we're at it."

Chapter 53

YESTERDAY'S RAINSTORM may have passed over, but its bigger and meaner brother wastes no time announcing its intention to follow up. Heavy clouds start massing far beyond the hill just after midday, a flat dark grey so uniform it looks like a background layer that failed to render, while the sunlit crown of the hill stands out in perfect high-resolution against it.

The museum's lawn is still in sunshine, but by mid-afternoon, the usual steady sea breeze has been replaced by unpredictable gusts from one direction, then the next. Anything light enough to be moved by the wind is sent bowling across the smooth green without warning. Bundles of discarded marker tape, bright orange tangles flapping and cartwheeling joyfully always a few steps ahead of their would-be captors; plastic cones spilling off their ordered piles and scattering in all directions. A bundle of paper forms thought to be secure in the site manager's hands gets whipped into the air, thankfully going no farther than the side of the porch before smacking back to the ground.

"That was a close one!" she murmurs, stamping on the pile before it can get any more ideas. A boot print here and there is preferable to a week's worth of timesheets disappearing into the ocean. "All done?" she calls to the team and receives a ragged but enthusiastic chorus of assent as they pick up their burdens and follow her back inside.

Viktor straightens up from collecting the last of the tapes he's been chasing, twisting it into a bulky knot with savage satisfaction.

"I think that's—"

Another scrap of orange tumbles past. He sighs, following it down to the boggy corner by the gate. At least it's stuck there, rather than leading him on a chase around the whole lawn like the rest of it.

"Got you," he snarls triumphantly, reaching across.

***

"Is Viktor coming back for his stuff?" Laura is itching to lock up for the day. "I can't hang on. I've got stuff to do tonight."

"Leave it then," Janice advises. "It's only a jacket. Security can let him in if he can't go a weekend without it."

"No, it's his rucksack and stuff as well. I bloody well told him I wanted to get away early today. Why is he like this?"

"Leave it," Janice calls in a singsong tone as she heads down the hall. "You know he wouldn't put himself out for you."

"Very true."

Laura abandons Viktor's gear without another thought, flicking the latch down and pulling the door firmly closed. Unconsciously, she adds a little nudge with her foot, just to double check that the latch has caught properly, victim of one occasion where she forgot to check and came back to a ransacked office. Once is all it takes. Now it's part of the ritual, leaving a small smudge on the brass kickplate at the bottom of the door. It's always gone by the time she comes back in the morning, the cleaning crew passing by with a duster and a *tsk* to erase the evidence.

Janice is almost out of sight at the end of the road by the time Laura reaches the garden gate and starts digging in her bag for her car keys. How can it be that you put the blasted things on top, and they're always somehow right at the bottom when you need them next? She stops and rests the bag on the low wall bordering the lawn, stirring the contents with her hand until she hears the telltale rattle of her collection of keyrings and extracts the bunch with a triumphant sniff.

The Path expands to meet her, a sudden wash of warm gold-green seeping under the wall and pooling at her feet. When it recedes again, the lane is empty.

***

"No security tonight." Evie frowns out at the shadowed back lawn. "Would have thought we'd have seen at least one of them on their rounds by now?"

"No-show on the night shift," Chris answers distantly from farther inside the office, sweeping the last of his scattered kit into a pile. "Jonas is on his way in to cover. Alright, I think that's everything. Shall we head back?"

She doesn't answer, so he heads back up to the doorway to repeat the question.

"Evie?"

He peers out to either side, checking along the path in both directions. No sign of her. What there is, to his horror, is a shining ribbon of light, bright silver-gold, scything through the air towards him like the loop of a whip. He stumbles back through the open doorway, the loop passing bare inches from his face with a fierce high-pitched buzz. Then it vanishes, leaving faint blue-black blotches in his vision and the taste of burning tin in the air.

Chapter 54

"SINCE WHEN DO you walk everywhere?"

"Since you've been sleeping on the job for several hundred years," Mainder jabs back happily. "Things have changed a bit around here, in case you hadn't noticed. Quickest way to fill you in."

Despite the sprite's grousing, he does seem to be enjoying the tour, exclaiming as he identifies traces of old landmarks and leaping up on the boundary wall to look out over the sleeping town. There are sparse pinpricks of light here and there already, a tiny handful of people starting their day at this early hour to beat the rush up to Exeter and beyond.

Ordinarily Mainder would enjoy the walk, too, the hush of grey pre-dawn before anyone else is about. He's not really feeling it right now, though. Even the view from the headland, normally a guaranteed emotional palate-cleanser, does nothing to lift his mood. Something feels wrong, and no matter which direction he's facing, the subtle itch doesn't subside. Well, he'll happily walk the whole damn town if he must to figure out what it is.

Ah. No need. There's a silver-green shimmer in the direction of Fairy Hill, spreading and creeping down the line of the old water leat. Now he's looking for it, he can see a faint translucent overlay of figures dancing up and down where the old shrine path used to be. They're not really there, he knows. Simple echoes of people and times past. They shouldn't be so clearly visible, though. If that's happening, then that means—

"Huh, Fold's open. Thought you said it was dormant?" Sweyn comments disinterestedly.

"It was," Mainder says tersely, breaking into a fast stride. "Come on!"

The closer they get to the museum, the more frantic he becomes. The Fold isn't just open; it's expanding. Faint silver sparks dance over every surface, a flimsy net of pale threads matching and hugging the landscape and shimmering as they move through it. He raises his hand and watches the threads sliding over his own skin, distorting and settling back as he clenches and unclenches a fist.

He all but sprints the last hundred yards, not willing to risk a glyph until he knows what's there, and skids to a halt in the lane. There's the Path, leaking up between the marker trees and out on both sides, wide open to anyone who passes by. The red-gold tinge to the sky isn't dawn, as he was vainly hoping; it's the aurora, Queen's Rage, clearly visible above the rooftops. Right now, the two sides are close enough not just to touch, but to virtually overlap. At this rate, if he steps any farther forward, he could well end up on his own doorstep back in the Realm.

"So . . . problem?" Sweyn enquires brightly.

Mainder ignores him, stepping back and calling *tren* for the second time in several hundred years.

***

"Over there somewhere." Chris waves vaguely at the stack of laptops piled against the wall. "That's Evie's on top. I recognise her stickers, so it must be under that."

Aaron starts dismantling the stack. "Sensors are still operational, right?"

"Mmm," Chris hums faintly, a distracted affirmative. "Evie said we might still need them, didn't say why."

Sheer luck, really. Any later and the laptops would have been on their way back to base with the courier, and they'd have no way of tracking what's going on, even with the sensor array still on site.

To be fair, even with that — plus certain highly specialised bits of software — they haven't advanced much further than *something is very wrong*. It's been — and the litter of drinks cans and food wrappers testifies to the fact — several hours now since Evie vanished.

"Room service will be about in a bit," Raj comments

wistfully. "We could give them a call? I could do with a coffee."

It's true, he does look exhausted, a far cry from his usual impeccable self, with deep bags under his eyes. He's probably had the worst of it over the course of a frantic night, unable to contribute to the technical discussions which sit firmly in the realm of Chris and Aaron's expertise. His main contribution has been regular trips to the vending machine at the end of the hall for calorific fuel.

"Maybe." Chris isn't really listening, frowning at the pinpricks of light dancing on his screen. Periodically, they refresh, throwing out a loop like a solar flare—exactly like the shining arc that nearly carried him off—before settling back to a roughly circular pattern, bright eye in the centre and three arms trailing on the outer edge. It looks like a tiny galaxy trapped in a box, dancing and shifting as it pleads to expand. He stares bleakly across the table at Aaron.

"I'm open to new ideas at this point," he says quietly. "Any sign of Mainder?"

"No word yet. I've left a bunch of messages."

"Someone will have to go down there. Raj? If we believe Vernon, he's probably not much into checking his demonic answerphone."

"If Vernon is right, can't we, like, summon him here or something? We have his picture in the system."

Aaron wilts a little under the stares from the others.

"No, seriously! I saw it in a film once. They had a picture of the witch and some of her hair, and they said some Latin or something. I mean we have his pass photo . . ." He trails off. "Anyway, it was just an idea."

"I seriously advise against it." Mainder's voice from the doorway makes them all jump.

He pauses for a moment to assess the effect and pulls the door shut behind him.

"Where is she?"

No need to question which *she* he's talking about.

"That's the thing. If you'd pick up your bloody phone, you'd know," Chris answers tightly. "Vanished last night. I was just talking to her, she stepped outside, and by the time I got to the door, she'd just vanished without a trace. We've been trying to reach you ever since."

"Fair," Mainder allows. "My familiar neglected to check my, uh, demonic answerphone this morning. You just can't get the help these days."

He's joking, a sardonic lilt to his voice, but under it, there's an edge of furious tension. He seems darker, more sharply focused than usual, and when he paces slowly around the table in thought, each person sits very, very still as he passes them.

The effect is almost completely ruined when he sighs and says over his shoulder, "Yeah, I'm talking about you, scumbag." There's nothing and nobody there that they can see.

"Anyway." Mainder claims a seat and leans on the table with both elbows. "You all need to be as far away from this as you can get, and make sure everyone else stays away, too. We don't have long."

"Why? What's going to happen?"

For a second, he looks distinctly uncomfortable; he takes a deep breath and says, "There are . . . doors, I suppose you'd say, that are supposed to be closed. Right now, they're opening up all over the place, and the people who should be watching them have dropped the ball."

"That's you, right? *You* dropped the ball."

Chris doesn't flinch under the shuttered, coal-black stare this elicits.

Then suddenly, over his shoulder again, Mainder mutters "Okay, I get it. Oh, you do? Well, maybe you can be his familiar from now on then."

Seeing Chris's blank look, he adds aside, "They already think I'm crazy, you might as well show yourself."

Chairs topple backwards as Sweyn's smoky outline appears in the air beside Mainder's head. Bright yellow eyes sweep the huddle of panicked youngsters, and he lets out a wheezing chuckle.

"Your wish is my command," he rasps with an exaggerated bow at Mainder and floats away to explore the corners of the room.

"Sweyn," Mainder explains with a thumb jerked in the sprite's direction. "He was just saying you were right, and he likes you."

Chris finds his voice. "Erm, thanks?"

"Yeah, I wouldn't get too excited. He'll be cursing you out and stealing your lunch soon enough." Mainder mimes patting his pockets for a missing wallet.

"Doors opening, you said," Aaron interjects. "Three of them?"

"Maybe," Mainder says guardedly. "Why?"

"Because that's what we're seeing here. Three spikes going out from the centre, and one happened exactly at the moment Evie disappeared."

He's barely finished the sentence before Mainder is striding behind him, staring intently over his shoulder at the pattern on screen.

"Well now," he murmurs in surprise. "Wish I'd known you could track it, could have saved a lot of trouble." He looks almost pleased, following the twists and shifts of the Fold's energy in real time.

"Yeah, we had—uh, there was a project we worked on before that, um . . . I can't share the details, can I?" At a firm headshake from Chris, he subsides. "Never mind. It turned out that it's possible to detect this type of energy. The whole site has been loaded with sensors since before they even broke the turf, so we have near-real-time readings on any fluctuations in energy levels. All of the usual human-detectable spectra, as well as some non-standard signals."

Mainder frowns slightly. "Didn't understand a word of that, but okay. What am I looking at exactly?"

The tension in the room dissipates. Confused, grumpy, middle-aged Mainder is far less intimidating than angry-slamming-through-doors Mainder, even with the disturbingly transparent monkey-cat-demon thing flitting under the table licking crumbs of chocolate from the discarded wrappers.

"It means we know when people are moving, talking, using

electronics anywhere on site. Luckily, we'd already packed up our gear ready for the next project, so we have everything we need to monitor."

The Fold sends out another flare, and Mainder straightens back up hastily.

"Okay, that's not good. Sónnarson's still staying up here, isn't he? Get him out of bed. He'll know what to do."

"The professor? Why?"

"He'll be happy to explain it to you." Mainder's evil grin suggests otherwise. "And while he's doing that, I'll be tracking down a lost child." He calls to the shadow head-first rooting through the wastepaper bin. "Just like old times, yeah? You still remember what to do?"

The shadow doesn't answer, but the smoky hand clutching the rim of the bin flickers briefly in a one-finger salute. Mainder chuckles briefly.

"One more thing I need you to do. Okay?"

Mystified, Chris spreads his hands wide in an invitation to continue.

"Good. Make sure you tell him I made my claim."

Sweyn emerges with the discarded crust of a ham sandwich in his mouth and stares at Mainder like he can't believe what he just heard.

He's not the only one.

"Gross," Aaron says sourly. "If you're talking about Evie, then I can't wait to see her face when finds out. She'll slap you into next week."

Mainder sighs irritably. "That's not how it is. The claim is, like, some kind of accountability, that's all. This is my fault, my responsibility, and the claim links me to her so I can find her and get her back safe. Whatever else it might mean, well — we'll figure that out once she's safe. What're you looking at, birdbrain?"

"Nothing," Sweyn lilts, stirring the pile of wrappers again in case he's missed something.

Mainder raises his hand in the air and slowly traces the glyph, letting it hang sullen red in the air for a moment before the Path sings into life behind him.

"Good. Get your sorry arse over here," he commands and steps back into the shimmering plane.

BOOK 3

Across the Divide

Chapter 55

MOVING WITH URGENCY, Mainder strides towards the door in the cavern even as he shivers away his mudside camouflage. His long coat parts and rejoins behind him, a tattered cloak with a wide cape-like collar of coarse black fur. Nestling on his shoulder is the muted gleam of amber caged in bronze, a sinuous salamander with its back arched and one oval stone set in its head. He's ready to go Home.

A glance at Sweyn brings the sprite obediently to his shoulder, clinging tightly to the fur, and then he steps up to the bright doorway.

If you didn't realise you'd crossed the Divide, the view that greets you on the other side wouldn't necessarily help you since it's a mirror image of the mudside cavern. The main difference wouldn't be evident unless you turned and looked back the way you came. Rather than twisted roots, the door on this side is inset deep in the trunk of a full-grown tree, fully five feet wide with smooth grey bark and massive twisted limbs disappearing up into the chamber's roof far above.

There are other clues, more subtle. No silt on the floor on this side, no scorch marks, no smell of damp and disuse. No battery lanterns heaped in corners flickering their last. The tunnels off to the left and right are whole and unblocked, dressed stone defining the arches with deep-carved symbols above marking their respective destinations. The whole chamber has the feel of having been recently swept. No torches sit in the bronze brackets, but it does look like they haven't given up entirely on this side, even after everything.

He listens for a moment, but the chamber and the tunnels beyond are silent and empty. The clean floor makes it hard to say if anyone passed through before him, but he's certain she'd have come this way. The alternative—that she's missing in some other way he can't do anything about—is a possibility that he files away as a future problem to solve. If he dwells on it even slightly, it'll be impossible to focus.

Small high windows set in the wall show him glimpses of the sky lit by the Queen's Rage, an aurora of bright gold and scarlet wisps churning high overhead. It used to have another, sweeter name, but after the Closing nobody dared to speak it. The current label is considerably more apt in any case.

Everything else is just as it ever was. He quickly reaches the Gather, a wide semi-circular balcony carved out of the rock face where travellers used to muster, ready for their crossing, and he indulges himself with a moment to take in the dark tangle of the forest and glints of the river road shining on the far side. The mountain beyond the river is wreathed in mist, the city up in the heights invisible. He'll have to head up there once all this is settled, make his report, but not yet. Not until he knows she's safe.

The moment stretches out, Sweyn beginning to fidget beside him, but he doesn't hurry. For the little sprite, it can only seem like a few hours since he was here, trapped as he was for all that time, but for Mainder, it's been centuries since he came this way. This used to be home.

This *is* home, he corrects himself. Exactly what he's been telling himself he's been longing for. Nevertheless, it doesn't feel right; the pull of homesickness is still present, the feeling of being out of place. That settles it. She's here somewhere, and he's close, but still not close enough.

Distant howls rise from the forest. That's not necessarily an unusual sound in the Realm, so quite why it should make the hairs on his neck stand up, he's not sure. It's with a deep sense of foreboding though that he continues down the tunnel and out through the dark cavern.

The lake ripples as he passes, even though he didn't touch the water, and Sweyn sits up abruptly to sniff the air.

"Vily girls are out and about. Want to stop for a bit and try your luck? Get rid of some tension? Have to say, you could do with it."

Mainder actually does halt mid-step, so abruptly that Sweyn

is almost thrown off, and he frantically digs his stubby fingers into the fur of Mainder's cape to recover his balance. The steely glare he receives in response makes him duck down and flatten his body until he almost disappears into the fur.

"I wasn't serious!" he whines.

Mainder's jaw clenches and unclenches a couple of times, then he starts walking again without a word. Sweyn settles himself awkwardly back into place and wraps his tail around Mainder's neck just in case, resolving to keep the jokes to a minimum for the time being. Evidently his old friend has suffered a major sense of humour failure in the last few centuries, or maybe it's just on the specific topic of this "special" *yasim* that he's lacking in perspective. Sweyn is half-eager, half-afraid to actually meet the girl if she's had this effect on him.

He wasn't wrong about the Vily, though. Before Mainder can pass out of the cavern, the waters shine with the pearly glow that heralds their approach, and three pale faces rise out of the dark surface and turn to watch him.

For half a second, Mainder almost thinks he's found Evie — although what the hell she'd be doing swimming in the lake at a time like this escapes him. Of course it isn't her, but the sudden surge of hope is chased by realisation. How did he not see it before? How much she resembles the water spirits he practically lives — lived — next door to for so long? The pale oval of their faces, the high forehead and the wide-set pale eyes, the slender limbs, and above all the supernatural calm, the inability to be rushed to action. If she's related to any House on the Realm side it has to be this one, and looking at the incurious stares of these three right now, he'd be prepared to swear the heritage is not all that many generations distant.

He acknowledges the faces with a short bow, a hand over his shoulder mark, and they bob solemnly in return.

"Somebody passed this way just before me," he says.

It's not a question, since that's not how you get information from the Vily. You make a series of statements, and they indicate whether or not they agree. Rarely they may even speak, but you soon learn not to rely on that. Three sets of silver-green backlit eyes blink slowly. That's an affirmative for the water dwellers who live here in the depth of the cavern, a nod that can be seen even in near total darkness.

"A pale girl with short hair," he states and receives more blinks.

"You helped her."

That statement hurts to utter, since he already knows it can't be true. If they'd done anything to help, she'd be home already or at least waiting safely here for him. The pale eyes stare unblinking, and he has to take a deep breath to quell the surge of anger. When did his people become so inhospitable? It never used to be so.

"*Adzo*. We do not interfere," the nearest Vila says, her incongruously deep voice vibrating the water around her in tiny, criss-crossing ripples. The statement is a pointed jab at him personally. Lost children are his department, always have been, and if they didn't lift a finger to help, then nobody would judge them for it.

"I will be grateful if you would bring me word," he bites out, and as he turns away, he hears faint splashes, one after the other, as they vanish back under the water. It's a faint hope that they've taken his suggestion to heart, but it's better than nothing.

The moon rides high in the sky, showing him long-familiar trails down the rise and into the forest. On one, there are footprints coming from the other direction, up from the river, and they turn aside at the last waterfall and take one of the smaller paths. He quickens his pace, following the trail around several twists and turns. Some of those footprints are inches deep, thick mud pushed up on all sides by the force of the foot landing and distorting the shape of the print. It looks too big a print to belong to Evie, but he needs to be certain. The individual prints are over a yard apart here, suggesting either a naturally long stride — or somebody running for their life. The last few in front of him look like the tip of the toe only, digging into the mud and propelling the bearer forward in haste, and at the bend there are signs of a scrambling slide. Partial handprints and deep gouges trail down the bank beside the path, someone cornering almost on all fours in terrified haste.

Just around that twist in the track, the undergrowth is beaten down by the passage of wide, clawed feet crossing the marks of the human's boots and erasing all trace of them from that point on. It doesn't matter, though. Beyond the mess of paw prints there's a low line of debris, lumps and bumps spread across the ground and a larger shape off to the side. It's difficult to make out the details here under the gloomy canopy of the trees, but the scarlet pool spread out around the scene is all too clear. Blood, lots of it, collected under the body and spattering up on all sides on the tree trunks and ferns beside the path.

Gorge rises, and he has to force himself to get closer. He has to know, but at the same time, he doesn't want to know, would give anything to not have to know if it turns out to be her. To his shame, he feels only relief when he gets close enough to see the bundle of keys glinting in the moonlight, hanging from a shred of torn fabric at the figure's waist. Near where the unfortunate victim's waist would have been, anyway. There's little else left of the corpse to identify, but the blood-soaked jeans and tan leather boots are unmistakably mudside in origin. He's curled up in a foetal position, arms wrapped around his head in a futile attempt to protect himself, but the hounds simply tore chunks out of whatever they could reach. He'd have bled out in seconds. Tattered remains of a t-shirt still cling in shreds to parts of the torso; exposed bone gleams pale against the gore, ribcage and spine clearly visible and picked clean.

Of course the hounds would have gone first for the organs, an easy treat for them, and left the rest for carrion or to return to later if they find no better prey. Which means that Evie is still in danger. The unfortunate boy's blood is still liquid, in these cool conditions no more than half an hour old, so he can only pray he still has time to find her before these beasts do. He rises swiftly and turns to look across the way, working out the quickest way to pick up the next trail.

On his shoulder, Sweyn stirs, flicking his trail nervously.

"I was only kidding back there in the cavern."

"I know," Mainder says tightly, already trampling down the ferns to clear his path.

"I could go and look along the other path. Cover a bit more ground, yeah?"

"Not yet."

Sweyn subsides, renewing his grip on the fur cape. It's not in his nature to be what you might call squeamish, but the sight of the corpse has shaken him more than he could have predicted. Mainder's well-being is consideration number one, no matter how much he might take advantage of their long partnership to curse him out when need arises. The protection of the Realm and any of its inhabitants comes a close second. After that, his priority is whatever Mainder tells him it is, and it follows that the protection of mudside intruders is only ever going to make that list if Mainder says so.

But this now … the Hunt was a dreadful tradition; an ancient form of Realm justice reserved for the very worst evildoers on both sides of the Divide, quietly abandoned long ago in favour of less blood-soaked methods. For there still to be remnants of the pack running around unchecked means very big trouble for everyone concerned.

Mainder brushes through one final barrier, the glossy hedge surrendering to his impatient trampling, and emerges at last beside the lake. There's his old bench overlooking the calm water, his favourite fishing and thinking spot. The path up to his cabin looks just as it ever did, he's relieved to see. What he's not happy about is the mess of footprints at this end of the lake, the hounds' passing churning up the mud in all directions. He spreads his arms wide, feeling for the barrier that should be protecting this place.

"They've taken down my ward somehow. No way they should have been able to get to here."

"What, the dogs?"

"It's more than the dogs." He closes his eyes, concentrating. "You feel it?"

"Dunno. It just feels kind of . . . dusty."

"Dusty," Mainder repeats thoughtfully and calls up a spark.

The air glistens around his hand, tiny particles igniting and spiralling upwards in a column above the flame. He coaxes the flame to full strength and sweeps his hand in an arc in front of him, watching the glittering dust pass over and billow towards the path to the cabin. There's no breeze and nothing is moving, so that dust is being directed somehow.

A single drop of water will wear a mountain down to nothing given a few thousand years, and a constant flow of tiny dust particles will eventually exhaust his invisible barriers if he's not there to renew them.

He lowers his hand, but the flame stays coiled in his palm.

"Someone's taking down the wards on purpose. Find her. *Now.*"

"What am I, a fucking spaniel?" Sweyn grumbles, hopping down and sniffing the paw prints. "Stinks of Miskin to me. Whatsisname, that huntsman, always smelled like wet dog. You remember? Better if I just have a look around."

He vanishes before Mainder can say anything else.

Chapter 56

HIGH IN THE cliff face, in a wide semi-circular balcony carved from the living rock, a girl sits staring out at a strange world: a distant river winding across the plain, a severe line of jagged mountains beyond, all cold and forbidding by pale moonlight.

The forest far below her feet looks like every fairytale ever about missing children just waiting to happen, deep shadows pooling under the tree canopy and a dozen tempting paths winding into the gloom. *Worse things out there than me,* Mainder's memory murmurs. She'd rather not risk entering the forest unless she can find some way to make light, but down is the only direction available to her right now.

There seem to be doorways in the path sloping down to her right, and after a brief debate with herself, she gets to her feet and heads to investigate the nearest one. When she reaches it, there turns out to be no actual door, just an outline inset into the rock less than an inch deep, with an ornate frame carved in the shape of braids and intricate decorative knots. It's too beautiful, too purposeful, to be nothing; maybe it really is a door, just one she's not invited to enter. She hesitates, laying a tentative hand on the stone just in case, but nothing happens.

She could simply sit still and wait there for Mainder to rescue her, but then he also said that without a token — whatever that means — there's no telling where somebody might end up. Even if he came looking for her any second, there's no way for him to know where she'd have emerged. She needs to keep going until she finds someone who might be willing to help her.

She's not blind to the possibility that the first person she encounters might be less than friendly. Checking her pockets for options for self-defence yields nothing in the way of weapons. She discounts her tiny penknife as more likely to close over her own fingers if she attempted to stab somebody with it, but if she can get down to the forest level, she might be able to pick up a big stick that she can wave threateningly. She laughs softly at herself; how quickly we revert to savagery when our home comforts are beyond our reach.

Speaking of home comforts, she almost automatically checks her phone. Plenty of charge, which is nice, but of course there's zero signal. It was probably too much to hope that the Realm had a nice, open, civic WiFi infrastructure. Out of sheer curiosity, she runs a network scan — you never know, after all. But there's nothing, and she puts the useless rectangle of expensive technology away. Perhaps in a pinch she can use it as a blunt instrument.

After a moment's hesitation, she retrieves it again and takes a hasty self-portrait with the balcony in the background. She doesn't like how her face looks, pinched and pale and anxious against the dark sky, but if the worst happens, at least she'll have left a record.

The tunnel curves down and around to the right, cut at intervals with small windows above and to one side. Moonlight slants in, bright ovals on the floor and wall like spot-lamps, lighting her way and illuminating more doorways on her righthand side. Some neat-cut and square, others water-carved and uneven, all of them unlit. They seem to promise adventure, but not necessarily safety. The very end of the tunnel is gloomy, the moonbeams giving out several feet before that point, but there's a faint, pale glow coming from whatever is next. She takes another picture of herself with the inviting dark behind her, then stows her phone, the better to have both hands free in case this turns out to be a terrible mistake. It doesn't feel like a mistake, but then she supposes that's probably what Hansel and Gretel said right before they started stuffing their faces with gingerbread. It's keep going or stand still, though, and for all the gloom and the watchful silence all around her, this doesn't feel like danger. Not yet.

At the end, the tunnel turns left and opens out into a massive cave, wide and shallow, with the sides disappearing into the dark on both sides and a still lake in the centre. It's eerily beautiful, a distant gold-green glow from somewhere reflecting off the lake's surface and delicately suggesting the arches of the dark stone above it. There are more passages off to each side, or more caves, but she follows the lake. It feels right.

Right does not necessarily mean safe, she reminds herself as she struggles to keep her footing on the slick stone. She begins to feel observed, watched by many eyes somewhere out there in the dark, although there's no sound at all apart from the steady drip of water from the stalactites hanging from the roof. It still somehow doesn't feel like danger, only watchfulness. Someone is watching her pass through their home or domain, stumbling foolishly around their familiar furniture and bumping into walls. As much as she wishes they would show themselves, even if to challenge her, she can't blame them for staying hidden. *You people are convinced we all have pots of gold under our beds.*, Mainder said. Little wonder she might not be a welcome guest in that case. She fights the urge to call out a generic apology for humankind's past transgressions and continues picking her way around the lake's edge. If she's not mistaken, that might be something more like moonlight up ahead again.

As soon as she focuses on the pale glow on the water, it vanishes, and she stops dead where she is. Was there something there, or did she just imagine it? She stares hard at the dark water until her vision begins to blur, but the light remains absent. She places her hand on the stone wall beside her before turning, just in case she loses her bearings, and stares back the way she came. The green and gold glow is still there, a little weaker now, but she can make out the tunnel she emerged from and the hint of the moonlight from the tunnel's windows. She's heading the right way; she has to be. The forest is up ahead.

When she turns back, there's a face in the dark on her left, just a momentary glimpse that could almost be her own reflection, but when her gaze flicks back, there's nothing there. She moves slightly back and forth in case it was a particular angle that captured her face in the water somehow, but it doesn't reappear. So she is being watched, but whoever it was isn't interested in making friends right now. She shivers and keeps moving.

The lake hugs the curve of the wall and disappears around the corner, and when she reaches it, there's the cave mouth ahead of her at last and a glimpse of the night sky, starless but with wisps of cloud lit by the moon and a flicker of green and red-gold like the strange aurora in her dream. She moves faster now, picking her way along the lake shore until the cave opens out to a rise leading down to the forest.

The lake ends here against a manmade barrier, an even line of smooth boulders damming the far end and forcing a series of tiny weirs to cascade down in irregular zigzags to feed another, larger lake beyond. This one forms an elongated oval like a spearhead, surrounded by tall trees and tangled undergrowth. The tree canopy is too dense to let the moonlight through.

Her hand closes over her phone again. *Thank you, flashlight mode.* She takes one more triumphant selfie against the cascade — if she ever makes it home, she's going to have quite the scrapbook — then she lights her way with the phone's mundane beam, sweeping it to all sides and checking for danger as she heads down the rise. Lost in Fairyland, saved by a smartphone.

Perhaps it's a little soon to claim she's saved, as at that moment a cacophony of howling starts up from deep in the trees. No, not howling; baying, the joyful sound of a pack let loose and picking up the scent. Her legs react before her brain can form a plan, sprinting not away from the sound but towards it and scrambling up the nearest tree.

The pack comes into sight bare seconds after she manages to fix her foothold.

Don't move don't move don't make a sound . . . She wraps one arm around her head and forces herself to breathe as slowly and as shallowly as she can, using the fabric of her sleeve to muffle any sound. Huge creatures, not quite dogs and not quite wolves, surge past right under her feet in a thunderous rush of fur and teeth and fury and disappear around the next curve without slowing. It's barely a pack, at that; there can't have been more than ten of the creatures altogether. Still more than enough to bring down a person.

The noise of the hunt gradually fades into the distance, but she doesn't abandon her perch just yet. She needs a plan of some kind if it turns out this place is stuffed with things that will want to eat her, and despite her earlier caution, she has, in fact, ended up in the wild wood, exactly where she'd aimed not to be. She could retrace her steps, but she already knows there's no help along that route; she could keep going and hope to find shelter somewhere. Or there's option three, which is to stay right here in this tree and wait for morning. Leaving aside the question of balancing while sleeping, it seems the safest choice. Unless there are also flying things that want to eat her, in which case all her troubles will be over sooner rather than later.

Footsteps on the path below break into her musings, and she's momentarily flooded with relief. Maybe this is rescue approaching.

The brief flare of hope is replaced half a second later by doubt when she sees the familiar thickset figure. Round face, untidy grey hair, bald spot, and above all, the ponderous step of a man in no hurry whatsoever, just doing his job. It's Clegg, or someone so like him they could be his twin, over here in the Realm. If it is him — well, as much as she dislikes the man, he is at least from her side of the Divide. Maybe he's not a complete monster.

On the other hand . . . maybe he is. He's not walking like a man transported against his will to Fairyland. He's walking like a man hoping to catch somebody out of place and make them miserable, exactly as he did over on the other side. It's a very specific brand of petty tyranny, the sort of mediocrity that seeks out just enough power to make people uncomfortable but not enough to have serious consequences. Not enough that you'll be missed if you get bored and move on to new victims. That no-show on the night shift must surely have been him, and no wonder. Here he is. If he turns out to be her only hope of salvation, she'd honestly rather be eaten by dogs. Her skin prickles even at the mere idea of letting him know she's here, let alone asking him for help and putting herself in his power.

He seems put out, peering into the trees and looking for something in the dark. If he is tracking her, then he's not doing any better than the hounds. He finds her footprints at least, crouching down to examine them, then turning to look in the direction the nearest print points to. With the overlay of the hounds' passing to camouflage her hasty scramble up the tree trunk, it must look like she carried on running in that direction and headed deeper into the forest. He rises again with a satisfied *oof* and picks up his patrol rhythm, plodding along, following the hounds with no interest in hurrying nor helping.

Evie holds her breath entirely as he passes underneath her feet, pressing her back against the rough bark of her hiding place until he disappears into the distant gloom.

Chapter 57

EVIE SCRAMBLES DOWN from her tree and moves cautiously along the dirt path churned up by the hounds, choosing the direction they've already covered. It ought to buy her some time.

By the lakeside, the brambles give way to a border of thick reeds and flag irises, delicate purple blooms nodding at the lake's edge. Ripples appear in the centre, and the moon's reflection on the surface, a bright perfect circle, splinters gracefully as they reach it. There are no stars in that mirrored sky, though, none at all, because there aren't any to be reflected. It chills her to realise just how far from home she must be. If you don't look at the sky, if you keep your eyes down and look only at the trees and the tangled bushes and thick leaf mould beneath, it's just a forest, just familiar enough not to cause too much alarm. However, the absence of the stars leaves her nothing to navigate by, no way to get her bearings. Where could you even be in this universe that has nothing hanging in the sky apart from the moon?

The more she looks at the broken fragments of the moon on the water, the more it looks like a road, silver-white paving on a bed of midnight blue, and her brain insists she could use that shining path to go wherever she chose if she just had the courage to step out on the water. *No need to navigate*, it seems to whisper. *No cause for alarm. Simply follow the path.*

She shakes her head to dispel the whispers. She hasn't eaten recently, that's the problem. Extreme physical activity on top of an empty stomach, it wouldn't be surprising if she started feeling a little lightheaded and having trouble focusing. She feels fine, though, not dizzy or confused. If anything, her senses feel sharper than normal, everything perfectly clear and in focus around her. Not that she'd turn down a meal if it appeared in front of her right now, although if she remembers her folklore correctly it would probably be a huge tactical error. She feels perfectly fine and yet at the same time has convinced herself that she could walk on water if she really wanted to. She skirts the lake well back from the edge and keeps her eyes fixed on the path to avoid further temptation.

At the far end, the lake narrows back to a point, and there's a low stone bench set slightly to one side, a rough construction with a single pale slab flecked with quartz that glitters in the moonlight. The paving slabs beneath are overgrown with moss and small pale flowers like five pointed stars creeping up and nodding wide open in the moonlight. A path leads from the bench up through the trees, no more than a faint track worn in the earth where somebody comes this way once in a while. That has to mean people — people who come and sit here often enough to decide they need something to sit on, whether to fish or simply to relax and to think.

It feels like more than a theory. It feels like a memory, a figure shrouded in a long dark coat or a cloak, sitting patiently still beside the moonlit water waiting for something or someone. A dream from long ago, perhaps, once upon a time back before she learned the hard way that nobody wanted to hear about her foolish dreams and her imaginary friends. But with the dream-memory comes certainty. This is the way.

The crowding trees to her left give way to a high hedge with glossy dark leaves, and on both sides of the muddy track, there are more of the pale star flowers, a thick border invading the edges and glowing in the moonlight, almost as if they were planted there to mark the way for midnight travellers. The further she goes, the more right, the more familiar and safe, it feels.

She starts as the howling begins in the distance again, rising to an eager crescendo as the animals pick up the trail and urge each other on. It's almost musical, a joyful rhythm picked up by one animal after another so that the sound never falters, a wordless round-song of blood and triumph. She freezes as the music collapses thread by thread to low growls and snarling, tearing, a distant scream cut off. They've caught something.

Some*one*.

She breaks into a sprint, choking back tears of mingled fury and shame. Whoever it was, they're beyond any help she could possibly give.

The path ends abruptly around the next bend, opening out into a wide clearing, and up against the forest's edge, on the far side — a house. A cabin, really, a tiny timber dwelling with no fence or wall around it, just the flower-edged track guiding her up to a door under the shingled porch. Lush moss grows over the shingles, thick weeds surround the door, but the structure looks sound. It'll do. She closes the gap to the door and lays a frantic hand on the metal latch, stumbling to her knees over the threshold as the door swings open at her touch. She scrambles back up and shuts the door, fumbling with the latch mechanism and searching for a lock.

There isn't one to be seen, but there is a thick metal bar leaning on the floor. It would make a good weapon, but the sockets in the door frame suggest it has another use. She hefts the bar up in both hands and drops it into place, and only then allows herself the luxury of a deep breath, exhaling heavily and sagging against the solid timber of the door with relief.

The respite carries with it space for the other emotions she didn't dare indulge, all of the fear and the anger and the shame put aside in favour of survival until this moment. She tries not to think about which poor soul the hounds might be eating right now in place of her and closes her eyes tight against the vile images shuffling through her head. What if that was Chris pulled through after her, chased down by the hounds, ripped to pieces? What if, not one of her friends, but even just someone else from the dig, maybe someone she'd sat and drunk tea with, shared a joke with, danced with?

She can't think about it; she dare not. Must not. Even if it wasn't someone she knew or cared about, still no. There was nothing she could have done. If she'd gone back, she'd be nothing but dog food herself right now. She had no choice but to run.

What if it was Mainder?

That's the thought that breaks her, though why the dam should burst for him and not for any of her friends, she doesn't have time to process. The unwelcome notion cuts the strings instantly, dropping her back to her knees again, a sobbing, heaving bundle curled up with an arm wrapped around her face, desperately trying to stifle the sound.

Chapter 58

THE STORM OF emotion trails away at long last, leaving
her blank, still sprawled against the door. A growing sting of
pain from her grazed knuckles demands her attention, and she
raises her hand and examines the tiny beads of blood welling
up through the smears of dirt. She can only hope she even lives
long enough for a cut to get infected, but there's no point
inviting trouble. She gets to her feet, wincing at the protest from
her bruised knees, and explores the dim cabin. To the left, a tall
bay window with a broad sill and a window seat. To the right, a
stone fireplace. Ahead, a bed with a carved wooden headboard.

She knows this place. She knows it, just like she knew the
bench, but this is something else. Something more recent, more
real. Despite her desperate situation, a tiny breathless laugh
escapes her, disbelief mingled with elation — it's Mainder's
cabin. Of all the places to end up, of all the sanctuaries, she's
arrived in the one place she could possibly hope to be safe
anywhere on this side of the Divide.

It's not exactly like it was in the dream. Then, the floor was
clean and swept, the grate laid with a welcoming fire, the bed
covers stretched out smooth and inviting. Mainder himself was
here, filling the space with his warmth and his mischief and his
smile. His absence now feels like a physical void, the familiarity
of the space all the more bittersweet without him here. The bed
is unmade, covers balled up and dropped to one side as if he
leapt up in haste to answer some call and never came home to
make it. The blankets smell musty, the wrinkled sheet cold
under her hand. On the floor at the end of the bed, she finds the
thick fur throw, tossed aside to land where it may, and she
shakes out the accumulated dust and spiders before wrapping
herself in it. It's a small comfort, but small comforts are better
than none.

There's no fire laid, but there is a stack of logs beside the fireplace, as well as a basket of kindling. She searches the mantelpiece, a broad oak beam worn smooth in one spot with many years of someone leaning there while they stoop to poke the fire, and she smiles as she rests her own hand in the same spot. Two small copper pans hang from hooks on the beam, one deep and one wide and shallow. A rough clay pot holds a bundle of rough spills, but no matches. Of course he wouldn't need them, would he. She searches her pockets again in case she has anything capable of making a spark, but there's nothing. Her phone can make light but not fire, no use here.

Phone. She pats her pockets again in frantic stocktake and finds it missing. She almost gives way to despair again at that point, her face threatening to crumple into helpless tears, but she takes a deep breath and scrubs fiercely at her face with one filthy hand. It's not as if she could have used it to call for help in this place, so its loss right now is no great disaster. She abandons the idea of lighting a fire for now and concentrates on what else she can find that might be of use. A poker sits in the grate, and she hefts it in her hand with a thoughtful look. The handle is no more than a rough lump of some brassy metal, pitted and corroded, giving the thing the look of a basic proto-hammer. A mental image rises irresistibly of Mainder using it to bang that nail into the beam to hold his frying pan because he couldn't be arsed to find a proper hammer. She smiles grimly, swinging the poker a couple of times to test its balance. It'll do, until or unless she finds something more compelling.

The rest of the room is bare and minimal, just one of each thing he might need within easy reach and no clutter anywhere else, no paintings or vases or ornaments of any kind and no decoration beyond the carved bedstead. There isn't even a mirror. A marble-topped dresser against the far wall holds a small basin and ewer and a wooden comb. The ewer at least contains water; she pours an exploratory splash into the basin and decides it's clean enough for the task at hand, even if it's been sitting forever on the dresser. There doesn't seem to be a sink or a pump in here, and she's not about to go out there to search for one.

A cupboard built into the cabin's timber frame reveals shelves with neatly folded spare blankets, a tall stack of tin plates, a line of four bright copper kettles identical to the one sitting in the hearth, a chipped brown china teapot and two dainty teacups. There's no cutlery other than a single silver fork, elegantly monogrammed with *AWV* on the handle. The bottom of the cupboard looks like the inside of Squirrel's Drey, boxes and baskets stacked on every inch of the lowest shelf next to a canvas backpack. A small crate packed with straw protects a china jar full of loose-leaf tea, a red-gold dragon chasing rolling clouds wreathed around the canister. She puts that back with extreme care, holding her breath until it's safely in its protective nest. Beside that, a stack of matchboxes and snuff tins hold twisted roots tied up with twine or leaves and dried flowers pressed in paper. They must be useful to be preserved so carefully, but she has no idea what they are or their possible uses.

She empties the pack next, swallowing a twinge of guilt at invading his space like this, rooting through his things without his permission. Will he mind once he finds out she's been here? She can only hope she doesn't end up unearthing anything too embarrassing. Anyway, he must have carried this around with him from time to time, so it stands to reason it should have the most immediately useful things to hand.

It's difficult to reconcile that assumption with what she finds. What she took to be a tool roll in soft leather unfurls to display satin ribbons in shades of sky blue, palest primrose, and sombre maroon, all cut neatly into swallowtails at the ends and hemmed with tiny stitches. Why on earth would he be carrying around little girls' hair ribbons? Underneath that, there's a cloth pouch that jingles when it moves. She shakes the contents out on to her palm and stares at the jumble of polished brass rings, plain bands like wedding rings in different sizes. Then there's a trio of small, bright-white metal ingots, no longer than her little finger, wrapped in a scrap of brightly patterned hessian. Scattered handfuls of flint arrowheads rattle around loose in the very bottom of the pack, scraping her fingertips, and right at the very bottom, there's the final item, another roll of leather.

It isn't ribbons this time. This one opens like an envelope, rigid, stitched sides unfolding to form a shallow square tray containing a jumble of metal pieces and scraps. It's a strange assortment to be kept together; the only thing that looks complete is a ladies' hat pin with a striped agate cabochon as big as her thumbnail, while the rest is a collection of coiled springs and short rods, and some curved segments of patterned bronze plate with notches in the outer edge and scored lines marking sections all the way along. It looks like something she's seen before, a vague memory picking at her conscious mind, asking politely to be acknowledged, but the penny doesn't drop until she turns the hatpin over. The stone is pretty enough, but on the back of its setting, stamped into the metal, there's the faint impression of a circle with three dots evenly spaced around it. It's the exact same maker's mark as the Hoard and the brooches. And now she looks properly, the curved pieces are almost identical to the ones turned up in the Hoard. Not a harness at all then; something more, a mechanism of some kind.

Fascinating though it is, it's not what she's looking for. She carefully rolls the leather back up and places it on the floor beside her, turning to the pack's deep pockets. The first one yields a crumpled wad of what feels like muslin, which she unravels with a restrained hiss of triumph, shaking out the length to examine her prize. This is exactly what she needs. Although, with a glance at the canister, a cup of tea wouldn't be unwelcome. For goodness' sake, Mainder, not even a tinder box? She can't wait to see him again and chide him for his lack consideration for guests. She has to hold on to the idea that she will see him again, that he's definitely not lying dead and mangled somewhere out past the lake, and he's absolutely certainly on his way to fetch her home to safety. He has to be. Because if he's not . . .

She refuses to finish that thought. One crisis at a time.

Returning to the dresser, she washes the mud off her hands, wincing at the sting of the cold water, then crosses back to the window to examine her injuries by bright moonlight.

That was a mistake. Right at the very edge of the clearing, dark shapes are clustering. Long and low, not humans but dogs or wolves or whatever hybrid those creatures are, churning around in the dark and turning to look at something behind them as if appealing for permission to advance. A darker shadow detaches from the murk under the trees and stands for a second, silhouetted against the path. It's Clegg again, his wide-legged stance and round figure unmistakable. They've traced her this far, then. Why haven't they attacked?

She has her answer when Clegg grabs one of the dogs by its scruff and its tail and heaves it forward over the edge of the clearing. There's a rippling flash of bright pale gold, an intangible net hanging in the air suddenly made visible, and the hound yelps and streaks through the man's legs to join its fellows in the comforting dark. Its anguished cries can be heard even from inside the cabin.

Clegg claps his hands together twice and turns away down the track, the hounds flowing after him silently until the clearing is empty again. Whatever that barrier is, they can't cross it. She was able to pass through easily. Why? Another question for Mainder if — *when* — he finally shows up.

Chapter 59

MAINDER ALMOST MISSES it, focused as he is on old-fashioned woodcraft, but the way the moonlight bounces off something sticking out of the ground draws him back in a tight circle. Tree roots are generally not that smooth, nor do they gleam with such perfect straight edges and rounded corners. He crouches down and scrapes the thick mud aside to reveal a sleek rectangle, its glass screen and single button smeared with dirt.

A hasty wipe with the hem of his cloak clears most of the muck, and he manages to jiggle the button just enough to get it to switch on. The lock screen lights up with a portrait of Evie at the edge of the rise with the Vily cavern behind her. It looks so odd to see her like that, transported to the Realm rather than against her more usual, mudside backdrop, but it's unmistakably her. She doesn't look hurt, though there's a grim determination in her face. He doesn't even know how he'd unlock the phone to examine the details, but it doesn't matter. This is unquestionably her phone. She made it across the Divide unharmed and with enough presence of mind to leave a trail, and at some point recently, she came this way. It's a start.

Something rustles behind him and hope flares brightly; he drops the hand he'd raised to summon the Path and spins to face the sound.

All plans fade to nothing when Clegg steps forward into the light. He's not mudside security, not anymore. His official uniform has been replaced by shapeless loose clothing in grey and brown, a clay-smeared apron tied tight under the bulge of his belly, and a short cape around his shoulders held in place by the bronze fibula from the dig. He's smiling, a gleeful smirk, holding in one hand a lump of clay formed into a rough lozenge. In the other hand, something slender and wickedly sharp winks in the moonlight.

"Carney? That you, boy? Hope your mutts enjoyed their

meal, such as it was." He's chuckling as he emerges but pulls up short and peers over at the figure framed against the lake. "Ah. Looking for something, are we?"

His smile widens, a spiteful joy that tells Mainder everything he needs to know.

"You know I am. Where is she?"

Clegg actually laughs out loud. "Who cares, Finder? All sorts of nasty things in this forest. Stupid moonchild won't have lasted five minutes."

It doesn't sound mystical, the way he says *moonchild*. It doesn't sound complimentary or admiring or indulgent. It sounds like bigots do when they say *half-caste* or *immigrant* or *foreigner*. It sounds like he's saying *tainted*. He seems all too pleased with himself, planting his feet wide on the path and smiling broadly.

"Never could work out what was wrong with you, chasing those dumb heifers mudside and pretending like they were real people. Makes it way too easy to mess with you." He looks down at the clay in his hand and scores a rune or two, like he's making idle conversation with a customer while he works. "You lost this one—but then, you've been losing this whole time, haven't you? Did my heart good to see you so busy chasing around after my leavings. I never could work out whether it'd be more fun if you knew or if you didn't. Doesn't matter anymore, though, does it? It's done. *You're* done." He holds up the lozenge and squints at the design, apparently satisfied.

It's done. Mainder doesn't like the sound of that; he's not even sure what it is that's done, but he has a growing suspicion that any scenario that makes Clegg smile like that is something that needs to be stopped.

"It's not done, though," he muses, picking his way around the words. "One more Vernon still to go. Right? I have my instructions."

Bring them to nothing, she said. No specifics, no caveats, just those four words. Given who she said it to, though—let's just think about that. The Queen of Faerie has many resources at her command, not least her own very considerable powers. So why would she choose him to be the instrument of her vengeance? What was she thinking?

If she'd set the smith to the task of revenge, the Vernon family might have been ruined financially in short order, project after project going massively over budget. The sculptor, he'd have made sure every statue magnified their every flaw, each wart and wrinkle and double chin faithfully reproduced. Carney would have patiently trained their horses to throw them in the dirt, their hounds to snap at their fingers and crap on the floor beside the bed. Mainder, though; he's nothing in the grand scheme. A nobody. A tinker, a fixer, a finder of lost children, half his power lost in the disaster that separated him from Sweyn.

The half he retained, however; that remained firmly centred around the very attributes that brought him into being in the first place. He didn't start off as a finder. He started off as a protector, a haven, a personification of the campfire that keeps the dark at bay and the hearth that warms the house. And the thing about protectors is this: they tend to develop an affinity for justice and mischief in equal measure. Often, they're the same thing. Which all means that he's had centuries to develop unconventional routes to justice, aided by his greatest power, and one that most people don't regard as a power at all: *observation*. The weakness in the grain, the pivot for the lever, these are his playgrounds.

"The last of them," he reiterates, watching Clegg's face. "He's got days left, if that, and I made sure he knew he was beaten before I left him. All his grand plans, all for nothing. I bet that stung. I'd have thought it would be devastating, wouldn't you? All that planning and he's still nothing, and he'll be even less when he goes into the ground. Bet his people are furious at all of their time being wasted like that. Can't say I feel sorry for them, if they chose to hitch their wagon to his shabby little scheme. I wonder what they hoped to gain? Pathetic."

And there it is. Clegg's face splits in an evil smile.

"What did they hope to gain?" he mimics. "Getting rid of you, for a start! That was my place, you smug bastard. My playground! All those gullible idiots coming to the wise man for their love potions and their good luck charms, all those dinners dropped at the shrine for their imaginary gods. Even had the occasional lord stop by to get my advice, polite as you please, not that you'd know anything about that."

"I save my courtesy for those who earn it." Mainder says lightly. "The wise man in the woods, eh? That was you? I can't quite see it, to be honest. Why would a fine lord be stopping by your door? Looking for tips on keeping the mildew off his boots, was he?"

Clegg's smile drops, and he jabs his wicked little spike in Mainder's direction.

"That's what I'm talking about. I was never good enough for you, was I? But one of those mudside lords wants a drop of fresh blood for his line, he comes to me. He treats my opinion with respect. Can you say the same?"

"No, because your opinions aren't worth respecting," Mainder retorts. "You started a war! What were you thinking?"

"It was supposed to make things right!" Clegg hisses. "What would you know about it? We had it all worked out—a marriage binding and her blood to rule the Fold forever. It would have made Alfriscombe ours, like it was always supposed to be!"

"Was letting her die all part of your masterful plan? Must have broken your heart when the babe didn't make it, eh? Was it your idiot idea to have her give birth in a locked room with no midwife?"

Sullen silence is his only answer.

"Typical," he says scathingly. "You didn't give it any thought at all, did you? Did it occur to you that managing something like that might be beyond your touch?"

"Right, like you stay in your lane? Lost children belong to the woods they wander into, and let their fate fall where it may. Not for you, though, eh? Trampling in and whisking them away so you can feel good about yourself. Anyway, you were only supposed to be kept out of the way while we got everything sorted. I'd've come and got you out again." Clegg smirks again, twirling the spike between his fingers. "Maybe."

There's no remorse in his face, no hint of empathy or sympathy for the children he stole or the damage he caused to his people on both sides of the Divide. No care for anyone's well-being but his own, as if nobody but him is a real person with feelings and needs. He should have seen this in the man, after so many years of being — as he thought — friends. It's an oversight he intends to put right immediately, before any more damage can be done.

"Look up," he says, and Clegg does so automatically. "What do you see?"

"What's this, some stupid riddle?"

"Maybe. Tell me what's in the sky right now."

"The clouds, the moon, the Sunlit Path," Clegg recites in a singsong voice, as if he's humouring a child.

"Ah, no." Mainder steps closer, his head tilted slightly and his arms hanging loose at his sides. Supremely relaxed, absolutely calm and unthreatening, and his voice is soft as he asks, "You haven't been home for a while, have you? You know what they call it now?"

Clegg opens his mouth to sneer again, but Mainder's hand is already at his throat, grasping the top of his tunic and twisting it tight in a choking hold. The skin of his fingers and wrist starts to twist oddly, blackening and shrivelling back like a dry branch at the fire's edge.

"They call it Queen's Rage." He answers his own question, looming over the sculptor and staring into his eyes. "Do you know why?"

Clegg couldn't answer, even if he knew. His senses are filled with the acrid odour of his tunic burning, scorching off the clay smears and crisping against his neck, and he doesn't dare look down to see whether the flames are real or just an illusion. He tries to bring his arm up to shake the hand free, to push this weakling salamander off him and quench his fire forever in the lake, but he can't budge him. Here, on honest soil, in the middle of the forest he's attuned to, he should be strong, invincible. Horrified confusion blooms in his face.

"My place, miskin," murmurs Mainder, a faint smile ghosting across his cracking lips. "This is my turf you're standing on, given to me to hold the Divide. Given to me to find the lost and return them where they belong." He twists his hold even tighter. "Or to avenge them."

He'll never forget, not if he lives another thousand years. It took him a mudside year of travelling through long-deserted back routes, torn by brambles and chased by hounds, to get back home, report the whole sorry disaster and make the sodden circuit back again. A year during which the child was held in a locked room at the hall, visited over and over again by the man who'd claimed her to wife, growing new precious life in her belly. A wasted, desperate year to get back and find they'd missed the birth, missed the deaths, and there was nothing left to rescue. He did what he could, and he's been doing it ever since, and here, finally, is the cause. Evie will have to wait. The Fold will have to wait. This *thing*, this treacherous walking talking well of evil intent, is all he needs to take care off right now. Time for an ending.

The flames roar behind his eyes.

Chapter 60

THE TUMBLED REMAINS of the mudsider caught by the Hunt are only vaguely on Sweyn's mind as he coasts high over the Path. Sprites, though intelligent, feel emotions only very lightly and care for them not at all. He's quickly back to what passes for equilibrium, and while his mission is clear, he's ecstatic to be free again, back home where he belongs and just itching to explore. The cabin is just up the rise, so surely there's no harm in just checking out the old place first before he goes tracking through the mud? He recalls he might have left a snack or two in his hidey hole under the bed. He could just nip in and grab something to sustain himself.

Doors are for other people as far as Sweyn is concerned, so he enters the cabin by the simple method of deciding to already be inside. He materialises perched on the mantelpiece, dislodging the clay pot which rolls off the edge and smashes on the floor.

"What the hell?" comes a voice from the bed, and the lump of bedclothes unfurls to reveal a girl with one bandaged hand clutching the poker in a decidedly threatening fashion. Not that it would do anything except pass through him in his current form, but the last thing he needs is to open this particular negotiation with any suggestion of hostilities. This has to be the girl they're looking for, and if she means anything at all to his old friend, then he needs to be on her good side as fast as may be.

He freezes, trying to look harmless. "Ah, talk about luck," he chirps hastily, waving his stubby fingers to demonstrate the lack of claws. "Finder sent me."

The poker doesn't move. "I don't know any 'finder.'"

"Yeah, you do. I dunno what you call him. Black hair, kind of scruffy looking, not too bright? Said I was to find you and make sure you were alright." He flicks his tail irritably. "Five hundred years stuck underground in a potter's turd and the first thing he has me do is babysit his paramour."

"Paramour?" she repeats incredulously, and the poker lowers a fraction. "I assume you mean Mainder, in that case. You seriously need to update your vocabulary."

"Not my first priority."

He hops off the mantel and disappears under the bed, emerging in triumph with a hunk of dust-covered cheese rind from his stash.

"Hungry?" He waves the rind in her direction, a peace offering of sorts.

"Starving," she sighs, but seeing how his face falls, she hastily adds, "but I won't deprive you. Looks like you've been saving that."

"Too kind," he mumbles indistinctly, already devouring the treat. "You know, you're not at all what I expected."

"How so?" she asks, unfolding herself and heading to the window. It's clear she's not wholly invested in his answer, peering down the path towards the lake, and Sweyn opens his mouth to reply before closing it again with a snap.

Mainder might believe his familiar has no more sense than a sparrow—and most of the time he'd be right—but even he knows better than to suggest to a lady that he'd been expecting to find someone prettier. Given how Mainder seems to have lost whatever good sense he ever possessed over this girl, he'd half been expecting some dazzling beauty. At the very least, she ought to have a decent bosom. Some of Mainder's past lady loves, he could have got happily lost for days in their cleavage.

This one is . . . well, none of that. Doesn't even keep her hair long. Can't expect to attract a man if you look like a boy. Obviously, that depends on the man in question, of course it does, but Mainder was never anything but traditional in that sense, especially when it came to mudside wenches. Tumbling locks and curves in all the right places, every time.

As he muses on this shocking departure from form, Evie turns back to face him, accurately decoding the reason behind his silence.

"You don't have to answer that," she says. "Anyway, we're doing this in the wrong order. Who are you?"

He shoots her an odd look. "Don't you mean, '*What* are you?'"

"No? Is that how you introduce yourselves over here? Hello, I'm human."

With the glint of mischief in her eye, he begins to see where her appeal lies. She's got something going on alright, even if she does seem a bit boring at first glance.

"Hello, human," he chirps, returning look for look. "I'm Sweyn. Normally when humans meet me in this form, they, uh, freak out a bit. You took me by surprise there."

"Ah," she says solemnly. "Yes, people can be stupid like that sometimes. Is Mainder on his way?"

Mainder, wrapped up in his own concerns, took mere days to decide Evie was his number one priority. Sweyn manages to reach the same conclusion in a matter of seconds. He hops up to the sill and points obligingly out towards the footpath.

"I left him down by the lake. He's really not happy, by the way. Someone's been messing with his stuff, and he hates that. He thinks there's an attack coming."

"Right," she says, twirling the poker in her hands. "Let's go and see if he wants any help."

She glyphs before he can process what he's seeing, leaving him standing foolishly on the windowsill with his mouth open.

"Well," he says to empty air. "Fuck me sideways."

Chapter 61

EVIE STEPS FROM the Path and recoils, hastily shielding her eyes. *Tren* has brought her where she needed to be, exactly as Mainder said it would, but rather than the moonlit serenity of the lakeside, there's a bonfire raging with two figures grappling inside the flames, lurching this way and that in a vicious struggle for survival. The soft mud of their arena has turned to baked clay, cracking under the weight of their scuffle, and the green of the forest's edge is wilting from the fierce heat. Through the fire, she can barely make out who's winning or even which limb belongs to which and who's punching whom.

At last, one of the figures seems to falter under the onslaught of the flames, missing blows and losing their grip, and they slump down in the clumsy embrace of the victor. It—he?—lets them drop on the steaming ground and stands back. The fire moves with him, and what remains is just barely recognisable as a man. He's a blistered oozing mess, flesh red-raw or a melted, bubbled grey, with shreds of blackened cloth clinging to his wounds and faint violet flames still licking at his neck. Incoherent, high-pitched moans escape him, with his lips burnt away and his tongue all but boiled in his head. One eye is gone altogether, boiled white and burst on his cheek; the other filled with blood, and his hands are twisted, blackened claws grasping feebly, still trying to put out the fire. It's sickening to watch. She can't believe he's even still alive with all that damage; he must be in agony. Why not finish him off? She feels an unwilling surge of sympathy for the beaten man. Whoever he is and whatever he's done, enough is enough.

She opens her mouth to say so and swiftly reconsiders. The figure standing over him isn't Mainder. If there ever was a mild-mannered shopkeeper in there somewhere, he's currently undetectable, subsumed into the flames and fuelling a nightmare. An unbound elemental stands in his place, a creature of flame with a core of pure, white-hot rage. It seems to have no form, no substance, only dozens of fiery wheels spiralling through each other, churning cogs generating a cape of oily black smoke. For a fleeting second, she thinks she can see Mainder still in the depths of the fire, something like the quirk of his brows above deep-set dark eyes, but then the wheels turn again and wipe the impression away.

The elemental steps towards her, and she automatically backs up a step. What if he doesn't recognise her? Will it even register her as a person, or is she just kindling? Its stance is watchful, wary, and she can see the wheels reforming and extending as if it's reaching for her. She turns and sprints for the cabin, not even bothering to try a glyph.

As she passes the bench, Mainder's voice, his normal voice, calls, "Evie, wait—" And despite the horror, she executes a skidding turn, sliding to a halt with one hand braced against the stone. He's just Mainder again, the flames gone and the wheels stilled, the smoke twisting away on the wind, and raw pain written in his eyes. He raises a blackened hand in a helpless gesture of appeal and apology, of resignation, and the last few sparks fall away from his fingertips and tumble down to die in the mud.

She cautiously straightens up and exchanges a glance with Sweyn. The little sprite looks shocked out of his shadowy skin, bright eyes round and pupils dilated to pinpoints, and he hops up to her shoulder again with his tail wrapped loosely around her neck. It feels like he's seeking comfort somehow, and the delicate weight of him there is a strange reassurance to her in turn. She puts a hand up to him and lays it gently against his chest, surprised to find that his transparent form has weight and texture, almost like petting a cat.

Mainder glances down at Clegg's still form and steps over him.

"Sweyn shouldn't have brought you here. I didn't mean for you to see that. Let's get you home," he says, his voice raw with remorse.

He refuses to meet her eyes as he comes closer, only holding out his hand palm-up to direct her. A mix of soot and sweat stains his palm, ingrained into the lines of his skin.

"This way."

She stares at the direction he's indicating, then back at him.

"Just like that? You're just going to take me to the door and, what, shove me back through without so much as a hello and goodbye? You scared the hell out of me. What even was that? Are you alright?"

A spasm of pain crosses his face, twisting his mouth as if he wants to reject the taste of the words even as he speaks them aloud. "It's not your problem, Evie. You need to go home."

She clasps the outstretched hand before he can withdraw it, stepping closer and peering urgently up into his face.

"Tell me you're alright."

'Sure. I mean, if you don't mind me lying to you. " He sighs. There's a hint of his usual smile flickering in his eyes, just a brief glimpse of mudside Mainder peeping out, and his hand tightens in hers before he firmly disengages. "I need to get you safely home. Maybe we can talk later."

"What the fuck do you mean—" she starts to object before they're both bowled off their feet by a heavy weight from the side. It's Clegg, somehow still alive. Not only that, but still moving. And not only moving but still, incredibly, on the attack. He's a mess of raw flesh and blisters, skin sloughing off in sheets, blood oozing from new wounds as he grabs Mainder's coat and shoves him into the churned-up mud at the lake's edge. He has to be in agony, and yet he keeps coming, rolling his enemy to the water's edge, grasping at his arms and pushing him down and down to the water.

Evie scrambles to her feet, staring in horror. "Aren't you going to do something?" she demands of Sweyn.

He shrinks back, sounding incredibly small and broken when he replies, "I can't. It's forbidden to act against people of the Realm."

"Are you serious? The more time I spend in this place the more I hate it," she says fiercely.

A few feet away, the poker gleams in the mud, dropped

from her hand when she came through the Path to find Mainder. With a scathing glance at Sweyn, she slides over to retrieve it and hefts it in her hand, its satisfying weight a lethal hammer ready for the right nail to present itself.

***

Mainder is almost out of time, and he knows it. Clegg's ruined hands may be clumsy, all finer sensation lost, but his desperate need for vengeance fuels new strength. He shoves the heel of his hand under Mainder's jaw and forces his head back into the mud-stirred shallows between the reeds. It's all he can do to bob his head back up for a frantic breath, and then he's under again, frantically twisting his hips and thrashing his legs, trying to unseat his assailant. Clegg may not have as much power in this place as he'd assumed, but he's still a dead weight on Mainder's more slender frame, pushing him down into the soft earth and sliding him inch by inch into the water. Both of them are severely weakened by the inferno Mainder unleashed just now, and here in the liquid mud stirred up by their struggle, Mainder fights to summon even a minor flame. Deep in the reeds, he can see pale faces popping up one after the other; the Vily, come to watch the show play out. So many of them. Surely they owe him aid, after all the lost youngsters he'd guided back safely to them over the years? Surely they'll do something.

It appears not. He chokes on another mouthful of brackish water mixed with seeping despair. He's going to meet his end here, drowned in his own lake in full view of the woman he swore to protect and with an interested audience of his own people, and the worst of it is that Clegg will be free to walk away, to heal, and to continue to put everyone he cares about in danger. He can't allow it. To his very death, he has to fight to prevent it. He goes limp, letting his mouth hang slack and unfocusing his eyes. One last chance to fight the miskin off, just one more before his strength gives out forever. Play dead and perhaps he'll let up for just long enough to give Mainder an opening.

But instead, Clegg lets out a gleeful rattle, a shadow of the triumphant bellow he'd normally be capable of, and leans heavily with both hands on the centre of Mainder's chest to push any remaining air from his lungs and finish the job. Ugly blue-black blotches appear at the edge of Mainder's vision, faint bells ringing in his ears, and he fixates on the red and grey blur above him.

Another pale shape hovers somewhere behind it, another face watching him breathe his last. One of the Vily, no doubt, looking for a better angle to observe. *A curse on you all*, he chokes. *May all your lakes be sulphur.* He's going to die here, he's going to die a failure, and worst of all he's going to die *angry*. There's nothing more he can do.

Suddenly, the weight on his chest is gone. The hands, gone. The blur of Clegg's ruined face, gone, and there are other hands behind him, under his head, under his shoulders, lifting him up out of the water and rolling him back to the safety of the shore. He weakly swipes the hands away and clutches instead at the shifting mud for support. There is none, but it doesn't matter anymore. He's back on dry-enough-for-now land, rolling on to his belly and retching miserably. His head pounds an agonising drumbeat of warning as he raises himself weakly to his elbows, empties his lungs and stomach of lake water and sinks back into the mud. It's almost comforting just to lie here for a moment with his cheek pillowed against the soft earth, almost like he could sleep now.

If it weren't for all the damn noise, that is. Frantic splashing somewhere nearby. Sweyn's voice piping in alarm. Waterlogged footsteps as someone wades in the shallows. He braces himself for the next attack, twisting his fingers to summon what's left of his fire.

It isn't needed. A pair of legs, mud-spattered and soaked to mid-thigh, come into view and stop next to him. The legs bend, somebody crouching beside him. A gentle hand touches his shoulder, and through the receding drums, he can hear somebody saying, "I think he's okay, no thanks to you lot.

Fucking useless."

Evie. He twitches, hand spasming against the mud, and shoves himself up a couple of inches to try to see her face.

"Clegg," he rasps. "Have to deal with Clegg."

"It's done," she says firmly, easing him back down. "And if a poker to the skull didn't do the job, my lovely assistants are going to hold him down until the bubbles stop.'. She looks past Mainder, out towards the lake, and calls in a clear, commanding voice, "And then they're going to hold him down some more."

Mainder twitches his aching head in that direction and sees a single Vila solemnly watching. She blinks slowly, and he swears he sees the flicker of a smile lift the corners of her mouth before she ducks back below the surface of the water.

Clegg is nowhere to be seen, but somewhere under the surface something is churning. Heavy swells break the moon's reflection into bright lines, racing to the lake's edge, and a swirl of tarnished silver bubbles marks a trail into the reeds.

Mainder manages to haul himself vaguely upright and settles himself in a miserable heap, wiping lake water and weeds out of his eyes. He can't even summon enough flame to dry himself out.

"Okay, look. This is unacceptable," Evie says, sitting down beside him. She sounds exhausted, and he notes with a jab of fresh concern the stained bandage across her knuckles. He draws breath to begin an apology, but she forestalls him. "No, you just shut up. I want this to be clearly understood, okay? If you ever, in the future, think you might end up wrestling in the mud with some mortal enemy in front of me, I want you to be absolutely sure you know you're supposed to do it shirtless. Are you hearing me?"

"What?" He gapes at her, trying to make sense of whatever that was. She cannot be joking, not at a time like this.

"Obviously you weren't to know," she advises kindly, patting him on the shoulder. "I don't make the rules, okay? Just remember for next time."

She's absolutely laughing at him. Damn it all.

As he finally manages to process the sheer nonsense of it, he starts to laugh, too, a helpless shiver of relief and unhoped for joy. Here at the lake, here in the Realm where nothing is ever nonsensical, where even the most ridiculous happening is purely a device to ensnare the unwary, here with the deadliest enemy he never knew he had lying dead at the bottom of his calm lake, this girl can find it in herself to make him laugh. What's more, she's capable of laughing herself, even after being transported to a whole other Realm, chased by the Hunt, and presented with Sweyn without warning. On top of that, seeing him in his altered state, pure destruction, and she's sitting beside him with the blood-spattered poker still gripped in her hand after saving his actual life and . . . she's still here. That she didn't turn tail and run screaming, that's some kind of miracle. He reaches for her and pulls her close, burying his face in her hair.

Chapter 62

HE HOLDS HER like that for a long time, it feels like. Maybe that's just an illusion caused by nobody actively trying to kill him for the duration, but he savours the sweetness of being alive, of her being alive and next to him, of her letting him feel like he's the one providing support when it's very much the other way round.

Movement on the far side of the lake brings them both instantly back to high alert. A tall, slender figure in dark green is pushing through the makeshift hole Mainder made in the hedge. Evie grabs the poker from the soft ground beside her and stands protectively over him.

"I had hoped to contribute to justice," Carney announces his presence, stepping out of the shadows. The hounds follow, clustered around his legs, but they look very different to the murderous pack from earlier. Now they look chastened, flinching and fawning around him as if seeking reassurance. With good reason—his long face, usually so calm, wears an unexpected expression of fury. His knees and sleeves are deeply stained with a mixture of grass, mud and gore. "I found the *adzo*, too late. I am sorry."

"Same," Mainder says, exhausted. "He never stood a chance."

Carney gestures at the dogs, and they immediately sit, fixed in place like a row of statues. Evie shivers at the display of subservience. If he can command them to stay, what else might he command them to do? And if he's one of the good guys, where the hell was he earlier?

"They will not attack again," he says, reading her apprehension. "And they would not have attacked you in any case. Is the border open?"

That last is obviously aimed at Mainder.

"It looks like it," Mainder answers, struggling to his feet.

"The Fold is exposed, at least one of the Paths blowing out all over the place. Smidur should be working on that on the other side."

"I see." Carney considers the implications. "I will be nearby when you need me." He glances again at Evie and favours her with a grave nod that's almost a bow. Then, without further fuss or fanfare, he disappears into the shadows with a low whistle, summoning the dogs to follow.

When Mainder doesn't seem to be in any hurry to explain, Evie breaks the silence.

"Friend of yours?"

"After a fashion. Haven't seen him in a while, but yeah. He's okay."

"What did he mean about being too late? The dogs got somebody, didn't they?"

"Yes," he says heavily. "I think it was Viktor. Must have been dragged through around the same time as you. I'm sorry."

"Oh," she says in a choked, small voice. 'I didn't like him much, but that's . . . That just makes it worse. Poor Viktor."

Since he had much the same feeling, he opts for a non-committal hum of assent. Tales of children lost in the woods don't always end in happy reunions and wicked stepmothers getting their just deserts, not in the real world, and he's seen too many tragedies to get misty-eyed over one more failure. But somebody somewhere will be grieving that boy, irritating as he was, and they deserve to know how the story ends. Some version that will make sense mudside anyway.

"We really should get you home." He cranes his neck, looking for Sweyn. "Where did that idiot go now? Sweyn! Where are you?"

"Here." And the sprite bounds into view with something clutched in his paw.

"What the hell is that?"

Mainder regrets the question when Sweyn triumphantly dangles the corpse of a tiny rodent by its tail, swinging it like a furry pendulum.

"Never mind. Cross back and find Smidur and see if he's got

the Fold under control yet. I need to clean up."

"Is it safe?" Evie queries with a note of concern.

"It is for me." Sweyn answers cheerfully. "The more it crackles, the more I like it, to be totally honest. I'll be right back."

He scurries a few feet away from them, swallows his furry snack whole, and vanishes.

Chapter 63

THE SHORT WALK up to the cabin almost exhausts him, trailing behind Evie and keeping an eye out for new threats just in case. The wards here are still in place at least, and as he shoves the door closed behind them and takes stock, it hits him just what a risk he took being away for so long. Anyone could have got in, and while he doesn't have a lot worth stealing over here, it would still have been an unwelcome invasion of his space. A vision of a would-be thief letting themselves in and immediately leaving again, disgusted by the dirt, brings a faint smile to his lips.

The cabin is a disgrace, no question. Thick dust covers every surface and is heaped in the corners of the room. The bed needs making — no, it needs wholesale stripping and remaking, as he comes close enough to smell the musty odour coming from the sheets. Did he seriously leave it in this state? How long has he been away, in Realm terms, anyway? He has no way of knowing until he talks to some of his own people. In any case, it's not the passage of time that's the issue, he's well-aware; it's entirely down to his own laziness in not leaving the cabin tidy for his return. To be fair, the last time he left it would have been in a hurry, under orders and under stress. Even so, a proper clean is well overdue. Too late to impress Evie, she's already seen it, but he can hope he'll have the opportunity to show her the place at its best another time. Basic comforts first. He kneels down with exquisite slowness, gripping the mantelpiece for support, and carefully lays a small fire.

While he does that, Evie settles in the chair and watches him with concern. He looks tired, battered, and bloodied and obviously in pain, but for some reason he's also somehow more *himself* than she's seen him before, more present and more real, like the difference between an old black-and-white movie and the digitally remastered version retouched with colour.

Something to do with being back on home soil perhaps. It takes him longer than she's happy with to complete the simple task, but she wills herself not to interfere. He needs to do this. Pain or no pain, he needs to feel effective right now. That notion is confirmed when he finally places the last piece of wood, sitting back on his haunches and closing his eyes briefly. He's concentrating, summoning the energy to call a small flame to his fingertips to light the kindling, and the smile that warms his face at even that small success rewards her patience. He sits still for far too long after even that small effort, though.

"Next time I come here, I'm bringing a box of matches," she announces, gently calling his attention back to the here and now.

He opens his eyes again and looks at her gratefully. "Good idea."

He stays where he is until he can see flames leaping up through the wood, then eases himself back up to standing and begins the fight to remove his coat. The heavy fabric clings stubbornly to his arms and back, but at last it releases its hold and he drops it to the floor with a sodden slap.

"Leave that there for now," he mutters to himself.

"Better," she approves from her ringside seat. "Shirt next. I'll help if you like."

He tries and fails not to smile at that. "I hope you're not trying to seduce me. I've literally just escaped certain death."

Her filthy chuckle fills the cabin. "Neither of us have the energy for seduction. Wet clothes off, right now, and then you're going to lie down while you have the chance."

He'd like to object, but she's not wrong. He desperately needs to rest. He laughs, a helpless wheeze, and begins the task of removing his shirt. It's fit for nothing now, anyway, even if he can get rid of the mud, and as he strips it off over his head he hears Evie take a sharp breath in. He glances at her strained face and follows her gaze to the marks on his stomach and ribs, mottled purple and black bruising from Clegg's weight on him and those jabbing fingers. There's blood too, smeared across his chest, and he prods experimentally to find the source. That's no help, since everything hurts no matter where he touches. It's a while before he can finally locate the cause, a scattering of tiny punctures under his left collarbone hidden amongst the ink of his tattoos. That wicked little spike Clegg was clutching when they met; that's the most likely culprit. He dimly recalls him lashing out with a closed fist during the beginning of their struggle.

"Huh," he says absently. "Didn't even feel it." He drops the shreds of his shirt to the floor and hesitates with one hand on the top button of his fly.

"I, um . . . This is the only other thing I have on," he says awkwardly. Talk about irony. Finally they have privacy, a comfortable bed, and at least one of them is getting naked, and it couldn't be further from his fevered imaginings. Nothing even remotely sexual about it. Between the pain, the cold, and the embarrassment, he's shrivelled to nothing in all the most crucial places, and that goes double for his ego.

She sighs and rises from the chair. "Right. I'll just be over here with my back turned, shall I?"

She crosses to the far wall and busies herself at the dresser while he tries to skin out of his trousers as quickly as possible.

It's hopeless, even worse than with his coat. The heavy twill seems to have soaked up half the lake and brought it back to the cabin with him, the moisture sucking at his skin as fast as he tries to peel the fabric away. He ends up balanced on one leg and then the other, easing each trouser leg off inch by frustrating inch while cursing fluently under his breath.

"Are you sure you don't want some help?" Evie enquires brightly. True to her word, she stays firmly facing the wall, but he can see her shoulders shaking with silent laughter.

"I've got this," he assures her with far more confidence than he's feeling. "Just let me — *damn it just fucking let go will you* — ah. There we go."

He abandons the heap of clothes and grabs the musty blanket from the bed, clutching it against his groin to preserve his dignity — a forlorn last stand after his performance in the battle so far. This is ridiculous.

"You are ridiculous," Evie echoes his thoughts, approaching with the basin balanced carefully in one hand and a bundle of torn fabric in the other. "Lie back and let me deal with that."

"This is all my fault, you know," he sighs, settling obediently back on the pillow. "I should never have let it get this far."

"Mmhmm," is the only answer. She's focused on his wounds, concentrating on removing a layer of mud to assess the damage beneath.

He shifts uncomfortably, twitching his shoulders so she has to stop momentarily, and she looks at him in concern.

"Are you okay?"

"Fine," he assures her. "I heal fast, dirt or no dirt. Listen, I should have prevented this, but I wanted to leave the Fold powered up so I could bring you here. You understand?"

"Not really." The linen lies forgotten in her hand. "What for?"

Her innocent question feels like being stabbed all over again. *What for?*

"So you could see the place. See if you liked it . . . " He almost flinches but forces the rest of the sentence out. ". . . enough to stay here with me."

She doesn't answer. He opens his eyes to see the effect of his words, and she's not even looking at him. Her gaze is fixed on the window, the path down to the lake, and he knows beyond all doubt that she's thinking about the hounds and Clegg wrestling him to the shallows.

"This is my place, Evie," he says desperately. "I can promise you nobody here wishes you harm. That thing with Clegg . . . " He pauses, touching her hand for emphasis. "Evie, that wasn't about you. It wasn't about that poor lad either. He was just in the wrong place. It was all to get back at me for something that happened centuries ago."

"That doesn't make it better. Viktor's just as dead." Her voice shakes as she says the word. "Doesn't matter if it wasn't personal. And if I hadn't been able to get in here, I would have been next."

"Clegg's gone. Carney has the dogs back under control.

You'd be safe here with me, I promise."

"And without you?" She looks back at him now, raw misery in her eyes. "Viktor never stood a chance, did he? Because he didn't have anybody invested in protecting him. You probably weren't even looking for him. Were you?"

Words refuse to form in his aching throat. She has every right to reproach him for that, every right to be wary of what he's offering. Every right to never ever want to see him, speak to him, set foot on this side of the Divide ever again. His whole chest aches, struggling to rise and fall and get breath back into his body.

"It feels like I'm only safe as long as you say so," she goes on. "That's not a good feeling. What if we fell out?" The forgotten basin tilts in her lap, slopping water over the bedclothes, and she catches it with an irritated *tsk*. "Let me finish getting you cleaned up. One crisis at a time, yes?"

She's right; he isn't going to argue. This conversation needs to be had once they're properly rested, and most definitely not in the emotional aftermath of this disaster. He can heal, yes, and much faster than the average human might after the same punishment, but that requires power and power requires fuel. Sleep, definitely. Food, maybe. Alcohol . . . Well, actually no, it has the reverse effect, but on the bright side it makes it so you don't care as much. Until the hangover kicks in, that is. It's immaterial, anyway. There's no food in the cupboard and certainly no whisky. Sleep is the only viable option, and he's rapidly drifting in that direction. Her touch is absurdly comforting—far from gentle, as she picks away at the caked-on mud and soot and uncovers the extent of his tiny wounds—but it's been such a long, lonely time since anybody was so invested in his well-being. He lets himself relax. They can talk later.

Chapter 64

HE'S A MUCH less troublesome patient once he starts snoring. Evie finishes removing the layer of dirt and leans closer to check the tiny punctures across his chest. Just as he said, they're rapidly fading. Even his tattoos are healing, pinpricks of dark ink blooming and expanding to fill in the breaks in the pattern as soon as the skin is whole again. It's an unsettling sight, the more so since she can now see the pattern clearly and knows what those interlocking spirals represent. At the same time, it's strangely beautiful. She swipes her thumb gently across the new skin, testing it, but snatches her hand away guiltily when he tenses and breathes out sharply.

"Sorry," she murmurs and collects the basin to return to the dresser before she's tempted to maul him again.

Adrenaline is one hell of a drug, but the withdrawal symptoms are a bitch. With no immediate threats and nothing pressing to do, it's as if someone has cut her strings. *Drop where you stop; there's no need of you anymore.* She eyes the fireside chair, wide and sturdy and stuffed with a haphazard arrangement of cushions. It would leave the bed free for Mainder to rest properly, especially if he's going to be weird about being naked near her. Plus, now she has time to think about it, she's still damp from wading in the lake. Being closer to the fire would be a definite advantage there.

She slips off her wet shoes with a sigh of relief, tiptoeing back to the bed for one last check. Still sleeping, and - damn it, he's lying on all the covers so she can't claim a blanket without disturbing him. There were spares in the cupboard though, she recalls. That'll do.

Before she can move away, a warm hand grabs her arm, and he sits half up in panic.

"Don't leave," he mumbles urgently. "Evie, don't leave."

His eyes are barely open, unfocused and dark. She lets out a breath on a laugh, easing him back to the bed. "Where would I go?"

"Don't know. Just don't." And with that he's asleep again, like a light flicked on and off. Unbelievable. With a glance at the chair, she accepts the inevitable. If he won't settle if she's too far away, well then he'll just have to deal with the awkwardness of it all once he wakes up. Serves him right for making it weird.

***

Dawn brings rain, blattering against the window in irregular bursts and driving sleep away. Mainder floats to consciousness in easy stages despite the noise, surrounded by the feel and the sounds and the scents of home and held securely in his feather mattress's loving embrace. Worth every mark of whatever it was he originally paid for it way back when. His waking brain politely serves up yesterday's concerns one after the other, as if not to overload him. There should be somebody here — that's right. Somebody he needs to keep safe, somebody who by rights should be —

Should be — *where is she?* He reaches out in panic, flinging his arm out clumsily until he at last makes contact.

He turns carefully, cursing the twanging white-hot pain across his chest, and reviews the situation. He's relieved to find her, and even more so to find her resting peacefully, but something feels off. She's too far away for a start, up against the far edge of the bed by the wall as if she's trying not to get too close. That's his own fault, his misplaced shyness last night probably making her feel she needed to create some distance. What's worse though is the position she's lying in, curled up at an uncomfortable skew across her side of the bed with her arms wrapped around herself as if seeking warmth.

He's an idiot. His dead weight was hogging the covers, so not only is she uncomfortable, she's freezing for the benefit of his foolish pride. He fumbles for the blanket's edge, throwing it over her body and closing the gap between them with a determined twitch of his hips so he can wrap his arm around her. As he settles back, he concentrates for a second and sends out a wave of heat, just enough to set the moisture still trapped in her clothing steaming off into the air. She stirs, an appreciative murmur of thanks, and gradually straightens her body out to a more natural position that brings her closer to him. One chilled hand creeps across and rests against his chest, fingers curling gently against his skin, and it feels like the most natural, the most right thing in the world. In both worlds. He tightens his arm around her and closes his eyes again, determined to savour every moment before the universe decides to fuck him over again.

***

Pressure on his bladder eventually rouses him again—a consideration even for elementals, since taking human form means also taking on the full range of human habits and needs and, sadly, weaknesses. The stinging sensation grows despite his best efforts to ignore it, signalling that it will resolve the situation by itself in short order whether he moves or not. There's no avoiding it. He cautiously eases himself over, raising a sleepy murmur of discontent from Evie, and begins the effort of extracting himself from the warm hollow of the mattress.

He manages to sit up and instantly regrets it; everything hurts, and underneath that everything hurts some more. He halts in place to breathe through the pain. Yesterday's wounds may be healed on the surface, but assorted body parts are making it known that there's still work to do before he's whole. Fading bruises still decorate his torso, mottled blue and yellow and tender to the touch, and an experimental stretch confirms that his right shoulder is vaguely misaligned, clicking alarmingly when he tries to rotate the joint. Not good. Next, he swings his legs out of bed and halts for a second, bracing for impact.

He should have braced more though, or better yet stayed off his feet altogether. Whatever is going on with his shoulder is nothing compared to the stabbing pain that shoots up his left leg when he tries to put his weight on it. Bending down to find the chamber pot that may or may not be under the bed is beyond him in this state, and things are rapidly becoming urgent. He grits his teeth, clutches the bedpost for support, and manages to make it out to the porch to deal with the most urgent business at hand. Anybody passing by this morning is going to get an unscheduled full-frontal viewing, but at least there will be no embarrassing puddles on the cabin floor.

The sun is just coming up above the trees, warming the damp grass and sending the morning's rain steaming off into the air. The only clouds in sight now are faint white wisps, scudding along in the distance over towards the river, and it looks set to be a beautiful day even by Realm standards.

He leans for a while on the door frame, taking in the sight, but eventually turns his back and returns to the — in his opinion — more appealing view. Evie is still sleeping peacefully. Faint tear tracks stain her cheeks, whether old or recent he's not sure, and the hand that was resting on his chest last night is now curled around the edge of the pillow like a child keeping hold of their favourite toy. She's been through a lot already, and she's still not safely home. Where the hell is Sweyn? If nothing is happening with the door just yet, then he'll need to make sure she's cared for here until she can return. It feels odd to be responsible for her in that way. But then, relationships are another area where he's desperately out of practice. Last time he had an overnight guest here would be . . . No, he's got nothing. He honestly can't remember, not name nor face nor details, and the only thing he can definitely say for sure is that she was on her way out of the door at first light without a backwards glance. And on the other side? He tries to calculate how long it's been and gives up when he can't even remember whether it was before or after he took possession of the shop. More than a century, anyway, and even then, it was a working girl. A transaction, not a seduction, and most definitely not a relationship.

That's the heart of it. Relationships end. Not just the romantic ones but the friendships, too, because the people on the other side are just too damn short-lived. Even if someone can hold his attention, they're aged and gone in no time from his perspective. Many's the time he's considered coming home, settling down if anybody here would want him and retiring if nobody does. But it doesn't appeal. His mudside friendships so far may have been all too short and inevitably tinged with regret, but his friendships in the Realm are virtually non-existent. It's a brutal realisation he's experiencing right now, gazing at Evie—a cruel trade of either keeping her here, using the Realm's energy to extend the time they can have together, or sending her safely home and never ever seeing her again because he can't bear to have it end like all the others.

It's a hopeless scenario. She already made her feelings on the Realm perfectly clear. Even if she thought he was worth staying for, she'd be miserable.

Chapter 65

EVIE WAKES TO the sound of muffled rustling, a door swinging open and creaking shut again, and whispers on the edge of hearing. It's not threatening in any way; rather, it's the distinctive cadence of domesticated man performing the "where the hell did I put that" dance.

She leans up to place the noise and sees Mainder, half-hidden behind the open cupboard door, reaching up to the top shelf for something. He emerges a few seconds later, moving with extreme caution and obviously favouring one leg. He's half-dressed, yesterday's trousers apparently considered fit enough to wear for now, and she frowns at the mess of welts and bruises on his ribcage.

"What happened to 'healing fast'?" she queries, and he spins to face her. The movement makes him grimace in pain, and he hops slightly to balance himself on his good leg before he answers.

"Better than it was, trust me. I just need a little more time and maybe some food. Until we find some, can I interest you in a cup of tea?" He waggles the teapot suggestively at her. "Kettle's on anyway, might as well take advantage."

"Tea," she breathes. "I'd love one . . . Wait, aren't there rules or something? Like if you eat or drink anything in Fairyland, you have to stay there forever?"

He lets out a crack of laughter.

"Half a story, as always. Used to be that your lot, when they crossed over, they'd end up sneaking into someone's home and helping themselves from the larder or the garden. Well, there are rules here. No supermarkets, no corner shops, so somebody taking food means someone else going without, you see? We take that sort of thing very seriously. The penalty for that sort of theft is that you owe the person you stole from some recompense, usually a term of service. Seven years, I think is traditional."

"Seven years for a cup of tea?" she demands incredulously. "What do I get for taking a biscuit?"

"Irrelevant," he says with a twinkle. "I don't have any biscuits. Tea, yes or no? I promise you will still be free to leave."

The scene is absurdly domestic as he places the kettle on its stand in the fireplace and starts laying out what he needs. A shelf from the cupboard serves as a low table, propped on two split logs from the woodpile. Aside from the teapot and cups, there's the tea canister, the red and gold dragon glowing against the translucent white of the china. He adds the shallow pan from the fireplace and extracts a handful of faded yellow petals from a tin on the mantelpiece, crumbling them between his fingers and scattering them over the bottom of the pan.

"Marigold," he explains. "Good for healing. How's your hand?"

She flexes her fingers, frowning at the grubby tinge of her disintegrating bandage and the spots of dried blood that had soaked through during the night.

"Stings a bit," she admits.

"Right. Tea first, and then we'll get that cleaned up."

She sits back and watches him bustle about the tiny cabin, and the strange impression she had earlier of him growing more real here spreads to the cabin itself, as if with his returning strength comes a return to the spirit of the place itself, spreading outwards from him. The room is still dusty, but somehow the wood block floor takes on a warmer tone under his bare feet. The wrinkled bedclothes stay wrinkled, but the white linen seems to brighten with each pass he makes near the bed. There used to be sayings, didn't there, about the fireplace being the heart of the home? The word *focus* literally means *hearth*, after all. He's the focus here, the fire that holds the place together, and it brightens the more he touches it.

The kettle finally comes to the boil, and he pours a measure of hot water first over the crumbled petals in the pan, then the remainder into the teapot.

"It's safe to drink, right? How long has it been there?"

"Good question." He looks struck. "I mean, it's been a few hundred years mudside — uh, on your side — but might only have been a few days here. Path energy has been all over the place."

"That's more than a few days' worth of dust," she says tartly, letting the "mudside" thing slide for now. "Although your little friend had a stash of something, cheese I think, under the bed. It looked a bit on the furry side, but it must have been okay."

"Maybe. Okay for Sweyn, perhaps, but that's not the same as okay for you and me. You seriously would not believe the things I've seen that little bastard eat." He chuckles to himself. "Trust me, you do not need the details. But if it was still recognisable as cheese, furry or otherwise, that means no more than a few months. Maybe a year at most."

The tea certainly smells okay. Better than okay; as the steam curls up to meet her, she detects a hint of bergamot in with the tannin.

"Earl Grey? You certainly know how to make a girl feel special. Where did this come from?"

"Oh, I had a travelling phase before I settled down in Alfriscombe. I used to do a circuit every few years up to London, up again to Liverpool to see what was coming off the docks, down to Bristol, and then back down this way. That was just around when coffee houses started to be a thing. Purely coincidentally —" he pauses to gently capture her injured hand, picking at the knot on the bandage " — that's also when I stopped coming back here so much."

"What, because of coffee?"

"Because of coffee," he confirms with a lurking twinkle. "It doesn't grow here, you see. I don't know why."

He keeps a firm grasp on her hand, noting her sudden pallor. Likely the emotional strain is making itself known, so he keeps up a flow of chatter as a distraction while he soaks a pad of clean linen in the infusion he's prepared.

"They make something they call coffee on this side, but you know what they make it from?"

She shakes her head faintly.

"Acorns," he announces with a disgusted face. "You know that old joke about bad coffee? Tastes like mud because it was fresh ground this morning? Well, that's acorn coffee."

She lets out a weak chuckle, and he takes advantage of the moment to squeeze the excess moisture from the pad and press it gently to her knuckles. She flinches at the sting, and he pauses his monologue to murmur, "Nearly done now. Are you okay?"

Her shaky nod is less than convincing, but he lets it pass while he finishes cleaning the grazes and binding it with a clean bandage.

"That should hold for a while. Finish your tea while I check something."

He moves the kettle and the copper pan to the hearth, then comes back carrying the leather roll from his pack and a slab of wood with four holes bored into it.

"Hope this still works," he murmurs, unfurling the roll and stirring the jumble of metal pieces with his finger.

"What is it?"

"It's an *otla*. A sensor." He retrieves a handful of the metal rods first and sets them into the holes, then repeats the search for springs. "It's a lot like a barometer, I suppose, for Path energy. It reacts to the phase differential on the Divide and tells us where we are in relation to the other side."

The springs slide over the pegs one by one, then the curved plates slot into place resting on three of them. The fourth peg has a shallow groove running halfway down its length, and he carefully slides the centre of the flattened copper coil into the groove before adding the hatpin and giving it a practised twist to set it turning. Fully assembled, it looks just like an instrument gauge, the needle sweeping back and forth searching for its mark.

"How does that work?"

"Smidur could explain it better. Sónnarson," he clarifies in response to her quizzical look. "Mechanisms and such are his speciality. It has to do with the stone in the counterweight—that was quarried and cut on your side. It sort of remembers where it came from, if that makes sense, and keeps the time from that place in mind. Once it's done a sweep to calibrate, it'll settle somewhere, and where it lands tells us which phase your side is at. We need to know so we can cross without losing time on either side."

The needle twitches on its spiral coil, idling one way then the next, like a compass seeking true north.

"Might be a while before it settles down. It's one of those things that won't happen if you're waiting for it, don't ask me why."

He busies himself at the cupboard again, rooting through the folded blankets on the top shelf and occasionally turning to peer over at the needle in case it'll move when it thinks he's not looking. It's almost comical, especially the rueful twist of his lips every time it fails to oblige.

At length, he finishes his search of the linens and emerges with a shirt that has seen better days, but at least no one appears to have been stabbed in it recently.

"Might as well be decent," he pronounces and tosses it over the bedpost while he closes the cupboard. "There might be another cup in the pot if you're interested?"

She hands over her empty teacup for a refill, and the needle chooses that precise moment to calibrate and settle.

"Told you," he crows. "We just had to pretend we weren't watching."

The needle vibrates gently a fraction of a hairsbreadth away from the indent at the very end of the gauge, with the coil it sits on wrapped tight around the central peg.

"Perfect. Stay right there," Mainder announces, whether to her or the needle she's not sure, and he hurries out the door, shrugging on the spare shirt.

Chapter 66

THE CABIN SETTLES back to silence, just her and her thoughts for company, but even with him gone, it still retains the glow he brought to it. It feels like home, like safety. But what about the world beyond these timber walls? Could she learn to like the place enough to stay here with him?

It feels like several steps at once, maybe a step or two too far. He seemed to be hinting that he didn't intend to come back, and that makes no sense to her. Something else must be going on. Surely he has far more available to him there than what she's seen here. As for her, what she'd be leaving behind — she almost can't count. The family business, just when Roger finally felt ready to retire. The people relying on her, the careers she's helped to start, scattered. Family, too. Roger and David counting down the days until her next visit home, so they can be waiting in front of Aberdeen airport with balloons and flowers and teddy bears to embarrass the ever-loving crap out of her in front of her fellow travellers. Angie, waiting to introduce her new baby daughter. She can't do that to them or to herself. Some responsibilities can't be dismissed with the wave of a hand, not even for "true love."

She stares down into her empty cup, tipping it this way and that to watch the remnants of the tea leaves swirl into different patterns. By rights, there should be some insight hiding in the leaves. A vision of some kind, a shape of her possible future. What is it you're supposed to see — a crown, a skull? Block capitals spelling out *EVIE GO HOME*? All she can see is fragments caught on a ripple in the glaze at the bottom that if she tilts the cup and squints look a bit like a WiFi symbol.

She huffs a laugh to herself; there's her answer, then. If she can't find a way to connect to home, then she can't stay. That was the real challenge she was picking at without even knowing it, of course. Can she be useful here? Can she be busy? Can she manage her other life, everything she has waiting for her on the other side, from a couple of logs and a shelf in front of the fire? As the ultimate in remote working, it has a certain appeal.

But it's like being on holiday — the difference between exploring some quaint little village on a bright summer's day with the hanging baskets all in bloom, and living there through a miserable, wet winter when the buses stop running and the corner shop is out of teabags.

A crow lands on the windowsill outside, tapping its beak against the glass, and she smiles and sits back to watch it. Not that there's much else she could do. Is Mainder in the habit of feeding the birds? If so, they're out of luck today; there's nothing in the cabin she could contribute. Not even a biscuit. She spreads her empty hands wide apologetically.

The crow cocks its head and expands in a sudden flurry of dark dust. When it settles down again, the shape at the centre turns out to be Sweyn, dancing on the sill to keep his balance before abandoning the battle and materialising inside instead.

He rolls over onto his back like a cat, scratching his back against the wood grain of the window seat.

"Fuck, that's better," he sighs. "Feathers are alright for a bit, but if they go the wrong way they itch, you know?"

Footsteps approach, the door swings open and Sónnarson/Smidur's voice floats through. ". . . not sure how long it may hold."

"It'll do for now," Mainder says, leading him in. "I'll finish repairing the damage on this side. Here she is," he adds as introduction, making eye contact with Evie with a faint lift of his brows. *Are you alright?* that glance says, and she returns him a slight nod of reassurance.

"He wants to get you home as soon as possible."

"We should leave now," Smidur confirms, leaning over the *otla* and touching a careful fingertip to the counterweight. "She will only have been missing for a few hours."

The cabin seems overfull now, with both of them standing around her chair and talking over her head. It sparks a memory, several in fact, and none of them good. Being small again, being shoved in a corner with a colouring book and some crayons and told to stay quiet while the grown-ups discussed what to do with her. There probably weren't that many occasions in reality, but she well remembers the sting of it, the remarks flying past about her, about just how gosh-darned difficult it was to know what to do with her. She keeps quiet now, just as she used to then, sensitive to some hint in the air that there are bigger concerns right now than her ego.

Her instinct is correct; Smidur digs in his pocket and extracts two small rectangles, which turn out to be security passes from the project.

"These are the others you need to find."

Mainder peers at the first. "Did you even look at these? *T. Clegg, Night Shift*. Look familiar?" He waits for understanding to dawn, then skims the pass into the fire with a disgusted flick of his fingers. It wilts instantly, burning with a turquoise flame until it bubbles and shrinks to a lump, falling through the bottom of the grate with a pathetic *tink*. "That saves me a job."

"Who's the other one?" Evie asks sharply, and he hands her the pass. Laura Monaghan, a young woman with long dark hair and a round face, stares back at her. The photo is missing her distinctive dimpled smile, but it's still a good likeness. "Oh, god, I know Laura. From the admin team."

"I've seen her before," Mainder says, taking back the pass and pressing a reassuring hand to Evie's shoulder. "Don't worry. I'll find her and get her home."

"You make it sound simple."

"It mostly is. It's like the crystal; she's not on the side she belongs on. Once I find her, I get her to the nearest Path back, and it'll return her to whichever door she crossed through."

"How very neat," she says lightly. "And then you'll be coming back too, right?"

Smidur already has the door open and is waiting anxiously on the threshold; no protracted farewells, then.

Mainder hasn't answered her question, but she doesn't press him. She keeps her eyes down, locating her damp shoes under the chair, grimacing as she slips them on. She finds herself strangely reluctant to even look at him; his face might give away the answer, and it might not be the one she's hoping to hear.

"Alright then. I'm ready."

The goodbye is left hanging, unsaid. That means it isn't really goodbye, doesn't it? It's more like *I'll see you soon*. It helps to think of it that way.

Chapter 67

THE CAVERN LIES in darkness, undisturbed other than distant ripples heard rather than seen. Somewhere in the dimness, water drips from the roof, so slowly that if you held your breath and counted, you'd run out of air before the next droplet fell.

Now scraping footsteps disturb the calm. Heavy boot soles clump against the rock, and what little light seeps in this far is blocked by a tall figure casting a long shadow before him. Eventually there's no light at all, twists and turns taking him deeper into the blackness.

He could easily choose to light his way if he needed to, could fill this hole in the ground with righteous flame to scorch the black away forever, but he chooses not to.

For now.

At the water's edge, only the faintest of sheer glows suggests that the Vily are nearby. Their non-appearance would usually signify that they're not at home to visitors today, but this is not a social call.

"A task for you," he announces sternly to the silent cavern. "Another *adzo*. Bring me news."

He doesn't wait for an answer, turning on his heel and stalking away.

"Not the most cooperative, that lot," Sweyn says. "You sure they'll help?"

"They'll help," Mainder responds grimly. "They fucked up, with Clegg and the hunt and all, and they know it. They owe me."

"Yeah, they ought to be embarrassed. I'm surprised they didn't figure it out when she came through."

Mainder isn't really paying attention, too deep in his own concerns, what with missing Evie already and being angry about just about everything in general. He hums something non-committal and steps back out to the cascades, tasting the air. He's uncomfortably aware how out of practice he's become.

"It's no big deal to miss the odd *yasim*," he says eventually. "It took me a while, too. She hides it well."

"No shit," Sweyn says incredulously. "You think she's only half-blood?"

"Of course. What else could she be?"

"*What else could she be?*" Sweyn mimics disgustedly. "Think about it. She doesn't have a token, does she? But she landed here without a scratch, bang on the dark water path, exactly where you'd expect if she was coming home. Didn't wash up somewhere at random like they usually do."

"That could be a coincidence," Mainder argues. "The boy that got caught by the hunt must have come through somewhere here. Or do you think he was one of ours as well?"

"Not a trace of him in here. Do you trust my nose or not? She's got an aura a mile wide. Moon on water, or I'm a one-legged sparrow. Did you go blind while you weren't looking?"

"Apparently so. I didn't—"

Mainder halts, brought up short by realisation. He did, though. He sensed something from day one. Wondering what she was about, what she was hiding, *why* she was hiding. Testing to get her attention. Arranging to be where she was, lurking in corners to observe. The constant creeping fear that something somewhere was out of phase. Staring at her face by moonlight, the fascination with her filthy laugh, the jealousy, the joy in her company . . .

Good news! You're not in love. Well, probably. The bad news is you're an idiot.

***

It takes a while to get to the river. Of course, he could just call a Path to wherever he needs to be right now, but he opts for the longer route to give him time to think. There are subtle changes all around, a marker of the time that's passed in the Realm while he's been busy across the Divide, and he's curious to see what's new. A couple of dwellings stand empty, windows dark and fences overgrown, where he'd have expected to see friendly faces, but farther along there's timber stacked and brambles cleared, hinting at new settlement.

As early as it is, there are only a few faces out and about to see him pass, but he gathers a few cautious nods as he heads along the steadily broadening path.

As he comes within sight of the river, a whispered "Finder?" stops him, turning back to see who wants him. A youngster in faded green is watching him warily from the undergrowth, long slender fingers twisting nervously in the hem of their shirt. They have the sallow skin and wide-set hazel eyes common to many forest families, and the dark red cloth cap draped on the back of their head only just covers the pointed tips of their ears.

He frowns, hoping for a spark of recognition, but nothing comes.

"That's me," he says at last. "You need me?"

"The girl in the water said you should know. She said to follow the flotsam path."

The child blends back into the green, mission discharged.

"Gods help me," Mainder sighs. "I give them a simple task, and they send me infants with fucking riddles. 'Flotsam path' — what even is that about?"

***

The river road is broad and calm, a shining ribbon splitting the Realm into its neat halves just as it ever did — day and night, light and dark. Behind him, the forest and the caverns and the still lakes under stone, home to the dark dwellers, the woodsmen and the misfits like himself. On the far side, a swathe of well-kept green, broad paths of pale stone picked clean of weeds winding between neat gardens and orchards and the tidy dwellings of their owners. On that side of the river, the residents have always been more inclined to precision and order, bending nature to their preferences rather than the other way round. Mainder doesn't hate it exactly; it's alright to visit, but there are many very good reasons why he chose to make his own home up against the forest's edge.

Barely a quarter of a mile upstream, the graceful span of a stone bridge offers a convenient crossing. There are boats, of course, but theft is severely punished here in the Realm. Not even the Queen's own Finder can get away with that. He heads that way, idly picking at an almost-realisation in his mind.

"Flotsam," he says suddenly. "Flotsam and jetsam. Isn't that what they call the trash that washes up after shipwrecks?"

Sweyn shrugs. "I'm not a fucking dictionary, am I. Why don't you ask a scholar? We're about to be knee-deep in them." He eyes the neat dwellings on the far riverbank with disfavour.

"No need," Mainder says. "Somewhere there's a place where people wash up. You said it yourself: somewhere at random. Except it wouldn't be, would it? The Path doesn't do random. It'll put them where it makes sense to put them. Wherever that is, that's where we need to be."

Chapter 68

THE CITY SHINES, clean and bright in the sun at the mountain's peaks. If anywhere feels like home, it should be here, surrounded by everything he's been working to protect.

Home. He wonders when that word stopped making him happy. *This is home*, he tells himself again. He's finally back. Back where he belongs, back in his proper shape and his proper attire, strolling down the broad, cobbled avenue from the tower, exchanging nods with familiar faces. He'd got unaccustomed to the sheer variety of people here, of different heights and builds and colours of skin and fur and feathers, and the sprites leaping about, riding on shoulders or scuffling in the dusty gutters. It doesn't feel alien, exactly; it's just that it's slightly too much of everything and, at the same time, not enough. There's a thinness to it all, a lack of depth, as if he's walking through a stage set. It's everything it should be and yet it's not.

The solution to that is waiting for him back on the other side of the Divide, or so he very much hopes.

The lower he goes through the streets, the less the city sparkles. Up at the peak, the Queen's tower, it's all fine pale stone and silver wood, serene and spotless and well-kept. Down on the lowest level, it's rough cob and bare rock, ramshackle huts pushed up against the curtain wall and patched with anything that comes to hand.

Much as mudsiders decorate their living rooms with exotic artefacts from distant cultures, so the inhabitants of the Realm liven up their surroundings with oddments from across the Divide. Through windows and open doorways, he glimpses road signs and Tupperware, paperback novels, and multiple yellowing posters from *Cottle's Travelling Circus!* tacked across a bare timber wall in lieu of paint. A few people are wearing heavy, black oval pendants, and he grins to himself as he recognises an Audi logo on one. Car key fobs, apparently the latest fashion. Whatever next? It raises a belated swell of affection for his people, even as it cements the feeling that he's on the wrong side.

Right at the furthest outer edge of the city, there's a neighbourhood of sorts, midway between the two lower gates. From here, you can't even see the gates themselves, only the towering wall and the cobbled street leading up to the higher reaches and the intimidating towers of the citadel. It's decent enough land, but it's mostly unclaimed, city dwellers preferring the neater plots lining the river and the road or, alternatively, to be up inside the inner wall with proper roads and gutters. But there is a road of sorts, a dusty mud track that hugs the wall, and it leads to a cluster of . . . He would say houses, but these structures hardly seem to fit the category. Lean-tos, perhaps, if every part was leaning on something that was leaning on something else, with no way of telling what was there first. Poverty and scarcity, this neighbourhood signals, put together with whatever goes unclaimed by anyone else. Even the Realm has its outcasts.

A gap in the frontage reveals an arch to nowhere, standing in the middle of a bare patch of ground almost up against the wall. The arch is neither beautiful nor graceful, though it has its own charm; something of an optical illusion, like a Möbius ribbon built from leavings and findings of a dozen or more mismatched types of stone. He can see familiar rough lumps of red sandstone exactly like half of Alfriscombe. There's granite in there too, and sea-smoothed chert with thick veins of quartz, leaves of dark slate, and the carved remnants of a trefoil window on the keystone at the top. There's even, when he crouches to examine the base, a chunk of mudside brick still embedded in mortar, a piece of somebody's garden wall.

It's a clever structure, but it seems to have no real purpose. There's nothing but blank wall on the far side, no doorways or gates, and no road unless you count the fact that the grass doesn't seem to grow quite as thickly underneath it. He stays crouched, sighting through the arch. If he's not mistaken, the shorter grass describes a footpath that leads up to this arch and then stops. The weeds grow tall on the other side, a separation as abrupt as if they'd been deliberately mown in a neat straight line. So . . . a path that goes this far and no further. Or, to look at it a different way, a path that begins directly under the arch without anyone having approached it from the other side.

"I think this is the place," he says. "The flotsam path. Look at the arch."

He tastes the air, half-expecting the stench of *tros*, but instead it just smells like mudside, of wintry sun on city streets, yesterday's newsprint, the earthy tang of beach sand, and a hint of saffron and diesel fumes.

Sweyn jumps down and hops through the arch and back again, but nothing happens. "Didn't feel anything," he reports. "Bit of a shiver maybe."

"Perhaps it only works from the other side." Mainder walks to the arch and follows Sweyn's example, stepping through braced for trouble. Nothing happens. He sighs and turns back, stopping dead when he sees what anyone else coming through the arch would see. Leaning against the shack opposite, there's a painted tin sign, a mudside artefact.

Beneath the text, a painted arrow has been added, pointing directly to the shack's open doorway.

"So they wash up here," he muses. "They come through the arch, and then they see that. 'Travellers welcome'. What does that look like to you?"

"I dunno, a welcome sign?" Sweyn picks at something in his ear and examines it closely.

Mainder strolls around the shack to the other side, and there he finds a shabby storefront, the window lined with driftwood shelves displaying the owner's wares. A child's lunchbox sits in pride of place, cheerful cartoon characters chasing each other across the green plastic lid. Pinned to a board, there are a dozen or more leather keyrings with bright metal tags in familiar shapes: Volvo, Audi, Volkswagen. *Good luck charms*, the sign declares. His eyes crinkle in brief amusement, but underlying that, there's a dawning bitterness.

"No," he says. "It's bait."

There's no movement in the storefront or the room beyond, but in the back somewhere, he can hear a woman singing to herself. He walks unhurriedly through the shop, touching the items on the shelves and silently tallying up how many souls must have passed through here to leave so much behind. A bright bead curtain covers the doorway at the back of the shop, and he stands very still next to it and listens, motioning Sweyn to do the same. The song is nothing, a nonsense melody with a gentle cadence that's almost a lullaby, hardly a siren call. It's uncomfortable to listen to for some reason, and after a moment, he understands why. It's not the song of someone singing for the joy of it, nor someone stretching their voice to train it to hit the notes. It's the song of someone who's been instructed to be singing, someone who's heard that sometimes people sing to themselves but has never learned what that sounds like when it's genuine. It's camouflage.

He breathes out sharply and lifts the clattering strings of beads aside. A woman sits at a table in the corner, every inch of workspace covered with trinkets and scraps, even the bleached walls beside her peppered with hooks holding coils of ribbon and string and tape. Her dress is nothing more than scraps and twists of fabric from a dozen different garments, a skirt made of a dozen or more silk scarves shifting around her feet in an invisible breeze. Beside her on a patchwork cushion, a bundle of fluff uncoils and blinks bright blue eyes at them, yawning ostentatiously to display its needle-sharp teeth, and settles with a wary eye on Sweyn. The woman is busy emptying the contents of a smart leather handbag, methodically checking every pocket, even pulling out the patterned lining to check she hasn't missed anything. Even the empty sweet wrappers have been carefully unfolded and smoothed flat. A tangle of bright ribbon half-hides a security pass, its smiling image the twin of the one in Mainder's pocket.

"That does not belong to you," he says sternly.

"The found are my charge. I have leave from the Queen," she replies calmly, not looking up. Her voice is deep and gentle, with a resonance to it that hums welcome. When she speaks, the listener feels that everything is perfectly as it should be. There is no wrongness here, there is only what she says there is.

No. He shakes his head to dispel the blurring harmonies her voice generates. "I doubt that very much. Where is the girl?"

"I put her on the path."

Again, it sounds like this is the only possible course of action, the only thing that could and should be done with lost travellers. They go on the path, of course they do. What else would there be? Mainder has to fight the impulse to accept her hollow reassurance and walk away. She seems to know it's working. She extracts a folding makeup mirror, opening it to smile at her reflection, and bright sea-green eyes glint at Mainder in the mirror before she closes it with a click and returns to her task.

"Finder," she murmurs, as if delighted to see him, and despite himself, he feels warmth spread though him at the acknowledgement.

"If you know who I am, then you know what I'm here for." The buzzing is louder now, trying to drown out everything he knows to be right and true.

"You are in my home," she chides. "What passes through here pays a toll."

That does seem fair; there are rules after all. She almost sounds sorrowful. What else is she to do if people will insist on stepping inside? Mainder can completely appreciate how she might feel at the constant intrusion. More than that, the imposition. Is it any wonder she should feel she ought to be compensated for her trouble?

He's halfway to the door when his gaze is captured by the plastic lunchbox again. Jen's grandson used to have one exactly like that, popular maybe fifteen years ago. It came with a matching drinks flask and some toy or other, some boy genius super-spy gadget wristwatch that made him the envy of his classmates. He used to stop in at the sweetshop on his way home from school with the goal of conning his besotted grandma out of a handful of free sweets, stepping out again swinging his lunchbox high in triumph with every step. He would have been what—eight years old? Mainder imagines him stepping through the wrong door, appearing under that archway, turning back in panic to look for grandma's shop and finding only the towering wall. Seeing the sign and entering this shop to be met by a smiling woman whose words made perfect sense. Trustingly handing over his treasured lunchbox, his flask, his pocketful of sweets on the promise of being taken somewhere nice and safe if he'd just be a good boy. The image revolts him and at last breaks the huldre's spell.

"A toll! For what? Why should they pay a toll when you invite them in?" he snaps, turning back.

"What passes though pays the toll," she says again. "Else how should I live?"

There's tension in her hands now, though, a faint tremor as she uncaps a lip balm and smells it.

"Your living is not my concern. Where is the girl?"

"I put her on the path," she repeats.

Her voice is becoming less soothing; she sounds impatient now, repeating a defence that's possibly never failed before. How many times has she tried this trick on people of the Realm? She should know better. There are rules about that as well. Her familiar climbs to her shoulder and nuzzles into her neck as if to reassure, and she lays a hand on its back to smooth its fur.

"Sweyn," he says lightly. "Just nip outside and see how sturdy that archway is, would you? I have my doubts about that keystone, if I'm honest. Smidur would have a fit if he saw it."

Sweyn sniggers and bounds to the door. The huldre's familiar growls a low sound and coils itself to attack, but she grips it tight to hold it back.

"Wise choice," Mainder approves. "Sweyn's eaten bigger things for breakfast."

Her beautiful mellow features twist to a snarl, eyes narrowed and dulled to a muddy green as panic dissolves her mask. "What are you doing?"

"Just a little scientific enquiry," Mainder says cheerfully, leaning on the door frame to block her path. "Call it idle curiosity."

"My living! You will destroy it!" she says desperately.

"Robbing children? Find another living!" he snarls. "Where did you send her?"

The hand touching the wood flames briefly, a scorch mark spreading rapidly along the grain.

"Shen holds the lost until there is a trade," she says hastily. "Shen is who you want."

The flame abates. Mainder lowers his hand, leaving a clear handprint still smouldering on the door frame.

"For the moment," he agrees. "And where exactly can I find this Shen?"

Chapter 69

PRACTICALLY UNDER HIS nose, as it turns out. Mainder shoves his way through the cellar door, making a frantic grab for the handle at the last second so as not to slam it against the wall and terrify the people he's supposed to be rescuing. They've been through enough. Calm and careful is the way.

But the spark of furious guilt keeps leaping up again regardless. How long has this been going on? Decades, if the huldre's shabby storefront is any indication. How many lost? And their hiding place, their prison, is right here almost in direct line of sight of the citadel itself. The tiny cellar sits underneath a popular bakery, with legitimate trade going on two floors overhead and customers in and out all day long while frightened *adzo* are held in near total darkness until they can be sold off. Call it what it is: slavery.

Half his fury is for Clegg, for the original builders of that lopsided arch, for the huldre and everyone in her whole sordid supply chain.

The other half is directed firmly back at himself. Clegg was right about one thing: he spent so much time caring about the few people he could see, back in Alfriscombe, he forgot what he was supposed to be looking after. The whole Realm was supposed to be his charge, holding the borders, not just the bits he personally cared about. He neglected it all to be a big man in a small mudside town. He's no better than Clegg in that regard, is he?

Well, he's here to fix that now. One mistake at a time.

Somewhere up above his head, an argument is raging about whether Shen gets her coin back from the huldre, all under the interested eye of the city guard. That's not his chief concern right now, though. Huddled on the grimy floor of the basement, with her arms wrapped protectively around her knees, is his charge. The tiny, barred windows set high in the wall allow barely enough light to see by, but her defeated posture tells him everything. He coaxes a small flame to life and holds it up to check her over. She looks pale and shocked, but otherwise unhurt. *She had better be*, he tells himself grimly. If she's been physically harmed in any way, this whole building will be a smouldering heap of ash before the end of the day. They say stone doesn't burn, don't they? But he's angry enough to test that fact to its limits right now.

"Laura," he says gently, as if to a child.

She flinches but doesn't look up, folding into herself to make herself smaller still.

"Laura," he repeats, placing her restored bag gently beside her on the floor. "Time to go home."

BOOK 4

Aftermath

Chapter 70

ARCHCHANCELLOR COOPER GLARES at the sheet of paper on his desk. What on earth is that still doing there? One of the early drafts of Vernon's eulogy, delivered and done with weeks ago. He certainly has no need of it now. He crumples it into a ball and tosses it neatly into the wastepaper bin. That association is over, and he needs no further reminders of the man haunting him now.

The funeral itself had been a pale, underdone affair. Apparently Vernon had left instructions for something far more grandiose, but that had been before the full extent of his debts had been uncovered. The executors were forced to pare it back to the absolute minimum. It's just as well. The expansive celebration of Vernon's life and deeds originally envisaged would have been entirely wasted on the five mourners in attendance, none of them family. It would appear Vernon didn't have any — not near and dear enough to mourn his passing anyway — and of the handful of people who did show up, two of them were Cooper himself and Vernon's lawyer. The others, whoever they were, didn't seem particularly distraught.

The proposed Vernon Foundation is a rapidly fading dream for much the same reason. There was no money set aside, despite their benefactor's grand promises, and no paperwork had even been drawn up, much less signed. It looks more and more as if he had never intended to go through with it, although how he'd expected to escape the consequences of such an outrageous scam, Cooper can't fathom. What remained of the estate has been eaten up by creditors, the contents of Vernon's sumptuous townhouse sold off piecemeal at auction as "the property of a gentleman."

Even his name erased, a final stinging irony.

Chapter 71

MEMORIES FADE. OLD hurts heal, past concerns subsumed by newer ones. The offices at the back of the museum stand empty long enough that they get turned into storage, boxes stacked high and obscuring the desks and the counters and the whiteboards. The lawn is restored, as far as these things can be, with the tunnel safely boarded over and new turf laid over the wound. The seams are barely visible. Time picks up where it left off and, gradually, Alfriscombe forgets.

The pooled dark under the elder tree shimmers, a flare of silver-green light that resolves into the shape of a man, tall and dark and wrapped in a long coat. He steps carefully around the pond's edge, fastidiously lifting the hem of his coat to avoid it dragging in the mud, and takes a deep breath.

"Home," he says experimentally.

The shadow draped over his shoulder raises its head and utters a quiet *pfft* of derision. It doesn't matter. He was right—this is home. It feels right, a major chord vibrating on the word spoken aloud, attuned to the deep contentment humming in his chest. In the Realm, that wasn't it. Alfriscombe is. This is where he's supposed to be, this is where he has a life of sorts and people to exchange smiles with, work to do and concerns to manage. This is where she is.

But he can't stay. Not just yet.

"You're certain?" he asks, in a tone that clearly says, *I'm not certain.*

"Like I said." Sweyn jumps down lightly to the ground and stretches like a cat. "Trust my nose, yes?"

"Right. And we have, what, eight hours until moonrise? That ought to be long enough."

"If you get your lazy arse moving, it might be," the sprite grouses.

"Alright, then. Let's see if you're right."

Chapter 72

YOUNG ROB AMBLED home from the pub one clear, spring night, keeping to the middle of the road so he'd be easily visible to any cars that might come round the bend. Not that there ever would be, not at two o'clock in the morning at the arse-end of nowhere, but still.

A full moon rode high over the sea, and periodically he stopped to lean on the turf-topped stone wall bordering the road and admire the view. Warmed by tonight's drinking and several hours in the fug of the pub's tiny taproom, he was more than glad of the cool breeze on his face. At his third stop, he struggled out of his thick sweater and carried it loosely in one hand.

Young Rob wasn't actually all that young—pushing forty, in fact—but some traditions defy logic. His father was Old Rob, and so he'd be Young Rob until the day he died or until he produced a Younger Rob of his own. Chance would be a fine thing, eh. No girls in this neighbourhood had eyes for anyone who's not either on the rigs or bringing home city money. His little garage paid its way alright, but he couldn't compete with that.

A few hundred yards from home, his boozy meandering was interrupted by the sight of something else in the road. Not a car, but a tiny child, clutching a handful of flowers plucked from the verge and toddling towards him, babbling happily to herself. She couldn't be much more than a year old; no nappy, no shoes or coat, just a rough sack of a dress that looked more like an old pillowcase with rough-hemmed holes for head and arms. Soft curls of primrose-pale blonde hair hung down to just above her shoulders, and aside from her muddy feet, she looked clean and cared for. He changed tack to intercept her, cornering with the fluid grace of the habitual Friday night drunk and sweeping her up in his arms to place her on the wall. She scrabbled to get down almost before he had her seated, and he had to grab at her leg when she made to crawl away. Her little limbs felt chill to the touch, though she wasn't shivering; he glanced at his discarded sweater.

"Let's warm you up, eh?" He held the knit above her head, and she obligingly lifted her arms so he could put it on her. The dark blue woollen swamped her, and when her tiny hand emerged at length from the sleeve, she'd lost her ramshackle bouquet somewhere in the folds. She made a small sound of annoyance, uncannily like the way his mother used to *tsk* at dishes out of place in her kitchen, and he chuckled as he lifted the hem to help her retrieve the handful of scattered stalks. "Now then, you sit tight."

He stared into her face, looking for signs of distress, but other than a faint pout when she realised she couldn't immediately get down from her perch, she seemed unfazed at being picked up by a stranger. Trusting little thing.

"Let's get you back to your mam, eh? She must be going spare." She babbled quietly in response. It didn't sound like any words he knew, but then she was barely a baby. Her tone suggested she was happy to go along with his plan, and that was good enough for him.

He peered back along the road in the direction of town, considering his options. Home was barely a quarter mile up the road. He'd be fit to get his front door key in the lock best out of three tries, but he was a long way away from being the most proper person to look after a wean overnight, even if he were stone cold sober. No, best thing to do was head back into town and raise the alarm with Ruaridh. He'd know what to do. Decision made, he picked the child up in his arms and wove his way back down the road in the moonlight.

The child babbled again, twisting in his arms to look all around. "I'll be dropping you if you keep that up," he grumbled and tried hoisting her up on to his shoulders instead. She evidently approved, squealing delightedly when he bounced her up and down a couple of times to test her grip. Satisfied that she wasn't about to fall off, he set off again.

The police station sat up towards the back of town, a tiny stone cottage up by itself overlooking the north road. He made his way through deserted streets, everyone else long since gone to bed, and came at last to the front door, grabbing the child down from his shoulders and settling her securely on his hip the way he'd seen his sister do with her own little ones. Always looked desperately unhandy, the way they'd squirm and reach for whatever she was trying to keep away from them, but to his great relief it worked and gave him a hand free to knock on the station door.

"We'll have to make some noise. He'll be in bed, eh? Like you should be, little mischief."

She nodded firmly with a sound like *ah*, staring solemnly up into his face; he could swear she was agreeing with him. He chuckled and banged his fist on the door a few times for a warmup. The little one cackled at the noise and leaned precariously over to copy him.

"Eh, you're trouble, aren't you. Like the big noise, heh? Bang bang bang?"

"Ban ban ban!" she agreed, reaching over again.

Ruaridh chose that moment to open the door wide, the words "what the fuck" clearly queueing up to be said, and nearly received a tiny finger up his nose. He flinched back hastily and peered at Young Rob, then back at the child.

"What's this about then?"

'Found the wean running in the road up past the castle. Nobody else about. I dunno where she's come from, but I couldn't just leave her, eh?"

"Naw, course not." Ruaridh stared at the child. "Come in for now and I'll make some calls."

Epilogue

IT WOULD BE a stretch to claim that Aberdeen is the most beautiful city in the world, but late summer sun bestows a golden glow on even its severe grey stone. It seems to have put the throng of shoppers in a cheery mood too, although the newest addition to the Linden family might have something to do with that. They haven't been able to get more than a few steps all morning without someone peeking into the pram and making admiring noises.

That currently includes her doting aunt.

"Who's the most beautiful baby Linden in the world? Who is? You are!" Evie burbles happily. "Auntie Evie is going to buy you *all* of the toys."

You'd be forgiven for thinking she already had, judging by the heap of carrier bags stuffed under the pram, but as she's already firmly explained in the face of all Angie's protests, she's on a mission. Roger couldn't come shopping today, busy running errands and getting David to his hospital appointment, but he'd pressed a wad of banknotes into Evie's hand before she left this morning with strict instructions to come back with none of it.

"Anything that baby needs today," he'd said, "you buy it. Got it?"

Evie has never been one to shirk a challenge. Mentally reviewing the mall layout ahead, she says, "Marks and Spencers next, do you reckon? They've got the cafe on the first floor, and I'm about ready for a coffee stop."

"Coffee sounds good," Angie allows. "Technically she's a Berry, though, not a Linden."

Evie accepts the correction. "Mama's right. The most beautiful baby Linden-Berry in the entire world," she assures the crowing infant. "Yes, you are. As soon as we stop for coffee, you are going to get so many cuddles!"

The cooing continues all the way to the baby clothes section, where more important considerations arise.

"Pink or lilac?" Angie asks, holding up two almost identical outfits on tiny hangers.

"Both. Grandpa's paying," Evie says firmly, stuffing them both into the shopping basket. "Does she need socks?"

"Lord, babies always need socks," Angie says despairingly. "I don't even know how she manages to lose them, but I swear we had a basket full of odd ones by the time she was a week old." A couple of other shoppers emerge from the aisle, and she wheels the pram back to let them pass. "Can you pick up one of those ten-packs? The plain white ones?"

But her foster-sister has stopped listening, staring blankly at the man who just passed by, tall and Scandinavian-fair and wearing a heavy tweed jacket despite the sunshine outside.

"Hmm?" she says distantly. "Oh, right, yes. Listen, go on up and get the coffees while I pay for this lot."

As soon as the elevator doors close behind them, she reaches down and unfolds the scrap of card dropped on the polished floor tiles beside her. It's a picture postcard of the moon rising over the sea with a ruined castle in the distance, and on the back it simply says, in forest green ink:

I think I found your door.

Printed in Great Britain
by Amazon

44295160R00179